The Lambs of War

Brian McManus

PEGASUS BOOKS

Pegasus Books
3338 San Marino Ave
San Jose, CA 95127
www.pegasusbooks.net

First Edition: October 2016

Published in North America by Pegasus Books. For information, please contact Pegasus Books c/o Christopher Moebs, 3338 San Marino Ave, San Jose, CA 95127.

Library of Congress Cataloguing-In-Publication Data
Brian McManus
The Lambs of War/Brian McManus– 1st ed
p. cm.
Library of Congress Control Number: 2016950340
ISBN – 978-1-941859-51-3
1. FICTION / Historical. 2. FICTION / Thrillers / Historical. 3. FICTION / War & Military. 4. HISTORY / Military / World War II. 5. POLITICAL SCIENCE / Genocide & War Crimes. 6. POLITICAL SCIENCE / Political Ideologies / Fascism & Totalitarianism.

10 9 8 7 6 5 4 3 2 1

Comments about *The Lambs of War* and requests for additional copies, book club rates and author speaking appearances may be addressed to Brian McManus or Pegasus Books c/o Christopher Moebs, 3338 San Marino Ave, San Jose, CA, 95127, or you can send your comments and requests via e-mail to cdeluca@pegasusbooks.net.

Also available as an eBook from Internet retailers and from Pegasus Books

Printed in the United States of America

For my family

"We shall draw from the heart of
suffering itself the means
of inspiration and survival."

Winston Churchill

This is a story of a husband and wife, living in Nazi Germany, 1943. Both orphaned at a young age and childless, Isaac and Flora Bloom become victims of a Nazi police sweep in their North Sea town of Bremerhaven. They live with Isaac's elderly boss; a well-respected food merchant. Isaac has been his right hand man in business, as well as his personal valet at home. Flora is a local seamstress.

They are ordered to Ravensbruck Labor Camp. Isaac's boss tries to keep the couple together, and asks an old friend to speak to his son, a camp officer, hoping that they will at least not be separated. Upon arriving at the all women facility, Flora is taken into the camp, as a common prisoner, but Isaac is used by the commander as his own personal secretary and houseman. The commander lives outside the prison gate.

Most of the Nazi administrators are diabolical, corrupt, sadistic, even hateful of one another. There is also a strong male/female rivalry, as many of the guards are woman and jealous of the male hierarchy. This hatred breeds mismanagement and possible vulnerability. Isaac observes, quietly.

After months of camp personnel infighting and criminal accusations, a murder of jealousy is committed. One evening, the chief female guard visits the officer's house, confronts him and kills him. This was in revenge for the mysterious murder of her female associate, who had been prying into the captain's strange behavior, concerning his theft of new prisoner valuables, for his own personal gain.

Before his death, the officer had signed an indemnity order, if any harm had come to him, while Isaac lived with him; Isaac's wife was to be executed, at once.

Isaac, who was hiding in the pantry, realizes he must act quickly. There is little time. He devises an escape plan, before the dead body is discovered. Using all the resources in the officer's house, the man drafts a plan to enter the prison, free his wife and flee to Scandinavia. The plan works. The story continues. The second part of the tale is the many adventures, close calls, and accounts of how the couple avoided being discovered and recaptured.

Chased through northern Germany, Denmark, as well as on the Baltic Sea, Isaac and Flora Bloom manage to outwit all Nazi pursuit for their escape, and also, the blame for the murder they did not commit.

The Lambs of War

INTRODUCTION
JULY 31, 1943

Salivating, grunting and panting from the effort, the young Nazi soldier gritted his teeth and focused with a drunken, blind determination. He was going to be in charge. He was going to dominate the exchange. The attractive blond fraulein was going to respond to his muscular cues.

He grabbed her limbs and held them down along her sides. A man always had more control when he wrapped his claws around the partner's wrists, paralyzing the strength in her extremities.

The situation intensified. He squatted, jutted his pelvis forward and pulled her frail arms close to his torso. Compliant, the girl jumped onto her partner's thighs, burying her red stiletto heels into his uniform slacks. It was a pain he could bear. The nineteen-year-old concentrated on the soldier, and with fear in her eyes, she climbed the front part of his body. It was her first time (performing such a bold manuver?).

He tightened his grip as her red heels dug into his uniform top. In one thrusting motion, the soldier became the physical fulcrum that enabled his partner to complete the dangerous backward flip onto the dance floor. There was no mistaking it—Nazi youth had a secret, unmistakable passion for the American jitterbug. The fervent crowd shreiked as the female dancer landed in her cumbersome shoes and transitioned to the next phase of the couple's choreography.

"American Big Band Music, Herman?" an older voice carrying Nazi authority bellowed while pounding his fist on the hotel manager's desk.

Herman Wohl, the night lobby man at The Lorelei rooming house and beer hall, looked up and froze upon seeing the threatening authority figure in front of him.

"Oh uh, Good Evening… Captain," the cowering desk man answered. "What can I say?"

He followed with a sheepish laugh and shrug. "The young people cannot get enough of it. They tell me it puts them into a trance-like mood. It makes them feel invincible."

"Very nice, Herman. I am elated it makes them happy. Unfortunately, it is the music of the *enemy*!" Wohl knew the officer meant those words. The concierge always treated the hot-tempered Nazi capitan with the utmost politeness, though he never knew how to read him.

The captain visited The Lorelei on most Saturday nights, always arriving with one or two army duffle bags and visiting the prostitute who had a steady room, booked for weekend employment. He stayed for only two or three minutes and departed with a small briefcase, leaving behind two bulky satchels.

Wohl knew better than to ever ask *Why*?

"I have an idea, Herman. How about we hang the American *flag* in your beer hall, and the patrons can sing *The Star Spangled Banner*—as long as you like playing American dance music so much?"

The Nazi sought a facial response, though Herman gave nothing but a hint of shame to appease the officer.

"Have you seen the papers or listened to the radio this week, Herman?"

"Yes, sir," the desk clerk answered, certain about where the conversation was headed.

"They estimate thirty thousand deaths just 75 kilometers northwest of here, in Hamburg. Thanks to the people who bring you Big Band Music… the Allied Forces! And yet they—" the Nazi sneered, pointing to the chaotic beer hall dance enthusiasts, "they would rather celebrate their Saturday night drunk dancing to *I Got a Gal in Kalamazoo!* It is that type of behavior that will cause our great country to lose this effort!" He took a breath, calming himself. "Now, is my *girlfriend* upstairs?" Wurtzmuller continued, still exasperated, his voice impatient, "and is she available?"

Herman was happy to advise the officer that the girl was free, as her last appointment was just descending the stairs. As the eighteen-year-old enlisted man passed the front desk, he returned a military soft cap to his flowing mane of blond hair, avoiding eye contact with the captain. The embarrasment turned his Aryan complexion to a soft pink.

"Hold it, soldier," the officer demanded as the young enlisted man passed. "Did they teach you how to greet an officer when you come in the presence of one? Or did they say to just walk by him, offering no acknowledgement of respect?"

The captain looked back at Herman Wohl as much as to say, *See what I mean?*

"Sorry sir,"

The soldier stood at attention, and with outstretched arm, he saluted the Nazi captain, ten centimeters from his face.

"Where were you just now, boy?" the officer asked. "You were upstairs with a prostitute, weren't you?"

"Uh… Uh… Y-Yes, sir, I was," the soldier responded, his rose complexion turning crimson.

"If I catch you here again, I will not only have you arrested, but I will personally call your mother and tell her exactly what her little boy is doing while serving his country—he is having fun visiting prostitutes! Do you understand?"

"Yes, sir!"

The teen soldier had never before experienced such a reprimand from a commissioned officer.

"Now get out of here, and write to Mommy. Tell her how much you miss her and how much you love her."

Herman watched in awe. The soldier ran out of the lobby like a wounded animal.

The captain refitted the bag straps onto his shoulders and began his weighty ascent up the stairs. Halfway up, he stopped and turned back to Herman Wohl at the front desk, laughing with disgust.

"The two biggest enemies in wartime are enemies that I have no control over, Herman—venereal disease and American jitterbug."

Herman, however, could not hear what the officer had said. *Elmer's Tune* by Glenn Miller was blasting to a deafening level on the public address speakers.

CHAPTER 1

That damned Vischnitz! Why did he have to get caught? His selfish behavior had managed to destroy the arrangement he had created within the community. The situation had changed overnight, creating local panic. Without his protection, there would be no one around to look the other way.

Commodore Adolf Ahrens was in a thoughtful mood as he stood, gazing out the window of his second floor library—out over the copper and stucco-tiled rooftops, down to the wharf district of Bremerhaven.

He could see the ships' masts and steamer funnels in the harbor. The vessels were in line, waiting to unload their bounty of cargo. Perhaps some of the imports would be heading to the commodore's warehouse in the market square. However, without the presence of the Nazi Police Street Captain, Hiram Vischnitz, things were going to be a bit tougher.

In return for two crates of oranges a month, Vishnitz did not report on the Polish escapees who loaded trucks for Ahrens. For another sack of Spanish olives, he did not "bring up" the commodore's driver, who was wanted for killing a sailor in Hamburg. All the Bremerhaven merchants knew and complained about the crooked street captain, but everyone who needed to maintain a peaceful life, uninterrupted by Nazi politics, tolerated his demands.

Low quotas for arrests and apparent accusations concerning graft plagued Vischnitz's record, which caused authorities to remove himfrom the Street Captain position and replace him with Karl Polmer, a no-nonsense neophyte who scoured the neighborhoods of Bremerhaven, looking to make a name for himself.

Within weeks, Polmer arrested hundreds of so-called enemies of the Nazi state, and every Monday, he filled three to four buses with detainees. Hundreds of locals, who had managed to avoid capture for the last five years, were being transported from Bremerhaven to civilian detention centers or to labor camps.

Local gossip suggested that Vischnitz had escaped imprisonment, but he was working in a lower military rank, somewhere in Warsaw.

* * * * *

Commodore Adolf Ahrens was one of the most respected businessmen in town. The unschooled entrepreneur was a member of the last generation of Bremerhaven residents to receive his education from world travel—aboard linen mast schooners, and later—steam-driven cargo liners. Ahrens was the proverbial "child of the sea." He became a cabin boy at age ten in 1888, and he worked his way up the merchant marine ladder to become a full captain of the *German Lloyd* and later, the commander of the *Bremen IV*.

In his later years, the well-respected seaman sought connections in all of the foreign ports he visited and began purchasing produce that was foreign to German markets. In 1931, he founded Ahrens Exotic Fruit and Vegetable Co., introducing Mediterranean and African foods to his North Sea town, and business thrived from the very beginning.

By 1943, however, with the war in its fourth year, the situation had become dangerously unstable. The old seaman thought that his earlier life had held risk and danger, including fighting pirates on the Ivory Coast to the death, shunning thieves in the Dardanelles, and even killing three men who tried to hijack his vessel in Sardinia. He never imagined that his very homeland would eventually be home to his greatest enemy!

Although the villagers respected him, the Nazi Party hated *The Commodore*. As a wealthy and influential capitalist, he was a threat, and since Vischnitz was not around to protect people like him, Commodore Adolf Ahrens had every reason to worry.

* * * * *

"Sir, I have brought your tea and two sweet rolls," the young man announced as he placed the silver tray on Ahrens' office desk.

"Has Flora left for the factory yet, Isaac?" the old seaman asked.

"Yes sir, she has—about an hour ago. Is everything fine, sir?"

Isaac knew his boss and guardian. And standing in the office, staring at Ahrens, sensed an ominous spirit that seemed to consume the older man, who continued staring out the library window.

"Isaac, please sit down," the commodore began.

Ahrens faced the wide-eyed twenty-nine-year-old. The difficulty of the situation reminded him of the time, years ago, when he was forced to tell Isaac the news of his parents' deaths.

Ahrens had met Stanislaus and Trinka Bloom in Gdansk. The two had worked in a food shop in the dock region. The couple had a fourteen-year-old boy, Isaac, who helped them run their business every day after school. For years, they pleaded with the commodore to let them stow away on the *Bremen IV*, so that they might escape the looming political and economic doom that now faced Poland.

On his last voyage before retiring, the commodore agreed to their request. The Blooms and their son Isaac, escaped, and they eventually began working for the veteran seaman's new produce business in Bremerhaven, Germany. Ahrens was pleased by their work ethic, as they ran his warehouse with the utmost precision. He felt lucky to have the Blooms in his life almost as much as they were indebted to the commodore for helping them escape to their imagined freedom.

Young Isaac took to the trade, and in no time, he was performing tasks more suitable to the talents of a seasoned business man.

Then came that horrific day—a mere six months after the Blooms arrived in Bremerhaven. A freighter, *The Lisbon Sea Wave*, which had been en route to Hamburg and Stockholm carrying a hold full of wine, olives, figs and cork, received a radio message to set anchor and dock at the closest port. The company, Ferriera Brothers, had claimed bankruptcy. Creditors impounded the ship and its contents and ordered the crew of thirty men off the vessel, subject to the forfeiture of two months' pay.

The angry and violently-disposed merchant seamen were thus stranded in the defenseless port of Bremerhaven. And so rioting their way back on board the *Sea Wave*, the seamen broke into the wine cases, so that by night fall, the angry crew became murderers.

The drunken mob killed twenty-six people that night. Stanislaus and Trinka Bloom heard the unruly horde in the wharf area. When the alarmed husband raised the metal door of the produce warehouse, a bearded, stocky fellow slashed his throat with the edge of a severed wine bottle. The man stomped on Trinka when she came to her husband's aid, and then he kicked her to death. None of the drunken murderers from Portugal were ever found or brought to justice.

Young Isaac slept through the crime frenzy and violent attacks. When Commodore Ahrens later awakened him, he told the boy about the life-changing incident. In that very moment, the widowed and childless sea captain vowed that everything he had would one day belong to young Isaac Bloom, all the while realizing that perilous day was perhaps nearly upon him.

"Isaac, as I told you, the policeman, Vischnitz, was replaced by another whose name is Polmer. This new policeman is totally different—dedicated to the cause of the Reich, unlike his predecessor. He has taken pride in, as he says, 'cleaning up' the dock area. He paid a visit to me yesterday."

As Isaac stood, the commodore accepted that his own greatest fear had been realized. The dormant presence of Vischnitz was over. After 13 years, the authorities would consider Isaac to be an illegal Polish immigrant, a Jew, and thus an enemy of the Reich. However, nothing was different as far as Isaac was concerned, except that Vischnitz was no longer around to look the other way.

"What did he say? Why would anyone bring *me* to his attention?" Isaac began in a defensive tone.

"What is strange," the commodore answered, "is that it wasn't *you* who initiated his inquiry... It was, rather, Flora."

"What! What *about* Flora?" Isaac asked, his voice rising in alarm.

Flora had been Isaac's wife for seven years. Sixteen-year-old Flora left her birth city of Bremen after both her parents died. She had moved into her aunt's house, which was in the building next to Adolf Ahrens.

Isaac had noticed Flora soon after she arrived, but he was too shy to speak. He was attracted to her long, wavy black hair and Mediterranean coloring, with fine Nordic features. Her piercing cobalt eyes, however, were her most striking gift. When Isaac looked into them, he fell into a hypnotic state. He imagined they were the exact color of the waters in the Great Coral Sea.

After six months, Isaac found the nerve to say hello, and the two began a brief courtship. Over time, they realized they had found in each other the love they had lost when their respective sets of parents died. After they married, they lived in the commodore's house, as his "unofficial" surrogate children.

"It seems Polmer had been at Flora's dress factory," Ahrens continued, "and he had asked the owner for employee records. The owner said that they had been stolen months earlier and tried to get past the visit as quickly as possible. What they do to get around this non-cooperative tactic is to begin asking questions of the workers. It is amazing how quickly employees begin selling out one another, thinking they are getting into the Gestapo's good graces. In any event, it appears one woman began telling them that Flora wore a Jewish star pendant to work several years ago, though not recently. Polmer said nothing to Flora, but he discovered that I employed her husband, so Polmer visited me as well."

Furious, Isaac huffed, his face turning red as his eyes bulged.

"Those bastards! They have nothing better to do than play detective, bothering innocent civilians! What did he ask you, sir?"

"He asked about when I took you into my home and how I became the employer of your parents. He asked about if I knew Flora's parents and if you and she were indeed Jews. He asked about why Vischnitz never pursued following up on these topics and why your parents left Poland years ago."

Then Ahrens stopped and looked down at the breakfast tray, seeming depressed.

"Then he ordered me to make sure both of you remain in my custody until I hear from him on Thursday, August 5th. He warned that if either one or the two of you left Bremerhaven, you would be considered common criminals, and I would be killed for aiding in your attempted escape."

"This is not happening… it is not!" Isaac blurted.

His whole young life darted before his eyes.

"I must get to Flora right away. I need to tell her to be careful… not to speak with anyone."

"Maybe it would be best to keep a low profile—until we hear from Polmer on Thursday," the old man suggested to Isaac, who was headed down the stairs to the front door.

"Polmer advised that he would handle the matter himself. I even offered him some crates of food from the warehouse. He refused, but I did not insult him, Thank God! Let us see how he responds."

His gentle words failing to elicit the desired response from the heated Isaac, the commodore pursued a more severe tactic.

"Or maybe we should just call them and tell them to come by tomorrow and kill all three of us… for no reason at all?"

"Isaac… Isaac!" Ahrens called, but it was too late. Isaac Bloom had already straddled his bicycle and was midway down the lane, peddling toward Flora's dress factory.

CHAPTER 2

One thing was certain. Polmer was thorough. By eleven o'clock that day, one of the policeman's subordinates had visited Commodore Ahrens. The soldier presented him with a preliminary notice that the people under his supervision, namely Isaac and Flora Bloom, should be at home on Friday, August 6th, for their reporting papers. If the couple were unavailable to receive the papers, then Adolf Ahrens would be responsible for seeing that the Blooms responded to the orders.

Ahrens realized the inevitable: German authorities planned to remove Flora and Isaac from Bremerhaven society and send them to a detaining facility, a concentration camp. In another bit of bad news for Adolf Ahrens—the two Polish loading dock workers had run away before they could be discovered by the Nazi patrol. Their absence left him short-handed for truck loading and product distribution. The commodore really did not blame the workers. It was only a matter of days before someone would have ratted on them.

Ahrens took the papers from the Nazi courier and studied them. The writing was vague—merely an order to await upcoming formal notices. He was glad he had sent Isaac out to collect on unpaid bills from local merchants, glad that Isaac did not have to deal with the messenger who delivered news that would definitely change or end his and Flora's lives.

That evening, mealtime was silent, except for an outburst of tears from Flora. She felt guilty, saying it was her fault that they were in such a hopeless situation.

"I know when this happened last week—when some SS soldiers were at the factory. There was a lieutenant who was questioning Mr. Shensul. Some girls were flirting with the other troops, and they began talking about various random things, just to keep the men there longer. One of the new women asked why there were still some Jews in town. She said she thought the Nazis were taking them away. Then another pointed to me and said, 'She used to wear a Jewish star, you know.' I walked away. No one said anything else after that. I did not think it would blossom into a full investigation!"

"It is like I said," Ahrens responded. "The Nazis like to intimidate and let the victims spill all the information out onto their ears. Unfortunately, the ones who think they are making friends are the ones who could very well be hunted by the same group next week."

No one ate much that evening. Isaac apologized for not making more of an effort, and every time he passed Flora, he rubbed her shoulder in a comforting gesture.

"Isaac, sit down," Commodore Ahrens ordered. "I have a plan. I do not know if it is a good one, but I cannot just let this happen without trying something."

Isaac sat next to Flora. They stared at the commodore, hoping his years of wisdom and survival on the high seas might bring some encouragement in such an overpowering predicament.

"When I commandeered the flagship, *Columbus*, from 1922 to 1928, my first mate was a gentleman from Bremen. His name was Otto Wurtzmuller. Over the years, we have kept in modest contact. He informed me, about three years ago, that his son was a commissioned officer with the Nazi Shutzstaffel. He is stationed in a working camp, somewhere north of Berlin. Let me call my old friend and see if he can do something about this? Who knows? It is always worth seeing if there may be another Hiram Vischnitz working within the Nazi hierarchy."

Ahrens laughed, though he received little more than a somber reaction from the couple.

"Sir, I made a phone call to a customer in Bremen this morning," Isaac responded, a sense of eagerness growing in his voice. "So communication is still opened from Bremerhaven to that district. Please do this tonight. With the latest raids, the lines could be knocked out at any time!"

"It is late, Isaac. I will call him first thing in the morning. If I do not get through, I promise, I will make the 30-kilometer journey to see him personally. I still want to think about just what I would like to say to him.

Isaac and Flora cleaned up the dining room and retired to their small living quarters behind the kitchen, which had been a maid's room long before they came to live with Ahrens.

Sobbing over the uncertainty of where their young lives were headed, Flora lay in their bed, falling asleep due to mental exhaustion.

They lay together in each other's arms. Isaac remained awake, realizing that night may be one of their last together.

On the next afternoon, Commodore Adolf Ahrens was able to make phone contact with the former seaman, Otto Wurtzmuller. Retired for ten years, Wurtzmuller had developed a small hobby business, selling miniature ships in bottles. He had learned the craft from an old, Norwegian sailor at the turn of the twentieth century.

He produced hundreds of the miniature ships a year, and sold the remarkably accurate scaled models to novelty store merchants in the sea town of Bremen. As he said, "it pays some bills, and revitalizes my loving memories of youth, during my maritime life."

The commodore spoke with his former first mate, reminiscing over their young, daring, adventures on the high seas. They spent the time laughing at the story when both got so drunk that they reported to the wrong vessel in Malta. They had to wait five days in Marseilles before their assigned ship rescued them. After several minutes sharing tales of years' past, Ahrens came to his point.

"Otto, I have called to ask a favor. I hope that I am not out of line, and I do not even know if it is an area for discussion... There is a young couple who live with me. I unofficially adopted them when they were young. There are no religious affiliations in my household, but both of them are of Jewish heritage. Last week, they were caught up in an SS sweep. It appears that they will be sent to a detention camp immediately—probably next week."

"And you want me to get my son, Heinrich, to get them off, right? Well let me tell you, Adolf—if I, his own father, was being sent to an SS prison camp, he would not help me out."

The old seaman laughed heartily at his own joke.

"He is my son, but he is my son second. He is a Nazi first. He considers any tampering with Nazi law to be an act of treason."

"No... No, Otto—" the commodore pleaded. "I do not want him to exonerate them from any crimes the SS feels that they have committed—which is none, I might add. I would like them to merely go to the same facility. They have been together for eight years—not one night have they been separated. They have no one, you see."

"My son's camp is only for women. It is a labor camp. They manufacture military things—mostly parts for weapons, uniforms, leather supplies. They also re-sole boots that they take from dead troops. I think he mentioned that there was a small men's prison on the distant grounds, but they do not mix with the women workers.

Believe me, this place does not treat the people like they are part of a household. They would not be living like husband and wife. They may be only eight hundred meters apart, but it would be no different if it were a thousand kilometers. I do not see how he could help, Adolf?"

"I would still consider it a favor if you could speak to your son and have them assigned together. He could certainly use the talents of this couple."

Ahrens was quickly approaching a begging demeanor.

"My man, Isaac Bloom, would be an asset to him. He is my personal valet, business associate, buyer, accountant, chauffer, bookkeeper and salesman. At home, he is my cook, launderer, cleaner and personal secretary. He does *everything*!"

"And the woman?" Otto asked.

"Well, she is a seamstress, if one of his products in this facility is uniforms?"

Ahrens heard silence from the other end of the line. After a few seconds, the old friend answered.

"I will try to contact him tonight, but I cannot promise that he can do anything. Even if he can, they will live in separation, anyway—no matter where they are sent. Give me their full names and the SS officer who processed their papers. If they have identification numbers on their forms, it would help."

Commodore Adolf Ahrens read Karl Polmer's name and the case numbers that had been typed on Isaac and Flora's initial notices.

"Otto, my comrade—I thank you for doing this for me. They are my children… that I never had!"

Otto Wurtzmuller seemed sincere in wanting to assist his old friend. However, he did not have faith in any Nazi—even in his son for accommodating such an unusual request.

"By the way, Otto—what is the name of your son's facility?" Ahrens asked.

"It is in the middle of nowhere, Adolf," Otto answered, "in farm country, thirty kilometers north of Berlin. It is called Ravensbruck."

* * * * *

On Friday evening before dinner, the three were startled by pounding on the door. Rather than using knuckles, the visitor used the side of his fist, a more impatient greeting. Thee noise came from the strength of an arm and the determination of a clenched hand.

"I will answer it."

Isaac hurried from his spot at the kitchen stove, and yet before he could get to the latch, the rapping grew more forceful. When Isaac swung the hinges open, there stood two soldiers with folded papers.

"Isaac and Flora Bloom?" the emissary shouted.

"Yes, it is us," Isaac answered.

One soldier handed him the documents.

"Monday, four-thirty a.m. Be at the wharf bus terminal. If you do not show, you will be considered fugitives."

The other soldier, who did not speak, handed the next group of papers to the one who appeared to be his superior. Then the men turned and left in a hurry.

"Let me see the forms," Commodore Adolf Ahrens shouted as he rounded the corner of the dining room toward the foyer. "Sometimes there are markings on the paper—special codes that give away information."

He sat at the table, scrutinizing the two papers, ignoring Isaac who leaned over his shoulder.

"Here, look at the box labeled 'DEST'. That indicates where you are being taken. It is the same on both papers, and the abbreviation letters are 'RVBK'. He *did* it! You are going to the same location! That is good, no?"

Ahrens was jumping to conclusions, but had seen enough paperwork in his lifetime to extract possible facts from the data.

"Provided that is what the letters *mean*, sir?" Isaac responded, showing shallow excitement.

Upset by the mens' reactions and the reality of the situation, Flora broke into a hysterical tirade.

"What is wrong with both of you?"

The young wife, showing a rare, frustrated semblance, threw the dish plate she had been drying, hurling it clear across the space, where it hit the dining room wall and shattered into pieces.

"See, that plate! That is our lives", she insisted, her voice becoming manic. "It is ripped into fragments. It is destroyed!" She cupped her slender hands over her face. "You make it sound like we received the same room at a hotel! Or we are going to the university! We are not! We are going to a prison! Have you ever heard of anyone *returning* from these places? If the *Nazis* do not kill us, we will probably be killed by the British or the Russians. We are doomed, no matter."

Isaac grabbed the frail girl and tried to hug her into calmness, but she pushed him away and ran to the bedroom, slamming the door.

Commodore Ahrens became self-conscious about his trite behavior in such a serious moment.

"Go to your wife," he told Isaac. "Console her. Stay positive both of you. I have tried to do some good."

Then the man of iron nerves, the merchant marine who survived 50 years of danger and deadly situations, slumped into his armchair, and like a beaten child, succumbed to quiet tears.

CHAPTER 3

Four impatient uniformed Nazi officers of the Shutzstaffel stood in front of the military vehicle garage. It was early Monday. They all smoked. Somehow it seemed mandatory to engage in smoking, as Nazi officers in particular were pathological about satisfying their need for nicotine. The habit seemed to accentuate their intimidating presence, if that was possible.

The officers were awaiting the arrival of their commandant, Major Fritz Surhen, who lived just outside the gates of Ravensbruck labor camp. As the head of this facility and unlike most of his subordinates, Surhen lived off premises in a 23-room Normandy-style villa on nearby Lake Schwedt.

"Wait until the old man sees this," the young, dark-haired, shorter lieutenant offered, refraining from laughter. "For two years, he has been after the Inspectorate to build him a chamber, and *this* is what they send him. He will shit!"

"Horst, you tell him he has to be the driver of this contraption as well," the taller of the two captains quipped. "That will start his week off well."

He then made a feeble motion imitating someone steering an imaginary wheel and honking a horn. The others hooted, but they immediately halted as Surhen's jeep pulled up to the snickering quorum.

"We will take a quick look at this," the major said to the two captains, Heinrich Wurtzmuller, and Horst Bitten, as he left his vehicle. "Then I want to see you two in my quarters, right afterwards."

"Lieutenant Volsgaard," the major called, "lift the door please."

The young officer squatted, and with all his strength, he hoisted the massive wooden front of the warehouse panel until it displayed an idle green military vehicle that had been backed into the vast garage cavity. Surhen looked at his crew in disgust. He was annoyed, so they were not about to taunt him with wise cracks.

Hands on his hips, he walked in a circular motion as he studied the bus.

"What the hell…" he sputtered and grimaced as he ran his hand along the green fender.

"Hello, sir!" the civilian mechanic shouted, wiping his grease-stained hands as he emerged from the garage office. "Would you like a closer look?"

Many locals had been employed by the Concentration Camp Inspectorate, especially as cooks, electricians, carpenters and common maintenance people, and yet others worked in more highly-classified projects, such as the garage. Unlike prisoners within the gates, the local laborers were allowed to return every evening to their nearby residences.

"What is your name?" Suhren asked the man.

"Schmidt, sir. Would you like a tour?" the amiable tradesman offered. "I will explain how it works. It is rather ingeniously simple".

"You know you are bound to silence, Schmidt, or else… right? Now tell me, Schmidt. Could you build me a gas chamber with your own hands—like I have been asking the people in Berlin to do for the past three years? Instead they send me a… a…" Suhren pounded the fender of the green van.

"A mobile, mass extermination vehicle, sir," the cautious mechanic gulped, answering the angry major.

"How many bodies can it hold?" Suhren asked.

"About twenty-five women at a time, all in a vertical position, uh, standing, I mean", the mechanic answered.

"I know what vertical means," Surhen snapped.

The four officers burst into laughter at their chief's obvious disapproval of what was being supplied in place of his requests. Schmidt understood and decided to move to a more technical level, explaining the vehicle's attributes.

"It is merely a converted military troop transport. The cab is totally separate from the passenger compartment. As you see, the back is windowless, welded to the point of being seamless. The walls are two-centimeter metal. The back panel doors have been equipped with gaskets, assuring an air-tight compartment when closed."

"So what makes this thing ingenious?" Surhen asked with annoying puzzlement.

Schmidt went into a physical drill, walking around to the rear of the transport and pointing to the exhaust pipe.

"Yah, so it is a tailpipe," the novice Lt. Volsgaard spoke.

"Look closely, sir," Schmidt began in his north German dialect. "The pipe flairs out at the end to a six-centimeter diameter, and it has been fitted with plumbing threads."

The worker then removed a six-meter rubber hose from a compartment under the rear bumper of the vehicle. Displaying the ends of the hose, he began fitting the collar on to the tailpipe, twisting it tightly.

"Now follow me, gentlemen."

The eager mechanic pulled down a metal flap on the exterior wall panel of the truck and attached the hose to the receiving collar behind it.

"On the interior wall of the van, there is a vent. The vehicle's own carbon monoxide has now become the fuel for emitting the poisonous gas into the airtight chamber. The driver up front is in a separate cab, unaffected.

"How long does the process take?" Suhren quizzed.

"Approximately fifteen minutes. Different time results will vary," Schmidt conceded, standing tall, proud of his demonstration.

Suhren looked back toward his associates.

"I repeat, I ask for a chamber to be constructed, and they send me a toy!"

He turned to Schmidt.

"I do not want my men touching this piece of crap until they are fully comfortable in handling it. You will be the driver, and you will teach them for the first few weeks. I want a tally of how many people it can terminate in a day's period. Do you live in Furstenberg, Schmidt?"

"Yes sir," the mechanic answered with a sense of pride.

Surhren's admonition surprised Schmidt.

"If I hear that you have been speaking idly about this vehicle to townspeople, I will have you killed. Do you understand, Schmidt? My doing so would be approved by the very people who are paying you. So I suggest that if you have already spoken to your wife about your little project, you better tell her to keep her mouth shut, or I will order to have you both killed. This is classified information, Schmidt."

The mechanic's stare was blank as he struggled to recall just how much of the project he had discussed with his wife.

"You two lieutenants—get back to your duties," the major called. "Heinrich, Horst—in my office immediately."

"Yes sir, Major," Horst Bitten answered.

"Could I bring my jeep to you someday soon, Schmidt?" Heinrich Wurtzmuller whispered as he backed away from the mechanic. "The brakes appear to be getting somewhat weak—when I apply my foot to the pedal."

"Certainly sir," the mechanic answered, still feeling nervous about the major's threat. "Which one is yours?"

"The one with the letter, 'W', white-washed on the spare tire, "Wurtzmuller laughed. "What can I say, Schmidt?—you come out of a beer hall drunk at two in the morning, and all the jeeps look the same— except for the one with the big white 'W'."

They both laughed.

"I will bring it in to you soon."

Captain Heinrich Wurtzmuller hopped in his monogrammed vehicle, started it and crossed the prison courtyard, headed toward the camp officer's building and his meeting with Major Suhren.

* * * * *

At the same hour that Monday morning, a bus filled with prisoners rounded up the week before in Bremerhaven pulled into the city of Bremen. It nosed into a military transport-designated parking area in the middle of the town square.

The transport halted to conduct passenger exchanges. The driver pulled the lever to open the front door, letting on one armed soldier and second soldier who was holding a clip board. The latter checked his roster and began calling names. Isaac and Flora watched in silence, fearing it might be their moment of separation. The armed soldier directed the five people whose names that his colleague called to another transport, waiting in the street.

Five new people then boarded the bus to occupy the empty seats. The soldier with the clipboard studied his list closer.

"Flora Bloom!" he shouted, and then he hesitated, showing the list to the driver. The driver passed a remark and they both laughed.

"And Isaac Bloom!"

The couple gathered their satchels and walked down the aisle to the bus exit. Once again, as they were exiting to the street, the soldier and driver passed a remark and laughed.

Outside the bus and on the pavement, another soldier questioned Isaac and Flora.

"Do you both have your orders?"

After they handed over their papers, the uniformed man called to the guard and driver.

"Yes, it is correct!" he nodded. "Both of you—follow me."

He walked the couple to the fourth bus parked in the street terminal and ordered them to board the iron-barred vehicle. Flora and Isaac stepped onto the green van with idling motor.

"Okay, you are ready to go," the armed guard shouted to the driver.

As they found two seats in the rear, Isaac noticed that everyone on board, except for him and the driver—happened to be female.

*****

Once back in the administration hut within the walls of Ravensbruck, Heinrich Wurtzmuller stood fidgeting in front of his commanding officer, Major Fritz Suhren. He picked up the wooden-handled automatic German luger that lay on Suhren's desk. With a courageous sneer, he pointed the barrel directly at his commanding officer's head.

The major stared back, his mouth pursed in a daring facial expression.

"Go ahead, Heinrich, pull the trigger. I dare you. Pull it!"

Slowly, Wurtzmuller squeezed the metal trigger until the gun's mechanism responded to the pressure of his clenched forefinger. On top of the barrel, a lid popped up from the shaft, and instantly the luger cigarette lighter sparked a brilliant blue and red flame.

The officer held it to the fresh cigarette between his lips, lit the end and inhaled an enormous draft of smoke. It had been his fifth cigarette in that early morning. Wurtzmuller flipped the novelty lighter back onto the major's desk, glanced toward his associate, Horst Bitten, and then back to Surhren.

"What was it you want to discuss with us, sir?"

"We will not survive if this overpopulation surge continues," the Major answered. "It has me extremely concerned. There are fourteen huts, with 240 bunks. You do the math. We now have over 5,000 women here, with two to three hundred new prisoners added every week.

"Berlin has no interest in accommodating us in a mass extermination program. We have production quotas, vendor agreements. If our output is affected by the conditions they continue to throw at us, we can only take the situation into our own hands. Women are getting sick, giving their diseases to other women. I cannot let people who have been trained to do a job for six months die off because their bunkmate who arrived last week has hepatitis."

Wurtzmuller and Bitten nodded as he explaind his rationale concerning business versus genocide.

"So, you want us to handle this?" Heinrich Wurtzmuller asked.

He was the facility financial administrator. All production reports, vendor-camp communication, bookkeeping, food ordering, supply operations and costs passed through his command. His associate, Horst Bitten, was responsible for the daily functioning of the camp. He was in charge of the armed soldiers within the complex, and the 250 female guards, called "overseers," who acted as monitors over female prisoners. Some of these non-military personel exemplified Aryan sternness, while others were nothing more than violent, sadistic Nazi thugs-in-skirts.

Bitten had another job that Wurtzmuller had grown to detest in grandiose proportions: an accomplished musician, Horst Bitten had created an all-women prison orchestra, which had become the darling program of the Concentration Camp Inspectorate and had gained much notoriety from the Reich powers in Berlin.

Unfortunately, as operations officer for Ravensbruck, Bitten often was absent for days at a time, conducting at concerts for government dignitaries and people of influence. The camp and the prison system received false accolades, depicting Ravensbruck as some type of cultural haven in promoting the Arts.

Little did the glittering women and bow-tied men applauding in the audience realize that the concerts were nothing more than propaganda, masking the filth-ridden lives these women would return to when the music ended. Nonetheless, Bitten was happy to have a reason to play his accordion and escape his duties at Ravensbruck at times. Unfortunately, it left the supervisory burden on the shoulders of his cohort, Heinrich Wurtzmuller.

"Gentlemen, going forward, I must propose the following: any new entry over the age of sixty will be terminated at registration, and there will be no exceptions. Any woman who is ill and has not been to her assigned factory for three days will be terminated. We will need full accountability from all the kapos.

"Trouble makers, thieves and anyone inciting acts of unrest will be singled out by the overseers and executed. If this does not keep our population down, I shall implement more actions. We will have to use that stupid death bus for the extremely ill and for the new prisoners.

"We will tell the women they are being transferred to an infirmary—just to keep the hysteria down. I have not decided the methods I will use on the others. I do not want guns firing all day long. That would be bad for production morale. Keeping the Inspectorate pleased with our output is all I care about. Do both of you understand?"

Wurtzmuller responded to the morbid topic with genuine enthusiasm.

"Sir, I have been working on a new project with Engel. Leitzner Pharmaceuticals in Frankfurt has developed a remarkable product that may be an interim solution: disposable syringes that have already been filled with the appropriate medical dose. You just remove the top, expose the needle, inject the patient and then throw it away. No one has this technology yet. You can administer the medicine ten to fifteen times faster than before."

"What medicines?" Suhren inquired.

"Whatever you want? They sent an entire menu of medicines that we could request the syringes be filled with—antibiotics, phenyl, tetanus, morphine, even experimental heroin!"

He looked toward Bitten, eyes wide with excitement.

"As an alternative, this could be an excellent method of euthanizing!"

"Has Engel ordered anything?" Suhren asked.

"So far, everything has been sent as samples. I know Leitzner Pharmaceuticals would love to have a military contract. Right now, they are giving us whatever we request." He paused, unable to resist. "Perhaps I can get some pre-packed heroin for Horst and his woman band," he jibed, poking Bitten. "You musicians are big into heroin, are you not?"

"We are not a band. We are an orchestra", Bitten sneered. "Berlin loves us. The generous patrons look at the orchestra, and because of my good-will ambassador musicians, everyone sings praises for our labor facilities."

"If they only knew," Wurtzmuller snickered. "May be you could transport them to your next concert in our new carbon monoxide van. Give tours of the bus. Tell everyone it has been acoustically altered for practicing inside."

"All right, that is enough, you two," Suhren warned. "I know your administrative duties are doubled when Horst is not here, Heinrich, but it is the Inspectorate's wishes are that these concerts should continue. They raise money."

"But not enough to build us a gas chamber," Wurtzmuller replied, his tone sarcastic.

Ignoring the remark, Major Suhren cleared his throat.

"On Friday evening, I am having a cocktail party at my villa. Many of our vendors will be there. The Siemans Corporation will be putting on some type of a demonstration. I want you both there."

"Sir, my group has a performance at the Banking Symposium in Cologne. We will not be returning until Sunday," Bitten volunteered. "The Inspectorate has informed us that we cannot cancel."

"Whatever!" Suhren sighed, annoyed. "Captain Wurtzmuller, I trust you will be present. You already know most of the corporate moguls."

"Of course, sir. Can I bring anything?"

"Just bring your best behavior," the major laughed. "Chief overseer Dorothy Boerner will be there as well. I know how you two *love* to be in one another's company."

"Now that is someone I would like to take for a ride in the carbon monoxide truck," Wurtzmuller quipped.

"And we all know you do not mean in the cab section? " Suhren replied, laughing. "You have to admit, she is a 'looker.' All the vendors asked if she would be there on Friday evening."

"Masochistic bastards," Wurtzmuller laughed. "I promise you, Major, I will behave, even if she attempts to castrate me in front of the entire crowd."

Suhren rose behind his large oak desk, looking at his watch.

"The first bus should be in by 11:00 a.m. I want the mechanic, Schmidt on notice. He will drive the transport and operate its exhaust mechanism until our men learn how to do it. If any of the new prisoners gives you or any of the guards a hard time, you are to have them killed immediately, but keep it discreet. Those are my orders. Overpopulation right now is our biggest enemy. I will not tolerate it. Keep the numbers down. Now, have a very pleasant day."

CHAPTER 4

The prison bus carrying 29 women and Isaac pulled off the side of the road outside the picturesque town of Boizenburg. It was a storybook village resembling the setting in a Grimm fairy tale, yet it was no fairy tale.

"We will stop here to piss!" the armed soldier shouted down the bus aisle. "You exit four at a time, and you will go behind the stone wall. When you return, the next four will go. We should be out of here in ten minutes. Leave your satchels on the bus."

Isaac and Flora exited with the last group. The husband walked several steps away from the women, giving them respect and privacy. He took in the country scenery. Near the river Elbe, the terrain was flat, fertile farmland. It seemed the three meter-tall stone wall had been erected to identify the property boundary, and behind it was thirty meters of grass that led to a fortress of corn stalks. In a few weeks, the crop would reach its maturity and be cut down. *But in irony, the corn was free to grow again next year*, he thought.

In an instant, one of the women turned and began running for the shelter of the cornfield. At once, the guard who appeared at the door of the transport deliberately raised his rifle. As she came within ten meters of the tall rows of corn, he took careful aim and shot his fleeing prisoner. She fell to her knees, tumbling forward, the head and torso of her body, covered by the stalks she was trying to reach.

"Everyone back on board!" the soldier called, as if this was a routine reprimand.

"Are you not going to get her?" one elderly woman called out from the rear.

"What if she is in pain?" another added.

"All of you, mind your business. You now have no rights to any questions or opinions. There are only two things you should know, right now: I am a marksman, and I have many more bullets."

The Nazi laughed as he looked through his sight, randomly pointing his weapon at the passengers. Isaac held Flora's hand, squeezing it as if to impart a message of strength. They both looked to the floor, afraid to make eye contact with the guard. Only five hours had passed from the time they boarded in Bremerhaven, and yet the couple already realized that not only had their freedom been stolen, but their identity as well.

Flora had cried herself into an exhausting sleep as the humming motion of the bus rocked her body in a to-and-fro motion. Isaac, on the other hand, remained alert and vigilant, studying the landscape, curious about where they were headed. They had traveled into the rural lake district of northeast Germany. The road meandered past what seemed to be hundreds of small bodies of water. Through the forest of pine trees that outlined the azure lake, Isaac could see billowing clouds of gray smoke, ascending into the sky.

Is it a fire? he thought. A toxic industrial smell permeated through the bus. Isaac knew it was not wood, but the odor was hostile, though he could not identify it. He was not aware that he had arrived at his destination, Ravensbruck Labor Camp, the Nazi facility for military supplies production. The smell was gunpowder.

The eight-hour journey ended as the transport came to a halt in front of the brown concrete wall, reinforced with barbed wire at its apex. The stretch of mortar seemed endless. The ten meter double-wood and iron-framed doors with armed guards atop the duel turrets said anything but "Welcome."

Isaac could think but one thought: *This is what Adolf Ahrens used his influence to help attain?*

"Get your belongings and line up outside of the transport, immediately. Stand at attention! You are now officially prisoners of the Reich, and you will obey all orders as they are given. Please remember what happened to the women in Boizenburg. From here on, exemplify your best behavior, because the guards inside are not as humanitarian as I am."

After speaking, the sarcastic soldier laughed with a sneer. The two armed men perched in the turret lookouts aimed their MP40 stationary machine guns down at the group, daring anyone to give reason to shoot.

Isaac looked away from the wall, and then to the scenery outside of the labor camp. He knew he would not see what freedom looked like for a long time. Flora clung to Isaac's arm tightly as he carried both of their satchels. There was a 24-hour security booth with phone access to the entire facility at the base of the wall, near the entry doors. A sergeant exited the modest office and approached the 29 new residents.

"Welcome to the proudly productive facility of Ravensbruck. As you go through our registration process, please follow all directions thoroughly and move quickly," he said, gazing at his watch. "It is getting late. I do not want you lovely people to miss the sumptuous dinner that the chef has planned for you this evening."

Isaac observed the guards in the turret laughing. Every Nazi he had to confront since this ordeal began behaved like an absolute sarcastic, sadistic thug. They all seemed to take delight in the misfortune of others. It was one thing to be a bully, but it was quite another to take joy at inflicting pain.

The new prisoners heard the start of a mechanical groaning and a cranking noise that came from behind the double-entry doors, which creaked at their hinges and for the first time, providing Isaac and Flora a full view of their dreaded future.

The cold brown brick-and-mortar uniform buildings blended into the late-afternoon overcast day. A voice on the far side of the courtyard, standing behind a group of desks, called out to them.

"Station One, here! You must come here, first!"

The group traversed the flat dirt yard, heads bowed, forming a line. Isaac and Flora could see a cluster of women who had just finished registration were shedding their civilian clothes in exchange for a mandatory uniform—a brown skirt and beige blouse.

"Isaac, I see no men here. What is going to happen?" Flora whispered.

She feared that one of the hateful guards might kill her husband and claim it to be a mere paperwork error. Clutching his arm even tighter, she knew it was a grasp of futility.

"You, mister... You wait over there!" a female *aufseherin*—the overseer guard to the women prisoners, called to Isaac, prodding him with a horse whip. "You see that old man, standing by the pails. Go wait with him until I come get you."

"Don't leave me," Flora pleaded, pulling his arm tighter.

"Flora, it will be all right. I promise," Isaac maintained in a calm voice, peeling her clenched fingers from his jacket. "Do what they say. Do not make them angry. I will be right over here."

He realized that the moment had come. Their separation seemed inevitable, but he did not want to strike an emotional scene.

"Where are your orders? Hand them to me, now," the first station soldier scoffed toward Flora, who dutifully complied, her head turning, still searching for Isaac.

"State your name, age, height, weight and occupation", the guard shouted, never making eye contact.

After she mumbled the words, he handed her back her orders and summoned the next registrant. Flora turned toward the place Isaac had been, but he was gone. A flow of bile surged through her stomach, bringing a feeling of sick abandonment. She looked all about the courtyard. Her strength had disappeared.

* * * * *

"I tell you, this is an outrage! I expected to be greeted by the camp commandant. Thus far, not even a commissioned officer has had the decency to speak with me."

Both Isaac and the female overseer stared at the elderly man, both amused by his recklessness. *How could anyone act in such a way when facing the eye of death? Was he someone important, or was he just crazy?* Isaac stepped a few paces away from the outspoken senior, distancing him from any involvement.

The gray-bearded individual continued to rant.

"The Military Inspectorate sends me here to advise the building of a tunnel system from your barracks to the Siemens plant, and this is the greeting I receive! This is preposterous, unacceptable! I want to speak with Major Suhren."

He had imposed himself within centimeters of the portly overseer's nose as he continued the tirade.

"You wait here until an officer is ready to speak with you. Do you understand? I have been given orders to detain all male arrivals at this location until that officer is ready for you."

Isaac noted that the woman guard was perplexed by the old man's nerve. She had probably never encountered such behavior from a first day prisoner. Though Isaac admired the fire in the man's delivery, he wanted no association to his cause.

Turning to Isaac, the male continued.

"Look at this place! Fortified walls completely surround the facility, and the prison section lies within an extra layer of barbed wire fencing! If anyone tried to escape from the barracks, they would have to pass though the electrified coils. Then either deal with the mortar wall and armed guards to the west, or the soldiers' residences to the north, or the factories and warehouses to the south—and my guess is the western area is where the incinerators are situated. This place is inescapable! The women live in the center, with a multitude of obstacles between them and freedom…"

As the man ranted on, Isaac refused to react, his expressionless face focused on the ground.

*****

"Do you have tuberculosis, mental illness or venereal disease?"

Flora had just completed the medical portion of her registration process, answering "No" to the three questions. The guards then ordered her to the next station—the last in the routine. An overseer pulled at Flora's arm.

"Give me your bag!"

"No!" Flora said resisting, pulling back, "The notification said to bring my valuables for safekeeping." However, when the guard threatened to whip her hand, Flora relented.

A seated soldier continued the demands.

"Remove your rings watches and jewelry. Place them in the bin."

"Not my wedding ring, no!" she pleaded, folding her hands.

The Nazi stood and grabbed her hand, squeezing it until she succumbed to his force.

"Now, change into this!" he yelled, throwing a uniform blouse and skirt at her. "When you are finished, throw your clothes on the pile," he finished, pointing to a mound of clothing behind his table.

"Where do I change?" Flora asked the soldier.

He glanced at another guard and the two grinned, ogling her.

"Right here—so we can look you over."

Flora wept at the ridicule from the soldier. Her integrity and pride had been ripped from her essence. She felt violated, spiritually. To her great relief, one of the ladies from a group that had registered before her called out.

"Come here. We will circle you. Change behind us."

Flora used their girth as a shield of privacy and threw her civilian clothes onto the pile.

"Too bad—I would have liked to see more of you," the enlisted man said, leering, as she passed his table. "You are going to make some of our overseers very happy. You are a cutie."

The other guard laughed at the wisecrack.

"Here—here is your identification triangle," the second soldier said, handing Flora a yellow, tri-cornered patch. This insignia categorized her as a Jew.

"Here is a pin also. Clip it on your blouse until it can be sewn."

* * * * *

"What do we have here, *aufsehrin*?" Captain Heinrich Wurtzmuller asked the overseer as he took the two mens' folders from her possession. "That will be all. Return to whatever job you were doing."

"Yes sir."

Turning to the elderly man who had acted so differently from any other prisoner she had ever encountered, she whispered, "Good luck" in sarcasm, laughing.

Yet before Wurtzmuller could begin his interrogation, the irate elderly man exploded.

"Who are you? I demand to speak to Major Suhren—not some second-in-command, errand boy who does not know why I am here! I have been sanctioned by the Minister of Military Planning to consult with Major Suhren regarding a building project. I am an architect. I was informed that I would only be detained as long as the construction period warranted."

"Both of you—follow me," the captain said. "I must go over to the warehouse area. It will be a bit more private. We can continue our conversation there."

The men walked behind the fast-paced officer. As he held both folders, he studied the sketchy information written on the men's orders. They reached a line of warehouses, away from the registration area, which were border edifices, separating the inner prison area to the auxiliary buildings. The wall behind them divided the overseers' barracks from the prison section. At the front of the warehouse area, there was a road and fourteen huts that housed approximately 4,300 women resident prisoners.

Wurtzmuller stopped in front of Warehouse #8. Before he could assemble any thoughts, he was once again subjected to the architect's acerbic tongue.

"Do you know Major Messerling? He advised me to speak only to Suhren!"

"Heinz Messerling?" Wurtzmuller asked? "Isn't he retired? He fought in World War I."

"Yes, when I received my detainment papers, he wrote to Major Suhren. It appears the Siemens company would be willing to fund the construction cost of a tunnel, connecting the women's residences to their factory. This would enable easier passage in the winter months."

"Wait! You are a detainee—and a retired army person was your recommendation contact for this whole project?" the impatient captain asked. "*That* is why you are here?"

"I do not have all day, and I am too important to be dealing with anyone other than Major Suhren," the feisty elder responded.

Heinrich Wurtzmuller walked over to Isaac Bloom, who continued to distance himself from the demeanor of the man.

"I have just one question, young man. Is this individual, in your estimation, disrespectful and annoying?"

Isaac was afraid to respond. The old man had obviously taunted the officer into a state of frenzy. He had only one answer.

"We are not together."

"I did not ask you that. All I asked was, in your estimation, is this individual annoying?"

"Yes sir, under the circumstances, I find his behavior to be dangerously aggressive."

"Me too."

With a single motion, the Nazi drew his Walther automatic and released one bullet in the temple of the defiant elder. Isaac cupped his mouth, jumping back as the flow of blood responded to the pressure of the metal entering the man's skull. The old man stumbled forward and fell to the pavement in front of the warehouse entrance, blood pouring on to the concrete.

Isaac shook in fear. The captain, unaffected by the incident, opened the folders that the overseer provided. Two male guards, responding to the gun blast, ran toward the incident from the lane that separated the two closest barracks.

"You two—clean this up. Put the body in that wheel barrow," he ordered, pointing to the cart left idle in front of the warehouse entrance. "Bring it to the pit, quickly. This area will be impassable in twenty minutes, once the women are let out of the factories."

Isaac had not witnessed two people being killed on the same day since the death of his own parents in Bremerhaven. His separation from Flora felt like it had been days earlier rather than a mere forty minutes. He wanted to search for her, but that was not possible.

"Now let's see," Wurtzmuller began. "You must be Mr. Horovitz, no?"

He scanned the folder, circling Isaac, as the soldiers dumped the lifeless body of the architect into the available cart.

"No. No sir, I am Isaac Bloom."

He pointed to the other folder in the officer's hand.

"Wait!" Wurtzmuller said, a bit disoriented as he studied the papers. "Let's see, you are the person whom my *father* called me about, correct? But your name is Horovitz?"

"No sir, I mean, yes sir."

Isaac was afraid to irritate the Nazi any more than he was.

"I mean, yes—I am the person whom your father spoke to you about, but my name is Isaac Bloom."

Isaac nodded to the body being wheeled away by the two guards.

"That man was Horovitz."

"Are you sure?" Heinrich Wurtzmuller asked, his voice mischievous. "*My* folder tells me that I just killed Isaac Bloom."

Isaac bent down and began searching through his satchel for paper identification with his name, so he might prove his identity. At that moment, a new group of six women prisoners, flanked by four overseers on each side of passed the two men. The cynical captain peered over to women and yelled.

"Welcome ladies. Look—"

He pointed to the soldiers who were pushing the teetering cart with the lifeless body.

"I just killed Isaac Bloom," he said, laughing at his own foolish joke.

Squatting over his satchel, Isaac remained somber. He did not find the humor one bit entertaining.

"Keep moving!" one of the overseers yelled as the group passed.

"So Bloom, it is? Wait in the jeep inside the warehouse. Face straight ahead. Do not move."

The captain glanced at Isaac's photo identification and returned it, instructing the prisoner to follow into the warehouse opening. Isaac obeyed and sat on the passenger side of the jeep. The officer unlocked and entered the office just inside the door opening.

Sitting there, Isaac began to think of Flora. He was starving, but felt nauseous. This was to be the first night in their eight-year marriage that they would not be together. He could feel the sinuses flooding inside his head, making his eyes water. Though tears ran down his cheek, he remained calm, brushing them away, hoping the Nazi would not catch him displaying such emotion.

He swallowed hard, gaining control, estimating that it was perhaps a good sign he was sitting in the car, but he could not figure out why. Wurtzmuller exited the office along with an old man and a guard. Then the Nazi returned to the office, leaving Isaac alone for ten more minutes. When the officer re-surfaced, he had a canvas bag slung over his shoulder. Climbing into the jeep, Wurtzmuller threw the bag onto the back seat and started the motor.

"Now… Bloom, it is?"

"Yes sir."

Isaac looked straight ahead, hoping the officer would not notice his earlier sobbing.

"My father says that you were the personal secretary for his maritime friend? Just what did you do for him, Bloom?"

"I was basically his business assistant, accountant, bookkeeper, purchaser, warehouse manager and chauffer—as well as his house cleaner, launderer and personal cook. Well, me and my wife—who I just left at the registration tables."

Isaac wanted the captain be aware that she was at the facility as well.

"Well, Bloom, she is going to be needed in our factories—more than you. What is it that she does?"

"She is a seamstress, sir."

Isaac hoped that they would be viewed as a team, so they could perhaps stay together somehow.

"She will be very busy aiding in the manufacturing of soldier uniforms then," Wurtzmuller answered. "It is you—I am wondering how we can utilize your talents."

The officer started the jeep, swung it out of the warehouse garage and began heading toward the prison camp courtyard, where Isaac had last seen Flora. Driving, he dodged women who were making their way from long work days at various factories. The impatient officer beeped his horn, threatening to run them over if they did not get out of his way.

"Just sit tight, Bloom. Look self-confident. Keep your mouth shut."

The military vehicle approached the main gate. Soldiers, recognizing the second officer-in-command, saluted and ran to turn the gear wheel that opened the huge, reinforced doors.

"Good day, men. I will see you tomorrow bright and early."

Wurtzmuller gunned the car from a dead stop and shot through the temporary opening.

"See how easy that was, Bloom? All you need to be is a big shot."

Isaac could not believe what had happened. He was suddenly on the free side of the ominous wall. Turning, he looked at the bag in the back seat. His first thought was Flora, but it was not her. Although free, he could not feel as elated—as anyone else might have felt. With his wife still inside, he was still inside.

After a short distance, the officer made a left turn and began heading down a small, tree-lined dirt road. Isaac recognized that they were heading to the lake the bus had passed earlier on the way into Ravensbruck. Wurtzmuller jammed on his brake in the middle of the dirt road, and pulled his pistol from his holster.

"Bloom, today you are the luckiest man within thirty meters of here."

As he held the weapon to Isaac's temple, Isaac closed his eyes, panting, thinking of how quickly the Nazi killed the older man, Horovitz.

"Promise me you will not embarrass me!" Wurtzmuller screamed. "Promise!"

"I promise!" Isaac pleaded, squeezing his eyes tight.

"Promise me you will remain faithful and not do anything underhanded!"

"I promise!" Isaac answered.

"Promise me you will do *whatever* I ask—and you will give me a full day of work!"

Isaac was so frightened that he could barely form the words.

"Yes! Yes sir, I promise!"

The officer removed his pistol from Isaac's temple and slid it back into his holster, finishing his demands with a final remark.

"Good, Bloom, because if you do anything bad, I will not only kill you—I will kill your wife."

Throwing the jeep into first gear, Wurtzmuller continued down the road.

CHAPTER 5

Chief women's overseer, Oberaufseherin Dorothy Boerner, sat on the edge of her bunk, counting the money she had acquired while on her weekend pass in Frankfurt. It only took a few minutes in the winding back streets of the theater and entertainment district. Meeting the right people beforehand in the Rathskeller was a several-hour investment, but once the contact was made, she was instantly 2,000 Reichsmarks richer.

Boerner folded most of the bills into a circular wad and shoved the green cylinder into one of her stockings. Then she buried it in her top dresser drawer. Walking to the bathroom door, the chief of all the overseers at Ravensbruck knocked, getting the attention of her cohort and roommate, Olga Deitzl.

"Here, here are 500 Reichsmarks for the sale. We need more paydays like this one. It was clean, simple and profitable. I am tired of promoting those stupid beer rackets and fights. This is real money."

"Dorothy, I will keep my eyes and ears opened if I see any opportunities," Olga chuckled, from their toilet. "Just leave it on my bed. I am afraid to look Bitten in the face. I may start laughing at that buffoon and give our deed away."

"Too bad—he takes a select group of prisoners to big dinners and top dignitary parties while we do their dirty work," Dorothy complained. "Prison laborers are in Berlin, having caviar and lobster, while we are back here, eating the cafeteria shit that his friend, Wurtzmuller, has ordered for us. Something is wrong, I tell you."

The supervisor pointed to the money, reminding Deitzl that it was there.

"I wonder if his friend went to The Lorelei this weekend?" Boerner asked. "I would give the entire treasure we made to uncover what he does there."

Exiting the bathroom in her uniform, the older and less attractive Deitzl ignored the question.

"Dorothy, do you think we will get caught for doing this?"

Boerner responded with the assuring posture of authority.

"Olga, there are only three people who know what happened—you, Max Engel and myself. Are *you* building a case to extort money from both of us?" Dorothy smiled, teasing.

"No, no, Oberaufseherin! I am honored that you include me in this whole arrangement. Are you sure you can trust Engel?"

Deitzl bowed her head, experiencing the first signs of guilt, remorse and the growing burden of paranoia.

"You leave Max Engel to me. All those doctors are the same. They are big men in their laboratory, but socially, they are still pre-adolescents. I will just stand close to him and watch as he gets an erection, while I whisper my orders into his ear. I will not even have to touch that medical weasel."

They both laughed, as poking vicious ridicule at the male authority at Ravensbruck was a regular diet for the disgruntled and unrecognized overseers—no one more than their chief, Dorothy Boerner. Olga Deitzl took a last look at her uniformed image in her dresser mirror.

"I will make coffee when I get to the office, Dorothy."

"Fine. I will be there in fifteen minutes."

Boerner gazed at her own beauty into the dresser mirror. Her extraordinary good looks had paved the way for her promotions—promotions that had had usually been bestowed by military males. Her diabolical and sadistic behavior had always been alluringly praised by some of the Nazi hierarchy, though they were viewed as sassy and fresh by others.

She studied her reflection, tilting her perfect, Aryan face to the left and then to the right and smiling at what she saw. With a strong self-concept, Dorothy Boerner looked into her own steel-blue eyes, diabolically contemplating how she would make her next sock-full of cash.

* * * * *

Flora and the four new arrivals to Barrack 116 stood before its front door. It was battered and scratched, with kick-marks and nail-digs. The only reason they recognized barrack 116 was because someone had gouged the gray-painted wood siding with the numerals 1-1-6.

The overseer, who seemed to be the leader of the other three, banged on the unsightly portal with the palm of her hand. As the door opened, the noise level from the interior flowed into the lane that separated the next barrack.

"These are my new women, aufseherin?" the tall, stern-looking house leader said as she peered out the doorway. "Tell them to get in here, fill a bowl with soup, take one piece of bread and return to the lane."

The five women, starving from the long day, followed the kapo's order. Within a few seconds, they had eaten the soup and bread and stood on the dirt in front of the barrack.

The boss, or "kapo," of the long, crowded building ordered a helper to retrieve the bowls and addressed the five.

"I am Tula Janaczeck, the leader of this unit. You will do as I say, or you will answer to one of the guards. You do not want that to happen. If I tell them to take you away, you will not come back."

"Rat!" a voice called out from the inside of the house.

"Piece of shit, snitch!" another followed, with a bellow of laughter afterward.

Tula Janaczeck maintained her composure and ordered the women to wash from a water spigot that jutted from the ground at the base of the wooden framed hut.

"Tomorrow we will rise at four-thirty. You will use the bathroom and clean up by five-thirty. You will eat and be ready for the day by six o'clock. You will have to share a bunk with someone. Pick anyone who will accept you."

The six new prisoners assigned to the barrack adjacent to 116 had been going through the same indoctrination. In a moment of chaotic frenzy—waiting their turn at the water valve—three broke away and drifted across the alley to Flora and the group at 116.

"Excuse me, miss," one began, wanting to make her statement quickly. "You were on line in the courtyard today after my group. You were with a man. Is that correct?"

"Yes, my husband," Flora responded. "Did you see where they took him? I do not even know if he was allowed to stay. I am so worried!"

"What is your name, ma'am?" the young girl inquired.

"Flora Bloom. My husband's name is Isaac Bloom. Why are you asking?"

The three from the next barracks looked at one another and murmured in a tight circle.

"You have to tell her," one of them spoke after turning to Flora.

"We were being led to our building after the courtyard, which was near the warehouse area, when we heard a gunshot. When we walked past the Nazi officer, he laughed and yelled, 'Ladies, I just killed Isaac Bloom!'"

"What? No! That is impossible!" Flora said in panic before letting out a scream of fear and anger, bringing kapo, Tula Janaczeck and several women of 116 out into the lane. Flora convulsed as her eyes lost focus. She was not sure if anyone caught her collapse as everything went dark and she fell unconscious.

"Stay away. Give her room to breathe. Wet this cloth!"

Flora came to several minutes later, her head in the lap of a woman in the house who had taken charge of the situation.

The three neighboring prisoners, who had delivered the story, hurried back to their hut. The only ones standing over her were the other four new women—including Tula Janaczeck and the Good Samaritan, tending to Flora's spell.

"Take it easy, little one. Take deep breaths."

"We cannot stay out here all night," the impatient kapo ordered. "Get this woman inside. Find her a bunkmate."

The strong-willed woman stroking Flora's forehead looked up at the callous Janaczek.

"Damn it, you! Her husband was just killed by your Nazi buddies on her first day, and you are pressed for time? Go to hell!"

"Watch it, Resto. Keep speaking to me like that and I will have you in the Nazi box in no time!"

Tula Janaczeck was no friend of the Romani woman, Risa Resto, but everyone knew Risa was too strong to be treated like all of the others. Deep down, the kapo had a fear of the dark, belligerent gypsy. She was well aware that in any other situation, Risa could kill her within a matter of seconds.

"Get her inside!" Tula ordered as she left the scene and went in to the other 300 prisoners who were preparing to bed-down for the evening.

Risa Resto helped the shocked Flora Bloom into the barracks. Some women gawked at the scene, showing little apathy, realizing it was just another day within the camp's walls. Risa told the women closer to the door area the reason for the new housemate's hysteria. These women seemed more understanding. The fact that Flora had the support and consolation of the gypsy, Resto, meant the same from others would follow.

"Let them pass ladies. They are going to Resto's bunk," Tula shouted as Risa supported the dazed Flora as they walked to her slot.

"You know, Resto," the kapo said, trying to get in the last word, "the Nazi's are not my buddies, and my husband too, was killed by them in 1939. And do you know what for? For throwing eggs at them when they paraded through our town!"

"They were probably your eggs!" the Roma woman fired back, sparking a cacophony of laughter and applause from the crowd between their voices.

"Funny, Resto…"

Tula Janaczeck knew Risa had won that round of the verbal duel.

"You keep that woman quiet for the rest of the evening. Morning comes early," the kapo prodded to keep the tender moment.

Risa bedded Flora, who had begun to gag from sobbing over the news. So Risa went back to the entrance and kitchen area of the barracks to face Tula Janaczeck, nose to nose.

"If you make this woman's day one bit more miserable than it has already been, I swear—I will kill you. Do you understand?"

Another cheer erupted from the women who were able to hear the threat in the 150-meter-long building.

Risa had come to Ravensbruck from the Roma gypsy slums of Bucharest, Romania. At nineteen years of age in 1939, she and a gang of unruly youths boarded a train in Bucharest. Poor and hungry, the group began robbing upper-class passengers. Someone had warned the authorites that the station security in Targoviste, the next stop, would be a target for criminal acts. When the train arrived, the gypsies were met by a hoard of Romanian and Nazi police.

After her conviction, authorities sent Risa to Auschwitz for three years. One day, as two prison buses were in the central courtyard of the Polish death camp with prisoners boarding, a silent Risa walked onto the line and boarded one of the buses. She was a resident of Ravensbruck two days later. Whenever she told that story to anyone afterward, she always ended, laughing, exclaiming, "Nazi assholes!"

Tula Janaczeck gave orders with every bit of authoritarian weaponry allowed her. Herself a prisoner, the kapo could only get the overseers or armed male guards involved if she was faced with a situation that she could not handle. Too many such situations, and she would be deemed ineffective at the job, and she would return to being just another prisoner. More important to her, she would lose all of the perks that the prison bestowed on her—the separate sleeping room, the special meals, the cigarettes and the freedom from slave labor.

With Risa Resto screaming into her face, Tula Janaczeck felt the matter with Flora was definitely a situation that needed some prison staff intervention. She opened the door to Barrack 116, calling out to the closest overseer in the lane.

"You—I need someone to handle this woman."

Dorothy Boerner, Oberaufseherin to all the overseers, turned to the kapo.

"You—is that a way to speak to any overseer, nonetheless the chief overseer?"

Tula was embarrassed after having been agitated by the aggressive gypsy.

"I… I am terribly sorry, Oberaufseherin. Your guidance would be greatly appreciated in controlling this resistant woman. She disrespects me, and the others cheer her on. She needs to be reprimanded!"

Dorothy Boerner came to the barracks entrance and walked up the two steps and into the front quarters where Risa Resto defiantly stood.

"This is the woman you speak of, kapo?" the chief overseer questioned, staring deep into the gypsy's dark brown eyes.

Tula Janaczeck stood to the side as Boerner walked around Risa, circling her like a bird of prey over a wounded animal.

"What is it that she did, kapo?" the overseer asked, using her best intimidating tactic on the Romani woman.

She tapped the palm of her hand with a leather horse whip, the disciplinary aid of choice, which was used by the female guards in Ravensbruck.

"She threatened to kill me," Janaczeck answered, "if I made a new women's life any more miserable than it has already been today."

Janaczeck expected Risa Resto to deny the accusal, but the Romani woman shouted instead.

"Her husband was killed by you Nazis today. I was trying to console her, but Janaczeck kept making it worse."

"Did you threaten to kill her like she says you did?" Boerner asked, cutting to the heart of the matter.

"Yes," the Romani answered.

"You would kill someone just because she made your friend's day more miserable? What kind of a person would do such a thing?" she asked the cunning gypsy.

"I find that question funny, coming from someone who is part of a group that would kill Jews, Romanians, and Jehovah's Witnesses for a lesser reason."

The section of the barracks that heard the response from Risa erupted with cheers and applause.

"Silence!" Boerner screamed to the others while banging her whip on the kitchen wooden utility table. "Silence, or your disrespectful friend will be the cause for you to lose tomorrow night's dinner privileges."

The crowd obeyed at once. Risa knew one of the tactics used by overseers was to turn the others against the troublemaker. The problem would always seem to self-destruct. She refrained from her wise remarks, letting Boerner continue. The overseer pondered some form of discipline as she strutted around the gypsy who stood at attention in the open kitchen area.

"Kapo," Boerner said, "I would like this prisoner to be treated like a dignitary—like a queen from a visiting country—our most welcomed guest. Do you understand?"

Tula Janaczeck gasped, interrupting.

"Oberaufseherin! What is this you speak? These are your wishes? Reward her for this behavior?"

The house kapo was thrown by the seemingly irrational command of the overseer. She was sure that Risa Resto would receive some type of discipline this time, even if her threat had been merely a display of bravado.

"I would like this woman to have whatever food she wishes," Boerner continued. "I will tell the soup wagon to deliver it with the other rations. She does not have to go to her factory until I say otherwise. She is to live a life of leisure and relaxation."

The chief overseer then looked into the gypsy's eyes.

"I want to fatten her up. She will need some meat on her bones."

Boerner then turned to Janaczek, who still showed confusion and dismay on her face.

"You are to follow my orders to treat her as a guest, or I will reprimand you as well."

By the time the Oberaufseherin left the barrack, night had fallen. The scene was calm, though strange. Janaczek was first to speak.

"Do not be happy, Roma. This is a trick. She has something planned. She is just giving herself time to think what it is."

"Do you think I am stupid, kapo?" Risa answered. "If she had killed me right now, she would have been doing me a favor. However, I am going to take advantage of her silly little plan. It has been four years since I have had an egg. Tomorrow morning, I would like eggs?"

When Risa returned to her bunk slot to check on Flora's condition, somehow the exhausted woman had fallen asleep. The front section of the barrack remained quiet, awaiting Janaczeck's response to the defiant Roma woman.

"Eggs! Eggs, you want eggs? Where am I going to get eggs for you tomorrow morning? Hah? Tell me, Resto? I ask you—where am I going to find eggs for you for your breakfast tomorrow morning?"

"I do not know," Risa called out, laughing from her bunk, for all to hear. "Maybe you can get them from your dead husband!"

CHAPTER 6

Isaac's opinion of Nazi priorities became quite confused after leaving the squalor of Ravensbruck and then viewing the magnificence of the structure facing Lake Schwedt. The lakeside house was once owned by a German baron, who had it built in 1919. He was an industrialist, but he had friends in high places within the Third Reich.

In 1937, when the Concentration Camp Inspectorate proposed the construction of the Ravensbruck labor facility outside the town of Furstenberg, retired baron Louis Seigmeyer had been approached by officials to sell his home of nearly twenty years to the government. Being a shrewd businessman, Seigmeyer managed to strike a deal with the Reich, trading his 23-room, Normandy-style mansion, situated on the banks of Lake Schwedt, for a warmer, more modest Italian villa that the German government had acquired on the attractive and desirable Amalfi coast.

Assigned to the remote, newly-constructed labor facility, the Reich allowed the commandant, along with his wife and an already existing staff of six, the residence in the offsite villa. It was within 500 meters of the front gate, just down a dirt road and to the left of the labor camp. It was off-limits to all personnel, unless formally invited. Heinrich Wurtzmuller sarcastically called it "the master's house."

"It is beautiful, is it not, Bloom?"

Isaac could not speak after having spent several hours within the Ravensbruck walls. He was thinking of his beloved Flora. Why could she not be with him? *This house could certainly hold both of them, easily.* They could have each performed any duties the Nazi officer requested.

"Yes, Bloom, it certainly is magnificent. Too bad it is not where we are going."

Fifty meters before the stately manor, the Nazi officer turned sharply and proceeded down a lane that was forged by tire marks etched over a grassy span of backyard.

"Here are my quarters, Bloom. Somewhat less impressive, would you say? I do all the work, but my boss gets the maids, the butlers and the room with the view."

Wurtzmuller expresses his bitterness with a somewhat harmless envy, Isaac thought.

The jeep stopped well behind the wooded backyard of the lakeside home. The modest A-frame chalet seemed like a comfortable dwelling, but it was shoved between the treed posterior of the villa and abutted a hill to its rear.

"This used to be the cook and caretaker's house, years ago," the captain apologized. "This is now my home and office. Not much to look at, but I never have to spend the night with the low-class behind the camp gate, and I do not mean the prisoners."

Laughing, Wurtzmuller parked the vehicle along the side of the house.

"I always enter and exit from the rear, Bloom."

Isaac entered with caution, but he developed a sense of relief that the Nazi, who had held a gun to his head earlier, felt assured that he made his point. Isaac kept thinking of Flora's well-being and hoped that his arrangement was only temporary. Perhaps he could visit her—or better, she could stay with him at the chalet.

The back entrance led into a hallway with two small bedrooms on the right side and a walk-in food pantry on the left, which also contained household supplies. Wurtzmuller pointed toward the food-filled room.

"Throw your bag in there, Bloom. There is where I want you to stay."

Isaac said nothing, but he wondered why he was not given access to one of the bedrooms.

"I said it was your lucky day, but never forget you are a prisoner, Bloom. You said you are a cook. You will sleep with your food, on the floor. I will get a blanket. Now follow me to my office. We have some matters to discuss.

The two entered the two front rooms of what seemed to be the former caretaker's home. Its living room had been converted to Wurtzmuller's office, with an entire wall lined with boxes, three deep, most opened.

"All of those boxes, Bloom, are samples sent to me from various companies that are seeking to do business with our facility. If a company lands a contract with us, they will become pretty rich. Think of it, Bloom. Think of how big the Reich is. Who would not want it for a customer? Now, please, sit down."

The officer pointed to the chair in front of his over-sized desk, which consumed most of the room. Isaac hesitated, confused by the man's cordial manner. He wanted to ask the question that had been burrowing through his brain. Could Flora join him here? It would make things so much better. Perhaps he would ask in a day or two.

Wurtzmuller sat in his desk chair, pulled open the top right drawer, removed a paper and rolled it into his ironclad black typewriter that sat on the middle of his office desk. As he set the bar to the precise spot on the paper, Isaac could see the memo heading read "Military Command Order."

"Now Bloom, what is your wife's name?" the officer asked without looking up.

A rush of exhilaration and relief overcame Isaac. *Was it really going to happen?* Otherwise, why would he care what Flora's name was? Wurtzmuller was obviously going to have her summoned to stay with Isaac. Could the captain really be the same individual who shot a prisoner in the head nearly two hours ago?

The Nazi typed for several minutes, re-read his entry and pulled the page out, handing it to his prisoner.

"Okay Bloom, read it aloud please."

Excited, Isaac tried to steady his shaking hand as he began.

"August 9, 1943, Military Command Order…

As a matter of national and military security, please know that I am ordering the execution of Ravensbruck prisoner, Flora Bloom, admitted to this labor facility on the above date, for the crime of espionage and endangering the welfare of the State of Germany. Now that I can no longer follow her subversive activities, I am posthumously ordering that she be hanged for treason upon the immediate review of this command.

I remain with total allegiance to the Reich,

Captain Heinrich Wurtzmuller,

Heil Hitler!

Isaac was dumfounded. He had frozen in fear when he first came to Flora's name and the order of her immediate death, but he did not understand the wording involving a posthumous order. He put the paper on Wurtzmuller's desk and looked down without making facial contact.

"Relax Bloom, at least for now," the diabolical officer commented. "We officers are given the right to execute a will—a last request, so to speak. They are on file in the commandant's office, right inside the camp wall. Tomorrow, this document gets added to my will, which leaves my father all my medals, and my guns and money to my brother."

He held up the paper, waving it.

"This is my insurance policy on you, Bloom. If you decide some night to kill me, know this provision exists, it just might make you think twice. If you decide ever to run away, I will just kill her myself. So Bloom—keep me healthy and happy. Don't ever think of killing me, and do not ever think of escaping."

The officer folded the document, slipped it into a military envelope and tucked it into his uniform pocket.

"My goodness, Bloom," the captain complained, checking the time. "All this planning for the future has made me hungry. As you know, I also procure the military food provisions for the facility. There are two large pieces of veal in the ice box. How about proving your culinary skills by making us both some wiener schnitzel."

Isaac explored the kitchen area in an effort to acquaint himself. After he cleaned a dirty frying pan, he searched the icebox for the veal. He could hear Wurtzmuller rustling papers and slamming drawers in the next room. Through the cracked door, he saw the officer studying what appeared to be items of jewelry on the desk top. It seemed strange to Isaac—bracelets, rings?

He found some acceptable ingredients and began the preparing the meal. How stupid he felt, to think that he was to be re-united with his wife! Yet the situation was as good as could be expected. His wife was of no use to Wurtzmuller. For the moment, she was in more grave danger than he was, and there was nothing in his power that he could do about it—except keep the Nazi captain out of harm's way.

Isaac poured breadcrumbs onto a plate, running his finger through the flakes while thinking of his wife and the life they shared only a week ago. He wrote a message to himself, having no idea about what he wanted to say, and yet when he drew back his finger, the only word that he could create through the disarray of crumbs was "S-U-R-V-I-V-E."

Isaac stared at the word. It seemed to infuse a spirit into his very essence. He viewed his situation as an opportunity for strength. He was determined to withstand any obstacle necessary to re-unite him with his spouse. For the time, he would use the small amount of freedom his situation provided in order to survive and find a way to get to Flora.

*****

One hour later, Wurtzmuller opened a bottle of Mosel wine as he savored the best meal had had eaten in months, earning Isaac favor in the opinion of the officer. The meal was not difficult for him, and the house was well equipped with the necessary food and tools to create what Isaac thought would be very desirable meals.

"Bloom, did you eat? By all means, make sure you enjoy the meals you create for me as well. Try not to make it so good that I die from its richness, because you know what will happen, no?" he said, laughing.

Isaac wondered if the letter was a bluff. Wurtzmuller's behavior was so accommodating one minute, and in the next, he was threatening Flora.

"Yes, sir. I ate in the kitchen."

"Sit down, Bloom," the officer ordered. "There are a few rules that I must discuss with you—if you are to live in my home—and they are to be strictly followed. I will not tolerate any disobedience. Number one, Bloom—never ever forget for a single minute, as strange as this may seem—that you are my prisoner, just as your *wife* is my prisoner. Since you were highly recommended by my father for your business skills, I will utilize them here. You will be my personal assistant. However, as I said—never forget you are *also* my prisoner.

"No one is ever to know you are here, Bloom. What I am doing is quite unorthodox. If my commanding officer or others find out that I have opened my home to a common prisoner, I would be reprimanded—and you, of course, would have to be killed."

Although his situation was unique, Isaac realized that his situation was not as fortunate as he had anticipated. Wurtzmuller continued.

"You are to be certain that the staff of the mansion does not see you walking around my house. Shadows on the windows could reveal this. You are to keep the curtains closed and the shades drawn, all day long. You are to stay indoors at all times.

"I will expect this place to be cleaned spotless. My laundry is to be done daily. My dinner is to be ready by 7:30 p.m. every evening. I will also leave you paperwork, reports, lists to be compiled and general office tasks that will need to be completed, with my approval."

The Nazi finished in a most rational and military fashion.

"Do you understand these demands, Bloom?"

"Yes sir. I appreciate this opportunity. I will perform my duties to your expectation."

Nervous and concerned, Isaac feared that his work may not meet the Nazi's expectations.

"The business tasks of which you speak, sir?—will I have the resources to handle them adequately? I mean, I may not be aware of the subject matter necessary to complete these tasks?

"Do not intellectualize this, Bloom. I am not asking you to create a military strategy to help Germany win the war. I will need lists compiled, purchase orders typed and bills submitted for payment. I am sure the assignments are well within your range of completion."

Isaac looked at the time, which was approaching 10 p.m. Grabbing a blanket from one of the samples in a box that was resting on the office wall, Wurtzmuller advised that 4:30 a.m. was only over six hours away.

"In fact, Bloom, this will be your first assignment. Rearrange these samples. Combine boxes. Get this section more organized. There are cans of food, medical supplies and parts for just about anything imaginable. Be careful. There may be some hand grenade canisters, bullets and gunpowder in some of the boxes. I would not want to jeopardize having no meal tomorrow night—now that I have had a taste of your cooking."

Isaac had already grown tired of Wurtzmuller's morbid references to his death and his wife's death. The officer had made his point. Isaac was not going to kill the captain or try to escape. He was going to focus on surviving and saving his wife. That was all.

As Isaac bedded down for the evening, he could not believe that, less than twenty-four hours ago, both he and Flora were in Bremerhaven, anticipating what the day would bring. In that day, he had watched two people killed in cold blood before his very eyes, and he was living in the house of one of the killers. He even made dinner for that man and had become his housemate. With his wife still behind prison walls, he was concerned for her safety and wondered if he would ever see her again.

He finally realized what Commodore Ahren's phone call had done for him. As he lay on the floor of the chalet pantry, covered in an army blanket, he could only wonder if the call had made any impact on Flora's life inside the labor camp as well.

CHAPTER 7

Captain Horst Bitten, Chief Operations Officer, sat distraught in the command center headquarters of Ravensbruck. He had the last rehearsal for his all-woman prison band concert—to be held in Cologne that weekend. However Edith Klein, his virtuoso violinist, was nowhere to be found. He sent out numerous guards and overseers to find her. He searched the boot factory, where she had been assigned since her imprisonment for the past three years. He searched the infirmary and barracks. The musician had vanished. The kapo of building #108, where Edith lived, informed the captain earlier that she never returned from her practice session on Thursday past.

He guessed that either that virtuoso violinist Edith Klein either escaped from the barbed-wire fortress of the labor camp, or she had been murdered. Since she had just turned sixty years old, and no one had ever escaped from the highly secure camp, the latter seemed the more plausible answer. Edith Klein had been a member of the Berlin Philharmonic Orchestra. A highly recognized talent, she was probably the best symphony violinist in all of Germany.

Many times, Bitten introduced her to audiences at performances, as many in the crowds knew of her esteemed reputation. After every concert, there would be no less than four or five patrons asking for her autograph. She was an exceptional talent. She was a star. And yet she was a prisoner of Ravensbruck.

Klein and the Berlin Symphony had just completed a 1940 summer performance at the Munich Opera House. The show had been highly acclaimed and the reviews were glowing. As the curtain descended on the last night performance, a Gestapo troop of three SS officers and twenty soldiers who waiting in the wings of the theater swarmed the stage and held them captive.

The civilian-dressed leader ordered ten of the musicians to remain seated, releasing the balance. The SS had been on a mission to "purify" what they deemed to be "the intensely liberal population of the Performing Arts community." That evening, five Jews—three known narcotics users and two homosexuals, orchestra members—were arrested and incarcerated. Gestapo authorities in Berlin had uncovered records and incriminating information about some of the muscians that they perceived as "crimes of the state." Within days, Edith Klein found herself offstage—a prisoner of Ravensbruck. After learning who she was, Bitten allowed the artist to retain her violin and began accompanying her with his accordion on hot summer evenings.

"She was the reason that I formed the ensemble, Lt. Volsgaard," a distraught Bitten sighed when his associate, Heirich Wyrtzmuller, entered the office.

"Captain, one of Captain Bitten's featured musicians has disappeared," the young lieutenant offered, trying to warn Wurtzmuller to be cautious in his remarks. "It is feared that she is dead."

"Does this mean I will not have to cover for you every weekend, Horst? This is fantastic news!"

Wurtzmuller availed himself the opportunity to joke about his associate's somber mood.

"Then I guess you will have to go to Major Suhren's cocktail party tomorrow night, after all? I will not have to go alone?"

"No, of course not. We will still be performing. It is not like I have to end this project, but I am so upset. She was the group's main attraction. There were many songs where she had solos. Now, I will have to improvise. I hope the rest of the women can fill in for this great loss, but I am definitely going.

"You know, she owned a violin that was second only to a Stradivarius—an original nineteenth century Sebastian Vuillaume. The instrument is missing as well. I think she may have been murdered, the violin stolen and her body discarded after our last practice. What a loss to music! She should have never been here in the first place!"

"Of course she should have been here, Bitten," Major Suhren called out from his office. "She was a Jew—she belonged here. If you are going to put your love for the Arts before your love for the Nazi Party, then perhaps we should disband your little group. Captain Wurtzmuller is right. You are making money for the Inspectorate, and yet when I ask for a chamber, they follow with that hideous carbon monoxide transport—which I might add will be in operation today."

The commandant looked at his watch.

"The first bus of new women should be here shortly. I would like to observe how discreet the registration staff can be while boarding the group that will be euthanized immediately. I do not want riots."

Wurtzmuller returned to the original topic.

"Who do you think would have done this, Horst?"

"It sounds like a guard, or an overseer may have killed her," Horst answered, "rather than another prisoner. If another woman was the murderer, it would have been extremely difficult to make the body disappear. Someone would have had to discard the body."

"Perhaps they could have dumped it into a barracks latrine," the young lieutenant ventured, trying to solve the dilemma.

"I would not be surprised if Boerner did not have something to do with this—or at least know who did it, Wurtzmuller commented. "She is constantly looking for ways to make quick money. You say the instrument was expensive?"

"In the thousands—maybe over one hundred thousand Reichsmarks," Bitten responded.

"And you let her walk the grounds with it?"

"The kapo kept it locked in the barracks bin. Klein practiced every day. This has been routine for three years."

Upon mention of the name, Lt. Volsgaard remembered.

"I heard that Boerner and a group of guards and overseers were having dog races a few weeks ago?

"Dog races? What kind of dog races?" Horst Bitten asked, trying to forget his situation.

"A group of about twenty were making wagers in the field by the soldier housing area," Volsgaard answered, "They used the camp attack dogs. Someone would dangle a dead rabbit in front of eight shepherds in a cage. Then they would carry the carcass about 300 meters to the end of the property. The dogs had numbers on their collars. They would release them and all would bet on which dog would get to the rabbit first. Boerner was the ringleader, of course, so no one was going to order them to stop, as she is the Oberaufseherin."

Wurtzmuller shook his head, squinting, marveling at her creative techniques for making money while inside Ravensbruck.

"Hmm, well the outer package really does not reveal what her undercoating is certainly made of, does it?"

The other officers laughed.

"That is certainly true," Major Suhren called from his office. "She could have *men* do that instead of dogs if she wanted. She is so pretty that she could even get away with murder."

"That is what I precisely mean, Major," Wurtzmuller called back. "Unfortunately, she is well-protected by that hatchet-faced assistant of hers—Deitzl. No men would be able get close to Boerner to see if she was trying to get away with murder…

"Well, if you gentlemen will excuse me, I must check on my own Inspectorate project in Warehouse #8. Horst, hang in there. I am sure that your orchestra will do just fine without the virtuoso. Dazzle the crowd with your accordion. Play some enemy jitterbug tunes—and dedicate the songs to Himmler."

The men laughed at Wurtzmuller's attempt at being sacrilegious—even the forlorn Bitten.

"Play jitterbug for the audience? Do you want me killed now?" he called to Heinrich Wurtzmuller as his friend left the command center for Warehouse #8.

* * * * *

The knock on Commodore Adolf Ahrens' Bremerhaven home was far less intimidating than the Nazi Gestapo sergeant's greeting a few days earlier. He could almost conclude that it was a woman.

"Frau Weber, good morning," he said as he open his door, greeting the elderly visitor from the brick townhome across the street.

She had been a very close friend to Flora's aunt before her passing, ten years prior. Ahrens was perplexed.

"What brings you to my home at seven in the morning?"

"I was wondering where the children have gone? I have not seen them here since Monday, so I was concerned."

The neighbors referred to Isaac and Flora as "the children" since their courtship, a label that had followed them into young adulthood. Ahrens had tried to keep the week's events in strict privacy, because he knew it was a wise thing to do when dealing with the Gestapo.

"And I wanted to ask what this was?" she continued, pointing to a notice posted on his front door.

He had missed it upon opening to greet her. Removing his spectacles from his jacket, the startled, aging commodore put them on only to be shocked by the image of the red, white and black swastika symbol, with the word "Achtung!" that fell into immediate focus. He ripped it off the wood, shrugged and retreated inside to study the warning.

Ahrens had seen such notices elsewhere—on churches, meeting halls and public buildings in town, but he had yet to see one on a residence.

The notice ordered that his dwelling was condemned and to be vacated immediately. Authorities cited Ahrens' home as a property associated with criminal activity and were turning it over to the SS authorities in Bremerhaven.

"I do not know what it is, Frau Weber? This must be a mistake, or some kind of a nasty joke. I know of nothing that would cause this document to be posted on my door."

Of course, the commodore knew that the SS was quite capable of doing whatever they pleased. He did, however, consider that the situation regarding the payoffs to former officials for overlooking Isaac and Flora's heritage may have had something to do with the citation.

Forcing himself to smile toward the neighbor, he shut the door and headed up the stairs to his office, which was the only room equipped with a phone. Ahrens dialed, knowing urgency was now an important factor in his actions.

"Ah, thank goodness, Kraus! You are there."

Sigmund Kraus, a loyal employee of the commodore for twenty years, answered the call. Kraus had undertaken most of Isaac Bloom's workload temporarily—until Ahrens found someone as capable as Isaac to assume the managerial position.

"Sir, I was just about to call you," Kraus stammered. "A unit of SS soldiers was just here at the warehouse. They have posted notices all over our doors and windows. They condemned the building and listed the company as an enemy to the Reich. They want us out by noon today. He said they would return. Do you know what is happening?"

"I am afraid I do, Kraus."

Ahrens was not naïve.

"Send the employees home immediately. Tell them to check Monday to see if we have reopened. Did the leader of the group give any more information?"

"They told me," he explained, "that the old Gestapo street leader, Vishnitz, had confessed to bribery charges, and that our company was under investigation for being one of his clients."

"But I heard he was sent to Warsaw as a punishment for his actions?" Ahrens muttered.

"Well, perhaps that is what they *wanted* everyone to think," Kraus deduced, "because the sergeant who was here confessed that Vishnitz escaped and was in hiding for his SS crimes. They had orders to shoot-to-kill, if he surfaced in the Bremerhaven area ever again."

Ahrens knew it was a matter of days, or even hours, before he and the employees of his company would be apprehended.

"Kraus, after you release the workers, remove all of the money from the safe. There are two suitcases next to my desk. Put the money in them and drive to my home. Use the unmarked truck—not the one with our company name. You must do this in five minutes, not longer."

Sigmund Kraus acted quickly. After sending everyone home, he filled the two suitcases with bundles of Reichsmark bills until the meter-high, glossy black iron safe behind Ahrens desk was empty. Kraus was widowed, and his children had left home to pursue their careers nearly ten years earlier. He could have run with the small fortune and faded into the chaotic German landscape, but he was honest. Ten minutes later, he pulled up in front of Ahrens' home in the unmarked produce truck.

Exiting the vehicle, he carried both satchels up the steps to the townhome and knocked on the door, which had been left ajar. Kraus pushed it open and called.

"Sir? Sir, I am here. I brought the money, as you ordered."

"Good, good—over here," a voice murmured from behind the dining room wall. "Come in here."

When Kraus turned the corner, he was greeted by Karl Polmer, the Gestapo leader in Bremerhaven—the officer who had replaced Vischnitz. At Polmer's feet was the slumped corpse of Commodore Adolf Ahrens. Polmer pointed his luger pistol toward the commodore's assistant.

"You have been very helpful, Herr Kraus. Now please put those two bags on to the floor."

Kraus stooped, placing the suitcases on the ground. Before he raised his torso to an upright position, the SS officer buried two bullets into the aging man's heart. Krause fell, knocking one of the bags over as his body tumbled next to that of his boss on the dining room floor.

Smiling from the kitchen, a portly hulk, dressed in civilian clothes appeared.

"Good work, Sergeant. One of those satchels is yours."

The man walked over and picked up the other bag.

"Now if you will excuse me, I have a commercial tanker for Spain that I must catch."

Polmer grabbed the handle of the other bag, seeming anxious to leave. As he made his way to the door, he turned toward his accomplice in civilian clothes, holding up the suitcase.

"You have a comfortable retirement, and I sincerely thank you for this opportunity, Herr Vischnitz."

CHAPTER 8

Isaac looked at the telephone on Captain Heinrich Wurtzmuller's desk. It rang once and ceased. It then rang a second time, stopping abruptly again. When it resumed a few seconds later for the third isolated ring, Isaac lifted the receiver with caution.

"Bloom, are you there?"

It was the first time Isaac had responded to the private signal that the officer had devised to identify himself as the caller.

"Hello, Captain."

The Nazi seemed pressed for time.

"Bloom, did you finish combining all of the boxes against the wall? I need more room for samples. I am expecting more pharmaceutical items and uniform material."

"Yes sir, there appears to be quite a bit of ammunition in those boxes. Do you want them to remain indoors?"

Isaac knew that he was out-of-line in questioning the small arsenal leaning against Wurtzmuller's office wall. However, he thought it should be addressed.

"They have been there for months, Bloom. That is not any of your concern. I have more tasks for you. I did not have a chance to give you these orders this morning, and I must attend a gathering at the Major's villa this evening. Remember what I said about casting shadows on the windows. There will be many people around our quarters this evening.

"Please listen closely, Bloom. There is a box on my desk. Do you see it? It has several fancy bags inside it…"

Isaac located the carton and the four velvet liquor-bottle bags that were lying at the bottom of the corrugated container.

"Yes sir, I have it."

"Inside are some articles that have to be counted, weighed and tabulated on paper," Wurtzmuller continued. "This must be done before you retire for the evening. Look in the upper right desk drawer. There is a small scale. It is for weighing precious gems.

"You are to weigh all the gold items and come to a total. Do the same with the gems and stones. If a ring has a diamond in it, you are to remove it from its setting and treat those diamonds separately. Do you understand, Bloom?"

Isaac could not believe the request. What was happening?

"Sir, how do I remove the stones from their settings?"

"Next to the scale, Bloom, is a set of jewelry pliers. This must be done as I request. I would normally do this task myself, but now I have you. That is my only explanation. Do you *not* want to do it?"

"Oh! No! No sir!"

Isaac could sense the officer's discomfort with ordering the chore, as it seemed quite unconventional.

"What else, sir?" he asked, trying to infuse his voice with a spirit of allegiance.

"There are watches as well. Please categorize the maker, the weight of each one—and if there are any gold content markings on them.

"When you have finished that," Wurtzmuller said, changing the subject, "there is a list of all the new women who have entered Ravensbruck this week. Please type their names and the corresponding barracks to which they have been assigned. Contrary to other camps, Bloom, I am quite thorough and want to know where people are located and that they can be quickly found.

"It appears that there were 230 new additions this week. I do not want my workers spending inordinate amounts of time trying to find one, should we need. I will be home by midnight. There will be no reason to cook dinner."

That being said, Wurtzmuller ended the call with same indifference that Isaac had come to expect over the last five days.

* * * * *

Inside the brick and barbed-wire walls of the Ravensbruck facility, Risa Resto of Barrack 116 tried to stay focused as she followed the unusual demands of Chief Overseer Dorothy Boerner. Risa was becoming bored with the idleness and all-day company of the building's "Snitch." Although resistant, kapo Tula Janaczek had complied with the gypsy's requests for the cheese, fruit and other foods that she kept in her own private bin.

"You know, they are doing this until they find the correct punishment for that mouth of yours. They are fattening you up for their kill. That is the only reason I am agreeing to this," the kapo scoffed in an attempt to defend her pride.

"The reason you agree to it is because you are a prisoner like me. They would sooner kill you. They have no respect for you, Snitch. At least they are a little afraid of me, and they need time to think how to deal with it. Now, get me two apples, some cheese and a piece of sausage from your bin, or I will "rat" on you to them. We can then see how much they respect you?"

Risa took the items that Janaczek had gathered from her personal bin situated in the kitchen area, next to her private quarters. The day was quiet. The only sound in the building was the continuous coughing and spewing of phlegm coming from the handful of sick women who had been segregated to the rear of the barrack.

The Romani walked toward the group of invalids and threw the food on a bunk, summoning one of them to retrieve it. Then she walked back toward Tula Janaczek.

"Make sure you tell your Nazi friends what I just did. I want them very angry at me, so I can stay equally as angry at you."

Risa walked out of the barrack, feeling little benevolence about the good deed she had just done. Instead, she assumed it a moment of emptiness and despair. Sliding down against the side of the wooden building, the Romani from Bucharest was hard-skinned, tough and belligerent. However, she began to feel distraught and defeated. Just what did the Chief Overseer have in store for her, and when would it happen?

As Risa Resto's mind wondered over the barbed-wire stanchions to the left, gazing toward the distant skies of freedom, a hollow feeling of insignificance and helplessness overcame her iron exterior. She began throwing pebbles at the adjacent barracks, trying to decode the diabolical and sadistic Nazi plan she knew she would eventually have to confront.

At that moment, a group of twelve new prisoners walked past the lane, en route to their assigned dwelling.

"Poor bastards!" Risa murmured. "Like a herd of defenseless sheep, responding to the rod of the shepherd. We are nothing more than the lambs of this war… one day to all be slaughtered."

* * * * *

The late summer weather delivered a crisp, cool evening temperature as the gentle breeze blew across the water of Lake Schwedt.

A mixed crowd of military administrators and civilian suppliers to the labor camp had gathered for an evening of camaraderie and contractual obligation. Major Fritz Suhren was sensitive to the value of maintaining strong relationships with his vendors, so the cocktail parties he hosted at his villa, overlooking the lake and the town of Furstenberg, were done with all the public relations etiquette of an industrial tycoon.

He always boasted that the productivity and success of his camp had resulted from the team efforts of his fine staff, the cooperation of the contracted suppliers and the hard work of the women prisoners of Ravensbruck. Unfortunately, the prisoner women were unrepresented on those festive nights, and no one had ever requested to view the camp's working conditions.

The evening, however, promised to be one of enlightenment and entertainment. There was to be a demonstration involving new technology from the Siemens Electrical Corporation and the Daimler group, which was expected to dazzle the guests and revolutionize weaponry.

Suhren was excited, as Ravensbruck would play a key role in manufacturing certain weapon parts that would be integrated into the success of the military endeavor. Captain Heinrich Wurtzmuller, who just entered the spacious ballroom and veranda overlooking Lake Schwedt, seemed anything but intrigued.

"Just what I need—more things to buy! Machine parts, dyes to make the items, metal sheeting, plastic molds and electrical cables—not to mention all the training sessions for our women! Why don't we just buy all this stuff assembled? Then we can just shoot the prisoners like at the other camps."

Major Suhren cleared his throat, downplaying the officer's frank and caustic remarks.

"Ah, always, such an unforgettable entrance! Gentlemen—you all know my assistant, Captain Wurtzmuller. He really *is* a team player. I do not know how the facility would run without him."

"Yes, of course we do," the tall, distinguished salesman from Sieman said, extending his hand.

Wurtzmuller could not resist the wise-crack.

"What? You mean that *you* do know how the facility would run without me?"

"No," the businessman responded, laughing. "I mean we met several times at symposiums and training sessions in Berlin, Captain. I am Rutger Von Blarcom of Siemens. I think you will find our demonstration this evening to be fascinating."

"Of course, it is my pleasure. This must be your lovely wife?"

Wurtzmuller clicked his heels and bowed to the attractive woman. Uneasy about the introduction, the seasoned businessman cleared his throat.

"This is a… friend—Frauline Wanda Taggerhaus. She has been kind enough to accompany me this evening while Frau Von Blarcom is in Munich."

"How do you do, Frauline?"

Major Suhren intervened before the officer could blurt out one of his barbs.

"And Heinrich, you know Victor Hamm of the Bavarian Leather and Textile Mills, Gunther Shultz of Daimler Motor Works?"

"Ah, Herr Shultz, here is ten Reichsmarks—" the quick-witted officer jibed, "could you look at my brakes before the night is over?"

Everyone laughed at Wurtzmuller vile tongue. The officer had a talent for dishing these insults out in a crowd—and yet even those on the receiving end felt that they had just experienced an old friend's verbal jab and were not offended.

Unfortunately, Heinrich Wurtzmuller spotted two individuals across the crowded room that would not be as accommodating to his degrading sense of humor.

Amidst several lower ranked officers and a select group of veteran overseers, the captain observed the dagger-like eyes of Chief Overseer Dorothy Boerner and her comrade, Olga Deitzl.

He smiled and silently acknowledged her presence by raising his fluted champagne glass, offering an olive branch of courtesy. He could not help but feel that she had passed on some disparaging remarks to the uniformed officers. Wurtzmuller didn't care what the overseer thought of him, but he bristled at the thought that his soldiers were being entertained by Boerner's character attacks on his persona.

"So Captain, I trust you will thoroughly enjoy tonight's program," Ruter von Blarcom, the representative of the Siemens organization said, recapturing Wurtzmuller's attention. "We are quite proud of our advancements with military technology. We feel thousands of troops' lives will be saved as a result. Ravensbruck will help make this happen."

The captain tried to maintain a proper business demeanor. As he spoke, he could feel that he was making eye contact more with von Blarcom's escort, Wanda Taggerhaus, than he was with the businessman. He caught himself.

"Well, Herr von Blarcom, I cannot wait to see your show. Would it be possible to get samples of your items? I always like to have prototypes or actual finished products of the supplies that we are considering."

Herr von Blarcom responded in full agreement.

"By all means, Captain, I will personally attend to this request sometime this week. Now, please come to the veranda balustrade. I would like you to see the military stage we have constructed for tonight's little demonstration.

Wanda Taggerhaus took both men's arms and escorted the duo out under the cool evening sky, to the panoramic front lawn view of the villa that was lit aglow with oil bamboo torches, creating an even more theatrical and impressive scene.

"Ah, what have we here?"

The officer scanned over the concrete railing, down to the grassy lawn. The Siemens crew had created a miniature battlefield. There were holes dug deep into the turf, two small bridges that spanned a temporary water hazard, a pile of rocks that simulated rough terrain and a live low-voltage wire, which crated sparks every few seconds.

At the end of the obstacle course, there was a newly constructed wooden shed. The crew had painted the Union Jack symbol on the building's side. The lit torches set an eerie glow on the lawn. The flames danced over Lake Schwedt, as did their reflections.

Wurtzmuller wanted to respond to the course with some sarcastic observation, but he was impressed with the efforts and ingenuity of von Blarcom's crew. Below, the men tending to the technical aspect of the evening removed a tarp from an object that had been sitting beneath the crowded veranda.

The captain recognized the machine.

"Herr von Blarcom, your demonstration involves the Goliath Drone Assault Module! This is already in operation?"

"Yes, but wait until you see the advancements that we have made to its striking capabilities," the salesman responded. "This will revolutionize the entire concept of infantry combat. We have already placed equipment in our factory in Ravensbruck. Your women will help produce certain parts for its operation."

The officer had been familiar with the Goliath. Similar in size to a sofa ottoman, the metal car resembled a tank, without any visible weaponry. It rode efficiently on its own treads, and a member of an infantry platoon controlled it.

The small vehicle forged the way into dangerous territory, ahead of the soldiers. Its job was to be the suicide machine that cleared the area of snipers and booby traps, while keeping the infantry at a safe distance from danger.

The drone was equipped with a detonating device, which had been situated on top of several explosives. The device responded to the soldier's radio transmitter at the end of electric cable wiring, two hundred meters away. The cable was the artery that supplied life for the steering of the Goliath, as well as the explosion command.

Until then, the weapon had drawbacks and received criticism, which involved tangled wires in trees and shrubs, its small size allowing the tank to get stuck in holes, and the most critical complaint—that the soldier who controlled the transmitter was too close to the unit while detonating it. He risked killing himself along with the enemy.

Major Suhren, realizing that everyone had made their way to the edge of the veranda, stood on one of the concrete stools, situated beneath the balustrade, overlooking the drama on his lawn. He shouted for attention and made eye contact to the Chief Overseer, Dorothy Boerner, beckoning her to join Rutger von Blarcom and himself.

"Ladies and gentlemen, I will turn this demonstration over to Herr von Blarcom, who will give us an explanation of what is happening. Ravensbruck is quite honored to be a part of this innovative project, Herr von Blarcom..."

The Siemens representative thanked the major for his introduction and began explaining the benefits and drawbacks concerning the remote-controlled Goliath assault vehicle's history. He could see Dorothy Boerner elbowing her way toward him, until she stood between Suhren and himself.

Wanda Taggerhaus seemed puzzled about why the uniformed woman wedged her slender body between the major and her date.

"Ladies and gentlemen, I would like all of you to imagine a battle where enemy soldiers show up to engage in warfare, only to find that they must confront machines—not men. Think of the lives that could be saved. Imagine military personnel controlling these machines from safe distances. Imagine them telling the machines what to do by radio transmitters. That is right—wireless machines—controlled by frequency waves. No strings attached!"

The guests snickered.

Von Blarcom held up a metal panel box, smaller than a briefcase. The crowd applauded as he raised the transmitter for all to see. Like a father hoisting a newborn for the villagers to behold, the proud businessman dazzled his audience.

"May I present the device that will revolutionize infantry combat. And *we* have this technology before our enemies. The remote-controlled assault vehicle equipped with detonation capabilities—it is a movable bomb, a suicide drone. Please enjoy the demonstration."

Von Blarcom held the box in one arm as he flipped the switch to the panel. A red light glowed at the unit's center. People reacted in awe as the small Goliath car, which had been idle beneath the veranda, suddenly came to life.

The salesman spun the ten-centimeter steering wheel at the center of the transmitter panel, directing the Goliath's path. At one point, it made a 360-degree turn on its axis.

"How cute is that!" a female guest shouted, causing laughter in the audience.

The tank-like weapon began its journey through the newly-constructed obstacle course. First it went through a large sewer pipe that had been half-buried, and it entered and exited with little trouble. It then climbed a tiny wooden bridge and a pile of rocks that sat on the lawn.

"It is a powerful little bugger!" Major Suhren confirmed, eliciting a stream of chuckles.

"Think of the range and potential of this weapon!" von Blarcom added as the tank splashed through a depression of water and over the simulated sparking wires.

"Here is an extra feature I did not mention," he noted, flipping a toggle switch, which caused a puff of smoke to emanate from the unit's body—the smoke created a deflection screen, making the weapon temporarily invisible behind a foggy cloud. The guests again applauded.

Travelling for nearly ten minutes over the grassy lawn, the Goliath finally stopped short of the wooden shed at the bank of Lake Schwedt. Rutger von Blarcom beamed.

"Now this is what technology is all about, ladies and gentlemen!" Steering the vehicle into the wooden framed hut, he finished. "Because radio frequecies are so varied, I must make sure that the transmitting waves in my panel are in agreement with the receiving waves inside the machine. I will have to turn this dial until my red indicator changes to green. Once it does, the frequencies are compatible. This also allows many Goliaths to attack at once, while each responds only to its own selected frequency."

"So when you push one button they all do not explode together!" Major Suhren shouted, embracing the concept.

"Precisely, Major!" Rutger von Blarcom exclaimed. "Now, Major, would you ask the prettiest woman in attendance this evening to turn the frequency dial, instructing her that once it becomes 'green,' that is the time to depress the detonating switch. We can all see how easy it is to operate."

Wanda Taggerhaus brushed her dress and stood at attention, awaiting the control panel to be handed over to her… to her surprise and embarassment.

"So let us give our support to *Oberaufseherin Dorothy Boerner*," Suhren blurted, "as she completes this simulated attack on the British occupied shed of Lake Schwedt."

Accomodating the request, and seeming to be in complete agreement with Suhren's selection, von Blarcom held the controls in front of the overseer as she attempted to locate the correct frequency wave. Embarassed, he recognized the anger in his escort's eyes—more for the remark rather than the choice.

Boerner turned the dial until the bright green light shown in the panel display, and without hesitation, she pressed the detonator button.

The resounding explosion blew the small structure fifty meters into the air in various directions. Flames shot out, as some wood fragments made its way on to the veranda. Von Blarcom found himself covering the face of Dorothy Boerner, rather than that of his date for the evening.

Some of the cinders drifted to the earth, sizzling, while others were extinguished in the cool lake water. Cheers followed, as the presentation had almost been as impressive as the weapon's effective result. Von Blarcom's crew ran onto the lawn, putting out small fires that had started from the shower of debris.

"Quite impressive, Herr von Blarcom! Indeed quite impessive," Captain Wurtzmuller said as he approached the businessman. "Please do not forget to supply samples of this mechanism to me? I always like to have samples of the finished goods that our facility assists in producing."

"Of course, Captain," von Blarcom nodded. "I will make sure you receive several transmitters and detonating receivers next week, but please be aware—they are easily activated. The batteries are already installed. All you need to do is just what I just did—match the transmitter with the receiver and detonate. The detonator is not that destructive, but if it is set off near other gunpowder, gasoline or explosives, a nasty chain reaction will occur."

"Or perhaps I can just get help from overseer Boerner, like you did," the officer quipped as Boerner came near von Blarcom and kissed his cheek, thanking him for requesting her assistance in the detonation of the Goliath.

"By the way, Captain—the steering of the vehicle is a whole other issue. You will have to speak to Daimler about getting a sample for those parts."

Boerners cohort, Olga Dietzl, joined the group, offering her congratulations to von Blarcom.

"Now Overseer Deitzl, if I was giving this demonstration, I would have picked you..." Wurtzmuller said to silence, as was obviously setting up a joke. "...to drive the little tank around the lawn, just so I could blow it up."

Rutger von Blarcom tried stifling his reaction, a challenge that became easier after the overseer responded.

"Go to hell, Wurtzmuller!"

Coming to her friend's rescue, Boerner sighed.

"Perhaps we will see you tomorrow night, Captain, at The Lorelei—when you visit your whore. You should come into the bar and have some drinks with us... after you are done with her."

"Visit *you*? But I will have already *been* with a... Forget it!" he jousted.

Uncomfortable, Rutger von Blarcom excused himself and returned to his angry date, preferring her clenched lips rather to the loose ones of the vial trio he had left.

With the evening's entertainment coming to a close, many of the guests began to leave the villa. Some had to face the 70 kilometer drive back to Berlin.

Wurtzmuller lagged behind, thanking the vendors for their partnership in the labor camp production.

"Your support in building machinery for us to take part in this great war effort is sincerely appreciated, Herr Schultz," he said to the Daimler representative.

"And your free labor enables both of us to achieve our goals, Captain," the man replied.

"Now if you will excuse me, sir. I must return to my hotel before I head back to Frankfurt in the morning."

Wurtzmuller finished the conversation with the phrase that unified their allegiance.

"Heil Hitler!"

After one of Major Suhren's servants appeared in front of the officer and presented him with his gloves and hat, he brushed Wurtzmuller's back, removing cinders that had settled on his uniform tunic.

"Don't forget to save me a dance tomorrow night, Aufseherin Boerner," Wurtzmuller called as she descended the stairway to exit the gathering. "But no jitterbug!"

Her response was inaudible, though he could tell by the roar from the crowd that her remark was a barb worthy of his wit.

"That is—if I can tear you away from that ape, Olga!" he called back in a final, cutting insult that hinted at her sexual proclivities. Several of the male guests, still descending the stairs, understood his inference, and laughing, seemed to agree.

* * * * *

Back at the captain's chalet, buried deeply behind Suhren's villa, Isaac had heard the explosion over Lake Schwedt and had rushed to the window, glaring through the wooded yard. Yet he was careful to avoid casting a shadow on the window curtain. *Very strange!* he thought. He heard loud, joyous cheers after the glowing fireball lit up the sky.

As Isaac walked back to the table where he had been tabulating the jewelry for Wurtzmuller, he had reason to celebrate as well. He finished the glass of wine that he had poured from Wurtzmuller's bottle of Moselle in the icebox, replacing its volume exactly with water from the sink tap. He was learning Wurtzmuller's paranoid idiosyncrasies.

He was celebrating for two reasons, and both he could hardly believe. While tediously recording the weights of the gold objects, as he had been ordered, Isaac discovered Flora's wedding ring amidst the pile of confiscated jewelry.

As he measured, weighed, tabulated every article, piece by piece, the wedding band he gave to his bride nearly eight years earlier just seemed to surface in singularity from the glittering mound of precious gems. The Initials "F.B" and the date 1935 proved to the young man that indeed he had found the ring he had bought for their wedding. Though he still lamented over their separation, it was like having a part of Flora back with him. He was elated.

After discovering the band, Isaac removed the shoe and sock of his right foot before rummaging through the sample boxes against the wall that he had categorized earlier in the week.

"There it is!" he whispered as he unrolled a spool of medical adhesive tape. Carefully measuring the length, he slipped Flora's wedding band on his middle toe and mummified the digit with the linen adhesive, wrapping it so secure that it looked like a legitimate wound to that area. As he once slipped his sock and shoe back on, he felt he had a piece of Flora with him again.

The other incident that excited Isaac was discovering that Flora had been assigned to barrack #116. Wurtzmuller's order to list the location of all prisoners after the registration process proved to be an enlightening task for the young husband. He had learned where she was within the prison walls, even if he could not see her.

Isaac did not want to confront the officer. He could hear cars leaving the lakeside driveway of Major Suhren's villa. It was only a matter of time before Wurtzmuller returned to the chalet.

Isaac scurried to the pantry, dropping his army blanket on the floor. He dragged a 25-kilogram sack of flour from the food supply shelf, which he used for a pillow. After bedding down, he hoped that Wurtzmuller would not require his services until the morning.

Isaac pulled the bulb string that dangled from the pantry ceiling, extinguishing the light. As he rolled onto his side, he used his other foot to explore the bulge on the taped toe as he thought of barrack number 116. Clinging to those two feeble facts, Isaac smiled for the first time in two weeks. His wife had no idea, but they were together that night, at least in his mind. Smiling at that thought, Isaac Bloom fell into a deep sleep.

CHAPTER 9

The veteran country physician, Neils Bracht, handed the medical folder to a couple who had driven twenty-five kilometers for the consultation. His demeanor was somber and defeated as he began the meeting.

"I am afraid that the news is as I had expected. The test results have clearly indicated that your daughter, Elsie, is suffering from a condition known as pituitary giantism."

"She is a big girl, doctor," the man responded. "That is good, no? She is strong. She can lift a milk barrel over her head. She can do this better than her older brothers. She will be an asset to any farmer in our area. Why is this a bad thing?"

His wife kept her head bowed, realizing that the situation had more to do than strength.

Elsie Honigsberg was five years old when she surpassed her nine-year-old brother in height. By her twelfth birthday, the young Westphalian daughter to Frederich and Leena Honigsburg was 200 centimeters in height and weighed over 86 kilograms.

Over the next five years, she grew another 25 centimeters, gained 40 kilograms and was forced to sleep in the barn with the livestock. She had outgrown the family dwelling, the furniture and her bed.

"You could take Elsie to the city, "Dr. Bracht suggested." I know a specialist who has worked in this area before. Perhaps they can provide help for Elsie's future. She will not be able to receive such assistance on a farm."

"Help? Why will she need help, Doctor?" Leena Honigsberg asked in a desperate tone.

"Cases like Elsie's have revealed that, as she gets older, certain parts of her body will grow at different rates, compared to other parts. Her skeletal system will grow by leaps and bounds, but her muscular system and joints will not be able to keep up with it. Consequently, she may need assistance with her mobility. Her heart may not be able to perform its circulatory tasks, because her body has become so large. This will affect her kidneys and lungs.

"We would not want her stuck on a farm one hundred kilometers away, should she need medical intervention. It would be best for her to be under a physician's watch for the rest of her life," the doctor concluded.

When Elsie Honigsberg turned eighteen years old in 1938, her parents finally came to terms with the fact that she needed special care. Reluctantly, they drove the family truck, with Elsie in a specially constructed wooden chair, on the flatbed portion, headed for the city of Hamburg.

Follow-up reports confirmed the rural doctor's diagnosis, and for the next few months, Elsie lived alone in a hotel room in the dank wharf district of the German port city. One day, the hotel manager knocked on her door along with a stranger.

"Elsie, this is Doctor Gunther. He runs a medical exposition a few blocks from here. He wants to pay you money for your talents."

"What is a medical exposition?" Elsie asked in her hollow, resonant voice, which was low as a result of elongated vocal cords.

Gunther explained that it was nothing more than a circus freak show, totally unrelated to academic medicine, as he was not a true doctor."

"I will pay you good money, Elsie," the fast talking charlatan began. "All you have to do is let people view your God-given uniqueness, and nothing more."

Elsie thought that it sounded too good to be true, though she accepted the offer.

One month later, she was billed as the "star" of "Dr. Gunther's Human Oddity and Strange Behavior Exposition." Elsie was the featured attraction in the dimly lit hallway of glass observation rooms that Gunther had built, perched beneath an existing restaurant along the Elbe.

Along with the usual fat woman, a sword swallower, and a strongman found in such base entertainment, Gunther also featured displays of dwarfs, contortionists and a South American Indian with hypertrichosis—better known as the "werewolf" syndrome.

Elsie completed his line-up of unfortunate human beings who would be gawked at and ridiculed, though sometimes drawing sympathy from people who paid to view them. The Germans even had a name for the behavior, which they called it "shadenfreude," meaning "to internalize a feeling of elation while viewing the misfortune of others."

Gunther introduced Elsie as "Mother Germany" to his cast and billboard advertisement displays along the shabby wharf district. She was huge, threatening, intimidating, fearless, and yet female—everything Germany should be, or so he thought.

The Reich, however, viewed Germany in a more masculine manner, as "The Fatherland." In 1938, Hitler ordered that all physically challenged individuals should be removed from society and killed, as part of the Nazi purification plan involved creating the perfect race.

Dr. Gunther's Exhibition was a sure target for Gestapo squads to invade and by orders, execute the unfortunate cast of characters. Fearing for his life, Gunther abandoned his handpicked group and escaped with the last three months' proceeds. Elsie had not even been paid a single time up to that point. Gestapo soldiers shot nine of the people dead, right in the restaurant basement, while most were still in their cubicle display rooms.

Only the contortionist, who hid in his own suitcase at the foot of his bed, and the tattooed Tongan, who the Nazis mistook for a paying merchant seaman customer when they encountered him in the hallway, managed to avoid assassination.

When the leader of the sweep reached Elsie's exhibit booth, the giant rose and stared down at the Gestapo officer. Frozen, he raised his hand to a halting position, ordering his men to hold fire. He stared into the lost eyes of the Westphalian woman. Her uniqueness and impressive girth paralyzed the officer.

He experienced a biblical moment of compassion, respect and wonder. The Nazi could not bring himself to harm "Mother Germany." Dressed in the barbarian, Germanic tribe costume, made of animal skins, and crowned with a silver helmet, supplied by Gunther, she epitomized a raw, primeval aura that the officer could not destroy.

Instead, the SS leader ordered a soldier to guard Elsie where she sat, defeated, in her display cubicle, next to her nine dead friends. The officer ascended the basement stairs to the restaurant to use the owner's telephone.

"Please, can I be connected with a Doctor Max Engel, Chief Medical Officer at Ravensbruck?"

It took several minutes for the military operator to contact the officer's old friend from the SS training facility in Berlin. They had met as officer candidates. After graduation, Engel shared that he would be stationed in the labor facility and would be in charge of human-experimentation projects. The information he would gain, using the prisoners as human guinea pigs, would then become criteria for the treatment of front-line soldier injuries.

The Ravensbruck physician had advised all his officer buddies to keep their eyes open for anything that they found biologically intriguing. He was interested in observing odd mutations and behaviors, and dissecting human subjectivity.

Once the Gestapo officer's eyes met Elsie's, he knew Engel would be interested. The next morning, a platoon of SS soldiers who were headed to Berlin wrapped Elsie in army tent material, tied it closed with rope and took her away.

They passed through Furstenberg, which was somewhat off their course, but as a favor to Engel, the platoon transferred Elsie onto a Ravensbruck utility vehicle. Eighteen hours after the phone call, "Mother Germany" was a common prisoner, and her new home was an observation cell within the camp's infirmary at the rear of the property. Only administrators, guards and overseers had access to the building, inhabited by the subjects used for experimentation. The facility behind the infirmary was the crematorium. And behind the crematorium was something that a select group of military personnel referred to as "the pit."

* * * * *

"Can I see her, Max?" Chief Overseer Dorothy Boerner requested of the Ravensbruck physician. "I have another opportunity for us. I was thinking next Wednesday. How is she doing physically? I was a bit concerned during the last match. It seemed that her joints were seizing up on her—half-way through the contest."

The Nazi doctor pointed out his office window, which served as an observational vista into the infirmary courtyard, flanked on three sides with chain-link fencing.

"Take a look for yourself. She is right outside on the grass."

Engel was the consummate Nazi medical practitioner. As a doctor, he was more interested in experimentation than the objective of healing. He deliberately tortured subjects by inflicting simulated war wounds, just to observe the effects of various drugs on the victims. He would pass his findings on to doctors treating the military-wounded in the hundreds of German field hospitals, dotting the many European war zones.

The only "sick" he tended to were staff members. Working alongside four others doctors and ten *krankenschwesters*, or nurses, Engel treated military when they needed assistance, but used the women laborers solely for experimental purposes.

Amidst the various groups of deliberately-wounded prisoners—some who sat tending to the injuries of their less fortunate mates—Boerner spotted the intimidating hulk of Elsie Honigsberg. She was stretching her legs, pushing against the metal link fence at the far end of the court.

"Let me out to speak with her. Will you need to administer any enhancers before she fights, perhaps something for her knees?" Boerner asked.

The overseer picked up what appeared to be a pre- wrapped syringe of medicine.

"What is this?"

"*This* is amazing," Engel answered. "Wurtzmuller found a pharmaceutical company that manufactures pre-filled medical syringes, pre-filled with the serum desired. You can get anything—penicillin, tetanus, cortisone, morphine, sulfonamide any antibiotic you may need. Do you know how much time this saves on administering the drugs?

"They will even fill the needle with phenyl if I want, for mass euthanizing. He showed me boxes of morphine and heroin syringes they sent him. They will supply any drug imaginable in this disposable needle. You just twist off the cap and inject. It is a major breakthrough for 'en mass' wartime applications."

Boerner threw the packet back onto Engel's desk.

"I will need to speak with the giant now."

She had heard enough praise of the drug company's innovation.

"Make sure you inject her with a performance-enhancer and with pain-killers before the event. I want her opponent *destroyed*—she is a real troublemaker."

The overseer unlocked Engel's door, went out to the grassy area and approached Elsie, who stopped her stretching and faced the aufseherin in a defiant pose.

"Where have you been, Boerner?" Elsie began in her resonant, throaty, tone, common for victims of giantism. "You had promised that I was to be freed after my last fight. It has been five years since they brought me here. Haven't I made you enough money? I cannot keep doing this. My joints are constantly killing me. They are killing me now!"

Dorothy Boerner treated Elsie like a complaining teenager. She knew how to diffuse the giant's negative behavior. She would always deflect the anger by ignoring her remarks and making idle promises— small threads of hope that would make Elsie focus on the future rather than the present or past.

"Elsie, when you came here, you were living in squalor. We have given you your own room, three meals a day and all the pain medicine you require. All I ask is that you perform once and a while, put on an exciting display, and take care of some prisoners who are dangerous to the other women in our camp."

Although Boerner tried to make the giant's services seem dignified and meaningful, Elsie seemed tired.

"I do not want to kill anyone anymore. I just want to leave. You promised that was my last fight, and then you would free me."

Elsie begged, believing that Boerner was looking out for her best interests and still had a legitimate plan for her future.

"I tell you what," the overseer assured Elsie. "We can talk after next Wednesday. In the meantime, I will see that you receive a radio for your cell. You will be able to listen to your favorite music. I will have our military supply person order a new one—just for you. Okay?"

"I will need a long extension cord to reach the outlet by the guard's desk," Elsie spoke as a further condition.

That being said, Boerner knew she had won the point.

"Next Wednesday—in the same place. Dr. Engel will give you medicine before the contest, and afterwards as well. This woman is average size. We will want her killed, just like all the others. How many is it now, Elsie?"

"Sixteen—one every three or four months since I arrived. I bring you lots of money, Aufseherin, but I still want to leave here."

The misfortunate giant had never forgotten her dream of earning the freedom stolen five years earlier.

"Elsie, we all do what we can for the Reich. You are doing a great service by killing these criminal women who are threats to our camp's safety. I will always be indebted to you for allowing me to complete their execution at the hands of your strength. Your efforts are greatly appreciated by your country and by Ravensbruck. Now, let me go to the office and put that order in for your new radio."

Boerner stood with assurance that she had conned Elsie Honigsberg to fight in another gladiatorial exhibition—one that would make her, Olga Deitzl and Dr. Max Engel a bit wealthier. She did the math in her head. The scheme would not out-earn the deal on the Frankfurt sale of Edith Klein's virtuoso violin, but the night always promised to be sadistically entertaining to the throngs of male guards and overseers who paid an admission, drank four to five kegs of Lowenbrau and wagered large sums of money on the outcome.

Elsie was always the odds-on favorite, so most of the bets involved the time when it would happen. Even Elsie had appreciated being the inflictor of harm rather than being the prey, which was a feeling she never achieved before coming to Ravensbruck. The pituitary giant had grown tired of the "Schadenfreude." It was much more rewarding to hear supportive cheers during the fight rather than pitiful sighs.

In a low, hollow tone, Elsie's called to Boerner before the overseer entered the infirmary.

"And don't forget the extension cord!"

CHAPTER 10

Werner Schmidt, civilian mechanic, chugged slowly down the concrete lane between the Ravensbruck warehouses and the women's barracks. The "gas wagen" had taken 138 lives the first week of its operation. As Major Suhren ordered, every new prisoner over sixty years, anyone who appeared to be a behavioral problem and women who were too ill to perform their jobs in the camp—all were executed by the carbon monoxide "deathmobile."

Schmidt had carried out the tasks for the first week schedule. The crew of four different soldiers a day learned the routine, and they were ready to assume control of its mechanical functions on Monday. It was their final day of training.

The short, mustached man from Furstenberg had a fight with his wife every morning since Tuesday. She had told friends in their town what her husband was working on within the prison walls. Suhren's warning to stay quiet, regarding the "gas van" project, had come too late for Schmidt. Everyone in their building, as well as local merchants, had become aware of Suhren's plans to exterminate prisoners inside Ravensbruck—thanks to Thelma Schmidt's tongue. Schmidt hoped that "the talk" would not cross from the public gossip barrier and into the military confidential realm.

After the van pulled up to the lane where barracks 116 and 117 were situated, Schmidt brought the vehicle to a halt, allowing the four soldiers to jump off the side panel runner. Two went to one building, while the other pair walked past to the second structure.

Saturday was like the other work days. The women rose early, tended to their toilet and washing needs and ate porridge and watered down coffee before assembling outside for the appropriate overseer to escort them to the factory.

Tula Janaczek was advised to have the sick group assembled in her barrack during the previous night. A van would come in the morning to take them to the secluded infirmary at the back of camp property. There they would be treated for their illnesses, given the correct antibiotics and either returned to their quarters or shuttled off to a larger medical facility.

Prisoners talked during the week. Some barracks informed others that none of their "sick" had returned from the infirmary trip.

All was quiet. It seemed the guards and soldiers were able to keep the project more classified than the Schmidts could.

"Resto, I will need your help in a few minutes," Janaczek said to the Romani woman who was standing idle by the kitchen table. "Do not get lost. The sick have to be brought to the infirmary. The truck just parked on the lane."

"I am supposed to do nothing until I hear from the overseer," Risa Resto fired back at the kapo. "Get someone else. There are plenty others who can lift them on to the truck."

"Shh! I will help you, Risa," Flora volunteered. "Don't start her. We can do this quickly."

"You will have to take me to my factory late, kapo?" Flora warned Tula. "They will punish me if I do not present a legitimate excuse."

"I will take you late," Janaczek agreed. "See Roma, this woman wants to help her sick sisters—not like you."

The kapo rubbed Flora's shaved head, which had already begun to display an ebony shadow.

"She is their true friend."

"I will help them. It is *you* I have no desire to help, Snitch." Risa scoffed, sneering at the barrack manager.

One of the male soldiers interrupted the three women when he appeared at the building door.

"Who is bringing out the sick to the transport? Let's get to it!" he barked, and then he screamed down the barrack corridor. "If you have to see the medics, everyone must leave immediately, or be ready to stay sick and die!"

Flora and Risa began assisting the patients who were congregated at the far end of the building, creating an infirmed section within the walls of their dwelling. They helped the women, one by one, out the door of 116. Most leaned for support against the wooden exterior as they ambled, some staggering, toward the rear entry of the van.

Flora had been so attentive to the needs of the infirmed, that for a bit of time, she actually forgot about her own situation concerning Isaac's demise. It took several minutes to help each of the sick or infirmed climb up the van steps and into the unit. Once inside, the women grabbed on to polls and straps that had been positioned for travelling.

"I cannot breathe, please! No more passengers!" one called.

"Quickly, I am going to feint!" another yelped. "Can we go, now? I am getting crushed."

Schmidt stayed in the driver's seat, not assisting the boarding procedure. The guards had gotten lost under a nearby tree, smoking cigarettes, while Flora and Risa helped the final patient onto the bus. While the other building contributed eight women to the roster, Barrack 116 brought out fifteen patients. Tula Janaczek took the task upon herself to slam the back air-tight panels closed, turning the latch, literally sealing the fate of the women inside.

Werner Schmidt hopped out of the cab and went through the motions for preparing the vehicle with the carbon monoxide gas valve adjustment. As Risa and Tula headed back to the building, the Romani woman stopped and looked around with a blank stare. With a shriek of fear, the gypsy ran back to the van.

One Nazi guard rushed to the truck and held his rifle in a defensive pose.

"Where do you think you are going?"

He pushed the stock and barrel through Risa's advance.

"The helper is inside! She is not a sick person. Open up, we have to get her out!" the Romani woman shouted in desperation. "Where are you taking them? She cannot go. She is healthy. We need her in the barrack. You must let her go."

Schmidt, the mechanic, was completing the tail pipe diversion. He now twisted the rubber hose on to the valve, which entered the back compartment. The vehicle was ready to administer its own deadly exhaust fumes into the gas van.

"Forget it, woman. You will see your friend later," the armed guard, said. He realized what chaos would ensue if the panel doors were reopened. "Go about your business. She will be released when the unit gets to the infirmary!"

Before Risa Resto could respond with either verbal or manual force, Helga Utzinger, the kapo of Barrack 117, shouted across the muddy strip of land that separated the two buildings. The woman was assisting a frail elderly prisoner who was stumbling to the mobile van, while several others wandered toward it, as well.

"Wait, I found five more! They were in the toilet."

The guard rolled his eyes as the other three began to prepare the rear panel doors to accept the added number of patients. Werner Schmidt hopped back in the truck awaiting departure, the motor not yet running.

Three of the soldiers hung on the truck step frame as the panel swung open, revealing most of the sick prisoners, piled atop one another. Several fell out on the pavement. One woman appeared to have fallen directly on her head and lay unconscious. On top of her was Flora's frail, petite body. Risa ran to her aid.

"Get up, quickly. Stand between me and Janaczek."

Flora blended into the trio. When one of the guards looked in her direction, Risa answered.

"This was the one who got stuck in there by mistake. We are okay now."

They backed and drifted off to the front door of 116, leaving Flora's would-be murder scene.

With the additional women packed into the back of the van, Schmidt sat in the driver's seat, enjoying the warmth of the late summer sun filtering through the truck window. All he had to do was to turn on the ignition. The carbon monoxide diversion hoses were ready to begin their deadly gas distribution into the compartment. He heard banging noises as well as screams and moans coming through the air-tight iron walls behind his head.

Thoughts of the argument he had that very morning with his wife about conversations with town people whirled through his brain. She had told several friends about the important project he was working on in Ravensbruck labor camp. She tried to lessen the severity of what she may have said, but he knew his wife, Thelma, could not refrain from gossip. His thoughts returned to the present when one of the soldiers slapped the side of the van.

"Herr Schmidt, we are ready. Start her up."

The mechanic turned on the ignition with the hose in place, redirecting the noxious exhaust fumes back into the airtight compartment containing the women. Schmidt heard desperate coughing, yelling and pounding erupting from the 28 unwitting women who had been sentenced to death by Major Suhren. The civilian operator drove along the side road between the camp warehouses and barracks. He turned right and went clear around the living quarters a second time and a third time. It appeared that twenty minutes was the minimal amount of time to expect the fumes to complete the extermination of the women.

On the third trip, Schmidt continued down to the security gate that led to the camp infirmary and eventually the crematorium and mass burial pit. One soldier hopped off the van and ran to a camp phone that was encased in a green metal box on the side truck bay of the crematorium.

"Yes, Lieutenant, this is Sergeant Fleigal. We are at the pit, behind the incinerators."

"Okay sergeant, you know what the major wants you to do. Call me, afterwards and I will take it from there," Volsgaard responded.

Volsgaard hung up the phone and picked up a letter, re-reading it. It was sent by a regional German humanitarian group, questioning cruel and unusual forms of inmate punishment, citing torture and mass murdering. The most precise incriminating fact however, was the mention of a "mobile gas chamber" in the letter. That information could only lead back to Schmidt—its obvious source. He threw the envelope back on his office desk, awaiting Fleigal's return call.

The soldiers gagged from the stench after the back doors swung open over the communal burial site in the rear of the labor camp property. The newly decaying bodies from yesterday's murders lying in the hole gave off the most hideous of decomposition smells. Schmidt sat in the van cab. His job was technical— only operating the vehicle and the gas valves. It was the job of the military to provide the muscle for disposing of the bodies. He could see them in the van side mirror, removing the prisoner corpses, one by one.

They pulled the dead to the edge of the back panel, dropping the bodies into the abyss. Without emotion or compassion, they dumped the bodies of 28 women into the hole, atop yesterday's rotting lot—women who would never feel ill again.

Fleigal ordered Schmidt to remove the van from the pit's edge and to drive it close to the crematorium wall. The soldier grabbed a can of auxiliary gasoline that was strapped to the gas van's bumper and invited the mechanic to join him for the final task of humane indecency. He had performed the same task on the day before, and the day before that as well.

Schmidt joined the four soldiers at the cavernous edge as Fleigal doused the newly murdered victims with a generous amount of the petrol. He then handed a book of matches to Schmidt and spoke as if inviting him in to some initiation rite.

"Herr Schmidt, you do the honors, today. You are a good teacher. We have learned much from you this week."

Schmidt opened the mach book, somewhat reluctantly, removed a wooden stick and struck it on the side of the box. Once ignited, he dropped it onto the closest body, who appeared to be a woman in her twenties. He stared as the flames began consuming her flesh spreading to the other bodies.

Schmidt swallowed hard. This was too symbolic—like the corpses catching on fire, Schmidt's guilt-ridden paranoia began to consume him. He sensed, in that very moment, that the military knew he had not kept the transport project a secret from others.

Two soldiers placed their hands on his shoulders while grabbing the seat of his pants. Then they threw Werner Schmidt into the burning pit, alive. He screamed, climbing over charred bodies, rolling to the area where there were no flames—except the ones being fueled by his own flesh. He eventually succumbed to unconsciousness. The mechanic's teaching days were over—thanks to his wife, the humanitarian society and himself.

"Good work, Sergeant Fleigal. We cannot have civilians too knowledgeable as to what we are doing. It can be a dangerous thing. Now, please find Frau Schmidt in town. Tell her that there has been a terrible accident involving her husband, and you will bring her to him. Have her transported in the gas van. Let her see how well her husband trained you. She can be your initial victim. Then dump her body with his."

Volsgaard hung up the phone, hoping that the damage brought on by the Schmidts would not continue. He was eager to let Suhren know that the couple was gone. He believed he handled the task his major had given to him in a most efficient manor, along with the Nazi signature of sadistic pleasure. He expected an accommodation for it.

CHAPTER 11

Heinrich Wurtzmuller stopped at the front desk of The Lorelei Rooming House hotel to make certain manager, Herman Wohl, knew that he was waiting for his engagement in Room 206 as soon as the visiting enlisted man was finished with his carnal appointment.

Once again, the place was hopping with locals, as well as Ravensbruck personnel, on the cool summer Saturday evening. Groups congregated in the lobby, on the street and, of course, in the beer hall. On that night, the house was so crowded that people could not even dance if the management had been playing "jitterbug" on the crackling public address speakers.

The hotel manager was relieved that there was no dancing that night. He could feel the musically critical Nazi officer leaning over into his space.

"My friend, Greta—how much sooner?" the impatient officer inquired. "I really do not want to be mingling with the "help," so to speak, Herman—very bad for my image. Do you understand?"

"It should not be too long, Captain. The soldier has been with her for at least ten minutes"

"Ten minutes? My goodness, Herman! If he was anything like me as a young soldier, he has probably had sex five or six times in these ten minutes—horny little bastard that he probably is."

The men laughed at his brief admiration of youth.

"Just curious, Captain—why were you so hard on the lad last week. Do you remember? The soldier who was descending the stairway—you told him to call his mother."

"Because he did not salute me. Remember, Herman? I could care less if he started a three-alarm venereal fire in his pecker, but damn it, I am a captain. Salute me, you idiot!"

Herman answered the phone.

"Ah, yes! Of course, Greta." He placed the receiver down. "This is even better, Captain. The soldier must have exited the back way, ashamed of his actions. Greta has asked for you to go upstairs."

The manager felt better about Wurtzmuller's lighter mood. Perhaps it really was the "jitterbug" music that threw him into the incendiary behavior.

"Okay, Herman, time me," the officer said, tongue-in-cheek, smiling as he jogged up to the second floor toward Room 206.

Greta Junkwalter had known what poverty and abuse was during her eighteen short years on the earth. Her father, the town drunk, had lost multiple jobs when she and her brothers were young. He beat up her mother for the nightly money she made cleaning local businesses in Furstenberg. Greta helped her after school, working sometimes until two in the morning. She met the staff and frequenters of the Lorelei while helping her mother, intrigued with the "good cheer" people displayed in the "bar-room lifestyle."

In time, Greta worked cleaning tables and rooms for the owners. Succumbing to the allure of alcohol, she found herself occasionally sleeping over in vacant rooms at the Lorelei. One night, a travelling salesman took advantage of her intoxicated state. The next morning, she awoke to find a bouquet of flowers and fifty Reichsmarks on the night stand.

In that moment, Greta discovered how to make money during the depressed economy of World War II. Unfortunately, much of it went to the purchase of single malt scotch. One year later, the Furstenberg woman realized gainful employment, every Friday and Saturday evening. The soldiers alone would keep her busy up to two dozen times a night. She brought money home and secretly gave it to her brother to save and to buy provisions for their mother. Because her work as a prostitute disgraced the family, Greta was not allowed at the family house when her mother was present.

Heinrich Wurtzmuller knocked on door 206. He turned, with both cumbersome canvas bag straps over each soldier. A congregation of locals and two soldiers were milling around the hallway. They appeared to be interested in Greta's services, trying to muster up enough nerve to make a move. The two army men stood at attention when Wurtzmuller stared at them. He said nothing.

"Aah, my Captain!" Greta shouted as she swung the blue door open.

The Nazi walked in, kicking the door closed behind him.

Mascara running down her sweaty cheek, the young prostitute threw her arms around Wurtzmuller, kissing him with a scotch smell on her lips.

"Captain, what did you bring me? When are you going to take me on a date? Please tell me."

The officer recoiled, reluctant to get closer to the amiable, attractive boozer.

"I brought you some good food for your family, Greta. Your brothers and your mother will be happy when you give them this sack."

He laid the larger one down against the wall by her window.

"There is plenty of rice, potatoes, canned fruits and vegetables. I even managed to get a baked cake from our officer's commissary. Some beer, soft drinks. You will need help. The bag is very heavy, no?"

In the same motion, Wurtzmuller threw the smaller canvas bag on the bed. It tumbled and lay still on the messy sheets where Greta Junkwalter had been working since last evening.

"You are too good to me, Captain. How am I ever going to repay you?"

Greta nuzzled closer to the officer and began to act in a drunken, coquettish fashion.

"Just do what you always do, Greta my love, and you will make me extremely happy."

The captain grabbed her hands from his neck and kissed them.

She pulled away, and exaggerating the sexy way she walked, sashayed over to the closed toilet door, glancing back over her shoulder at the officer with sultry eyes, enhanced by intoxication, before closing the door behind her.

It was a Saturday night ritual that she and the Nazi shared. When he looked at his watch, it was the only time Wurtzmuller took his eyes off the door. He could hear her movement in the bathroom.

When the hinges creaked open, the person who exited the bathroom was a short, round, aging man with glasses, wearing a stained sport jacket and portly trousers. The trousers were held up with red suspenders. Greta was gone.

Heinrich Wurtzmuller clicked his heels, bowed and shook the hand of the man one would not have expected to exit from the bathroom of prostitute, Greta Junkwalter.

"Herr Bergeron, how are you this fine evening?""Aah, Good evening, Captain."

The round man, with a benign tone to his voice, seemed genuinely happy to see Wurtzmuller. He threw a beige brief case on to the disarrayed bed.

"Is the girl safely in your room?" Wurtzmuller asked. "Did you lock the door from the toilet side?"

"I most certainly did, Captain, but I must say—it is getting tougher out there. Hamburg was a much better area for us than Frankfurt. It is way more difficult getting the prices we want in Frankfurt, but we did pretty good this week."

Pierre Bergeron picked up the briefcase, letting Wurtzmuller peek at the bundles of Swiss francs that he had tied together in small denominations.

"That is a direct result of an increase in diamonds, and diamonds alone. The gold statues and candle holders—you can keep. They are heavy and not worth lugging around to sell. I know you are trying to vary the items, but diamonds are going to make you and me so much richer than large gold artifacts, Heinrich. We must think small—gold watches, gold rings and precious stones. All small stuff—the smaller the better. But mostly—think diamonds!"

"I have hired another man. He is going to weigh everything, categorize the items, separate the gems from their settings and assist in presenting them in a more marketable approach," the officer remarked.

"He does not know what we are doing, does he?" the cautious elder asked.

"Herr Bergeron, no one knows of our business. Greta still thinks we are funding an Alsatian resistance group with the money we make from our endeavors. I bound her to secrecy, advising her that if she were to tell anyone, the Reich would have to kill her for treason. Besides, I bribe her enough to keep her mouth shut. She really thinks, in a way, that she is a patriot."

Wurtzmuller laughed, shaking his head.

"Everyone thinks I am in here screwing her in bed. The only one we are screwing is Hitler, who is in turn screwing all of Germany."

The men laughed.

"I am supposed to administer the confiscation program within our camp, and turn everything over to Berlin, without paying myself for the wonderful job I do? It is not me living in a 23-room villa on a lake!"

"How is my old friend, Fritz Suhren?" Pierre Bergeron asked, laughing. "I miss the camp's business."

"You never would have lost it if that bastard from the Inspectorate didn't sway his brother-in-law's company into the fold.

And I am supposed to stand idle while everyone gets rich except me?" Wurtzmuller asked, qualifying his actions.

"Well, you and I are much better off as a result of our new partnership," Bergeron said, placing his hand on Wurtzmuller's forearm, assuring him that he had made the right choice in their private business model. "Now I will get back to my room and get Greta in here to say her 'goodbye' to you, and you can be on your way."

Nodding, Bergeron grabbed the smaller canvas sack and disappeared back into the shared toilet of the two rooms.

Wurtzmuller never questioned Bergeron's commission. He knew that his partner worked hard, fencing the jewels and gold in the maze of undesirable neighborhoods throughout the big cities. The captain was compiling his cut of the money in suitcases back in the chalet for his own retirement.

He hoped that one day, after the war, he would cross the Swiss border to live a life of complacency in a mountainous canton somewhere within the pristine, neutral country. Adolf Hitler got most of the stolen valuables profit from the prisoners, but Heinrich Wurtzmuller was going to take a small portion for his own future and hopefully go unnoticed while doing it.

His wandering thoughts became more rational when Greta Junkwalter appeared at bathroom door opening.

"Phew, his room smells from cigar smoke. It is disgusting," the prostitute complained, waiving her hand in front of her nose. "Are you done with your business, Captain? Why don't you stay with me for a while?"

She grabbed Wurtzmuller by his crotch, attempting to pull him closer.

"No Greta, I must be getting back to my house. I have much work to do before the night is over."

He reached into his pocket and handed the girl thirty Reichsmarks.

"As ever, Greta, you are to speak of my meetings with Herr Bergeron to no one. Our cause is a top-secret mission. If information were to fall into the wrong hands, your life could be in grave danger. So hush."

He kissed her hand that held his cash before picking up the beige briefcase and smiling a sinister grin.

"And I have brought you a gift, a gift like you have never encountered."

He reached into his tunic and threw six-packs of disposable syringes on her bureau.

"What is that? Medicine?" she asked. "I do not need medicine, Captain. I am not sick."

"Greta, my love, this is a mood enhancer. Musicians use it to relax. They say it is so effective that it makes the 'high' of alcohol just seem like a mild case of dizziness. These are samples, like the food I bring you. I get it for free. Tomorrow night, when you have finished your weekend, try it. Just inject it into your arm and relax. If you like it, I can bring you more."

Wurtzmuller knew the weak-willed girl would test anything new that would alter her state of mind. When she did, he would have more control over her pathetic life.

"Now, I will be here next week, but there have been rumors of a pending 'blackout'—at which point, I am afraid no one will be enjoying Saturday night frivolities."

As he exited, the six-packs of heroin syringes lay visible on her bureau.

Outside the room, the intimidating officer stared down the same group in the hall who were mumbling and attempting to stir up enough nerve to knock on the prostitute's door. He offered no quips this time as he descended the stairway, bulled through the lobby crowd and outside, easily found the jeep with the "W" whitewashed on its spare tire.

Greta stashed the officer's gratuity into a floral dress that hung in her closet, leaving the packets of heroin syringes on the wooden chest of drawers. She was grateful for the meetings the two men had in her bedroom. She asked no questions and really did not care what their intentions were. She enjoyed the tip Wurtzmuller always threw her way, but she was really excited about the free food he gave her family.

The sack usually fed her mother and brothers for a week. That meant she did not have to turn any of her funds over to the family budget. Greta gazed at the cans peeking through the cinched rope of the bag as a pounding at the door shook the bedpost and lamp on the nightstand.

"*Horny bastards!*" she thought as the rapping got louder.

"Keep banging like that, and you can wait to go last!" she blurted, rubbing the smudged eyeliner away from her tear duct. "Now why the racket?"

As she opened her door, the force of overseer, Olga Deitzl's, shoulder jettisoned her frail, drunk body across the room. Greta careened off the outer window wall and fell next to the canvas satchel that Wurtzmuller had brought. In a boozy hysteria, the young whore began to cry, anticipating physical danger.

"Please, please, do not hurt me! I do not do women, but I can get a friend who does. Just do not hurt me, please."

She was rubbing a bruise to her head that had hit the room window sill.

"Shut up," Olga Deitzl warned as Dorothy Boerner followed her subordinate into room 206, locking the door behind her.

"Hey, we were next!" one of the privates, standing in the hallway shouted, his complaint ignored by the pair of overseers now in Greta's quarters.

"What kind of contraband have you got in here?" Olga Deitzl demanded, grabbing Greta by her flowing blond locks.

She pulled her away from the canvas duffle bag and loosened the cinched rope.

"Well I'll be damned—cans of food! More cans of food, sacks of flour, rice…" Deitzl looked up to her chief. "That cheap prick, he pays for sex with our camp food?"

When they took a brief moment for laughter, Greta sensed some relief, hoping they would bring her no more harm.

"Where is the other bag, the smaller one?" the overseer said, as Deitzl once again pulled Greta's mane of hair.

"I do not know what you are talking about!" the sobered prostitute offered, as the violent overseer slammed her head against the closet door.

"We saw that officer carry *two* bags up the stairs and return with a briefcase," Deitzl shouted. "Where is the *other* canvas bag? Tell us, you whore!"

She slapped Greta across her mascara-smudged face, and then a second time.

"Maybe he brought it somewhere else before he came to me. I do not know. Please! You must believe me. He brings me food for my mother and brothers before he pays me for having sex with him.

He treats me nice. Is that a crime? Please do not hit me anymore," the sobbing prostitute begged.

"How do you know that officer?" Boerner demanded. "Why does he treat you nice? Why does he want to come to you every Saturday night? He can meet you anywhere at any time. This is a matter of state, not of desire. You are doing something for him. Olga—search the room."

Boerner looked under Greta's bed and in the bureau drawers, while Deitzl scoured the shallow room closet. She then walked over to the toilet door.

"This room has its own toilet. You do not have to go to the communal hall bathroom?"

Greta answered with a blank look.

"I am a whore! A communal toilet would be extremely difficult to conduct business successfully, would it not?"

"Don't get smart with me. Where does this go?"

Deitzl tried to open the locked door to room 207—the room that Pierre Bergeron used most Saturday evenings.

"That is an adjoining room. We share the toilet," Greta explained, hoping she had sold its anonymity.

"Who is in there?" Boerner spoke up. "Can you open it?"

"Both toilet doors lock from the outside side, for privacy. It is just some old man in that room. He stinks."

Greta was convincing. Deitzl exited the toilet and slammed the door.

"Young lady, we will continue to follow your behavior. If you are caught doing anything underhanded—even with an officer of the Shutzstaffel, we will make sure that your actions are immediately reported to the Gestapo, and you will be arrested. Do you understand?"

Boerner tried the rational approach.

"And if you are found guilty of any wrongdoing, you would probably be executed."

The chief overseer spotted the closed packets of syringes on the battered and scuffed bureau.

"So, you are a drug addict, as well?"

She examined the writing on the clear bag, indicating the content of the syringes was heroin.

"He also pays you with Ravensbruck medicine?"

"He just brought me that today, never before. He thought it might help me to relax after working," the prostitute explained, hoping to avoid any more physical responses from Boerner's assistant.

"Relax?" Deitzl chuckled. "You work by lying in bed. Why do you need medicine to relax?"

Boerner laughed at her friend's twisted remark.

"We will be back, whore, next week, and the week after. This is a warning. Be careful."

"I have done nothing wrong, I swear," she sobbed as she felt the inquisition coming to a close.

"Well for your sake, I hope so. Olga—say 'goodbye' to this pathetic leach of a whore, and maybe we will have better luck next time."

Boerner oozed a sadistic inference in her tone, though she let Deitzl have the final word. The unattractive overseer prefaced the remark by giving Greta an unexpected punch in her stomach.

"Incidentally, if you did do women—you might find that a much more rewarding experience than the likes of Heinrich Wurtzmuller—who you will never speak to about our little interview."

Greta doubled over in pain. She had never experienced such violence from any of her male customers at The Lorelei. The frail girl from Furstenberg collapsed in her room, vomiting the four glasses of scotch she had consumed since five o'clock. She would not be able to resume her schedule for the remainder of the evening. Instead, she lied to manager, Herman Wohl, and she still gave him his usual cut of a full night's work. The last thing she wanted was to lose weekend rights to Room 206.

The battered girl climbed into her rooming house bed alone for the first time that evening. She rubbed the pain and bruising on her skull and stomach alternately as she pondered her new dilemma. Should she report the incident to Heinrich Wurtzmuller, or fear being injured, or even killed, if she did?

CHAPTER 12

The Vorwerk Kobold Model "T" hummed like a lone Messershmidtt, circling the German sky. Its droning noise was monotonous and hypnotic. Isaac could not believe that Wurtzmuller owned the very same vacuum cleaner that Commodore Ahrens had purchased years ago in Bremerhaven.

The officer had acquired six of the machines for Major Suhren's mansion, two for the administrative offices in Ravensbruck, and one for each of the twenty overseer and soldier houses on the outer grounds of the camp. He threw one in for his own chalet, but he rarely found time or interest in plugging it in to the outlets and using the upright cleaning tool.

It is almost inane, Isaac thought. Yet the familiarity of the same vacuum gave a feeling of continuity in his life. It brought a brief acceptance of normalcy in his daily routine. The vacuum was like an old friend— something from his past was still a part of the present. The hum relaxed him as he directed it across the office rug and wood floors. For a moment, it drowned out the Nazi silence he sometimes found unbearable as he stayed locked up in the chalet.

The weighted woven sack that ballooned from the base of the Kobold's motor began to signal it was time to discard the dirt and grit accumulated there. After turning it off, Isaac detached the reinforced cotton sack from the upright pole and made his way to the rear door that Wurtzmuller instructed him to use. He released the bundle of filth into the isolated wooden area in the back of the chalet by the tree-lined hill, where it seemed to be unnoticeably harmless.

"Hello, young fellow," a well-dressed businessman announced, taking him by total surprise. "I hope I did not startle you?"

Isaac was not only startled. He dropped the cotton receptacle and tried to form words, but nothing came out of his mouth.

"Sorry, young man," the older gentleman apologized. "I know Captain Wurtzmuller likes frequenters to use the back entrance. My name is Rutger von Blarcom. I promised the captain that I would drop off some samples. I was going to leave them on the step, but since you are here, it would be much better to receive them into the house. They are potentially dangerous—explosives. I trust you will apprise the Captain that they were delivered?

"And who might you be, lad?" Von Blarcom asked, not expecting anyone to be inside the chalet during the daytime, and yet he was pleased to get his dangerous delivery indoors.

"Um, uh, I am the cleaning person," Isaac answered, hoping to sound legitimate. "I come once a week while the Captain is in Ravensbruck."

Von Blarcom appeared to have bought the story.

"Well, the army spends money much more freely than when I was a soldier. A cleaning man?" he laughed. "I have four boxes of samples that the captain was expecting. I will retrieve them from my car, if you would be so kind as to accept them?"

Still shaken at encountering the visitor, Isaac recalled Wurtzmuller's warning to never allow anyone to discover his presence while living in the backyard chalet. *Of all the times to run the Vorwerk Kobold, and have the electric motor drown any exterior noise, in this case, a car's motor!*

He took two of the sample boxes from von Blarcom and brought the detonator receivers and transmitters into the office, placing them in the room corner. The Siemens rep went to his vehicle for the other two corrugated containers, only to return a minute later.

"I have a paper for you to sign, young man—a receipt," the salesman stated, "just as proof to my company that I delivered these four boxes to Captain Wurtzmuller."

Isaac realized it was one thing to be discovered by a man delivering samples, *and now his presence was to be documented with a signature!* The situation was not good. What was he to do? What name was he to sign? He could already feel the ire of Heinrich Wurtzmuller. How was he to explain his being discovered by von Blarcom? What form of punishment would ensue? The young man picked up the Vorwerk model "T" dirt bag and threw it back into the house.

"Here you go, kind sir," the Siemens rep said, placing a paper under Isaac's nose.

While the page had something written on it, Isaac could only concentrate on the word "Quantity," and next to it, the number "4." Reluctantly, he placed a large "X" on the page.

"I never attended school," he explained.

Von Blarcom smiled, offering no subjective ridicule. He was a gentleman.

"Now, I must tell you, these are potentially dangerous items. Will you see the Captain later?"

Isaac nodded.

"There are instructions in each box—not that he will need them. Nonetheless, be careful. As you are probably aware from cleaning—I know he has grenade canisters and petrol products inside—these samples can create quite an explosion if the transmitter and receiver are aligned and detonated. They will cause a chain reaction. Please remind him to take their presence seriously. You will tell him that?"

"Yes sir," Isaac answered. "He does not want me to leave until he returns this evening, so I will tell him."

"Well good day, young man. I am sorry to have interrupted your tasks."

Rutger von Blarcom left as quickly as he came. Isaac stared at the carbon copy of the delivery receipt stared, bewildered, at the large "X" where it said "Signature." He dreaded the wrath of the officer.

Isaac retrieved the vacuum bag and decided that he would begin Wurtzmuller's laundry, when there was another knock the door. He could see that the salesman's car was still parked next to the house, so he cautiously opened the back door again. It was von Blarcom.

"I realized that I had an extra opened box, consisting of one transmitter and receiver. The other cases have two of each. The Captain may as well have this extra set. I do not want to drive around with it in my trunk."

Von Blarcom smiled as if to convey something had accidentally happened.

"There are instructions in here as well," he said while handing the article to Isaac. "They come with a battery already installed. Please remind him of that, as well. Now I will be out of your hair, young man. You can continue with your cleaning. If the Captain needs me, he knows how to reach me. Have a nice day."

Once again, silence possessed Wurtzmuller's small home. Isaac retreated to the chalet office and sat, looking at the partial box of electronic panels. The lid flapped, as if to beckon the man to look inside. He still held in his hand the signed receipt for the four full cases.

Without thinking, Isaac gambled that Wurtzmuller would base his acknowlegement of the delivery on what was on the signed receipt: four boxes only. He took the contents of the partial case and hurried into the pantry. Finding the near-empty sack of flour that he had hid toward the rear of a food shelf, he took an inventory of the canned foods, meat knife, hand grenade canisters, command order papers, flairs and other survival articles he had retrieved from the office sample room.

He slipped the transmitter panel and the receiving detonator into the woven flour sack, but not before flipping the toggle switch on one of the mechanisms. Abruptly, it glowed a bright red color. Heeding the warning, he deadened the control and grabbed the instruction paper, rolled it up and shoved it into his pants pocket. He knew that if the Nazi officer found his growing survival aids, he would be killed at once.

Isaac reached into the sack and brought the meat knife back to the kitchen drawer, replacing it with a much smaller dinner knife. The misplacement of one out of twenty pieces of cutlery would be less noticeable than a significant kitchen utensil.

He hid the burlap bag behind a group of five new flour sacks and concealed it with large cans of lard and coffee on either side. Wurtzmuller did not seem to be a fan of the pantry. Isaac had not seen him enter the room once since he had taken it as his quarters. He hoped the sack would go unnoticed.

Seven o'clock came very slow for the young prison boarder. Wurtzmuller came home at that hour with what appeared to be more confiscated valuables from a new group of camp laborers.

"I will need all of these articles categorized, weighed and recorded by the weekend, Bloom."

"Sir, a man came to the house today. He brought samples."

Isaac thought it better to announce the incident in a tone of factual banality.

"His name was von Blarcom."

"What, Bloom? Someone saw you here? You let him into the house? What happened?" Wurtzmuller asked, drawing closer.

Isaac could feel the tidal wave of reaction approaching his space.

"I was emptying the vacuum bag on the back porch. He had arrived already with samples," Isaac answered, trying to play down the severity of the incident. "Sir, I told him that I was your cleaning man. I cleaned your house once a week. He seemed satisfied with that fact. He wanted the samples safely inside, once he found the house was occupied."

"Oh he did, did he?"

Wurtzmuller cocked his arm and backhanded Isaac's mouth, drawing blood. The young man fell over into the boxes that still supported each other's weight along the office wall.

"What did I say about being seen, Bloom?"

The out-of-control officer shouted, dragging him up by his shirt, only to smack him down into the pile of samples again.

"Von Blarcom has a big mouth. I am not supposed to have a cleaning person. If Suhren finds out that and I did not pass this luxury through him first, I could be reprimanded, and you could be killed! Do you understand, Bloom?"

The irate officer grabbed Isaac by his shirt and shook him as if he was mugging a defenseless street victim.

"I, I am truly sorry, sir. I was vacuuming the floors. The sound covered up his car motor noise. That was the only reason there was a breech in your request. I will be more careful, I swear…"

Isaac apologized, sobbing, his hand covering his mouth to keep the bleeding contained. The Nazi was ready to fly into another rage of anger when the phone's ringing interrupted the action.

"Great!" he warned Isaac. "This better not be pertaining to what you just told me or you are a dead man."

The Nazi officer raised the receiver to hear the hollow, weak tone of a drugged woman.

"Captain," barely audible, "Captain, I need to see you. There may be a problem."

The phone went silent and a man's voice spoke.

"Hello Captain Wurtzmuller, this is the front gate. This woman was delivered by a taxi, which has since left. She would not return to Furstenberg unless I let her speak with you. She appears to have been beaten up. What would you wish me to do?"

The guards were always confronted with locals who had problems: men who accused soldiers of wrongdoings during town card games; torrid lover spats pursued by local women looking to get retribution by showing up at the gate with their brothers; someone inquiring about stolen property; and the ever famous shylock, demanding he speak to his deadbeat borrower.

"Tell her I will be right there, in two minutes. Keep her in your booth. Keep her calm. I am on my way."

Wurtzmuller seemed to have already forgotten Isaac's situation.

"Start working on the gems and jewelry. I want this completed by Friday. You are lucky, Bloom, that I have other things to worry about. My life is turning into shit!"

After he slammed his door, Isaac could hear the jeep ignition churning and its motor coming to life in the yard.

Hmm, now that car motor I heard. Never again will I vacuum. The rugs can stay filthy! he thought, rubbing his jaw.

CHAPTER 13

"Mother Germany" tended to herself in the converted cell room within the Ravensbruck labor camp infirmary. The giant carefully wrapped her knee joints and wrists. The medical linen tape added the much-needed support, giving strength to her lower body and arms. She remembered the time she applied the reinforced tape to her feet, which hindered her sure balance and caused dangerous sliding. She refrained from ever making that mistake again.

Elsie Honigsberg prepared while enjoying her new tabletop radio. Wagner's *The Ride of the Valkyries* rallied her psyche and created the conquering mood she sought before all the brawls, which were sanctioned by Dorothy Boerner. Her last ritual in preparation for the evening involved a red bandana. She had worn it in all the other fights. She called the guard for a mirror, and she strategically tied two of the corners behind her head. The third right angle stretched across Elsie's giant cranium, displaying the white and black swastika, directly over her heavily calcified brow.

"Mother Germany", whose life had been stolen five years earlier by the Gestapo squad in Hamburg, who had been delivered to Ravensbruck as a scientific freak of nature, who had been considered a detriment to the super race, who lived in an experimental probing cell for years—now fought proudly under the very Nazi symbol that removed her from German society. Still searching for acceptance, Elsie found her survival "hold card" as a fighting machine money-maker for Dorothy Boerner. She fought to live under the Nazi flag.

"Elsie, I have some pain medicine for you before the contest," Dr. Engel shouted through her room door.

The clanking of keys near her lock caused the giant to glance up.

"How do you feel? Are you ready for a victorious evening, Elsie? I know Oberaufseherin Boerner would like you to play with your victim a while before ending the fight. So, I have brought some medicine to enhance your performance and to make you feel comfortable as well as invincible."

Elsie held her fifty-eight-centimeter arm horizontally toward Engel, anticipating several injections. This was the final preparation for the contest. The fights always promised to be such a rout in Elsie's favor. Wagering by the crowd merely consisted of how long the opponent would last. Elsie's victory was not even part of a formal bet. Boerner had devised odds, indicating only the time frame her opponent would be defeated. Engel fortified the giant with every pharmaceutical advantage, assuring victory. It had worked sixteen times before.

Elsie began to feel nimble. Her range of motion grew as she held her arms up to the ceiling of her cell and then squatted twice—manuvers she could not attain without medicinal assistance.

"That's it, Elsie, limber you muscles. Prepare your body," Max Engel urged as he heard his office phone ringing.

He left the female hulk stretching within her room as he hurried to answer the call.

* * * * *

An elderly overseer accompanied the armed male guard as they approached the door of Barrack 116. Tula Janaczek had left it opened. Women were returning from the ten-hour workday at the various factories. Flora's group, the uniform makers, was usually the first to return to the building, at 5:30.

"We have come for the woman, Resto," the guard informed. "She is ready? She is to bring a friend—someone to assist her, should she return."

The order was given by a boy of eighteen years. Tula Janaczek smirked, staring as his helmet danced around his head while he asked questions. The overseer just looked on. The kapo had never seen either of them before.

"I will bring her to the front," she answered as she spotted Flora returning. "Bloom, she will want you probably. Go with the Roma to her big event. I hope you are strong enough to help her back to the hut."

Janaczek laughed sadistically as she disappeared into the building to find Risa.

Flora said nothing. It was because of the kapo that the event was taking place. She knew that Risa's mouth was as equally to blame, but they had become so fond of each over the last few weeks. Flora wanted to be with her gypsy friend, to help her through whatever was in store. She feared the next few hours, but she would never forget Risa's deep compassion as she consoled her through Isaac's death on her first day in Ravensbruck.

Resto appeared at the front door of the barrack.

"You and your helper—walk with the overseer, and keep your eyes forward," the armed soldier ordered as the four departed toward the lone wire gate leading into the guard quarters.

They passed through the locked barrier. Once on the side of the soldier quarters, Flora could sense a sane and acceptable life pattern. Her first observation was the grass, bushes and trees that accented the spacious area. The prison side consisted of dirt, mortar, filthy huts and walls of barbed wire.

The overseer's section, although military, was planned to offer a more comfortable life style. The dormitory buildings encapsulated a large wood framed structure at their center—a pavilion. It was raised off the ground and kept dry by beams and pilings. Thunderous noise, shouting, cheering, vibrated out to the lawn.

That was where the four were headed. Well-lit, the building seemed to be the center of guard activity. Large groups of unruly soldiers, obviously off-duty, stood outside the raised wooden structure, drinking ceramic humpens of beer and pushing one another as they boasted war stories concerning women rather than the battlefield.

"This must be her!" one of the soldiers shouted as Risa climbed the steps, with Flora following.

"I hope you asked God for forgiveness?" another chided as the four entered the hall.

"I want to change my bet—to ten seconds!" still another mocked, his friends bellowing a hysterical retort.

Flora studied the room. It had been constructed as a gymnasium for the sedentary staff of Ravensbruck. Removed from the frontlines of action, the male guards at Ravensbruck were instructed to maintain a strong physical regimen, in case they were ever transferred to a more demanding assignment.

Ropes descended from the ceiling, while barbells and climbing apparatus were stored in the corner of the amply-sized center. Two horses for vaulting had been temporarily utilized for holding numerous uniform tops, while the undershirt-clad soldiers clanked beer steins, spraying suds over each other.

The most striking piece of athletic equipment, however, was the large pugilistic ring gracing the center of the pavilion. Above it, hanging from the rafter, was a two-meter-tall banner of Adolf Hitler posing, his arms folded in defiance. Sighting the banner, Risa turned to Flora.

"Their fuhrer looks like an ass. That stupid moustache, it has no character—it looks like snot just fell from his nose."

Flora knew it was Risa's way of saying, "Do not worry, everything will be okay."

Flora giggled nervously after Risa's strange observation.

"Ah, here is the Romani opponent!"

Elbowing her way through the already drunken group of rowdy soldiers, Olga Deitzl and her boss, Dorothy Boerner, greeted the two.

"Here, put this on," Boerner ordered, throwing a pair of overseer gym shorts and an army issued female undershirt at Risa. "You are to wear this for your fight."

"Where am I supposed to change?" the confident Roma shot back at Boerner.

"Go to that corner," the chief overseer suggested with little sympathy. "Have your friend hold up a towel if you are ashamed. We must get started. When you are ready, get into the ring at once!"

Flora helped Risa attain as much privacy as possible. In no time, the gypsy was in the ring, along with Deitzl. Flora saw that Boerner had taken a control stand on a platform, overlooking the evening's event. She was definitely in charge. There were piles of money on tables in front of her, as the wagers had been made.

Soldiers and overseers in attendance had seen these bouts many times before. Drunken buddies clanked humpen mugs and more elaborate steins, all in a gladiatorial spirit. Some threw their half-filled brews at Risa, but most missed, falling back on to Flora, who tried to rally her friend from the lower corner of the canvas ring.

The "boos" were deafening and depressing, but amidst the antagonizing sound, Risa heard some of the onlookers begin to offer a rousing cheer of support. She glanced around to understand the sudden change. When she saw her opponent, she felt her heart sink, deep into a hollow region of her stomach. She had never expected her opponent to be the most remarkable person she had seen in her short life.

Elsie took strides of two meters in length. Supported by Dr. Max Engel on one side and a nurse on the other, the giant smiled as audience members patted her back and shook her extended fifteen-centimeter hands that reached over heads, three deep into the crowd. She widened the elastic ropes and entered the ring.

Some of the drunken enthusiasts scorned Risa, giving the awe-stricken gypsy thumbs down gestures. Others continued to hurl wild streams of beer at her, laughing at the fear in her eyes.

Flora began to cry, wiping tears that were mixed with alcohol from her sullen cheek. She stared at Elsie Honigsburg, who stretched her arms across nearly the entire width of the canvas while pointing to the Nazi swastika kerchief on her head. As the crowd roared with approval, Flora could not bear to think that on that night, her friend would be killed.

Deitzl went to Risa's corner of the canvas with the rules.

"Roma, there are no rules. You fight until one of you cannot continue. 'Mother Germany' has killed sixteen women before you."

She then turned to Elsie.

"Giant, are you ready?"

The mammoth hulk nodded.

The overseer gazed at Boerner for approval and left the two women alone in the square fighting zone. A loud bell sounded from beneath the raised structure when Max Engel hit the circular dome with a workman's hammer that had been lying on the floor, and so the fight began.

Risa circled the arena, assessing Elsie's mobility, first to the right, then to the left. In doing so, she was able to determine if the giant was more comfortable revolving clockwise or counterclockwise. The gypsy made a fake to the right and then reversed direction. She lunged forward and then pulled back.

Elsie Honigsburg may have fought and killed sixteen women before meeting the street-smart woman from Bucharest, but none had possessed the tough and savvy history of Risa. Survival was an art to the Romani prisoner. She took hand-to-hand combat seriously, and she had scars all over her thin body to prove it.

Elsie moved one foot forward, following up with the second. Her eyes were level with the giant's belly button. Like a tank moving slowly with unrelenting pressure, every time she approached Risa, the much smaller woman spun to make "Mother Germany" start over again. The crowd, becoming impatient, began booing the tactics of Risa Resto.

One minute had already passed. Historically, Elsie had finished off five of the sixteen victims within the first minute. Yet Risa did not let the cat-calls influence her strategy. She knew most of the negativity was coming from people losing wagers.

Then it happened. As the feisty opponent moved under Elsie's outstretched arm, eluding her grasp, the Roma tripped over the giant's fifty centimeter bare foot and fell, face first to the canvas. Elsie picked up the fallen prisoner by her arm like a child's doll and clasped her, suspended in air, against her gigantic body, enveloping her frail opponent in her massive arms, applying a bear-hug. The crowd erupted. Like a predator awaiting a mistake, the giant took immediate advantage of the literal misstep.

Flora watched her helpless friend, cupping her mouth, a scream erupting. Risa could feel the oxygen being squeezed from her lungs, a feeling that became surreal, as pain seemed secondary. The deprivation of air superseded the nerve damage Elsie was inflicting.

The giant, still seeking the entertainment approval of the crowd, released her from the death hold and spun Risa's body around, holding her up, as if displaying some sacrificial offering to the hoard of drunks. She was obeying Engel's directive, playing with her victim to lengthen the time of the fight.

As she orchestrated this display, showing Risa to the crowd, the Bucharest-bred street fighter snapped her head back and butted the bridge of Elsie's nose, breaking it. The giant's nose gushing forth blood, she dropped her opponent and grabbed her face in an attempt to stop the stream pouring from both nostrils. Onlookers erupted with approval. In the sixteen previous battles, they had never seen Elsie wear the mask of war.

Risa scooted behind the hulk, and in an unorthodox move, she pulled the giant's trunks down to her ankles. The room jeered the humiliation and followed with thunderous applause. The betting crowd seemed to have forgotten their losses. They were witnessing Ravensbruck history, and they knew it.

Elsie ceased tending to her nose wound and bent down to quickly retrieve her dignity by pulling up her oversized fighting trunks. Yet while she was temporarily off-guard, Risa ran, full force with her shoulder into "Mother Germany's" buttocks, catching the giant off-balance. Elsie fell, headfirst through the ropes, the lower half of her body still within the ring.

One guard poured his humpen of Lowenbrau over Elsie's head, mocking her awkwardness. Another pulled him back, insulted that the sudsy brew splashed on her Nazi bandana. They began fighting until a third managed to separate them.

Risa Resto shot a glance at chief overseer, Dorothy Boerner, who quite indifferently, appeared to be counting the money that no one would claim. Risa knew that on that night she might be Boerner's hero, but on the next day, the aufseherin would be just as angry with her for destroying the giant's mystique and income potential.

Elsie tried to rally. Four minutes passed. No opponent had ever lasted so long, but the contest was far from over. Risa, while lying on "Mother Germany's calves, remembered something she had witnessed once while cheering on two Bucharest street fighters.

With Elsie squirming, the gypsy imbedded her teeth into the Achilles tendon of the giant's bare foot. Elsie writhed in pain, but she was too exhausted to lift the lengthy appendage. As the champion lie in near defeat, no one stopped the barbaric behavior. Risa broke skin with her strong bite and grinded until she heard a loud snap. The woman's heel was now unattached to the rest of her leg. Elsie was immobile, and her threat diffused. She would never fight for Boerner again. Risa Resto had done what sixteen deceased opponents could not do. She had defeated the giant.

Elsie Honigsburg pounded her hand in pain on the red-stained canvas. Hitler stared down from the poster, arms folded, seeming more annoyed than defiant. Boerner and Deitzl whispered as the chief overseer rounded up the money and abruptly left the gymnasium. Soldiers poked at Elsie, pouring copious amounts of beer on her head, which still remained outside of the ropes.

Dr. Engel, along with his nurse, tended to the wounded hulk. Risa stood exhausted, bloody mouth, chin and undershirt, while displaying her battle scars. No one seemed appreciative of her performance. Flora could not help but think that her friend had merely postponed her death to another day.

The building cleared out. There was no ceremonial award for Risa Resto. If she had accomplished anything, it was to defy the symbolic strength of "Mother Germany." Even she knew that it was only a matter of time before Dorothy Boerner punished her for winning. For the moment, punishment was imminent for Elsie Honigsburg. The barely-conscious warhorse of Ravensbruck's gladiatorial evenings had become useless, her value void. Engel knew what had to be done.

A group of eight guards entered the ring with a canvas stretcher, and rolling Elsie's quivering body onto it, they carried her from the gymnasium and placed her on a flatbed utility truck. Ironically, it was the same vehicle that Elsie was transported on from Hamburg five years earlier.

The doctor she had so relied on during her five-year residence leaned over the hysterical giant, bearing a fake concern.

"Elsie, I am going to give you a sedative to ease your pain."

The grateful, wounded giant nodded, thanking the camp physician as he injected "Mother Germany" with three disposable syringes of phenyl, the camp's euthanizing medicine of choice.

No one recognized Risa or Flora's presence for the past twenty minutes. If there had been an open gate nearby, they could have walked to freedom, unnoticed. After a couple minutes, the aging overseer who had escorted the two from the barracks earlier appeared by the corner of the boxing ring.

"Okay, aufseherin Deitzl wants you out of here."

The group of three left the gymnasium, heading to the barbed wire gate, which led to the labor camp prison area. When the elderly guard opened the portal, she stepped to the side.

"You can get to your building from here. You do not need me."

Risa and Flora entered the less-manicured part of the concentration camp. Flora held her friend's clothes, and together they walked to 116.

Risa proudly gasped, "I cannot wait to see the look on Janaczek's face when she sees that I am still alive!"

* * * * *

The flatbed truck entered the secure area of the camp infirmary and crematorium.

"Stop and let me out before you go to the pit," Dr. Engel ordered.

The driver complied, and the physician left, speechless. He did not know if he was a tad sentimental over the death of his five-year relationship with the only pituitary giant known to exist under the Reich's domain, or if he was merely angry that her money-making potential had abruptly ended.

The truck drove another thousand meters and arrived at the pit behind the camp crematorium.

"Let's make this fast. It stinks back here," the driver yelled to the two soldiers who rode on the platform with Elsie Honigsberg's body.

They discarded the giant corpse quickly. It fell atop the pile of other murdered souls. Once in the open grave, "Mother Germany" did not seem to be as huge as she was in life. Perhaps it was because of the dark setting, and perhaps it was because death was not impressed with one's grand size or magnificence. Death accepted everyone as equals.

In her brief twenty-three years on this earth, Elsie had been a misfortunate enigma. She was always noticed, yet never appreciated. She had impressed everyone who knew her, but she was also an oddity, which made her a target for the Nazis. The last five years had been a gift in a way. Engel had merely extended her state of execution, during this time, she achieved the respect she so needed, as a result of Dorothy Boerner's self-serving efforts. In reality, however, Elsie always knew she was never anything more than a prisoner.

During those years, it was impossible for the giant to ever achieve a social acceptance. Exploited, studied, observed and ridiculed, Elsie was never allowed to pursue a peaceful existence. Risa Resto did not realize it, but on that night she was instrumental in helping Elsie escape the "shadenfreude" of the world and be delivered to the one that offered inner peace.

CHAPTER 14

Heinrich Wurtzmuller exited his jeep before it came to a full halt. The guard met him at Ravensbruck's front booth, eager to diffuse the ranting of Greta Junkwalter. Seeking approval from his superior, the guard offered a formal salute before relaying details of her hysterical behavior to his captain.

"She came by taxi. The cab left after a few minutes. She would not leave until we summoned you, but I calmed her down with some coffee. She said nothing about why she was here, only that it was a matter of your concern, and no one else's. Do you want Sgt. Eigerhahm and me to leave the booth while you interview her, sir?"

The young guard was cordial to the officer and eager to accommodate him.

"No thank you, Private. I will take her back to Furstenberg immediately. Women—they are stronger than any male, any size, any rank. They can bring all of us to our knees—even the Fuhrer. I will remove her from your hair. Thank you for calling me. I owe you one, soldier."

The guard felt that Wurtzmuller had approved of the way he handled Greta's surprise visit to the camp.

"Now, just let me go in and get her," the captain said. "She can take her wrath out on me, but not you. I deserve her ire. Never let romance gain control of your life. Never promise a woman something you cannot deliver."

Both laughed. Wurtzmuller was hoping the guards did not perceive the real circumstance for Greta's visit.

"Hello, my love," he said as he entered the shack, "let's allow these soldiers do their job and leave them at once, okay?"

Winking at the other guard, who had remained in the booth with his Furstenberg Saturday night associate, he smiled.

"Thank you, Private."

The humiliated officer picked Greta up by her thin bicep and walked out of the hut and to the "W"-marked jeep, sitting in front of the gate.

"I will see you tomorrow, boys… God willing."

The soldiers laughed. They thought it refreshing to witness a problem between a woman and an officer. It affirmed the human errors in relationships of all men, no matter their rank. It was Wurtzmuller's intention to come across as a bit embarrassed, to show the guards that officers can have "woman problems," just like them. He sped away on the lake road, heading for Furstenberg.

Blood boiling, the Nazi officer spotted a clearing between a group of pine trees that led down to the lake's shoreline when they were half the distance to their destination. He pulled to a stop in a place where no one could see the idle jeep from the road. Grabbing her arm with significantly more force than in the guard booth, he yelled.

"Are you crazy? Taking a taxi to the front gate of Ravensbruck? Those bastards are now looking at me like I am some kind of fool! Why would you do such a thing? Tell me!"

Wurtzmuller slapped Greta's sobbing face with his palm.

"Tell me, what this is about? Did one of your boyfriends get you pregnant? This has turned into one shit of a day! Tell me now!"

Greta pulled back her wavy hair that was covering up the bruise on her temple and lifted her blouse, displaying a black and blue mark, extending from her groin to just under her breast. She cried hoping he would bear some sympathy for her wounds.

"What happened? Who did this to you? Why did you come to me?" he demanded, knowing that he had been somehow implicated in the attack on the woman.

"Let me see this, better. Get out. Stand in front of the headlights."

Greta obeyed, showing her wounds under the lights in front of the vehicle, and then she climbed back into the jeep.

"Two woman guards came into my room right after you left on Saturday night. They wanted to know why you always bring two canvas duffle bags, but you leave with a briefcase."

"How did you answer? I want to know everything you said to them. Was one quite pretty, and the other wretched-looking?"

As she nodded, he knew who his pursuers were.

"Yes," the ugly one was the one who hurt me. I swear captain—I said nothing. I swear!"

Greta had questioned her own conscience for two days, wondering if she should tell Wurtzmuller about the visit. After her admission, she felt the burden of indecision lifting from her body.

"Well, Greta, you must have had to say something. I want you to tell me what that was. Do not worry if you have done nothing wrong."

The Nazi calmed, realizing what the situation had become. Boerner and Deitzl had crossed the line. He was an officer of the Shutzstaffel, and they were merely female guards, who were not even military. He would not let them bully him overtly. He could have had the duo terminated. However, he did not want them floating around the prison circles, spreading stories to significant personnel about what they had observed.

"They asked where the second bag went," Greta continued. "I told them that you only brought one, filled with food to me for my family. I said that if there was a second bag, like they stressed, that perhaps you delivered it elsewhere. They also made fun, thinking that you paid me in army canned goods for sex."

"Did they get into Bergeron's room?" he asked.

"No. They tried. I told them that a strange old man used that room. They were satisfied, but threatened me with harm if I was in assisting anyone in illegal actions. Then, as they were about to leave, the ugly one punched me so hard in the stomach that I had to end my appointments for the night."

Wurtzmuller could see the pain and fear in the young woman's eyes. Her battered face and alcohol-impaired speech certainly betrayed her age of twenty years.

"I want you to remember everything, what else?" he pressed. "Why did you wait so long to tell me all this?"

"I was afraid, but most of all, I used the heroin that you brought me to ease the pain. I remained in bed for three days. Do you have more?"

Greta could not hide her weakness from Wurtzmuller. She was dependent on any mind-altering substance available. He was shocked that, in such a short time, she had used all the syringes he had given her.

"I will bring you more, but I will have to stop with the duffle bag of food for your family," the officer conceded. "The predictability of bringing you food has created such an offensive inquiry by these two that I do not wish to continue."

"No! Please do not punish my family, Captain! We live on that, week to week."

Greta wept at the thought of losing of the officer's nurturing gift. With rations becoming scarcer as the war entered its fifth year, the bag of food was better than any other customer's payment.

"Look, you will have to trust me—but also trust yourself," he consoled.

"What do you mean, 'trust myself?'" She demanded, confused by his comment.

"Instead of actual food, I will give you cash. It will be up to you to purchase food for your family and not be tempted to spend it on booze. Do you understand? You must gain control of your own destiny, Greta."

"Will you bring me more heroin? It helped me through the last few nights. I promise I will use it wisely, Captain."

"Heinrich Wurtzmuller was now beginning to have little faith in the success of his weekly transactions with Pierre Bergeron. He would need some time to assess the precarious situation created by Boerner and Deitzl, but he would be damned if common overseers would destroy his personal goals!

"I may make some adjustments concerning our rendezvous procedures, Greta," Wurtzmuller said as he removed a wallet from his uniform jacket and handed the battered prostitute fifty Reichsmarks. "In the meantime, this is for you and for maintaining the secrecy of our funding the Alsatian Resistance Group. Remember, you possess a key role in securing the success of the Reich's efforts. I am proud of you, standing up to those two women. And I am prouder that you maintained the secrecy of our valiant mission to secure victory in the Alsace."

Greta always felt like more than just a common prostitute with Wurtzmuller. He seemed to find qualities that elevated her self-worth and made her feel important. In truth, the officer was using her to achieve his own selfish goal, but he did have feelings for the girl. He abhorred Deitzl for the beating she had bestowed, and he began to focus on how he would deal with that.

He delivered Greta Junkwalter to her mother's residence, kissing her farewell and promising to call her before next Saturday's meeting at the Lorelei to review any changes that he may have made for the visit. As the broken woman left his jeep, she reminded the officer to bring some syringes filled with heroin.

He realized that in one short visit he had created an addiction. People like Greta could not face life's crucial moments on their own.

By becoming her source for drug dependence, Wurtzmuller realized he had even greater control at manipulation—even more than with money and alcohol.

He drove the ten-minute journey from Greta's Furstenberg home back to his chalet, contemplating the dangerous situation regarding the team of Boerner and Deitzl. He could not believe that they had so much anger for him and his command. Why? It was definitely time to deal with them, but how?

Exhausted, the puzzled Nazi sat in his parked jeep, alone, in the front of his home, staring at the night sky for an answer. The afternoon problem involving Isaac Bloom being discovered by Siemens salesman, Rutger von Blarcom, had virtually become a non-issue.

Then it hit him—like a bolt from the sky, causing the Nazi to bang his hands on the steering wheel.

"That's it!"

The idea seemed perfect, manipulative and valid. Heinrich Wurtzmuller hurried into the back door and called for Isaac, awakening him from his floor bed in the pantry.

"Bloom! Bloom—wake up! We have work to do."

Isaac opened his door, expecting a continuation of reprimand due to the afternoon's events. The manic officer, however, had something else on his mind.

"Bloom, go through the boxes. Find the ones that have samples of Gestapo police uniforms that we have made for the government. Find your size and try it on. Show me when you are wearing it."

"What, sir?" the sleepy prisoner asked. "I do not understand? You mean now?"

"Yes Bloom, now!"

The captain rubbed his head, disrupting his hair.

"Like it or not, Bloom, you are going to become an emissary for the Gestapo. You are going to put the uniform on and do as I command," he insisted. "You have a problem with that, Bloom? Perhaps I should have killed you this afternoon when you were discovered by von Blarcom?"

Isaac was speechless.

"Hah! Being a Nazi now looks pretty good, as compared to the alternative" the officer continued as he opened a fresh bottle of Reisling that had stood for several days on the table next to the sink.

Isaac rolled his eyes away from the wild officer and began moving the cartons.

CHAPTER 15

The wire pen, just within the front gates of the Ravensbruck labor camp, barely held the two dozen local townspeople who were workers. They arrived every day at six thirty a.m. and stood in the cramped cage until various military guards or overseers escorted them to their work areas. Some skilled workers assisted the prisoners on factory assembly lines, while others cleaned, cooked or helped maintain on only the military segment of the camp.

They left in groups, except for the one local—Reinhold Freund, an aging man in his sixties who had been in trouble for most of his life. Arrested over twenty times for crimes such as theft, vagrancy, disorderly conduct and other petty offences, the old street robber and hustler warranted the only private escort to his job every morning.

The armed soldier usually greeted him with just a nod. They crossed the courtyard and reach their destination at the warehouse section of the camp, just beyond the prison barracks. The line of warehouses bordered the wall separating staff residences from the prisoner quarters.

Freund and his guard waited there every morning for access to the windowless and securely locked office, just inside the warehouse truck bay.

"Ah, *there* is my favorite crook! Good morning, Herr Freund. I hope you are not hung over? Will you make your Fuhrer much money today? Ha? What do you think?"

"Good morning, Captain," Freund answered, amused at Wurtzmuller's sarcastic tongue. "We seem to have had several rewarding days recently. I trust Hitler will be satisfied with Ravensbruck's contributions to the Inspectorate's account."

"Just remember, Freund. It is never enough. Whatever you uncover today means you should uncover even *more* tomorrow."

Wurtzmuller always stressed to the old man that he was being observed continuously, keeping Freund on his toes and accountable. Whatever happened, Freund knew that the captain was always watching him.

Wurtzmuller knew Freund from town and the Lorelei. His street intelligence and criminal background qualified the old thief to be Wurtzmuller's "expert" for uncovering any concealed valuables that women were trying to bring in on registration day. Every piece of luggage and clothing that was confiscated from the new prisoners on the first day of their incarceration passed under Freund's criminal scrutiny.

Unaware that all belongings would be appropriated and they would be required to don the uniform of the prison, each woman's personal items were turned over to Nazi jurisdiction, and Freund was the initial stage of the conduit that channeled their modest possessions into to the Reich's growing fortune.

Meticulously, the crafty Freund sat at eight flat tables, which had been combined to create one giant surface. Piles and piles of women's clothing lay to one side. One by one, Freund would single out garments, running his hands along every centimeter of hem and seam. If he felt an inconsistency, a lump or an indication of re-stitching, he slashed into the garment, and more often than not, he would discover a hidden treasure.

"As usual, do not take your eyes off him. If in any way you *think* he may have stolen something, call me. I will be in my office. If you actually *see* him take something, contact me for sure. I would like the honor to kill him myself, in the name of the Fuhrer. Five cigarette breaks, nothing more. Please search him before each break—hair, pockets, pant cuffs and mouth. I will spare you looking up his ass until the end of the day."

All the while, Wurtzmuller's delivery was stoic, assuring Freund he meant business.

"Don't you get tired of saying the same thing, day in and day out, Captain?" the thief asked. "I have been performing these tasks now for quite some time. Do you not trust me?"

"I know somehow you have discovered a way to steal something from time to time, Freund. I want you to realize that the one time you are caught, you will be shot. Please know that I have a second worker reviewing your daily findings. He weighs, tallies, and records everything. It will not be necessary for you to remove the precious gems from their settings any longer. This can improve your speed for uncovering the goods. Our population is growing, and we are running out of time."

Freund had realized that his concern for separating the gems from their pronged anchors might have been picked up by the officer, which it was.

"But Captain, I can still remove some of the stones from the rings. I do this quickly, no? Why?"

"Why?" the captain answered. "Because they are easier to steal after separation."

Wurtzmuller turned to the guard.

"Remember, any suspicions—notify me at once."

New to this post, the young soldier stared at Reinhold Freund with eyes brimming with aggression.

Go ahead, I dare you! Steal something or even try to do it!

He sat behind the old man, just to the right, near the locked door.

Wurtzmuller left the men alone and went about his administrative duties. He meant all that he had said to Freund, and yet he knew it would be difficult to replace him should the crook be caught pilfering from the belongings that had already been stolen.

Having a civilian performing this daily job assured the Nazi officer that he would have to answer to no one in the military as far as compiling the treasures. All he had to do was report Freund's results. No one ever questioned Wurtzmuller's numbers. They were never double-checked. Instead, the confiscated valuables that women were trying to secretly keep after entering Ravensbruck were welcomed by the Concentration Camp Inspectorate. The amount was never questioned.

Freund lifted a carpet bag, which had transported someone's belongings. It was empty. The crafty veteran thief rubbed his fingers along the black silk lining, listening to the sound, as if it was a bank safe. He turned to the guard and winked.

"I cannot believe people would be so stupid as to think that this would go unnoticed."

He took a pair of shears and punctured the lining. Cutting the material, Freund removed what appeared to be thousands, in Reichsmarks. He neatly piled it onto the table and then placed it in a large glass food jar.

"See, I do not steal," he quipped to the guard over his shoulder. "But I probably could have stolen this—" Freund added, holding up a gold pendant that had been stashed in the satin wall. "You did not even see that, did you, young man?"

Freund laughed, challenging the soldier's accuracy for observation.

"Shut up, old man. I could easily kill you for trying to steal that, rather than having you insult me for not noticing it. Try that again, but if you do—I dare you not to show it to me. I want to find it on your person, just so I can see you get shot. Then we shall see who laughs."

Freund went back to his job. During the first two hours, he uncovered diamond rings—hidden within hollow shoe heels, he found necklaces and bracelets—sewn into dress hems, paper money—flattened to the back of framed pictures, and teddy bears—stuffed with nearly everything imaginable, and expensive.

"Ten o'clock, young man, cigarette break."

Freund studied the guard's "break behavior" before attempting to conceal any contraband. There were usually three other guards who shared warehouse duty. Two were easy to steal from, while the other a bit more thorough.

He held up his cigarette pack and matches, motioning to exit the room and enjoy his smoke on the warehouse dock.

The guard stood, and facing Freund, looked into his scalp, ordered him to invert his pants' pockets and shake his cuffs. He then ordered Freund to open his mouth, raise his tongue, and lift his lips away from his gums. Satisfied, the private unlocked the office door, following the vintage thief from the stuffy, isolated interior, and both took their respective smokes, standing on the bay entrance.

Freund looked over to the novice soldier and smiled. The sentry had been quite serious since Freund's earlier remark. He was not amused or happy to have been given this assignment. He was bored, and the old man could see that. It was a plus for him. *Boredom bred incompetence*, Freund thought.

The soldier finished his cigarette first.

"Hurry up, old man. I do not want to be reprimanded for your tardiness."

"Very well," Freund answered, flicking his butt on to the concrete walk.

The young soldier had neglected to see Freund slip an errant gem into his cigarette pack earlier, while gathering it from the inspection table. When he took the pack out into the open air, Freund tapped the bottom of the package, receiving one cigarette into his hand, along with the unnoticed sapphire. With his back to the guard, he placed the tip of the butt into his mouth, along with the valuable gem. He swallowed it in order to retrieve it later—after it had succumbed to the mercy of his peristaltic clock.

When they returned to the room, Freund realized his guard was just a "hot shot" novice. The soldier could berate him all he wanted. As the old thief felt the scratchy gem depart from his lower esophagus into his gut, he knew he had beaten the guy.

All mouth, no brain, Freund thought. He could hardly wait for his next cigarette break.

CHAPTER 16

Between the hours of six to seven-thirty p.m. every day, no one could locate Heinrich Wertzmuller if they ever needed to reach him. During that time, the dutiful captain was locked within the confines of the warehouse office he created specifically to uncover the confiscated articles stolen from new prisoners. The project was under his command only.

For his productivity, he received accolades from SS hierarchy in Berlin, and his productivity allowed him to accumulate his own personal wealth for retirement. However, it was also because of his productivity that he would be ridiculed and questioned by his ever-present nemeses—Boerner and Deitzl. They were the metaphorical thorn in his side that could potentially destroy his nearly perfect project.

All alone within the ten-meter plaster fortification, Wurtzmuller inspected what Freund had uncovered within the piles and piles of prisoner clothing, suitcases, and bags taken from the first day victims. As ordered, everything was placed in used candy and cookie tins, which made excellent receptacles.

Wurtzmuller thought there was something peculiar about their sound. He could hear the scattered scramble of the precious gems as they danced across the metal floor of the tin boxes. If the volume was heavy, the pitch of the noise made by the stones resonated lower. The Nazi could tell, and that day was profitable. Then he went to the safe in the corner of the room, dialed the secret combination and combined the day's entry, adding it to a larger, heavier tin. As he removed the "four-dozen butter cookie" tin, it hardly made a sound at all because it was so firmly packed with valuables.

Next, the officer checked the boxes of artifacts and the money. He shook his head, distraught at the bounty of gold candlesticks, ornate picture frames and piles of silverware. So much weight in gold, and yet Pierre Bergeron, his associate, advised him to cease bringing any of these items to their Saturday night meetings. It seemed a shame that he could no longer profit from them. Ahh, but the pile of paper money stacked on the far desk made things so much better!

Wurtzmuller perused the pile, hoping to find some precious Swiss francs that he so desired. It was his favorite currency and the currency he would rely on after his retirement. He retrieved half the francs, leaving the rest. He understood all too well how to skim from the top of the treasures without creating suspicion. Thus he helped himself to copious amounts of Reichsmarks, in all denominations.

After that, Bergeron performed his magic, and in one short week's time, the lesser-valued Nazi money was transformed into the greater-appreciated Swiss notes. He may have had to exchange much more of the faltering German currency to get the Swiss money he wanted, but there was an unlimited bounty of Reichsmarks lying on the table. He helped himself to one-third of the day's find. Banding several piles of the notes, he stuffed them deep into his briefcase. Then he reviewed a tray of bracelets and watches, securing five of each and placing them in a brown paper sack.

The captain dedicated the last forty-five minutes of his private session to studying the category of articles that had been retrieved from the mound of clothing that sat in four laundry bins along the office wall. He removed a glass, glistening pickle jar from the safe.

He could not tell, but there had to be thousands of bare diamonds filling the cylinder to what seemed to be forty percent of its volume. The Inspectorate emissary who collected the diamonds and other treasures would be by sometime next month.

Being careful, Wurtzmuller checked to see how much in treasure was reported during last period and how many new registrants were involved during that time. He did not want to create an inquiry about why his tally might have decreased during a given period, if the population had actually increased.

He opened the jar, and with reverence in his eyes, was entranced with adoration at its exquisite contents. In his callous way, had no remorse for pilfering the gems from the defenseless prisoners, nor did he plan on sharing it in his Saturday night transaction. The content was all his.

Bergeron requested him to focus on diamonds. But how would he take from the bounty? Just grab a pile? No. He would be much more discriminating. Wurtzmuller saw the remains of a woven carpet bag that Freund had gutted earlier, which still had its handles and was able to hold some contents. He put the diamond jar in the bottom of the satchel, placed the bags of the other valuables atop the glimmering jewels and prepared it for transport back to his chalet. He returned the day's other treasures back to the safe, locked and spun the dial closed.

No one, not Freund, not Suhren, not Bergeron, and certainly neither Deitzl nor Boerner knew of this stash of diamonds. It was to be Wurtzmuller's insurance. If anything happened to his other holdings, or if they ever diminished, he would have thousands of diamonds to sell later in life.

The officer then picked up the desk phone, dialed and hung up. He dialed a second time and repeated his action. A voice answered his chalet phone on the third attempt.

"Bloom, what size boot do you wear?" he asked.

"I guess just a medium, sir. Why do you…"

Wurtzmuller hung up the phone, assuming the answer, and left the isolated chamber of stolen goods in his jeep, making a stop at the camp leather factory.

* * * * *

Isaac stood in front of Wurzmuller, insulted and not amused that he was wearing the uniform of a Gestapo policeman. It was the very SS uniform style worn by Polmer, who had him sent to Ravensbruck. He detested wearing it, but he had no choice.

Wurtzmuller rolled in laughter as he swigged from a stein of Lowenbrau and cut into the delicious breaded pork chop.

"Look at you! My little Jew Nazi! Stand up straight. Look proud—at least try, okay? You are going to have to be convincing Bloom, or I will not need your services. And then you know what happens."

Isaac began to sense that Wurtzmuller's threats were even becoming less and less authentic, and yet he knew he'd best do as the officer commanded. The officer removed the glass jar of confiscated crystal jewels from the woven bag that was decorated in a tapestry floral design. Isaac's eyes widened in awe as the officer placed the jar on the on the desk.

"Beautiful, is it not, Bloom? The colors of the rainbow! So small, yet so expensive! It is nature's way of letting everyone know that the earth is still the dominant manufacturer of wealth."

The Nazi captain seemed to sober from his two giant steins of beer.

"Listen to my instructions, Bloom. I want you to take an inventory on this whole jar. Separate the diamonds by four categories: very large, big, medium and small. Leave the small and medium in the jar when you are finished. Place the very large and big diamonds in this velvet bag."

Wurtzmuller threw a crimson liquor pouch at the young Nazi-dressed prisoner.

"Leave everything on my desk. Practice your Nazi disguise. Tomorrow, we are going to Furstenberg, you and me. I will give you instructions as to what your assignment will be when we get there. It will be relatively simple, but it must be followed to my exact orders. After you clean the kitchen, you can start categorizing the stones in the jar, and do not be foolish and think you can take some without me finding this out. I am going to bed. It has been a tough week."

The officer removed his boots and climbed the stairs to his loft bedroom. Isaac could hear the guttural belching and farting, Wurtzmuller's approval to Isaac's culinary efforts.

Isaac thought about the captain's last remark—about how he would find out if his prisoner took any diamonds. He gave a serious review to the small arsenal of survival items that he was accumulating in the pantry, and how the officer had not missed anything over the past few weeks. Nor had he noticed one of the kitchen knives was missing and later returned to the drawer. Isaac cleaned the kitchen after Wurtzmuller's meal and decided to take a closer look at the mesmerizing jar of stones in the glass receptacle. Cautiously, the young man unscrewed the lid to the converted pickle jar and decided to dedicate two hours to sorting before he retired for the evening to his pantry.

At the same hour, on the Markt Street, above Fromm's Bakery, in Furstenberg, Reinhold Freund had just finished his dinner of burnt strudel and crumb pastry that he had uncovered from the alley garbage bin. He was pleased that he had passed the final stone he had stolen earlier. While scouring the belongings of the new prisoners, he thought about how similar that task was to his method for acquiring dinner. His life was merely one of rummaging. He was the lowest of low. Nearly sixty-five years on this earth, and all he could do was sift through the discarded belongings and food of others.

The old thief cupped the day's "take" of five jewels in his hand, went to the far side of his one-bedroom hovel and placed the stones into an old sock that he used as a bag, which held about eighty gems of various sizes. Freund dug up a slat of wood flooring and buried the woolen stocking in its hidden crevice, replacing it, and he crossed to his cot. He lay down, hoping that he would get the same guard to watch him " tomorrow." Pondering that premise, he flashed a smile as he began to doze. Amidst the squalor, Reinhold Freund gazed at the flooring by his widow, feeling like a wealthy, wealthy man.

CHAPTER 17

People who were congregated in the lobby of The Lorelei parted and deferred to him, creating a safe gauntlet for the young Nazi policeman. It was as if he possessed a rare communicative disease, or he was about to wreak havoc on their Saturday night festivities.

Isaac did not mind the respectful avoidance. He rather enjoyed the cowering of the masses. *If they only knew*, he thought. How many, would beat him up and remove his disguise, just for laughs. He forced through, holding only one small duffle bag, and ascended the stairs to Room 206.

Heinrich Wurtzmuller had phoned both Greta Junkwalter and Pierre Bergeron, informing them of his change in rendezvous plans. As long as each received what the officer brought along on the Saturday night meeting, they were fine with the new procedure. Wurtzmuller sat, unnoticed, in an alley, halfway down the Markt; his jeep nosing out to the road. He saw Isaac safely enter The Lorelei and observed his ascent to the second floor. Perhaps now, his own exposure would reach the level of invisibility that he had hoped.

Isaac pounded on the door to 206. He tried it again. On the second time, there was a response.

"Wait your fucking turn, damn it!" a muffled male voice shouted from the other side.

Isaac could hear the unlocking of the bolt before the badly worn door to room 206 flew open. An irate private was pulling up his pants, his visit shortened by Isaac's presence.

"Who do you think you are? You are supposed to wait until the desk man tells you it's…"

The plebe stopped his rant as his eyes came within three centimeters of Isaac's swastika armband. He swallowed hard, studying Isaac's gun and holster, proudly hanging on his uniform top. The irate soldier did not have to know that the Walther P38 was empty and that his confronter was actually a prisoner of the SS. The swastika armband was enough of a statement to make the embarrassed soldier refrain from continuing any display of temper. He left the room, pulling his pants over his rump and securing his military belt.

"Oh, is this my new little captain?" the benign but intoxicated young prostitute announced. "Hello! You are cute."

After she kicked the door shut and threw her arms around the Gestapo impostor's neck, Isaac felt embarrassed that another woman was showing him affection. No other woman had displayed any interest in him since his marriage to Flora over eight years earlier. It had been three weeks since he had seen his wife, so he was embarrassed that he felt aroused.

"How is the captain? Did he give you something to give me?"

Isaac could now see, in better light, that the girl had a defined abrasion on her temple. She had tried to cover it with facial make-up that had worn off from her recent appointment.

"He is fine. He gave me this to give to you."

The SS uniformed courier reached into his pocket and presented Greta with a money-filled envelope.

"But I am in a hurry. I am supposed to meet with a man who is next door?"

Wurtzmuller had briefed Isaac over and over again about this part of the plan. The young Greta transferred the money into the room closet and shoved it into her non-working wardrobe.

"I will get Herr Bergeron for you," she promised as she slipped into the shared toilet.

Isaac stood alone, next to the bed, clenching the duffle bag he was to deliver only to Pierre Bergeron. A few seconds after Greta had disappeared, the common toilet door opened and the portly salesman entered, holding a beige leather briefcase—the same style that Isaac had seen in large quantities strewn throughout Wurtzmuller's chalet.

"You are Heinrich's emissary, yes?" the old businessman asked, seeking affirmation.

"Yes sir, and I must leave immediately. He is awaiting my quick return."

Isaac could not believe that he welcomed the caustic company of the Nazi officer over the moment of independence in the Lorelei. *How different my priorities have become!* he thought.

"Here is the bag he had requested that I deliver. I will take the briefcase, if you do not mind," he said in a hurried tone, as he did not want Wurtzmuller to become concerned about the length of time that he was taking.

"Very well, young man. I guess I will see you next week."

The veteran salesman picked up the duffle bag and threw the strap over his shoulder as Isaac started to leave.

"No, no—wait until the girl returns. She will show you to the door," he reminded Isaac. "We must never leave either room unattended—even for a second. Adieu."

The old Alsatian disappeared into the toilet, and Greta returned a few seconds later.

"Tell my captain I said 'hello' and thank him for my envelope. Tell him I feel much better, now that a meeting has occurred after the last incident."

Isaac looked puzzled at her remark.

"He will know what that means," she laughed as she hugged Isaac again. "And if you ever want to go on a date, just come by. Any friend of the captain is my friend, too."

She stood on her toes and kissed his cheek.

Isaac was so embarrassed being propositioned that he opened the door to room 206 and started into the hallway—without the briefcase.

"Hey, do not forget this!" she yelled in a sing-song voice. "That is why you came," she laughed. "Did I make you nervous, Mister Gestapo man?"

Isaac thanked her and departed quickly with the beige bag, happy to be away from the artificial and financial romantic overtures. He darted down to the lobby, which was so crowded that he was forced to bull his way past the front desk area of Saturday night revelers. This time, his uniform did not part the multitude, but he managed to reach the street with no major confrontation or delay.

Hustling between the bumpers of speeding jeeps and sedans, full of soldiers celebrating the Saturday night wildness, Isaac managed to survive the onslaught and spotted Wurtzmuller's jeep poking out of the alley.

"Did everything go as planned, Bloom?" the officer questioned. "The woman and Bergeron, they were the only two who spoke with you?"

"Yes, I spoke with no one else. That place is mobbed with people. Many stared at me, but no one said anything," the young man offered as he removed the swastika armband, which made him feel ill from just looking at it.

"Amazing what a uniform can do, Bloom, no?" the Nazi said as he started his vehicle, headed back to the chalet on Lake Schwedt.

"People think you are Gestapo, and the seas part, like you are Moses." he laughed. "Now when you get back to my house, hang the uniform up neatly in your room, keep that shine on those boots, put my gun and holster back on the hall tree and do not forget to reload it with the bullets that I placed on my desk. Then cook me a big meal, while I investigate the contents in the briefcase. Tomorrow is Sunday. I have over twenty orders for you to place with vendors and as many bills to process for the Inspectorate's accounting department. So get a good night's sleep after you clean up."

* * * * *

Flora and Risa had finally settled into their bunk on Saturday evening. Overcrowding had become more and more of an issue, as some beds accommodated three women. On Friday, Ravensbruck had accepted its first trainload of new prisoners. The Reich had transported over 680 more women by rail from Berlin—the largest single-day addition to the camp in five years. Population had greatly exceeded its planned limit.

As two overseers patrolled the barracks earlier in the evening, they had performed a superficial check on all the new women. Those who were older or poor in health and those who were angry and belligerent were given a swipe of indelible ink on their forearm.

"Like bad food or poorly manufactured goods, they are certain to be discarded," Risa Resto whispered to Flora. "They are destined to be loaded on to that truck and we will not see them again, for sure."

"There are not even jobs for all these new women. What will they have them do?" Flora asked." As it is, they do not feed us enough food. What is to happen now?"

"Just as with our beds—we will be forced to share and make do. You know they will not increase any of our rations just because there are more women," the astute Romani answered. "Whatever happens, no matter how you feel, we must not complain, and we must not miss work. If they think you are of no value to them, they will kill you. I was lucky. If the kapo reported me now for my mouth, the aufseherin would probably have just had me shot on the spot. There are so many people entering here, they will not think twice before killing any of us. Each day becomes more dangerous."

Flora hated to admit it to Risa, but without Isaac, she did not care about her life. Yet her bunkmate was right—it was about personal survival. It was nice to have a concern for others, but it was either them or you. Tired, she stroked Risa's brow and kissed her on the forehead.

"Thank you for reminding me to stay strong. I love you for that," she whispered before turning away and falling asleep.

CHAPTER 18

Major Fritz Suhren sipped his black coffee, studying the document that had been signed at the bottom as coming from the Concentration Camp Inspectorate headquarters in Berlin. He read and re-read its content. The letter had been constructed with precise accusations. If requested, he would have no problem showing it to them.

"They are here, sir" the always accommodating Lt. Volsgaard advised the commandant, sticking his head through Suhren's open door. "Do you want them to wait?"

The major took a last review of the paper, dropped it on his cluttered desk and responded.

"No, send them in, but please bring in another chair. There is only one visitor's place to sit."

Volsgaard acted quickly, and while he was finding a second office seat, Chief Overseer Dorothy Boerner and Olga Deitzl slid into the Major's large office.

"Good day, Major Suhren,." Dorothy Boerner beamed.

"Good day, sir," Olga Deitzl followed.

"Oberaufseherin Boerner, aufseherin Deitzl—please be seated."

His offer was simultaneously met with Volsgaard supplying the second chair.

"How is your command coming along, Overseer Boerner? Has the increase in population been a problem for your staff? Are there any suggestions you may like to offer? Now would be the time to voice them. Things will soon be quite stressful and demanding for your staff and the soldiers. Do you feel we will need an increase in overseers, as a result of this influx?"

Suhren kept the beginning of their meeting formal and cordial.

"It is too soon to say, sir. Housing for the overseers and guards is limited. We do not have room for any more staff to live on the grounds unless new facilities are built. Perhaps we can purchase a residence already built in Furstenberg in order to house them."

"Yes," he answered, "however, the CCI budget has been sharply cut. I do not think they would spend money on guard housing. They are not even letting me build a gas chamber for the overpopulation problem. Very well. Do you ladies know why I summoned you, this morning?"

He focused first into Boerner's striking blue eyes, and then he looked into Deitzl's, trying to detect some indication of strategy or surprise, but they seemed unaware about why he had called the meeting. They looked at one another and then back to Suhren. Boerner shook her head, Deitzl shrugged.

"I understand that earlier this summer, you both took a weekend forty-eight hour pass and spent that time in Frankfurt. Would that be correct, ladies?" the crafty officer began.

"That is correct, sir." Boerner answered in a matter of fact voice. "Why do you ask?"

"As you probably are aware, Captain Bitten had a member of his orchestra, who had been a virtuoso violinist. Even though she was a prisoner, she played a very important role in our image. She was probably our most important incarcerated woman. To put it mildly, she made the CCI lots of money. The wealthy socialites adored her and contributed in thousands—mainly because they claimed we had been promoting The Arts. Captain Bitten had worked quite professionally and successfully at building a prison orchestra around…"

He shot a gander down to the letter.

"This Edith Klein—I understand she was a renowned musician, a celebrity, unfortunately for her, also a Jew. One evening, after band practice, Edith Klein just disappeared…"

Deitzl looked over to Boerner, urging a response.

"How does this involve Olga and me, sir?" the attractive chief overseer asked in a sweet voice. "We do not know how this woman disappeared. Certainly you are not implicating the overseers in any wrongdoing!"

"Do either of you know a man named, Marcus Klepperhaus?" Suhren inquired.

"No, no I do not."

"Me either."

"Who is this man, Klepperhaus, and what does this have to do with us or the Edith Klein story, Major?" Boerner answered.

The officer studied the letter as he prepared to answer.

"It appears that a man named Klepperhaus—or perhaps that is not his real name—was arrested by the Precious Art and Treasures Department of the Reichsbank. He had passed himself off as an art and antique dealer, but he had been found with stolen property on his possession. It was famous works of art and furniture that had been destined for display at the Fuhrermuseum. Somehow, during the havoc in Hamburg prior to the invasion, Klepperhaus managed to raid and plunder the warehouse where the articles were being stored and transferred—everything to a location in Frankfurt.

"I still do not see why this is of any interest or concern, Major," Boerner interjected.

"One of the items that Klepperhaus was guilty of illegally acquiring was a nineteenth century Sebastian Vuillaume violin. It had been registered as property of Ravensbruck Labor Camp and the Third Reich. Captain Bitten was astute enough to apprise the CCI of its presence and its use in his band. This automatically made it property of the Fuhrer. After Klein was presumed dead, Captain Bitten reported its theft to the SS, as a stolen or missing artifact belonging to the Reich. In essence, someone stole Adolf Hitler's priceless antique violin."

Major Suhren could see Olga Deitzl's complexion become pale as she took a gulp—the first reaction that he had noticed from either of them.

"We do not know anyone named Klepperhaus," Dorothy Boerner answered.

"Well, he claims to have met both of you. He claims to have paid you over two thousand Reichsmarks for the antique instrument. He claims to have bought it from, and this is a quote, 'the best damned looking jail guard I have ever seen. She could beat me all day. I would ask for more.' And then he asked his interrogators, where is Ravensbruck, anyway?"

"Where is this man, as I would like to contest his lies?" the chief overseer returned in rebuttal.

"I am afraid you cannot, Oberaufseherin Boerner," Suhren answered.

"And why, I may ask?" she asked with some defiance.

"Because several minutes after his confession, he was executed by the SS," the Major revealed.

The head of all Ravensbruck overseers looked down and then shot a glance to her partner, Deitzl.

"Look Major, we are all doing our best. I stole the instrument only to counter the behavior of others within these walls. There are men in high command using the system to gain personal rewards.

You cannot convince me, otherwise. Do you really think that violin or half of the reported art ever made its way to the Reichsbank? There is so much corruption within our system.

"What am I to do? Sit back and watch male officers attain the 'Good Life' from all the opportunities presented to them? I am the head of 250 women guards. I live in the same apartments as they live. True, you are in charge of the entire facility, but there are only 150 males. You live in a mansion on a lake. Bitten is constantly, attending caviar parties in places like Heidelberg. Wurtzmuller is, well, I would rather not say—just that his actions put everyone else's to shame. If I committed a major crime, then have me and Olga punished, if that is your desire."

Suhren was intrigued with the overseers' contained anger and revenge tactic. He was not at all interested in hearing about his soft life from someone who was unaware of his three bullet wounds from the Word War I, Battle of Verdun, or the Iron Cross medal he had received for overall military bravery. Yet, like every man who was a sucker for beautiful women, he answered.

"Oberaufseherin, I am not one bit in sympathy of your lowly, discriminated life among German military. How dare you equate me or any officer of the Shutzstaffel to you or your aufseherin group. If you feel the system is unfair to you then, please leave, and leave now, before I have you arrested for stealing the rightful property of Adolf Hitler.

"Please understand a war is going on and our main concern is to win it, not to make money on the side. I am concerned that your grudge for others may be restraining you from performing your job to an optimum level. We have a prison to run. We have more and more women entering our camp every day. It is your job to oversee your overseers, not to fence expensive violins in Frankfurt. That, and assisting in the victory of this war effort should be on your mind rather than selling a vintage instrument."

Major Fritz Suhren rubbed his chin as he rose from his seat.

"Stay here, I have to make a call to Berlin. Your fate will rest on this conversation. Neither of you move."

As he opened his door to depart from the duo, he could hear Deitzl whisper to Boerner.

"Why did you have to tell him? You should have just denied any wrongdoing. Now we are in big trouble!"

Once in the hall, Suhren motioned to Horst Bitten and Wurtzmuller to convene in the latter's office. He slammed the door shut. The three sat as the Major began to laugh.

"Did they admit to it, Major?" Bitten began.

"Oh yes, it was them. I did not even get into the murder of the prisoner, which they probably committed. But they definitely stole and sold the violin. They think I am speaking to someone in Berlin regarding their demise. Stealing from the Fuhrer is a capital offense, boys. And all of us are guilty of it, according to them."

Heinrich Wurtzmuller's smile quickly left his rugged face.

"What do you mean, sir?

"Well as far as Boerner is concerned, I am living a life of unnecessary pleasures. Bitten is gorging himself with gourmet foods and aged wines everywhere in Germany, except Ravensbruck. She did not even want to get into your illegal wrongdoings, Heinrich, which I may add, put ours to shame, according to her.

Wurtzmuller's face fell to a stare of uncertainty. That was Boerner's last straw. It would only be a matter of time before she verbalized her speculative remarks to Major Suhren.

Suhren genuinely seemed to dismiss Boerner's remarks, but Wurtzmuller knew he must take action.

"When you return, sir, do not forget to bring up the "guard dog" races and the wrestling match rackets that she and her friends sponsor for wagering. And if you word your argument correctly, perhaps you two can figure out in what way she could ever repay you for saving her life."

All three laughed at his implication. Underneath his wisecrack, the captain understood that he had a serious enemy within Ravensbruck. Boerner's fast quips and verbal jabs were becoming viscious. One accusation too many, and he could find someone investigating his actions.

Suhren re-entered his room and sat, facing the accused overseers. He sat back in his red leather chair and rocked, adding to the drama of the meeting.

"The problem has been diffused, ladies."

"Sir?" Olga Deitzl asked." Do you mean we are okay to leave?"

"I mean I lied for both of you to the Concentration Camp Inspectorate. I committed fraud. I told them it must have been someone else using your identities. I told them you were both with me that weekend, discussing the overseers' increase in responsibilities due to our growing population problem—that is, unless you are not happy with that lie and you would rather state a better one to the Inspectorate."

"Thank you, Major. We are humbly indebted to you for doing this," Dorothy Boerner smiled.

"That is not all, Oberaufseherin Boerner. Both of you will be on a period of probation for 120 days. You are not to leave the facility for more than two hours at a time, and you are not to continue your displays of gambling or money-making events for your entire length of stay in Ravensbruck. Do you understand?

"But everyone else can?" the still angry Boerner fired back.

"Shhh, what is wrong with you?" the more contrite Deitzl warned, poking her supervisor, stressing their indebtedness to Suhren. "We will abide by your demands, Major," the grateful aufseherin promised.

"I will put Lt. Volsgaard in charge of monitoring your behavior. If he reports any negative feedback involving either of you, I will be obliged to release you of your duties, file for insubordination, and you will never work in any labor camp capacity. Do you understand?"

Suhren felt that he had made his point, and Captain Bitten was satisfied that the mystery had been solved, although it would not bring Edith Klein back. Her murder by the two did not amount to any dialogue or reprimand.

"Now please return to your duties, perform them well and without complaint, and expect constant supervision from Lt. Volsgaard, who will be reporting back to me daily."

Suhren did not expect that they would be cooperative. The women stood, saluted Suhren, which seemed an insincere gesture, considering their guilt and the insubordinate behavior. They walked into the hall, passing Heinrich Wurtzmuller's open office. He kept his head down and tried to avoid their passing.

"How are you, Captain Wurtzmuller?" Olga Deitzl fired into the room. "I see you now have a Saturday night courier visiting your whore friend with the complementary bags of goodies. What is the matter? Are there too many inquisitors asking about your bag exchange with the Lorelei prostitute?

"That is no concern of yours, aufseherin. And be nice to me—Lt. Volsgaard is under my command. You would not want him to give me a poor report with regard to your antics, would you now?"

He winked, implying he also had control of her destiny.

"Well, I am surprised at your selection for delivery boy. He looks no more like a Gestapo policeman than my ass does. You could have paid someone more convincing."

She and Boerner laughed at her brash comment, rather comfortably, only minutes after Suhren's scolding.

"Do not sell yourself short, Olga. Perhaps if it was blond and a little more clean-shaven, your ass would make an excellent Gestapo policeman," Wurtzmuller volleyed, causing the offices of Horst Bitten and the two junior lieutenants, Joseph Volsgaard and Neil Grauptner, to erupt in laughter.

"Never think you are going to insult Wurtzmuller without getting destroyed in the process," the astute Grauptner advised his friend.

Wurtzmuller laughed to himself at his own jab. However, the remarks concerning his name and his questionable behavior would churn in his stomach all day. He knew the feeling would not abate until he found a permanent solution.

CHAPTER 19

Many of the Furstenberg townspeople in attendance that beautiful spring day remembered the fanfare, the colorful display and the energy that spun through the vortex of the mild April winds.

There were thirteen horses lined up at the starting banner. It had been the final race of the short season for all the qualified three-year-olds bred in the northern region horse farms. Two thousand fans stood entranced behind a series of ropes and fences, separating the grass track from the spectators. They wanted to see local history in the making.

It had been the first time since the inception of the event that one horse, The Pride of Prussia, if successful, would have won all seven regional races in one season. The horse's reputation had become the main sports story in North Germany, attaining even more press than local soccer clubs.

The Pride of Prussia was a beautiful roan-colored stallion, with a flowing brown mane and tail. He sported a triangular white mark between its eyes. Racing fans cited that he was perhaps the most beautiful entry since the multi-colored mare, "Cleopatra," who had been by far the most successful winner, nearly five years earlier. The new champion, Pride of Prussia, ran with similar dignity and delivered equally handsome winnings to its owner and all who wagered performances. Could he complete his perfect racing season and defeat all the challengers in this three-kilometer run through the Furstenberg Field of Schlossgart?

The level track was nearly one-and-a half kilometers, out to a lone elm tree that stood just before the land began a decline into a valley, around the vast spread of its trunk and back to the starting point. The weather was good, as there had been no precipitation for the past two weeks. Baron Yeager, the horse's owner, reported to all the papers that his stallion was in the best of shape, and after this race, the magnificent animal was scheduled to retire to a twenty-year life of grazing and studding. The arrogant and boisterous owner equated breeding the equine superstar to Hitler's creation of the Master Race. He bragged and jeered about how his horse made him loads of money on the track and joked, in the future, the horse would do the same "in bed".

The race lasted four minutes. The Pride of Prussia did not only lose, but he crossed the bannered finish line sixty meters after the horse that would have been last. Bettors screamed, "fix!" Racing aficionados who had travelled hundreds of kilometers to witness history left disappointed, and Baron Yeager saw his stud farm dreams answer an abrupt wake-up call.

Dolf Volks, owner of the winner, Stand Tall, a three-year-old mare from Furstenberg, had nothing but praise for the valiant effort put forth by Yeager's stallion. People commented about how he spoke more of his opponent's loss than his own victory.

In no time, an investigation led to the finding of a suspicious muscle relaxant drug in Pride of Prussia's blood after the race. The poor performance of the champion spurred talk there had been foul play, which indeed there had been.

The night before the Furstenberg event, locals testified seeing a town low-life and criminal, Wilhelm Goerthe, loitering near the paddock where three of the entries were stabled. Although the lanky, balding and awkward Goerthe was never found guilty, he was known to perform menial jobs for the owner and race winner, Dolf Volks. In particular, he worked for three years as a stable hand until a negligent and drunken Goerthe accidentally started a fire, killing five of Volks' animals.

Many suggested that the Furstenberg ne'er-do-well had a historied past with drugs, and he had injected the sure winner with a serum, supplied by Volks—if for anything, to absolve himself from the earlier mishap.

* * * * *

Heinrich Wurtzmuller sat cautiously in his jeep, tapping the steering wheel with his index and middle finger, losing patience. It was the correct place he had agreed to wait. He was positive about that: two kilometers on the main road, west of Furstenberg, at the dilapidated, uninhabited red barn—just as he had been ordered. The officer studied the swinging shutter as it teetered on one hinge, ready to crash down at a sudden gust of wind. It reminded the Nazi of the way life had been treating him, making him unhinged and about to fall.

Wild grass grew through one of the many broken windows. The barn had been red, but the grey weather-beaten planks had overtaken the original color. He was beginning to wonder if his plan was a good one. Just then, a tall, gaunt body came from behind the decrepit building.

"Captain Wurtzmuller?" Wilhelm Goerthe confirmed. He had never met the officer. Wurtzmuller's reputation had reached Goerthe's ears via his "sometime" friendship with street buddy, Reinhold Freund. The captain had asked his camp employee to arrange this meeting, and Wurtzmuller lied to Freund, saying that he needed someone to remove the unmanageable growth of weeds around his chalet. He offered the job to Goerthe, that is, if he was interested in making some fast money.

"Yes, Herr Goerthe," the stoic officer answered. "Please get in, quickly."

The neat and formal officer, along with the disheveled and seedy looking Goerthe rode still, farther west for another kilometer. The officer directed the "W" labeled vehicle into the beginning of Furstenberg's farm area. Stalks and stalks of corn, as far as one could see, graced the darkening landscape. Dusk came hard in mid-August. The hours of daylight were decreasing. The late summer sun descended slowly, seeming to appear five times larger than at noon.

Wurtzmuller found a field of corn that had yet to be harvested, and veering onto to the less-travelled road, he drove between the wall of corn and the adjacent trees of a forest. Well off the thoroughfare, the officer turned his vehicle directly into the labyrinth of corn stalks, hiding his jeep, making it indiscernible from every angle.

After mowing ten meters into the giant plants, the captain came to a halt, leaving the motor running, though he turned off the headlights. The corn stalks all around his jeep created a perfect womb of privacy and suspense.

"Am I in trouble, Captain?" Goerthe asked with some concern, becaue the military vehicle was fully concealed.

Wurtzmuller laughed, as the chosen destination truly did look like a setting for an execution. He understood Goerthe's fear.

"No, no—not at all, Wilhelm, but I want you to take this meeting very seriously. Listen carefully, and know that whatever is discussed is within full secrecy. Our national security is at stake. If you discuss this matter with anyone—anyone, and the Reich finds out—you will have to be assassinated. And if you make an attempt to escape after disclosing our meeting to others, you will be hunted down like an animal and killed. Trust me on that, Wilhelm."

"Yes, but why me, Captain?" Goerthe stammered, confused about why the military had any interest, whatsoever in his vagabond existence.

Wurtzmuller sat in the driver's seat, comfortable, arms folded, looking into Goerthe's eyes.

"You know, Wilhelm, this war is taking funny turns. As the years extend, people forget their goals and their principles. They become impatient. They start to complain. They think they can do better than the bosses. And what is worst, they share these thoughts and organize their dissention with other angry individuals. Are you aware that there have been many recent plots to assassinate the Fuhrer, all instigated by none other than the Nazi military itself?"

Goerthe seemed surprised. Wurtzmuller knew his companion was not the smartest of villains, but he was more concerned in winning the man's confidence and friendship. He thought that his narration was a good beginning.

"And why are you telling me this, Captain?" Goerthe asked, puzzled that such detail would ever be shared with the likes of him, a common criminal.

"All I know is that, if I was a younger man, I would ask to be sent to the front lines and fight for my Fuhrer. Who in their right mind would want to kill our leader?"

Wurtzmuller realized that he had established the beginnings of a patriotic bond with the man. He then explained why he had requested this meeting.

"Herr Goerthe, a few months ago, you were accused of injecting a prize winning stallion with a drug, causing it to lose a very important race," Wurtzmuller began.

"Now wait a minute, sir! I had absolutely nothing to do with that," he contested, meeting the blunt accusation with a defiant denial. "Those stories were never proven to be truthful, Captain. Are you bringing this up because you lost money on that race and want to blame me? How does that even have any bearing on what we were just discussing, sir?"

"So, you had nothing to do with that heinous crime of injecting that defenseless animal with a performance altering drug, Herr Goerthe?" the officer asked.

"Absolutely not, sir. I would never stoop so low as to inject serum into an animal!"

Goerthe refused to admit any wrongdoing, even secretly to a military person who had no past association with the Furstenberg racing debacle.

"Hmmm, too bad. I was hoping that you did," Wurtzmuller answered, catching the criminal by surprise. "I would have been able to offer you some good money."

Wilhelm Goerthe's ears picked up and his entire persona stood at attention.

"What? Excuse me. What did you say, Captain?"

He was ready for an explanation to the captain's disappointment on hearing his claim of innocence, and of course, the offer of money.

"Are you interested in working for me, Wilhelm Goerthe? Though I must inform you, if you say 'yes,' you cannot change your mind at a later date. I would have to treat that the same way as if you broke your vow of silence to me. I would have to have you killed."

The Nazi watched Goerthe's eyes widen, displaying fear. The German officer's demeanor was so intimidating that even a hardened criminal like Goerthe knew he meant it. Both men played by "no rules," but the low-life street criminal understood that he would be no match for a representative of the German government, should anything go wrong.

"Can I ask what it is that you want me to do? And just how much money we are talking about"?" he inquired as he pushed a wayward piece of an annoying corn stalk from his face.

"Of course you can ask both questions, Wilhelm, but not until you tell me if you will accept my offer. That is the first point of business. If you want to work with me and the government, you must say 'yes' before we move on."

"And if I say 'no,' Captain?" he asked.

"Then you are of no use to me, the Reich or your Fuhrer, Wilhelm," Wurtzmuller smiled sarcastically, staring straight into the deep-set eyes of Goerthe.

The unkempt criminal knew exactly what the cool officer was suggesting. It was an offer he could not refuse.

"I will gladly accept your offer and work for you, Captain," he answered, knowing that a negative response would have only expedited his execution, right there in the cornfield. "You said that you would pay me?"

"Before I explain your duties or your payment," the captain answered, "I must now stress that you are working for the Reich. I am your supervisor. This operation is top secret. I will kill you if you speak of this to anyone. And believe me, Herr Goerthe, that is the truth. I swear that on the life of our Fuhrer. Now get out of the jeep."

The men brushed away the jagged yellow crop that invaded the jeep interior.

"I am turning on the headlights."

The officer reached under his seat and removed a paper file. After crashing paths to the front of the jeep from different sides of the vehicle, they stood in the light source, hidden in in the cornfield.

"I will show you the photos of five military people from this area," Wurtzmuller began. "They are subversive and involved with the potential overthrow of the Reich. If you recognize any of them, I will ask you to state that. I will only ask for your assistance in dealing with the ones that you recognize."

He handed Goerthe the military photographs, the first of three who were males. They were fellow officers of Heinrich Wurtzmuller many years ago. Two of the three had been killed, serving the Wermacht at the beginning of the Polish invasion of 1938, and the third was currently somewhere on the Russian front.

The criminal studied the faces, scrutinizing the dead officers' photo. Handing the photos back to the crafty officer, he answered.

"No, no sir, I do not recognize any of these men. I am sorry. I thought I may have known one, but I was mistaken."

"Do not be sorry, Herr Goerthe. I will find another volunteer who is interested in serving his Reich as a civilian assistant to this mission. How about *these* individuals?"

The Nazi officer then handed the man ID photographs of overseers, Dorothy Boerner and Olga Deitzl. He carefully saw the criminal's eyes widen with an affirmation that he anticipated making some money.

"Ahh, now these two I know! I see them in town on the weekends. They are always together. They are drinking in The Lorelei every Saturday night. Men are always asking the pretty one to dance, but she never does. I think there is something going on with these two, no?"

Goerthe fell right into Wurtzmuller's "set-up."

"You mean they are part of this underground movement to kill the Fuhrer?"

"Well, they are part of the group dedicated to the downfall of our regime, Wilhelm. I do not think they are capable of getting close enough to the Fuhrer to kill him. But yes—they would like to see him dead."

"Lousy bitches," the disheveled low-life fired back, displaying patriotic emotion. "Well yes, those two I do recognize. Does that mean you want me to dispose of them? I only see those two in crowded situations. I have to think about what might be the best way to complete this mission, safely and securely, Captain. It will involve some planning. It may prove to be somewhat difficult."

Wurtzmuller smiled at the instinctive efforts of Goerthe, introducing a danger level to boost his pay for terminating the two annoying adversaries.

"I trust you can do it successfully, Goerthe. Have you ever served time for killing a person?"

"No, of course not," the criminal explained.

"And have you ever killed anyone before?"

Goerthe declined to answer. He looked away from the officer, responding.

"Perhaps that information may be top secret as well, sir," he snickered.

"Good, good answer, Herr Goerthe! From this moment on and moving forward, you are to act like this will have had never happened—especially after you complete this mission. Now get back in the jeep. There is just one more matter to discuss."

The two brushed the invasive stalks away from their path and hopped into the vehicle. Wurtzmuller stashed the five photos under the jeep seat. In the same motion, he took a brown paper bag that he had previously packed before leaving his chalet.

"Here is the weaponry that will be used for this mission, Goerthe."

The officer opened the sack and removed four acetate packets, which contained the disposable syringes that he had attained as samples from the Leitzner Pharmaceutical Company.

"You have probably never seen this before, Wilhelm."

The criminal's eyes widened as he was unable to identify the articles within the frosted paper wrapping. Wurtzmuller tore the top off one package and withdrew a syringe containing the lethal agent, Phenyl, which was the euthanizing medicine of choice by Dr. Max Engel and the medical staff at Ravensbruck. Goerthe looked at the small needle, already loaded with its lethal ammo. Wurtzmuller was right. The Furstenberg man had never seen this before.

When the criminal injected the stallion, Pride of Prussia, months earlier, his task had involved a larger needle and a bottle that was the source for housing the performance-altering relaxant. The injecting procedure was multi-tasked and cumbersome: insert the needle into the source, draw back the depressor, fill the syringe and prepare for injection. This procedure, however, was without precedent.

"So this syringe is ready for use, and the medicine was already put into it?" he asked like an awestruck kid seeing something for the first time in his life.

"Exactly! You just twist the cap off the needle and it is ready to use. The whole thing is made of plastic. After you use it, you merely discard it. It has been filled with an agent that will induce immediate cardiac arrest. The army has been experimenting with this medicine as a more humane procedure for killing enemy prisoners, or traitors, rather than the more traditional firing squad or hanging."

The Nazi would never admit, even to the likes of Goerthe, that it had become one of the methods used in prison extermination.

"You are holding a gun without a bullet, a firearm without a bang. This is the business of espionage, Herr Goerthe. You will pick your moment, complete your task, and fade into the mundane landscape, a true unsung hero to the German cause… Any questions?"

"When do I get paid?" was the only thing that mattered to the streetmercenary.

"I am giving you five thousand Reichsmarks tonight," Wurtzmuller stated, "and another five thousand once the two are killed and all indications point to the success and secrecy of the mission. And Herr Goerthe—if everything is as I wish, I may have more jobs for you, which of course means more money for you."

Wilhelm Goerthe shook his head with approval, eager to complete the job and accept the five thousand more Reichsmarks. Unfortunately for the old scoundrel, his military counterpart had no intention of paying him the balance, and had no other victims to kill other than his two arch enemies, Boerner and Deitzl. He planned to meet Goerthe, perhaps in the same corn stalk maze after the deed, and he would thank him by putting one maybe two bullets into his chest.

"One thing, Captain—why did you give me four syringes if I am to kill only the two women?" Goerthe inquired, suspiciously.

"Very good observation, Goerthe. I figure you would want to try one on an animal subject to make sure for yourself that it works. Then there are the two syringes for the victims… and the final one is for you—if you fail or break our vow of secrecy."

Wurtzmuller was every bit as good in such situations as the most intimidating criminal. *Whatever you do, don't leave them laughing. Leave them shaking in their boots. Let them know who is boss and who calls the shots.*

"Now here is your money."

He took five thousand Reichsmarks from his uniform pocket and passed it to his new associate, and then he handed over the four packs of phenyl syringes while staring directly into Goerthe eyes, who realized that Wurtzmuller was every bit as despicable as he was.

"For the preservation of the Reich and for the successful goals of our Fuhrer!" Wurtzmuller nodded.

The officer dropped the criminal back off at the dark hovel of a barn where he picked him up an hour earlier. They did not talk during return drive, the silence amplifying the moment's drama and the importance of secrecy, Wurtzmuller thought. Upon reaching the destination, Goerthe departed for the abandoned dwelling and took his new employer up on his suggestion at once.

The recluse discovered some food from a box lying on the barn floor—food he had found in a trash can by a restaurant in town. He acquired most of his life sustaining nutrients by rummaging through other's garbage cans. Once the pathetic indigent found a goodly amount of rotting waste, he threw it into a ceramic bowl and placed it on the ground by the barn entrance.

He took an opened acetate bag from his pocket, and removing the syringe that Wurtzmuller showed him earlier, he waited for one of the area's stray dogs to meander into the yard. The Nazi officer was right. Goerthe needed to see for himself that it was indeed a lethal dose of fluid within the syringe.

After two minutes, the smell of the rotten pile had attracted two mangy, homeless mutts, who began to snarl and fight over the odorous meal. Tipping up in silence, Goerthe approached the canine equivalents to himself, halted while contemplating, and chose the brown one over the black one.

CHAPTER 20

Major Suhren had been trying all evening to contact Wurtzmuller. Isaac ignored the ringing phone, as it was not in the recognized three, two, one, sequence that the captain created. When the Nazi officer arrived home after his secret meeting with Goerthe, Suhren was calling for the fourth time.

"Hello, this is Captain Wutzmuller," he called into the receiver that Isaac had removed from its console and passed to the frazzled captain.

"Where the hell have you been, Heinrich? I have been calling for two hours. Something has come up. I must leave for Berlin tonight—the Camp Inspectorate. We just received approval for the construction of a 200-person gas chamber, so I am getting down there fast and signing those papers before those asses change their minds. Horst is in Nuremburg with his band. Volsgaard is driving me. I will return late Sunday or at sunrise Monday. You are in charge. I trust you will keep a steady course."

"I'm sorry, sir. I was visiting someone in Furstenberg. I…"

"Well I hope she was pretty," the commandant interrupted, laughing.

"It will be good to get rid of those two carbon monoxide, piece-of-shit gas-wagons! They could not possibly keep up with the influx of people the Gestapo keeps dropping off at our gates," Suhren sighed without humanity, as the efficiency of mass execution was his only concern. "Some prisoners have had to be beaten into the vans. They are definitely aware that those vehicles have nothing to do with medical treatment. They're only good for new registrants, who have no idea they are climbing into a death chamber."

"And you think they will not catch on to a brick *building*?" Wurtzmuller asked, perplexed.

"Perhaps, but the effort involves two hundred victims as opposed to twenty. Trust me, Heinrich. This is necessary if we are to fulfill all contractual obligations with our vendors and the Wermacht. We are a working camp, and yet the SS is compromising our productivity and quality goals. Women who have been trained to assemble missile warheads die because new women are arriving with typhoid.

"I cannot tolerate this, I tell you. Some have to stay alive if we are going to deliver our quotas to the Army. Now I told no one that I was going except you, and of course, Volsgaard. My houseman just informed me the jeep is here. I will return as soon as possible. Keep the ship afloat."

After the major hung up, Wurtzmuller shrugged, muttering.

"It is not as if his presence is all that apparent anyway."

He turned to Isaac who was reheating dinner: sauerbraten and dumplings.

"Did you complete the twenty-five purchase orders, Bloom? I have to sign them."

"Yes, sir," Isaac answered. "They are on your desk, and uh, sir—I already signed them. You advised the importance of processing them quickly."

"How could *you* sign them? They will recognize right away that it is not my signature. They will be refused, Bloom."

The officer took an invoice from the desk, studied it. He threw it down and looked at a second, and then a third before turning to his assistant.

"So now you are a forger? How have you managed to duplicate my signature, Bloom? Is this something you acquired in Bremen?"

"Bremer*haven*, sir," he countered, correcting his superior.

"Wherever! Is this some type of parlor trick? Did you write yourself checks from my father's friend's account? Seriously, if it was not so well done, I would have to physically discipline you."

Wurtzmuller looked at additional purchase orders.

"Tell me how you were able to do this?"

Isaac was ambivalent in his response because he was uncertain about whether the officer was impressed or angry. He had performed his job, thinking that it was no more than the proverbial "rubber stamp." Again, the Nazi's take on his signing the documents was one of paranoia.

"It was easy. I will show you, sir."

Isaac sat in Wurtzmuller's desk chair, his arm reaching under the drawer, where he removed some papers from the trash pail wedged underneath and thumbed through several discarded letters until he found one that the captain had signed before discarding it.

"Here, see this?" Isaac held the pristine piece of paper. "See, you had already signed it."

Taking a pencil from the cup that was teetering on the corner of the desk, Isaac placed the aborted letter paper onto another piece of white paper. He sharpened the pencil with a razor blade that Wurtzmuller had sitting on his desk, solely for that purpose. After whittling a fine tip on to the shaft, he blew the dust into the air.

"This is how I did it," Isaac revealed as he pressed the pencil over the trail of Heinrich Wurtzmuller's established signature, pressing hard, though keeping the point intact.

Removing the top page—the one he had migrated over the officer's name with the pencil—he held up the white paper beneath. Wurtzmuller was quick to critique.

"So, the paper is still blank. Big deal!"

"Yes, but look," Isaac continued. "There is a perfect impression of your signature on the clean page. Now I will take your ink pen and glide it through the tracks of your exact signature. I just let the valley of your own penmanship guide my hand through the swirls as it leaves a trail of ink to the last letter, and *voila*—a perfect reproduction of Captain Heinrich Wurtzmuller's signature."

He held the paper up, proudly displaying his method to the Nazi captain.

"Reproduction? You mean a perfect forgery! We kill people for doing that, Bloom," the security-minded officer commented with a sly grin. "But you can redeem yourself by feeding me at once, okay? Then I need all jewels, diamonds, watches and the like weighed, categorized and tabulated—like you did for me last week. I will need this completed by five o'clock tomorrow, and I will need you to be dressed in your SS uniform, boots polished, and ready for our little excursion to The Lorelei. I will wait in my jeep in the same alley. But for now, Bloom," he said as he sniffed an aroma he immediately recognized from Isaac's former menus, "sauerbraten… and lots of it!"

* * * * *

Major Suhren left his luxurious lakefront villa and met lieutenant Volsgaard, who was parked under the front portico of the mansion. The lieutenant had erected the canvas roof for his jeep in case of rain during the seventy-kilometer journey to Berlin. Volsgaard was young, eager to please his commandant and ready for any promotion that Suhren might recommend.

"Do you know what, Lieutenant?" Suhren said as he stood next to the ride, gazing at his wrist watch. "I have changed my mind. With Captain Bitten out of town, I think it is unfair to dump all duties into Captain Wurtzmuller's lap this weekend. Please return to the camp. He will be commanding officer while I am gone, but you are more needed here, assisting him, than driving me. I will make this journey myself."

The major stuck his head into the covered military vehicle, examining the dashboard.

"Are you sure, sir?" Volsgaard asked. "I have placed all my expected tasks into the hands of Grauptner. He has assured me that he will have everything under control."

The eager junior Nazi officer was anxious to spend forty-eight hours in a bustling metropolis, with good food, pretty women, great beer halls and entertainment—as well as the chance to rub elbows with the upper-class CCI personnel.

The major was certain. He seemed to have abruptly changed his mind after hanging up the phone with Wurtzmuller.

"Ludwig, please bring around the Benz to the front. I will be driving that to Berlin this weekend."

The butler never questioned his superior, but he knew that the major rarely succumbed to sudden changes of plan.

"Very good, Major. Will Frau Suhren be accompanying you on this journey, sir?" the servant inquired.

"No, Ludwig, not this weekend—she would assuredly be bored with the events planned for my stay."

The commandant turned to Volsgaard a final time.

"Now be off, Lieutenant. I am sure you can keep busy here these two days. I will be fine. I will call you or Heinrich tomorrow to see how everything is coming along."

The young officer saluted his superior, and disappointed, he turned the ignition key. Revving the engine, Volsgaard headed out the circular driveway and proceeded to the main gate at Ravensbruck.

As the loyal and obedient, houseman, Ludwig drove up to the front portico simultaneously to the departure of the junior officer.

"Is the tank full?" Suhren called toward Ludwig.

"Yes, Major. I had one of my men replenish the fuel in Furstenberg yesterday, after taking Frau Suhren to the hair salon."

"Excellent, Ludwig."

The aging commandant climbed into the attractive white Daimler-Benz auto. He did not drive much, as he did not have to. Major Suhren was the chief—the prime executive commander for the prison camp, so his mild-mannered attendant thought it strange that his boss would pass up the opportunity to look like a big wig, in the comfortable passenger side of Volsgaard's jeep. Instead, he would drive the tedious, seventy kiilometer journey to Berlin as his own chauffer. His behavior was out of character. Yet he waved as Suhren, a capable driver, left the front lawn area, circled past Lake Schwedt and eased up the trail past the front gate of Ravensbruck.

* * * * *

Wanda Taggerhaus had sat waiting for over one hour on the hard wooden train station bench outside Furstenberg, her long legs crossed. She peered into a compact mirror from her purse, touching up the blood-red lipstick to pursed lips. A feminine overnight satchel sat perched next to her buttocks. It had been an hour and a half hour journey from Schwerin. She was, however, used to waiting for her men, as most of her dates were important, busy individuals. She saw herself as part of their schedule rather than as a partner whose time had to be recognized or respected.

The Friday evening station remained idle. The next train passing through would arrive at six the next morning. Wanda glanced up at the clock, rubbing her neck to relieve the aches of her early evening ride.

"Ah, my beautiful lady! Are you ready for a lovely weekend?"

Major Suhren's voice shouted from the Daimler-Benz convertible as he pulled the car to the edge of the vacant station. He exited, walking to her bench, reaching for the small overnight bag, which was still at her side.

Responding like the true professional escort that she was, Wanda said nothing and rose, wrapping her thin arms around Suhren's neck and whispering into his ear.

"It was worth every minute waiting for you, Major. I forgot just how handsome you looked in your uniform. Thank you for inviting me on this weekend. I am sure we will have so much fun. How can I ever thank you for letting me be a part of it."

"Oh, I am sure you will think of a way," he answered as both laughed in a risqué manner. He wrapped one arm around her waist while holding her bag as they rushed to his car.

"We will be in Berlin by midnight, my dear. My meeting will run from eight a.m. to ten. Then the rest of the weekend will be ours to have as much fun as we can."

Wanda placed her hand on his inner thigh, rubbing softly.

"You are the commanding officer," she insisted as she slowly trailed her playful tongue over soft lips. "I will follow any order you give to me."

She laughed, moving closer to the aging officer, making him feel like he was twenty-two again and on his first forty-eight hour pass.

"I hope this sits well with my friend, Rutger von Blarcom? I mean, I did not tell him I was contacting you. I have not spoken with him since the remote control demonstration at my villa."

The Major really did not care. He was merely plumbing her thoughts, and true to her professional instincts, she told him exactly what he wanted to hear.

"Major, I am friends with many men. I am so glad you called me. I do not speak to any of my male friends about others. Herr von Blarcom is a very good acquaintance of mine, but he is not the only man of influence that I date. I do know this weekend he is in Melk, with his wife. What is more important to me—this weekend, I am in Berlin with you.

"Von Blarcom and everyone else who I am friends with will never know that. This weekend belongs to just you and me, and I hope it is the first of many."

She made Suhren feel like he was the only man on the planet when she placed her arm through his and hugged tightly.

"But I must say, Major," she said as the zooming Benz broke onto a larger two lane road, "I had so wished that you picked *me* to explode the little hut that night of the demonstration at your villa. You announced that that you were giving the privilege to the most beautiful woman in attendance at the party. I was so admiring you that evening. Then you selected a woman in uniform. I mean, she was beautiful—even as she was dressed like a man, but I wanted you to like me even then."

"Do not worry, my dear, I will make it up to you this weekend," the tactful officer followed. "You see, there are many ongoing fights and arguments within my little Ravensbruck community. I sometimes play with that fact and am somewhat of a troublemaker myself.

"You were no doubt the prettiest, but I was making her feel attractive. The truth is I do not even know if that is important to her, but I was deliberately teasing her arch-enemy, Heinrich Wurtzmuller. He and she have this love-hate relationship."

"They do?" Wanda asked, confused by the remark.

"Yes, they love to hate each other," the Major explained, laughing at his own joke.

"He is a very funny man, Wutzmuller—quick with his insults. He must be a good officer."

"The best, but I will never let him know I think that," Suhren confessed. "He is the one I left in charge while I am with you, my dear. You know, he lives right behind my villa on the lake, in what used to be the cook and matron's dwelling—years ago, when it was owned by a wealthy baron."

"I did know that, Major. When Rutger brought him samples he informed me that he was not at home. He had to leave them with his cleaning person," Wanda innocently answered.

"His what? He does not have a cleaning person!" Suhren chuckled. "The CCI continuously wants to dismiss *my* help in the mansion. It is only because of my threats to retire, that they keep them in employment," Suhren assured the young woman.

"I am just repeating what he told me, Major. I remember because he followed with, 'How the army has changed'," she said in a low voice, imitating a man's delivery. "Well, whatever! This weekend is not about him, your captain or a house cleaner. What are we going to do, for fun?" She whispered coyly into Suhren's ear, "Besides making love?"

Suhren's carnal thoughts returned as he smiled, glancing down at her ample cleavage and then into her Aryan blue eyes.

"How about midnight caviar, oysters, champagne, at the Hotel Kaiserhof; oh and yes, I almost forgot, S-E-X?"

"Oh Major, I can hardly wait for you to be inside me. I am tingling just to think of it!"

Wanda Taggerhaus seemed sexually interested in a man old enough to be her father. If she wasn't, it certainly fooled Suhren. It was more likely that she wanted the finer things in life that a vintage male could offer—material wealth, champagne and caviar—unlike a young man's stein of Lowenbrau, fried bar treats and slobbering of hormonal juices exuding all over her.

Whatever—this was Suhren's youthful, illicit weekend away from his wife and away from the demanding grind of Ravensbruck. He hoped that he would not forget about his meeting at eight a.m. involving the construction of the new gas chamber. He had hardly given it a thought for the last hour. But at that moment, he was just hoping that he could perform formidably for his young escort. That was the only thing on the Major's cheating mind.

Like a younger, more aggressive, driver in the night, Suhren worked his clutch. He threw the Benz into second gear as he rounded a sharp curve and then eased it back into third once he was on the straightaway. Wanda planted a big kiss on his weathered cheek, causing him to sit up tall in the driver's seat, feeling youthful. He put his arm around the escort's attractive, slender body, holding her closer to him. As both glanced at the road sign they were passing, Suhren smiled with elation, his heart beginning to pound to a beat of perverse romantic excitement. The sign read, "Berlin—22 kilometers."

CHAPTER 21

The Luftwaffe air corpsman and the stocky young guard from Ravensbruck labor camp had squared off on the busy Saturday night, Furstenberg, Havelstrabe. Several local fraulines were holding each other, trembling. Two drunken military soldiers were fighting to be the "boyfriend" of the curly blond who was being consoled by four friends.

The crowd, unimpressed by the unruly display, gave the fighters a wide birth. Some were already keeping beat to the dance music that they heard coming from inside the beer hall. It was Benny Goodman's *Sing, Sing, Sing!* A dutiful waitress held The Lorelei public address microphone to the console record player as she swayed to the naughty American jazz, picking up every crackling signature from the vinyl disc. Saturday night was in full swing.

"Gestapo—why do you not stop those two assholes in the street? They are bound to hurt an innocent person," an anonymous shout bellowed from the group jamming into the lobby of The Lorelei.

"Let them kill one another. Who cares?" another voice added.

Isaac ignored the remarks as well as the drunks as he attempted bypassing the line that was blocking any free passage in or out of the hall. As he looked back across the Havelstrabe, he could barely see the front bumper of Wurtzmuller's jeep, concealed down an alley, where it was parked on the perpendicular street, the Markt.

The entry process was taking longer than he had anticipated. The bulky duffle bag filled with money, jewelry, watches, gold artifacts, and other confiscated valuables, was also not conducive to moving freely past the clogged doorway. When he forced himself through the three overseers who happened to be right in the portal entry, one fell to the floor.

"Oh, I am so sorry," he said as he stooped to help her off the ground.

As he did, he heard another say in a low tone. "It is a miracle; an apologetic Gestapo. What will we see, next? The Fuhrer praying in church?"

The group around the voice roared at the sarcasm. Isaac finally broke through the obstruction of bodies, straightening up as he got into the lobby and made his way to the stairway.

"Did you remember to bring me some heroin? You did not on the last visit," was the salutatory greeting from Greta Junkwalter as she opened the shabby, battered door to Room 206. "Come in, little friend of the captain. Tell me, did he give you some heroin to give to me?"

The prostitute appeared jumpy—not as smooth as she was one week earlier. Her face was drawn and seemed older, if that was possible. She did not even bring up issue of her family money.

Isaac threw the bag onto her bed and advised he was somewhat delayed getting past the crowd in the lobby. Thus it was prudent to summon Pierre Bergeron immediately. He reached into his shirt pocket and found the envelope of Reichsmarks that Wurtzmuller prepared.

"Thank you," the young woman sighed, stashed the envelope in her robe. "But did you bring the medicine? It really relaxes me? Please, did you bring any?"

He presented six packs of syringes, four—labeled heroin and two—morphine.

"What is this, 'Morphine'," she asked. "Does this give the same effect?"

"The captain has both on hand. I believe they are the same opiate-based medicines."

Isaac tried being helpful, but he was nervous.

"Now please summon Herr Bergeron at once!"

He walked toward the bathroom door, hoping to hurry her to fetch the portly salesman.

The novelty of last week did not appear to be present. It made Isaac realize why the captain welcomed someone else performing the ritual. The night had been a challenge so far, unpredictable—not as fluid as last week's maiden journey to The Lorelei.

The knock interrupted his thoughts.

"Come in," the young Gestapo imposter called to the toilet visitor from room 207.

Bergeron entered, holding a new beige leather brief case. He flapped it on the bed, shaking the messenger's hand.

"Isaac, is it?"

"Yes sir. Here is the bag prepared by Captain Wurtzmuller. He has left no other information for me to relay to you this evening. So I will just remove this and be on my way…"

There was a knock on Greta's door.

"Hey, you have had enough time with the whore! Hurry up!"

Bergeron and Isaac laughed.

"I will get the girl. Do not open it until she is back here and all doors are locked. See you next week, lad."

The man skulked back into the common bathroom. Isaac could hear an exchange of door slams. He lifted the briefcase. In an instant, Greta was back. A bit calmer, she became amorous, throwing her arms around Isaac's waist, kissing his cheek.

"Remember, you have an open invitation. I will even do it for syringes, instead of money."

He pulled away from her advance.

"Thank you. I will return next week," he whispered, blushing again at the overture. "Do not forget, you have money for family food. The captain wanted me to remind you to use it for those purposes."

Just then, another pounding erupted on to the door of 206. Isaac unlocked quickly and pulled it open. A young, intoxicated private, clinging to an overflowing stein seemed startled. He drew back, taking homage at Isaac's uniform, especially the intimidating swastika armband. It blasted a "no nonsense" message in the face of the impatient soldier.

"God damn it, Private! Wait your fucking turn!"

Isaac grabbed the cowering soldier by his lapel and shook him forcefully. He could not believe his behavior was beginning to reflect his disguise. He was ashamed to admit as much to himself, but after seven weeks of imprisonment, it felt good. The soldier had fallen to the ground where he began slurping from his ceramic mug. Isaac walked over him.

"You are a disgrace!" he shouted before heading down to the lobby.

At the third step from the bottom, the scene became a five-second blur to Isaac Bloom. A loud scream filled the lobby, which could have come from one, or possibly two females. The dense crowd parted, becoming a circle of bodies. In the middle, the slumping form of a uniformed person, braced by the arms of two civilian men, was slowly guided to the floor.

"Hurry, call a medic, physician, ambulance, something! This person is convulsing. Someone hurry!" one of the civilians yelled out to the dispersing crowd.

Isaac looked away and pushed the front door of The Lorelei open, exiting to the Havelstrabe and across to the Markt, locating the hidden jeep. He turned to see a man running behind him, shouting for someone to call for an ambulance.

"The medical facility is two blocks from here. Someone run there get an ambulance," he called, his voice echoing off the cavern of brick walls.

Wurtzmuller's disguised messenger made it to his destination and hopped in.

"What the hell is going on? What happened in there? Why all the screaming? And why were you so long? Did this ruckus involve you?"

"No, no sir. I do not understand. It was difficult getting into the hotel. The crowds were uncontrollable. I tried to move things along. I do not know what just happened. Someone feinted, or died, while waiting to enter the beer hall. I really did not comprehend. I wanted just to get out of there."

"You're sure the uproar does not involve you?" Wurtzmuller inquired again.

"No, no sir. I don't think it did—No, I mean I know it did not."

Isaac had been rocked by Greta's behavior, the drunken soldier, and the final incident in the lobby.

"I just think there may have been an emergency medical issue with someone. But I did see that the person was in a uniform of some type."

Wurtzmuller turned the ignition switch and pulled out the dark alley. He circled at the far end of the road to the next corner and went back to observe the scene in front of The Lorelei. There was a dense crowd around what appeared to be a covered body, lying on the sidewalk. He sped past the mob and turned back onto the Markt.

As the two drove back toward the chalet, the captain returned to his matter of business.

"You have the briefcase?"

"Yes sir."

Isaac held it up from its resting place between his legs.

"Ah, I hear the ambulance siren. Do you?"

Both heard the approaching and pulsating shriek of the German vehicle, on its way to The Lorelei. Isaac nodded. Wurtzmuller looked toward his Gestapo-clad passenger.

"Well perhaps whoever it was, they will survive."

CHAPTER 22

Oberaufseherin Dorothy Boerner, though being crushed by the Saturday night drinkers and jitterbug enthusiasts, pushed away the grinning male soldiers and civilians, who felt lucky to be pressed up against her shapely uniformed body.

"Olga, I cannot take this pushing. I refuse to get in the beer hall and have to go to the bathroom after a few minutes. I am using the toilet in the restaurant now."

She made a face to her friend, indicating that the man to her rear was not totally innocent, blaming the crowded conditions for his frontal rubs against her shapely buttocks.

The chief overseer departed from the rocking mob and rambled to the ladies' toilet, situated in The Lorelei dining room, abandoning her cohort Olga Deitzl, leaving her to fight her way into the rathskeller all alone.

The September weather was always unpredictable. Sometimes it was comfortably autumn, while at others, the temperature still possessed the heat of July and August. On that night it was the latter, making the hoard of revilers all the more unbearable to endure. Overseer Deitzl swayed in motion with the mob.

Someone screamed, "Lowenbrau, now," as another bellowed, "Free beer here if you are pretty!"

The hoard tightened as more and more people entered the lobby, the sheer number seeming to create individual isolation. So many bodies brought a singularity to the moment—so that one felt alone amidst such a crowd.

Aufseherin Deitzl was not groped in the fashion that Boerner had been. Yet the crowd still smashed her body tightly against those who surrounded her. As she moved along, closer and closer to the doorway of the beer hall, she suddenly felt a pinch or a prick through her uniform skirt, stabbing her outer thigh.

The forceful overseer turned to scold the man in the direction of the poke, and yet before opening her mouth, Olga Deitzl contorted her face grasped her chest as she went into a cardiac arrest, collapsing into the arms of a male of about twenty-five years, and an older person—being none other than her murderer, Wilhelm Goerthe.

"Let her down gently," the younger called. "Everyone stand back—give her some air!"

Herman Wohl, the desk manager, ran out from behind the counter to assist the situation.

"You," he ordered Goerthe, "go outside and see if you can get help. Get a doctor or an ambulance!"

The murderer could not comply fast enough. The lanky, older criminal left the scene of his crime and made his getaway out to the Havelstrabe. He was the very man who was running down the street to the hospital to report the overseer's collapse, ordering that an ambulance be sent. His concern to help Deitzl would definitely rule out any suspicion about him, should authorites discover the actual reason for the overseer's death.

A minute later, Dorothy Boerner emerged from the dining hall bathroom, and she instantly noticed the person on the ground was wearing an overseer's uniform. Frantically, the petite, chief guard began pushing people out of the way, trying to reach her fallen roommate.

"My God, my God… Olga! Are you all right? Speak to me! Please say something!"

In shock and dismay, she slapped her friend's cheek.

"I do not feel a pulse," the young man assisting in her care called to Herman Wohl.

"Get her outside," Wohl ordered his staff. "Let her get some air. She will be near the ambulance when it arrives. You men, help please!"

Within seconds, Olga Deitzl's body was lying on the sidewalk, a rolled up sport coat propped under her head, shadenfreude crowds standing around, unaware that a murder had just been committed.

In the distance, the shrill of a German ambulance grew louder as it arrived, to no avail.

Olga Deitzl was secretly executed by paid assassin, Wilhelm Goerthe. No one, as they were all gawking at the slain overseer, recognized the "W" jeep turning off the Havelstrabe and on to the Markt. Wurtzmuller himself had no indication that the chaos at the curb he was passing had been the result of his death deal with Goerthe.

As good as the hardened criminal was at exercising his task, it was only fifty percent complete. Goerthe left the hospital ambulance bay and walked back past the crime scene, turned on to the Markt and found refuge in a dimly-lit, smoke-filled bar called The Black Eagle.

The sweaty old local, shaking as the reality of the last ten minutes finally settled into his brain, climbed onto an empty bar stool.

"Scotch, a double, straight."

Taking a large gulp from the glass, Goerthe began to contemplate how he might approach and kill the pretty one—the one that was still alive. He fumbled through his dirty jacket and *Eureka!*—he discovered half a cigarette. Grabbing a complimentary book of matches from the bar, he struck one. He inhaled, hoping to calm himself after the lead-up and execution of his act of murder. He downed the remaining alcohol. If the cigarette did not work, the scotch certainly would, so he ordered another double.

"Hey, hello old friend! I have not seen you in a while. Where have you been hiding?"

The "zoned-out" man looked up, feeling a bit high, but he was not in the mood for bar talk. He tried to seem inconspicuous as he nodded to his town acquaintance, Reinhold Freund.

"Hello Freund, can I buy you a drink?" he offered.

Plopping on the bar stool, Freund smiled.

"Of course! What—have you come into some money? I never turn down a free drink!"

* * * * *

Boerner held onto her friend's lifeless hand. The body lay still on a cold stainless steel gurney inside the Furstenberg hospital morgue. The chief overseer began to display seldom-seen emotions, those totally unrelated to the callous and almost inhumane behavior that she displayed inside Ravensbruck.

Olga was more than her friend. Everyone knew their relationship had been more than military-oriented. Deitzl was also her comrade, her business associate, her roommate… her lover. Boerner rubbed her dead partner's hair away from her still-sweaty brow, which was becoming cool to the touch. What could have happened?

The overseer had appeared to be in excellent health. One minute, eager for an evening of music and drinking, and the next—dead on the floor, her heart stopped. It did not make sense. She began to vacillate between melancholia and rage. A hospital nurse entered the room to remove the fallen overseer and place the corpse into a drawer that was one of twelve on the morgue wall.

"I am so sorry for you and your friend," the medical assistant, wearing white, said to console Boerner. She placed her hand on the chief overseer's shoulder.

"I will help you transfer the body," Boerner volunteered. "I want her to know that I was with her right to the end, if that is okay with you?"

"Of course, if that is what you wish," the nurse nodded.

The krankenschwester locked the wheels of the gurney and took control of the dead body upper torso. She put both arms under Deitzl's armpits, while Boerner secured the lighter bottom area, raising her friend's legs. The women moved the corpse onto the morgue drawer slab and straightened it for an easy closure.

As the chief overseer lifted her fallen cohort, a clicking noise of something rolling onto the stainless steel gurney echoed in the sterile emptiness of the morgue.

"What was that?" the nurse asked. "Money from her pocket, a pen?"

"No!" Boerner fired back.

She squeezed the object tightly into her hand, closing her eyes, almost feinting from her startling discovery. Then the oberaufseherin hurried from the room, leaving the nurse and the still-visible body. In the hallway, she opened her palm, studying the expended syringe that she realized had delivered the lethal injection into her friend's body—the very same type of newly invented needle like the ones she had seen Dr. Engel's desk!

The doctor had explained that it could be filled with a euthanizing drug for camp extermination. It was also the very same type of new disposable syringes she had seen in prostitute Greta Junkwalter's room at The Lorelei. The common denominator for both sightings, the enraged overseer deduced, was her long time camp adversary—Heinrich Wurtzmuller.

Boerner stormed out of the morgue, forgetting her promise to the nurse and totally abandoning her final farewell to longtime friend, Olga Deitzl.

CHAPTER 23

Goerthe was too drunk to make it back to his decrepit barn outside the Furstenberg city limit. He and Freund celebrated Saturday night, especially since both men had money in their pockets, though Goerthe had significantly more. They closed The Black Eagle Bar and staggered to Freund's small apartment above Fromm's Bakery.

Before he went upstairs, the older Freund advised that he was first going to see what the baker Fromm left for a late night snack in the alley trash bin. Goerthe followed his drinking partner and helped himself to a badly burned strudel, wrapped in wax paper. The alcohol did its job, making the murderer forget that, just five hours earlier, he had executed someone he believed was an enemy to the German Reich. Yet he was sober enough to maintain the secrecy he had vowed to Captain Wurtzmuller.

"Nightcap?" Freund asked as they entered his one-room apartment. He grabbed a half empty bottle of whiskey off his table, along with two filthy mason jars.

"Sure Freund. Do you have to work tomorrow?

"No, I only work six days a week in the Labor camp," Freund admitted. "I work for a captain there. I hunt down all the valuables that the prisoners try to sneak into the camp, and I turn them over to the administrators. It's not much, but it helps me get by."

"Well, I hope you manage to steal something while you are doing this job?" Goerthe grinned, getting at the potentially criminal aspect of the job.

"Never! If Wurtzmuller caught me, he would probably kill me on the spot," Freund laughed.

"Did you say Wurtzmuller?" Goerthe asked, picking up on the name at once. "*Wurtzmuller* is your boss for your work?"

"Yes, he practically runs the camp. You do not want to mess with him. He is a tough customer," Freund explained. "He has told me that if he caught me stealing something—like jewelry from the confiscated articles—he would kill me on the spot. Do you know him?"

"Uhh no—no I do not, but if you ever need an assistant, please tell him that I would be interested," Goerthe answered.

Freund snickered. He knew of Goerthe's reputation around town, and he knew that Goerthe was a bigger criminal than he could ever be. The fleeting thought of Goerthe and Wurtzmuller ever crossing paths would be one to laugh at—just knowing of the incendiary results.

"The toilet is behind that curtain. You can sleep on the floor. Do not wake me if you get up first. Here is a blanket."

Freund threw a filthy woolen wad of material at his friend, and Goerthe plopped his head right over the loose wooden strut where Freund had buried the stolen goods from his job. Yet Freund felt secure that the "drunk" would not realize that he was no more than a few centimeters from a bag of expensive gems. He giggled over that fact.

"If you do get up early, tomorrow, Goerthe, it is Sunday."

"So what? I should attend services?"

"No, but Sunday is a big day for any bakery, and I am sure Herr Fromm will be throwing out a lot of cakes that your pallet may still find worthy of eating."

* * * * *

Aimless and angry, Dorothy Boerner ambled through the streets of Furstenberg. She did not know how to begin her plan for retaliation, but she wanted to accomplish it as quickly as possible. She went back to The Lorelei Rooming House and Beer Hall. She played dumb as to the cause of the death as she re-questioned manager, Herman Wohl, and the remaining locals who were still in the beer hall at 2:00 a.m.—after the rowdier dance crowd had disappeared for the evening.

No one had seen anything suspicious earlier, other than a feinting woman being laid on the floor in a congested lobby. Forlorn, Boerner sat on the front steps of the rooming house, still in shock. She did not want to report the death of Deitzl or her findings of foul play to authorities—not yet.

The krankenshwester from the morgue entrusted Boerner to notify the camp officials in the morning so that appropriate military procedures would be followed, but Boerner had no intention of following that plan of action, since the head camp official that weekend was none other than Heinrich Wurtzmuller—the very person she believed had orchestrated Deitzl's murder.

She cried herself to sleep while sitting on the front step, resting her head on the cooling wrought-iron banister, missing the departure of the drinkers who closed the beer hall at three a.m. She stayed asleep in a sitting position until daybreak delivered normalcy to the Havelstrabe. Bodies began appearing, with church goers the first to be seen, which was followed by children, doing early chores for their parents. Women swept dirt out the doorways with straw brooms, while an occasional delivery truck sped down the street.

The chief overseer squinted, confused about why she did not return to her dormitory at Ravensbruck. She did not know if she could face her room, alone for the first time in five years, or if she even wanted to remain after the sight of Olga Deitzl's last breath. Whatever—she was exhausted.

A stray dog wandered up the steps, nudging the lamenting overseer. She patted its head, noting the loneliness in the wandering animal's eyes.

"I have no food."

The dog scooted away, but not long afterward, a boy delivering sweet rolls and pastries to The Lorelei restaurant handed a cherry Danish to the pretty though disheveled woman.

"Thank you, but no," she said, rejecting the offer. "I am not very hungry just yet."

Something then made Boerner spring to her feet, as if seeing a ghost. Holding the wrought iron railing, she felt a jolt of vitality.

"You! You there, in the brown jacket," she called. "Wait! I must speak with you!"

Walking down the Markt toward her and the Lorelei was a man displaying a very tired swagger—Wilhelm Goerthe. He rocked side to side with the unsure, unattractive gait of a pathetic hangover.

He did not see her emerging from the toilet on the previous night as she pushed her way toward Olga Deitzl, but he immediately recognized Boerner as his next victim, from Wurtzmuller's photos. He could not attempt anything then. He was too shaky, and there were too many observers.

"Who, me?" the crafty lowlife shouted back, as he crossed the Havelstrabe. "Yes, what is it that I can help you with on this early Sunday. It has been a late night. I am walking home after staying at a friend's house. Late night of drinking and all, you know."

"I saw you around the crowd when one of my women collapsed," she commented. "You were quite near her. Did you see anyone acting strange?"

The reeling in shock overseer never thought of considering Goerthe as a possible suspect to the murder. Although he did not look like proper member of society, the old street dweller seemed harmless and not the threat he actually was.

"No, no it was so crowded. I saw nothing, but I was just glad to help her from injuring herself more from the fall. Have you spoken to her? Is she feeling okay?"

Boerner did not answer. She wanted to keep Deitzl's death a mystery, and she certainly was not going to discuss details with the likes of Goerthe.

"Excuse me, but I must return to my facility. It was a long evening for me, and I need rest. Thank you for your help."

Boerner avoided the inquiry. The overseer eyed her jeep that was still parked in the middle of the next block. She was unaware that she was just within meters of the concealed murder weapons in Goerthe's pocket. The two remaining syringes of phenyl were still wrapped and ready for an opportune moment for attack. Fortunately, the busy morning street had helped prevent Boerner's untimely date with death, and Goerthe's securing another payday.

CHAPTER 24

Wurtzmuller went into his command center office within the Ravensbruck facility on Sunday morning. Without the presence of Major Suhren and his fellow officer, Horst Bitten, he felt that the increase of over seven hundred new prisoners that week to the labor camp warranted formation of new barracks occupant lists. He realized that the overpopulation problem was making it impossible to track where all of the women were being housed.

However, Wertzmuller still demanded organization to the facility. He tried to maintain it as long as was possible. The officer ordered his staff out to each barrack kapo to demand a list of current dwellers. He would later have Isaac tabulate the names and document the women's presence within the various houses. He was also surveying registrant ages, reasons for being incarcerated and health issues. While he awaited his subordinates to return with the information, the disgruntled Wurtzmuller pondered on the progress that Fritz Suhren may have made with the Gestapo gas chamber committee.

He hoped the major would convince them to begin construction immediately, or would bureaucracy take control of the project they had been discussing for three years.

He closed down at four p.m. and decided that he would return to his chalet to spend some time working for his own selfish interests. He retrieved the briefcase that Isaac had received the previous night from Pierre Bergeron, counted the money and began his exchange plan for the next week. He did not even wait for Volsgaard to return with his findings.

Wurtzmuller called Isaac and ordered him to prepare the bratwurst, red cabbage and potato pancakes so that dinner would be ready by seven p.m. He also ordered several bottles of Lowenbrau to be placed next to the freezer block of ice.

By Sunday evening at six o'clock, the chalet was emanating an odor of fresh veal links, pungent root vegetable and cabbage aromas, along with onion potato pancakes. Wurtzmuller arrived, removed his uniform top and sat at his desk, his suspenders holding up his jodhpurs. The captain downed a stein of brew in the comfortable t-shirt while anticipating a better than normal amount of Swiss francs that weekend.

"I will dine in one hour, Bloom," he called to his busy valet in the kitchen as he peered into the briefcase.

* * * * *

Dorothy Boerner had managed to get a few hours of rest. One more journey to the crime scene might prove to be enlightening. The chief overseer thought that perhaps someone visiting The Lorelei on Sunday might have passed vital information to the lobby manager, Herman Wohl. She drove the fifteen-minute trek and found Wohl reading the paper at the front registration desk.

"Ah, hello, aufsehrin. Did you manage to rest, today?"

The man had heard through bar gossip that Deitzl was indeed dead, though he did not bring up that specific information

"No one came forward with any more information if anything seemed suspicious last evening during the mob scene in the lobby, Herr Wohl?" Boerner asked.

"No, but if I may ask—if your friend died for whatever reason, why are you concerned about witnesses to her collapse? It was a death of natural causes, no?"

Neither Wohl nor anyone else had any idea Deitzl had been murdered. He thought it strange that Boerner was so inquisitive.

"Just wondering, Herr Wohl. My friend was so healthy. I cannot believe that she is gone."

Hearing only the mumbled dialog, bar sot Wilhelm Goerthe observed Boerner's whole conversation with the desk man. His fingers played in his pocket. The two packets of phenyl syringes were still at his side. The old criminal sipped his whiskey, never taking his eyes off his next pretty victim. He was ready to make Captain Wurtzmuller and the Fuhrer proud. But most of all, he was ready to accept the five thousand Reichsmarks in payment that the officer had promised, once both executions were completed.

Boerner now knew what she had to do. She would directly confront Wurtzmuller, the only person she could connect to the silent murder. She had been unsuccessful finding the hired assassin, so she would surprise the Nazi officer with the empty syringe, which she had wrapped neatly in a handkerchief and stashed at the bottom of her shoulder bag. She made it to her jeep parked out front, planning to catch Wurtzmuller by surprise. Pulling onto the Havelstrabe, she circled the lake road and headed for the officer's chalet.

* * * * *

Goerthe made a beeline out The Lorelei as well. Frantically looking along the street, he saw a BMW sedan idling in front of the flower shop next to the rooming house. In one smooth motion, the old but agile hood hopped into the available car and floored the accelerator, in pursuit of Dorothy Boerner.

The killer's plan was to run her vehicle off the road, then complete his job by injecting the attractive overseer with one of the needles. He stayed behind her jeep as she sped along, assuming that she was heading for the labor camp. He hoped the overseer would not get to the front gate before he intercepted her.

The taillights of the pretty overseer's jeep beckoned Goerthe. He could see that he was getting closer, but he could also see the approaching walls of Ravensbruck and front gate activity, compliments of entrance security. A sense of failure overtook the criminal until Boerner took a sharp right turn just before the entrance to the camp and directed her vehicle onto a dirt road, heading toward Lake Schwedt. Her sudden change in course infused Goerthe with a feeling of hope, redeeming his sense of imminent failure. But where was the "pretty one" headed?

He turned his front beams off as he steered the stolen vehicle down the dark, tree-lined path, as he did not want Boerner to discover he had followed the jeep past the camp entrance. He cut the engine and coasted, using gravity as his means of acceleration. As he got closer to the water, he could discern the outline of a mansion facing the lake, but the overseer turned before reaching the impressive structure and seemed to be headed toward a smaller house behind the villa.

The crafty criminal wheeled past the lane and came closer to Major Suhren's residence. As he rolled to a stop in the stolen BMW, Gorthe looked around, welcoming the quiet of the late summer Sunday evening. Everything seemed harmless and still. He started the engine, nosed the sedan into the lakeside reeds, backed the vehicle up and buried it and himself behind thick brush, facing Wurtzmuller's chalet… and the final sighting of Dorothy Boerner.

Patiently and methodically, the murderer of overseer Deitzl and hired killer of Wurtzmuller removed one of the two remaining packets, containing the syringe of phenyl. He placed the plastic cartridge between his lips as if it were a knife. When the overseer emerged from her visit to whoever she was visiting, Goerthe would strike somewhere on the desolate road leading up to Ravensbruck. Like an animal, he would wait as long as was necessary to complete his end of the deal.

CHAPTER 25

The impatient, aggressive pounding by a clenched fist was becoming all too repetitive to Isaac Bloom. The intrusive drunken soldier in The Lorelei, the stern, indifferent street captain who brought his life to a profound halt—and now someone at Wurtzmuller's front door, all displaying the rudeness defiance and anger that had become synonymous with Nazi behavior. It was a sound he was now hearing much too often. This pounding, however, seemed to have less muscle behind the thudding noise.

Wurtzmuller looked toward Isaac with alarm. He motioned, bringing his finger to his lips to indicate silence, while pointing for Isaac to retreat into the pantry. Isaac tiptoed, leaving the officer alone at his desk, returning all valuables into the desk drawer. The plate and stein remained.

"Who is it?"

Wurtzmuller tried to identify the visitor, but there was no answer.

The officer, clad in t-shirt, suspenders, jodhpurs and boots, reached the front door and whipped it open with a gesture of annoyance.

"Oberaufseherin Boerner, what a surprise! What brings you to my humble dwelling this late summer evening? I guess since Major Suhren is not in his mansion this weekend, you thought that you would see how the lower-in-command get by in such modest surroundings."

"Cut the crap, Captain. Are you going to stop the bullshit and let me in?"

"But of course, Dorothy. How can I help you? You have never visited, so I have to be me—you know, and have some fun. As you may know, the major is in Berlin. He left me in charge. Is everything all right? I was at the facility most of the day. All seemed quiet, yes?"

Wurtzmuller spoke with sincerity in his voice, still unaware of Goerthe's attack on Deitzl.

"You tell me, Captain. Last night, Olga Deitzl was murdered in the middle of the crowded lobby at The Lorelei."

The chief overseer began with the shocking statement so that she could study the officer's facial reaction and body language as she awaited his response. Wurtzmuller, for his part, knew he was being scrutinized. He knew that his reaction to the news should conform to the nasty relationship he had with Deitzl. Too happy, and he would appear suspicious—too sympathetic, and he would appear as suspect in her death, so he displayed a neutral reaction.

"You say murdered? How? What happened? It was in a crowded lobby? Are you sure she was murdered? Who could have done this? Was she shot? Stabbed? Beaten?"

He showed surprise, as he certainly was.

"Please, Dorothy, sit down," he said, offering her a seat, and then he went back to the chair behind his desk.

"Have you notified her family? The CCI? Why did you not inform the camp of the incident sooner?"

"Frankly, before I did any of that, I wanted to speak with you… to let you know that I know *you* were involved in her murder, Captain Wurtzmuller."

He paused, regrouping, realizing the hostile intent of the visit. She sat in front of him as she always had—the enemy.

"Dorothy, I am fully aware that you have had a completely devastating experience. I am sorry for your loss, but please know that I will not tolerate another remark like that. You have not even convinced me that she was murdered. Now I want remarks like that to cease immediately. Do you understand?"

Wurtzmuller raised his voice to a commanding volume, yet he could definitely sense that Boerner was officially dangerous. He was also sure that Goerthe had completed half of his strike.

"Now if you are so sure Aufseherin Deitzl was murdered, I would like to know how—especially if you are convinced I did it? I was not even in town, last night."

He asked in order to see just how determined Boerner was to bring her accusation.

"Who is your new Gestapo messenger boy, Captain? Why have you stopped visiting your whore friend on Saturday nights?"

Isaac's ears picked up the conversation as he held one against the pantry door. He was amazed that he had been noticed. He also realized that this visit involved whatever happened as he was leaving The Lorelei the night before. Fear entered his body. Were they trying to accuse him of the wrongdoing? He strained to listen.

"I have been performing highly-classified work for the Reich. It is no concern of yours or anyone else's. The introduction of a

Gestapo courier was suggested by my supervisors. I am certainly under no obligation to explain my actions to an overseer, but seeing as you see fit to ask, I must order you to not pursue this topic any further, or I will have you relieved of your command. Is this why you came to my house, to accuse me of military misbehavior, or to accuse me of your friend's death? In either case, you are not making much sense, Oberaufseherin Boerner, but please continue."

Boerner studied the top of the captain's desk. She searched for any clues that might have supported her accusation. His attitude was certainly confrontational, but Dorothy Boerner knew she had come to pursue a confrontation. Her sights locked in on what she was hoping to observe. Lying on the messy desktop, the overseer discovered exactly what she had come to find.

Wedged between the pencil holder and the corner of the blotter sat an unwrapped, unused, disposable syringe. She did not care what medicine it contained. Boerner reached for it and held it in Wurtzmuller's sight.

"Do you recognize this, Captain?" she asked.

"What do you mean, 'do I recognize it?' Of *course* I recognize it!"

The captain squinted, realizing she was trying to follow a trail to a solid accusation.

"You are friends with Engel—you know that we are using this item at the camp for various situations. You have probably seen this item on your many trips to his office. Look, Overseer Boerner, where is this leading? Your friend is dead. I am sorry. She was not my friend. Why are we talking of disposable needles."

"I will tell you why, Captain."

Boerner reached into her uniform pocket and presented the empty syringe that had been dangling on the uniform of Olga Deitzl while her body was being transferred from the gurney to the hospital morgue slab.

"This was found sticking onto Olga when she died. The needle was filled with a lethal drug—the very same syringes that you supplied to your whore in The Lorelei."

"Did you also accuse your friend, Engel, or am I the only one you seem to want to blame?"

He was hoping that the anger he expressed for the stupidity and sloppy execution of Goerthe's actions did not show. Wurtzmuller pursed his lips as he steamed at the poor performance by his hired assassin. *How could he leave the weapon behind? That idiot!*

"Many people have access to this medical breakthrough, Overseer Boerner. Please do not link me as the sole source for pre-filled syringes. Just because I have samples in my office does not make me a killer. Besides, I was not in Furstenberg last evening. I will appreciate it if you stop this fantasy, and I would like you to leave. I will advise Major Suhren tomorrow of your accusations. I am sure he will request your resignation for your statements. In the meantime, you can expect to be punished for your slanderous efforts. I am sorry for the loss of your girlfriend. Now leave!"

Proud of his defense to the remarks, Wurtzmuller could not resist taking a final shot at his accuser, and he could not wait for her to leave so he could go out and find Goerthe. He wanted to kill him on the spot, even before he finished his job knocking off Boerner.

Isaac stood vigilant, ear to the door listening for a cue, as Dorothy Boerner rose, incensed at the "girlfriend" remark. *How dare he insult their relationship and belittle Olga Deitzl's passing!*

"You are crooked, Captain. You know that Olga and I were aware of that. You had her killed and you probably have my death planned as well. You fed the prostitute with camp food, and you supplied her with drugs to act as an accomplice to your crimes. What is in the little bag you leave with every Saturday? My guess is that it is money."

"How dare you come into my home and accuse me of murder! And now theft! I must be insane. Suhren left me in charge of the entire camp while he is in Berlin. I find your behavior completely treasonous!"

Wurtzmuller stood.

"I will give you a choice, Dorothy. Leave my house and Ravensbruck tonight, or face charges in the morning. The violin confession and your ongoing antics for personal fundraising will be enough to bring you to trial. Now, your accusations about my behavior as acting commander of the facility could surely bring you imprisonment.

"Must I remind you that you are neither a member of the SS nor a member of the Wermacht. You are a nothing more than a monitor. You just happen to be the head of all the monitors. Now get out of my house and think hard about your future!"

Wurtzmuller had a fire in his eyes and a vocal command that Isaac had never heard used since he arrived at the chalet. The officer seemed even angrier than when he killed the architect Horovitz on

Isaac's first day at Revensbruck. Yet his volatile persona did not seem to faze the overseer.

He wanted her out of his house at once—primarily so he could comb the Furstenberg streets for Goerthe. The raging officer wasn't sure if he would kill the old villain on the spot or just beat him senseless. Little did he realize that the hired assassin was, at that moment, only a few meters from his home, lurking in the lakeside overgrowth, waiting for Dorothy Boerner to exit the house.

Isaac Bloom listened for every discernible noise that would serve as a clue to what was taking place just outside the door. Silence... stillness—an eerie void made him strain to hear something, but there was nothing.

* * * * *

Goerthe thought he heard a door slam inside the small house. He sat up in the BMW driver's seat and started the motor, ready to pursue his victim if indeed it was she leaving, but there was nothing.

Isaac fell to his knees, fearing what his ears had just audited. The muffled door slam that Goerthe had heard a hundred meters away—Isaac processed rather as a gunshot. It had come from the office. It was an exclamation to the preceding litany of verbal attacks, and after the boom—a return to total silence.

Panicked, Isaac strained to listen. Should he leave the pantry? Where was Wurtzmuller's voice? He listened for a call to come out to the office. Perhaps he was in shock. The silence had continued long after the blast. The suspense was unbearable.

After what seemed several minutes, though it had been only seconds, Isaac lifted an iron skillet from one of the pantry shelves. He unlatched the door and cautiously peered out the crack. There was a shuffling of footsteps. The slight man raised the skillet to shoulder height and pushed the door open, tiptoeing into the hall.

He held his breath and moved up to the corner of the wall that led into Wurtzmuller's office. Rounding the door, the captive houseman gulped at the sight he feared. Lying in a heap between his desk and bookcase was the still, lifeless body of Heinrich Wurtzmuller, staring up at the ceiling, a bullet hole situated in the exact center of the officer's forehead. He was shot right between the eyes, and a stream of blood exiting the circular wound had begun to collect on the area rug beneath the officer's desk.

The derrierre of Dorothy Boerner, prominent and shapely, was in Isaac's face. He could not believe amidst the terror, how much he noticed its attractiveness. How, he thought, could such a thought even cross his mind? The overseer stood after examining the murder victim. She turned, showing the Walther P38 pistol that she had swiped from his hall tree. Isaac's presence startled her.

The flat side of the iron skillet caught the overseer's right temple. Isaac swung with conviction, and Dorothy Boerner groaned, falling on top of Wurtzmuller's corpse. The frantic prisoner looked down, not knowing what to do next. His nearly two month stay with the officer had abruptly ended. Should he run?

A bile-like nausea invaded Isaac's insides. He recalled Wurtzmuller's "last will" letter, formulated for insurance purposes, on his first day of incarceration. Flora would be singled out and killed should Isaac try to escape or if anything happened to Wutzmuller. The young man ran to the sink and heaved the churning worries in his stomach.

"Oh my God!" he murmured.

He kept repeating it, looking down at Dorothy Boerner, who was beginning to regain consciousness after the blow to her head. *Who would have thought these events would have ever taken place?*

"Survive, survive!" Isaac mumbled, remembering his own advice as he attempted to take control of the moment. He began sifting through the pile of samples against the wall in the office. Uncovering the medical syringe box, Isaac reached in, examining various packets of disposable needles.

Dropping most on the floor, he collected five morphine packets and three marked heroin. Frustrated and afraid, he threw the remaining box across the room. He then found a box of clothes line rope that had been ordered for the overseer and guard population laundry lines.

Using a kitchen knife to cut three two-meter segments of line, he first tied Boerner's wrists securely behind her back. He then did the same to the overseer's ankles, immobilizing the woman. As an extra measure, Isaac then attached the bound hands to her bound feet. Dorothy Boerner was hog-tied, and with the help of three syringes of morphine, entering a state of neural delirium minutes later.

Isaac Bloom looked at the wall clock, showing the time had crept to eight-thirty. A plan formed in his mind, coming from a disarray of thoughts that swirled in his head. The wild though focused prisoner dragged the overseer's limp body out to the middle of the office floor, making space behind the desk. He then placed Wurtzmuller's typewriter front and center.

Finding Captain Heinrich Wurtzmuller' signature at the bottom of a delivery receipt, the clever prisoner began his forgery trick. He located a command order form in the second desk drawer on the right, and taking it, he pressed hard on Wurtzmuller's signature, carefully guiding the pencil across the receipt. Shining the desk light on the blank order form, he identified the wavering depression of the officer's signature. He then glided a fountain pen through the swirling channel, completing a perfect reproduction of the officer's name.

He rolled the "command order" form into the typewriter and thought as he constructed a memo.

> FROM THE COMMAND OF MAJOR FRITZ SUHREN AND CAPTAIN HEINRICH WURTZMULLER,
>
> THIS SS POLICE COURRIER IS TO BE ADMITTED INTO THE LABOR
>
> FACILITY AND REPORT TO BARRACK 116 FOR REMOVAL OF PRISONER NAMED FLORA BLOOM, WHO IS WANTED FOR QUESTIONING.
>
> RE: HER INVOLVEMENT WITH AN EXTREMIST GROUP ENDANGERING THE SECURITY OF THE GOVERNMENT.
>
> SHE WILL BE RETURNED WHEN THE INTRROGATION SESSION IS COMPLETE. THIS ORDER IS TO BE EXPEDITED AT ONCE.
>
> Captain Heinrich Wurtzmuller

"Hmm," he murmured to himself. "Those words seem like they could have come from Wurtzmuller's mouth."

Isaac looked down to his left at the cold, dead stare of the officer.

"I only hope it works."

He then ran back to the pantry, and knocking items off the lower shelf, he found the partially filled sack of flour that he used to store the supplies he had been acquiring over the last few weeks. He pulled an overnight canvass bag from a bin and began transferring items from the flour sack—first the remote-control transmitting panel that he had swiped the day Rutger von Blarcom paid the surprise visit while he was vacuuming. Next, he carefully placed its detonating receiver unit, along with five hand grenade canisters of explosives on top of the first panel. There were some road flares, more syringes of morphine, tape, cans of beans, peas, other foods and a can opener. Yet there was an ample amount of room left in the sack.

He went back to the office, checked the still body of Dorothy Boerner and threw the bag on the desk. Isaac remembered that Wurtzmuller stored large sums of money under his bed in the upstairs loft, so he hurried up there and found a traveler's suitcase. When he opened it, he discovered neatly banded bundles of Swiss francs, in all denominations. He grabbed as much as he could, making three trips to bring the piles down to the canvas satchel.

The wall clock displayed 9:15. He took a deep breath, examining himself in the room mirror.

"It is time!"

There was no response from Heinrich Wurtzmuller or Dorothy Boerner.

CHAPTER 26

The transformed Isaac Bloom straightened his Nazi swastika armband and placed the SS cap on his head. He hated the way he looked, but his hate would motivate his performance. The determined young man folded the contrived command order that he typed and placed it in an official Ravensbruck envelope. He had everything to gain, but Flora's death was imminent should his plan backfire. Once the dead officer's body was discovered, Flora would be executed. He could escape alone, but without Flora, his life would be in vain.

He brushed his Nazi uniform as he stared into his own eyes in the mirror.

"Flora, I am coming for you. Hopefully, I can do this."

* * * * *

The "W" jeep started right up. Wurtzmuller had the tank filled earlier in the day at the far end of the camp property, where there were two giant petrol tubes. He always filled the jeep on Sunday's. Isaac knew the tank offered at least 300 kilometers of fuel. How great it would be if he could save Flora, and this time tomorrow, be far from Ravensbruck. In the jeep, he chugged through the chalet driveway and turned on the upward slope to the labor camp's main gate.

* * * * *

Wilhelm Goerthe skulked behind the wheel of his stolen BMW that had been buried in the lakeshore bushes. He waited for the army jeep to turn, but quickly aborted his attempt to follow. The criminal could discern the uniform and stature of a male. It was neither his mark, Dorothy Boerner, nor her vehicle. He could see it was rather a man driving Wurtzmuller's "W" jeep. He slumped back into a stalking posture and peered down the lane where he had last seen the overseer headed.

This must be where the Nazi officer lives, he deduced. Boerner must be in the house having a meeting with him. His plan about how he would kill the overseer began germinating in his mind. If the woman left the house alone, he would intercept her car on the lane before she reached the main gate area. He would ditch the BMW, which could not be traced to him, and inject her with his lethal syringe. Then he would dump her pretty body and jeep in Lake Schwedt, close to Furstenberg, and walk to town. On Monday, he would be five thousand Reichsmarks richer, courtesy of Captain Wurtzmuller.

Little did the local vagrant know that his slipshod handling of Olga Deitzl's execution was the reason Dorothy Boerner was visiting the tiny chalet, that his contractor was dead, and his next victim was lying unconscious on the cottage floor. Destiny had nullified Goerthe's payday, but had possibly saved his life.

* * * * *

Isaac could make out the threatening front gate and wall of the labor camp as he reached the top of the lake path. He swung right and skidded to a sharp halt, as if to make a statement to the guards that his mission required speed and immediate attention.

Departing from the officer's army vehicle, Isaac walked to the booth at the exterior side of the camp wall.

"Yes, can we help you?" the sergeant on duty offered as he approached Isaac, perplexed about the strange visit at nearly 10:00 p.m.

Once the town laborers exited the camp at the end of the work day, there was never a visitor until the 6:00 a.m. bus brought them back. The only exception was on Saturday evening, when soldiers were returning from the night of drinking in Furstenberg, but it was Sunday.

"I am Volk, with the SS Police Unit from Berlin. Captain Wurtzmuller and Major Suhren have issued a Command Order to summon a prisoner for questioning. The Inspectorate has uncovered a serious intelligence breach of security, and they have to interrogate a particular woman, whose name has been associated with the plot."

Isaac handed the envelope to the guard, who opened it and read the message.

"There is a group from Berlin, right now, down at Captain Wurtzmuller's house, and they are in a hurry."

"I saw a sedan and military jeep shoot down there about two hours ago…" the soldier chimed in.

"Yes, that was the group," Isaac nodded, letting the sentry's memory lead in the ruse."They have to return to Berlin tonight, so they are in a rush. I was told to not waste any time. Can you expedite this, Sergeant?"

Isaac tried to be assertive but polite, hoping that the latter would be the correct demeanor.

"I will verify this order with Wurtzmuller," the thorough sentry relayed as he turned back to the booth in front of the walled facility.

Isaac was forced to react quickly.

"I would not bother them, sergeant. They were in a pretty horrible mood when I left the house. Major Suhren was totally irate, screaming at me not to take any more time than was necessary, or he would see to it that I would be reprimanded. I am not going to let you put me in jeopardy for that to happen. Please allow me to complete my orders at once, or I must blame you for the delay. I do not think you want that to happen. Do you?"

The guard slapped the envelope with his hand, as Isaac's threat had changed his mind. He turned to the guard atop the turret and gestured to have the interior crew unlatch the wooden structure. He then handed the order back to Isaac.

"The women's huts are to the right. Most barracks have their numbers scratched on to the outer walls. One sixteen is down the left side, two buildings from the end."

Isaac backed up to Wurtzmuller's jeep, hopped in and revved the motor. Within a few seconds, the dark abyss of the camp interior greeted him as he sped into the facility. He hoped the guard did not follow up with a call to the chalet. He could hear the doors closing behind. After seven weeks, he was once again within the walls of Ravensbruck.

Sunday evening, at this late hour, was as he had expected it to be. There was no activity. Several overseers huddled in a group, who were smoking and trading tales of the day events, took notice at him driving through the courtyard and to the left aisle of barracks. He saw a prisoner emptying a bucket onto the muddy ground in front of the first building. She disappeared back into the hut as he approached.

Isaac took note of loud yelling, laughter and a unified sense of camaraderie coming through the windows of the barracks as he passed. The women were surviving, he figured. *How strong they must be?* The general tone seemed to be one of coping and positive support.

He slowed to identify the etching "110" scratched on to a hut. As he turned to face the lane, was forced to jam on the jeep's squeaky breaks. A female prisoner had darted in front of his vehicle with two overseers chasing her. They ran, wielding their horsewhips, cursing the unfortunate fleer.

"Stop, you two" he yelled to the women guards.

He thought he would buy the young prisoner some extra time before getting caught. "Where is number 116? Who is the house kapo?"

The taller overseer pointed to the second hut beyond that point.

"The kapo is called Janaczek."

"What did the girl do?" Isaac asked, showing an official Gestapo interest.

"She stole extra bread at dinnertime," the other guard answered.

"I am a special Gestapo emissary for Major Suhren from Berlin," Isaac shouted. "We need all prisoners healthy to produce products for our soldiers on the front. What are your names?"

"Hilda Vorst," the taller guard answered. "Ida Milderbauer," the second followed.

"Let this woman be. If I hear harm has come to her, I am holding both of you responsible for the hindering of camp productivity. Do you understand? If not, I will report your names to Oberaufseherin Boerner and personally have you transferred to a Polish facility. I have the power to do that.

"Some women are committing crimes far worse than stealing bread. In fact, I am heading for one now. You two obviously missed her crimes because you were too busy chasing the bread hoarders."

He took personal delight in his brief performance, smirking as the guards halted their pursuit and changed direction.

"Hmm, Janaczek, Janaczek," Isaac muttered to himself.

He brought the jeep to a halt near the side wall of Barrack 116.

"Hopefully, I can be as convincing to her."

He walked around the corner of the hut, straightened his uniform, breathed deeply and knocked on the wooden entrance, banging hard and with authority, showing the defiant Nazi attitude he had witnessed in the past few weeks. A sheepish, young girl of about sixteen opened the door a crack. She stared in fear at his SS uniform, which was even more of an alarming sight at 10:00 p.m.

"Get me your kapo, Janaczek. Hurry!" he ordered.

The door shut, and a few seconds later, Tula Janaczek opened it, peering down at the Gestapo officer standing in the muddy lane.

"Who are you? Why are you here at this hour?"

"Please step down here."

He did not want his identity to be recognized by any of the women who may have remembered him from registration day. He also did not want Flora hearing his voice.

"I am an emissary from Berlin Gestapo. Major Suhren and Captain Wurtzmuller have summoned a woman from your house. She is wanted for questioning regarding a spy ring. I am to gather her and bring her to their residence immediately."

"That is odd. It cannot wait until the morning? I have never witnessed such a request."

"Perhaps you would like me to take you to them so you can share your mixed thoughts. I am sure you will be shot on the spot. My guess is Wurtzmuller would be the one who would gladly do it. Now are you going to create such a delay so I can tell them of your uncooperative behavior, Janaczek?

"Who is it you want?" Janaczek asked, backing down and becoming compliant.

Isaac opened his envelope, as if he had forgotten.

"Flora Bloom."

The kapo let out a roar of laughter.

"Some spy ring! What were they stealing? Secret recipes?"

"Just get her, kapo. I will be in my jeep, around the corner of the building. Get her at once."

Isaac did not want Flora blowing his Gestapo cover. Making his way to the "W" jeep, he hunched over in the driver's seat, pulled his cap down atop his brow and gazed toward the barrack wall to avoid showing any facial features. He could hear the door around the building corner creek open, and the muffled voices of two women.

"There he is," Janaczek said. "If you bring her back late," she called, "I am not getting the door. She can sleep on the grass for the night."

Isaac waved, not turning his lowered head, and made a thumb motion, directing his prisoner, Flora, to sit in the back seat. She was still in mid-air when he gunned the jeep, leaving Janaczek shaking her head as she returned to the barrack hut.

It worked! Flora still did not recognize him. After a moment, she shouted up to the front seat.

"There must be some mistake. I do not know of any spying people. I sew for a living. Where are you taking me? Please tell me. I am not an important prisoner. Please!"

Isaac halted the vehicle along the fence that separated the women's buildings and the infirmary. He exited on the driver's side walked around passing the "W" spare tire, and surprising his vulnerable wife, he cupped his hand across her mouth, preventing her from screaming.

"Flora, Flora, do not scream. It is me, Isaac. Please do not make a noise."

Fear in Flora's eyes greeted his stern request. Her cobalt-hued irises assured him that she would obey. He wished he could have held her, hypnotized by the beautiful blue eyes he dreamed of every night for the last two months, but their lives were still in grave danger. He slowly removed his hand from her lips, while she grabbed his neck and began kissing his face, gasping for air in an effort to speak.

"Isaac, my Isaac! They told me you were dead—shot by the Nazi officer friend of the Commodore. It happened on the first day. You were *killed*, they were sure you were! Oh my God, Isaac!" she wept, kissing him again.

"Flora, it was another man. The Nazi officer mixed up the folders. I have been secretly living as his houseman outside the camp property."

He was overwhelmed by a yearning to be with her. He wanted to make love to her there in the jeep, against the barbed wire wall, but his senses reigned over his desires.

"Stop! Stop—I have a plan."

Flora recoiled as she recognized the uniform.

"Did they make you join the Nazis?" she asked with an innocence that made him chuckle.

"No, but we will have to disguise ourselves if we are to have any chance of escape from this place. Now make believe I am taking you out for questioning. I have fooled the guards at the front gate. Just sit in the back and say nothing. This will either work, or we will die together."

She pulled him closer, hugging and kissing him, disregarding his requests to stop, but he grabbed her wrists, removing them from his nape.

"You are to sit and say nothing, do you hear? The guards think that I am a Gestapo policeman, taking you to the officer's house for espionage reasons. I escaped from his chalet because the Nazi and a woman overseer got into an argument, and she killed him. I drugged her and tied her up. We must return there, get into disguise and leave immediately."

"Wait, Isaac, please hear me. Please," she begged, processing only part of his directive.

Once again, he gazed into her eyes, where he could see concern, a plea of some type. Even in that extremely dangerous moment, he knew that she was going to ask for the impossible.

"My bunk mate, a Romani woman—we have to bring her with us!"

"What?" he mouthed in a barely audible whisper. "Flora, this is out of the question. We are probably not going to get out of here ourselves. We cannot have a third person to jeopardize our escape!"

Minutes later, the couple sat next to the side wall of Barrack 116. Isaac stared at Flora, smiled and shook his head, admiring her veto of his decision.

"What is your friend's name?"

"Resto—Risa Resto. Isaac, if it were not for her strength, I think I would not have made it through the past weeks. You will see. She is strong. She will help us be successful. I know it!"

"I will make up a story. Stay in the jeep. I want to be at the gate in two minutes."

Isaac returned to the door and banged, shouting.

"Kapo Janaczek, Kapo, hurry!"

This time, Tula Janaczek swung the entrance open with an annoyed greeting.

"You? What now? You got who you wanted."

"I now need Resto. Bring her out here quickly."

The suspicious kapo looked at him with a cautious eye.

"Of all the women here, and you need her bunkmate?" she questioned, insinuating deceit.

"I was unaware that she had a bunkmate. They may have shared stories. The committee will need to question her as well. If they are satisfied with their innocence, I will return both later."

"Resto! Resto—out here, now! You have been ordered to go along with Bloom. Resto!"

The kapo wanted these annoying intrusions to cease, though she was quite willing to present Risa to the authorities for any reasons that might be brought to light. Getting the Romani woman in trouble was an act that Janaczek enjoyed assisting.

Flora Bloom's gypsy bunkmate presented herself at the door, saying nothing.

"Go with this Gestapo. You and Bloom are wanted for questioning," Janaczek said with a pleasant sneer. "If the door is locked when you are finished, bang on the window. Disturb someone else. I am not getting up to let you two inside. Do you understand?"

Risa said nothing, staring at Isaac with a defiant, defensive stoicism.

"Please sit in the back with the other prisoner. If you try anything stupid, you will be punished," Isaac said in his most official tone.

He could hear the door slam behind as they turned the corner. Risa though, was stymied that a Nazi policeman would use the word "Please." After the second woman climbed into the parked vehicle next to her friend, Flora pulled her closer, whispering a concise explanation about the situation.

"So, he is not dead? Did he join the Nazis? What is going on, Flora?"

The gypsy kept her ear against the happy wife's lips, trying to process the confusing information. After further explanation, Risa Resto sat back in her seat and blessed herself.

"I am glad I had no time to think about this plan. Let's just try to get the hell out of here."

The trio crossed the courtyard. Isaac halted Wurtzmuller's jeep at the red and black "Achtung" sign, which hung on the interior wall of the camp gate. Its warning intimidated all who viewed it, just over the wheel and latch barricade.

The same guard who had greeted Isaac when he entered, thirty minutes earlier, emerged from the camp's interior wall booth. Isaac then realized that both small posts were connected, so guards could man the entering or exiting checkpoint simultaneously.

The thorough sentry held up his hand for the jeep to halt. Isaac obeyed, thinking the soldier would have something to say about the second woman prisoner. He did.

"Gestapo, can I please see your paper, again?"

Isaac obeyed, seeming to know what was to follow.

"Your request was for one—Flora Bloom only. Which of you is Bloom?"

Flora raised her hand in a sheepish motion. Nothing was going to slide by this guard. Isaac was only glad that he had not taken the extra step to phone Captain Wurtzmuller's residence.

"Why is there a second woman? This was not stipulated in this Command Order."

Thinking quickly, Isaac responded.

"Part of the espionage has involved a group of Romanians. The captain asked me, if it was at all possible, to also bring an interpreter, who can translate Romanian to German, but if it created a time delay, forget it. That is why it was not definitively on the order. If you want to call him, go ahead, but they probably will not even answer the phone."

Risa looked at Flora. Isaac's performance was an eye-opener for both women.

"No, that is okay."

The guard handed the order to his cohort and motioned to two other soldiers to open the cross beam structure that kept the camp inhabitants contained. He looked at Risa, shooting her a condescending glance.

"Say something in Romanian!" he ordered, in his only attempt to confirm Isaac's explanation.

"*Imbuca rahat tu mundar majareste*" the forceful gypsy blurted in a cadence that anyone not knowing Romanian would identify as an insult or curse, by the way the words rolled off her tongue.

The guard laughed, knowing that given a chance to say something and not be punished for it, she had a licence to tell him what she thought of him.

"And what does that *mean*, Roma?" he challenged.

"It means, 'Have a wonderful evening.'"

He laughed to himself, realizing that she was lying, though he had no way of checking. He waved the three prisoners through the gate, calling out.

"Give the officers my regards, Gestapo."

Isaac twisted in the driver's seat looking back over his shoulder just in time to observe the girth of the wooden doors converge back to a closed position. The sound of the latch wheel, turning, resonated from the freedom side of the barbed-wire walls. They held their breath until they reached the road that turned down to Lake Schwedt.

"My God, I cannot believe what just happened!" Flora exclaimed.

Isaac stopped the car and hopped out, vomiting on the dirt lane.

"Why are we going down this road?" Risa asked." Let us get as far away from here, as quickly as possible. Four minutes ago, I was half asleep in my bunk. Really! Let us get away from here!"

Isaac cleaned his bile-filled mouth with his uniform sleeve.

"I must warn you of the sight you are about to see. There is a dead officer, with a bullet in his head, and a heavily -sedated woman guard, lying on the floor."

"Why didn't you kill her, too?" the gypsy asked.

"I didn't kill anyone. She killed him. And we are not going to take part in murder."

He hopped back in the jeep and headed down the lane toward Lake Schwedt.

"We will get into disguises, grab the provisions that I have gathered and take the overseer with us. Somewhere far away, we will discard of her on the road. Until then, I plan to keep her heavily-drugged."

The vehicle chugged in the late night silence of the rural area. He turned on to the tire-marked lane that led to the chalet. All seemed as he had left it.

Lurking behind the high sea grass stalks of vegetation, Goerthe threw the stolen driver's license and identification papers he had been reviewing, back into the BMW glove compartment. The passing of Wurtzmuller's jeep startled the crook, as he gave immediate attention to the three figures making their way to the chalet. He could not identify the prison uniforms, but the figures appeared to be women, and definitely not Dorothy Boerner. The old criminal slumped back in the driver's seat and remained vigilant, expecting his victim to eventually leave from the small house behind the lakeside villa.

Once inside the captain's residence, Isaac orchestrated the trio's quick departure. Flora studied the blank non-responsive stare of Heinrich Wurtzmuller. Over the past two month's she had seen the same death mask on several corpses in Barrack 116—usually, the older women who had not been able to survive untreated illness. Her fixation on the dead officer's corpse was interrupted by a yelp from Risa, who stood over the other body lying on the floor.

"Flora, my God—look! Look who it is. It is the Oberaufseherin who made me fight the giant. It is Boerner. That bitch!"

Risa peered down at the fallen and sedated overseer, who moaned and rolled on the rug, the sedative slowly wearing off. Isaac walked closer.

"You know her?"

"She is the chief of all the women guards, Isaac," Flora answered. "Risa had to fight her giant woman fighter because she told off our kapo. It was their way of having her killed, but Risa won. The giant had slain sixteen women before fighting Risa in exhibitions that this overseer conducted for betting."

"She made money, wagering bets on the giant, killing innocent women," Risa explained, "but I spoiled her little game. Put me in charge of her! Please?"

The gypsy snapped her fingers in front of the overseer's non-responsive face.

"Okay, but you are not killing her. We are better than these bastards," he said, glancing toward his wife.

"Flora, help me take off Wurtzmuller's pants and boots. I will wear his complete uniform and drive the jeep. Risa—untie the overseer. Remove her uniform. Flora, I need you to wear Boerner's clothes, and put your prison uniform on her. Risa—you can wear my Gestapo outfit."

He began taking off his police shirt and pants. He could not believe that their charade had gone so far. He left the uniform in a pile for Risa.

Once Dorothy Boerner was free from her bounded state, Flora dressed her in the prison attire, while she slipped into the overseer's uniform. Risa changed into Isaac's old Gestapo policeman's wear.

"I thought there were no women in the SS?" she asked.

"Hopefully, you will not get close enough to anyone who will notice," Isaac answered. "Anyway, your new haircuts are now an asset," he remarked as he added more gold statues, candlesticks and frames to the large duffle bag.

"I want to have different forms of items, besides money and jewelry—in case we meet someone who wants us to pay them in gold."

When the weight of the bag seemed to be at its limit, Isaac turned and leaned over to the bookcase. He grabbed the large road atlas from the top shelf. During his time there, he had thumbed through the book, often wondering where distant and safer lands might be. He daydreamed and wished he would be reunited with Flora, living in one of those places, somewhere far away.

Turning the pages, he discovered the section that depicted routes heading north—to and beyond the Denmark border. Finding what he wanted, he tore out five pages and folded them into the pocket of his uniform.

"We have to know where we are heading. I do not want to speak with anyone regarding directions."

As thoughts for survival kept swirling in the young man's head, he opened the desk drawer and was met with the chilling and radiant, prismatic glow of the food jar, filled with nothing but diamonds. He halted. The sight was both beautifully brilliant yet painfully mournful, as well.

He had been separating and categorizing the gems at Wurtzmuller's orders. The dazzling beauty and insurmountable wealth in that the jar was overshadowed by the knowledge that its magnificence had only been achieved due to the despicable act of confiscation from innocent women.

He was sad because the jar's radiance displayed the treasured keepsakes and the valuables of all whose lives had been penetrated by the sword of Nazism.

"I will be damned if I am going to leave this behind," he whispered, and in one motion, he slipped the precious jar into the smaller canvas bag.

Wearing the uniform of a captain, he took the satchels to the jeep and placed them in the small storage area behind the back seat. He returned to the women to help with the removal of Dorothy Boerner.

"Before we lift her, I have just one more thing to do."

Isaac rummaged through the box of disposable syringes, and finding two units of morphine, he opened the packet, broke off the needle cover and injected more of the sedation into the overseer's already limp body.

"Okay, let's lift her. Risa—we will put her on the floor of the back seat. You will stay with her in the rear. Flora—get two or three blankets out of the open box that has samples." He motioned with his head. "Cover her body with one of the blankets. We may need them as well. It is becoming cold at night."

Risa and Flora lifted Dorothy Boerner's feet while Isaac held the overseer, under her arms. The three carried Boerner out the back door and heaved the lifeless body onto the back seat floor of the military jeep.

"Her head will make a nice foot rest," Risa Resto said, laughing.

Flora smiled and shook her head at the remark, while Isaac hopped into the vehicle.

"When we go past the gate, do not look in the direction of the turret or booth. They are expecting the group from Berlin to be leaving. Let them think that we are that group. Keep your heads down. I will try to scoot past them before they even notice that anyone is passing."

The group left the chief overseer's jeep parked next to the empty chalet and once again drove at a modest speed out to the lake road, where Goerthe lay in wait for a glimpse of Dorothy Boerner. As the jeep turned and headed to the main road, the old criminal observed what he had been waiting for over the last several hours.

It seemed that Heinrich Wurtzmuller, Dorothy Boerner and the SS soldier he had seen earlier had left the small house down the lane and were heading elsewhere. He started the BMW and bolted through the overgrowth onto the lake road in pursuit of the vehicle. He was determined to complete his mission and collect the money his contractor had promised.

The escapees darted past the gate and camp guards, who turned on the flood lights, only to catch a glimpse of the rear "W" whitewashed tire. Seconds later, the black stolen sedan also zoomed by the front area. Goerthe played the very delicate game of following close enough, though not close enough to be discovered.

"That must be the group from Berlin leaving?" one of the guards said.

"Yah, I wonder if they took or killed those two women?" the second asked.

"Who cares?" the first answered. "Do you have a cigarette? I'm out."

Isaac came to the junction in the road where he had turned left to go to Furstenberg and The Lorelei. He observed the sign on the opposite side of the road that read, "KIEL, 110 kilometers, HAMBURG 80 kilometers, FLENSBURG 160 kilometers (DENMARK BORDER).

"Hang on. Here we go!"

They turned right, accelerating to a high speed, headed north.

"By the way, Risa, what did you say to the guard in Romanian?" Isaac inquired.

"*Imbuca rahat tu mudar majereste?*" she asked.

"Yes, what does that mean?"

"Eat shit, you filthy swine!"

As they laughed, Flora and Isaac exchanged an intense glance. The cathartic joy could have easily turned into tears from their suppressed anxiety. It was the first time either had laughed in nearly three months.

CHAPTER 27

Freund sat alone within the civilian holding pen just inside the main gate at Ravensbruck. It was 10 a.m. Three and a half hours had passed from the usual time that Captain Heinrich Wurtzmuller or an assigned guard would have summoned him for reporting to the warehouse office. The situation was unprecedented. The gate sentries were avoiding his constant inquiries about where the captain was, and about why no one had come to get him.

The nervous worker had observed some activity around the fortress doors. There appeared to be several officers as well as guards, gathered in heated discussion. The major of the whole facility—Fritz Suhren, who Freund had only seen once before, stormed from the administration quarters.

He got into a jeep, driven by a lesser officer, Freund assumed, and they drove out the camp, followed by two more army vehicles.

"You," a guard called into the gated yard where Reinhold Freund waited. "Your services will not be needed today. Go back home."

"What, what do you mean?" Freund asked, confused by the order. "How am I to get back to Furstenberg? There is no bus until tonight. What is going on?"

"I do not care how you are going to get back to Furstenberg. Just leave. Get out of here, now!"

The soldier poked him with the butt of his rifle and used the barrel to direct the old man to the gate and out to the road. Freund, angry that he would make no money today rummaging through the confiscated belongings, wondered why his boss, Heinrich Wurtzmuller, was not around to challenge the guard's actions.

Disgruntled and mumbling, the old thief began walking on the road around Lake Schwedt, hoping that a generous soul or an army vehicle would give him a ride back to his village.

* * * * *

"I leave the camp for 48 fucking hours, and all hell breaks loose. Who could have done this? Who?" Major Fritz Suhren shouted rhetorically toward Lt. Volsgaard, his driver, as he left the jeep. "I arrived home at seven o'clock this morning. When did you discover the body?" he asked the jittery officer.

"When he did not answer his phone for two hours, I had a guard come down here, sir. The back door was open. He entered and discovered the body."

Inside the chalet, they gazed down at the bloated corpse of Heinrich Wurtzmuller, still resting precariously between his office desk and bookcase.

"Shot by his own gun, between the eyes. No witnesses?"

"None, sir.

Suhren put his head into cupped palms, rubbing his eyes, as if hoping to rub away the morbid sight he was facing.

"I do not want the Concentration Camp Inspectorate apprised of this until we accumulate as many facts as we can. There I was, in Berlin, trying to negotiate the construction of a gas chamber with the very people that I will have to report this crime to. They will think I have no control over my own facility—a fucking laughing stock. I want the guards ordered to keep this silent. They will be court marshaled and executed if found guilty of disclosing this crime to anyone. Do you understand, Lt. Volsgaard?"

"Yes, sir," the sheepish officer answered.

"Now, go get Dr. Engel. I would like a forensic opinion as to what may have happened. Do not tell him why he is coming down here. Tell him Major Suhren will let him know when he arrives. And no excuses—he must come with you, at once."

The senior officer leaned over the body, studying the bullet hole in the corpse's head, wondering why the body was wearing only underwear.

"Oh, and Volsgaard—have someone find our old friends, Dorothy Boerner and Olga Deitzl. Perhaps they may be able to offer some insight into this tragedy. We all know how much they loved and admired the captain."

Suhren began his investigation. First, the astute commander located Wurtzmuller's Walther P38, which had been in its holster, draped over the hall tree at the entrance. He removed the pistol and smelled the barrel. The strong sulfur odor indicated that it had recently been fired. He looked around the messy office and quickly located one expended shell casing near the desk.

The officer also realized that the boxes of samples had been of some interest. They were moved, thrown, and had been invaded for their contents. Someone had especially helped themselves to the pharmaceutical samples. Many syringes were strewn across the floor.

"Hmm, perhaps a drug addict?" the major deduced, until he noticed that there were still many packets of morphine and heroin for the taking.

He perused the room, while reflecting occasionally on his romantic weekend in Berlin with escort, Wanda Taggerhaus. It was a pleasant distraction from the horrendous task he was conducting. While searching, his eye caught something strange, rolled up in a ball, lying in the kitchen sink.

"Now why would a woman's prison garment be shoved in the sink?"

He picked it up, shook it and threw it back. Also, lying on the bookcase, the officer zeroed in on an open road atlas. The other books were neatly displayed on the shelves, but the atlas had been savaged and thrown onto the ledge. He could see that some pages had been torn from the book, so he read the glossary. The missing maps involved all routes in northern Germany—up to and including Denmark.

"Hmm. Interesting," the major mumbled to himself.

All the other maps to the east south and west were still intact. Suhren's thoughts drifted back to his stellar weekend, though the memory of making love to the young, vivacious escort were ever extinguished by the magnitude of the crime scene. How would he explain such an event to his superiors? A possible solution jolted his brain just as he heard a knock on the chalet front door.

It was his lieutenant, Dr. Engel and a soldier, looking rather meek.

"Why is *he* here? This area is restricted. He is to stay outside—far away."

"Sir, this soldier was on the front booth last night. When I went for Dr. Engel, I asked the gate if there had been any suspicious activity. He has some information," Volsgaard insisted.

"Wait outside on the grass, soldier. I must speak with the doctor. I will be to you in ten minutes. Go have a smoke."

Suhren tilted his head, ordering Dr. Engel and Volsgaard back into the chalet.

The subdued, yet diabolical camp doctor, who was capable of his own medical havoc and callous practices, approached the corpse with a fearful blank stare. Suhren studied his posture. He could tell the physician was not only surprised, but emotionally panicked by the murder.

"This is a cold blooded execution. Who would have committed such an act?"

"Tell me something I may have missed, Max. Why was he killed in his underwear?"

"He wasn't, sir," Engel advised.

"Now how do you know, Doctor?"

"Look at the band of his underpants," Engel explained, using his forensic experience, but also common sense. "It is pulled way down in the back. Someone undressed him after the Captain was killed. Pulling off his pants also caused his underwear to ride down as well. I would guess it was done so the killer could wear Wurtzmuller's uniform as a disguise."

"Now you see, Volsgaard—that is why you and I never would get into a medical school!"

Suhren seemed pleased with learning a fact that might help solve the murder.

"I found a woman's prison uniform in the sink. Do you think a prisoner may have done this then, dressed up as Captain Wurtzmuller?"

"A woman, sir? I doubt it."

Engel coughed befor beginning a story foreign to the findings in the chalet.

"Major Suhren, I am afraid that I have more uncertain news for you. About one hour before Lt. Volsgaard came for me, I received a call from the Furstenberg hospital morgue. It seems that on Saturday night, Aufseherin Olga Deitzl collapsed and died in the lobby of a beer hall. She was rushed to the emergency room, but the staff could not revive her. Oberaufseherin Boerner was with her and signed the papers to have the body transported to Ravensbruck. I knew nothing of this until I received the phone call. Boerner has not been heard of or seen since."

Fritz Suhren sat in the chalet living room couch, removed his spectacles and began rubbing his worn eyes. Deep down he wanted to believe that these were isolated incidents, but he had forty years of experience with such morbid coincidences, so he knew there was a definite connection.

"Have someone get Deitzl's body. On the way back, stop here and pick up Heinrich's. I am not going to report her death to anyone, and I am going to call his a suicide. We will have their bodies cremated by Wednesday. I refuse to deal with the Inspectorate over this—especially since it was because of them that I had to leave the camp. Lt. Volsgaard, when Captain Bitten returns this afternoon, have him come see me immediately. I am disbanding his prison orchestra. I need him here—not squeezing his accordion two hundred kilometers away. Both of you look around for any more clues that may help explain what might have happened here. I am going outside to speak with the guard."

The private dropped his lit cigarette and stood at attention when the commandant emerged from Wurtzmuller's residence.

"At ease, son. Relax. Forget protocol for the moment. I want you to explain thoroughly and precisely what it was that appeared strange or suspicious to you last night. Have another cigarette, if you must."

Major Suhren was aware that his presence was such an intimidation that an enlisted man might let rank cloud his accuracy. The officer put his hand on the guard's shoulder, assuring him that if his observations prove to be significant, it may lead to a promotion.

"You speak nothing to anyone about our discussion, soldier, or all bets are off. Do you understand?"

"Yes sir."

"Now what happened that you find questionable?" Suhren asked, reaching into his own jacket to remove a pack of cigarettes before joining the young guard in the ritual of a smoke. The two stood as equals for a brief moment, with the guard's information being the variable that raised his level to that of the commandant.

"Well, last night, sir, at about ten o'clock, an SS police courier showed up at the front gate. He presented an order from Captain Wurtzmuller, requesting that a prisoner be summoned for questioning at Captain Wurtzmuller's house. It involved the uncovering of a spy ring by the Camp Inspectorate. He said the woman may have had information. He also said that you were part of the interrogation, sir."

"So you just let him inside, with a bogus order form?"

The nervous sentry reached into his pocket and presented the skeptical officer with the actual form that had been forged by Isaac Bloom.

"I kept the form, sir."

The guard stared down because his next bit of information might potentially cause him more harm than good.

"There was a second woman who left with the emissary as well."

"But the order explicitly requested one prisoner."

He gazed down at the form with the perfect signature of the dead officer.

"One—Flora Bloom! Why did you allow a second woman to pass?"

"Sir he said the process needed an interpreter who spoke Romanian. He was to present the interpreter—only if one could be found. That was why the request was not on the order."

The guard glanced toward Suhren, expecting some form of a reprimand, but it did not come.

"Soldier, did you see them after this meeting?"

"No sir. Well maybe—about forty minutes later—I saw the Captain's jeep leave. He was driving. There appeared to be an aufseherin and the SS policeman with him as well. Then, a few seconds later, a sedan drove past behind them."

"Are you sure it was Captain Wurtzmuller driving?"

"Well sir, I could see that it was his uniform, but I did not see a face. The top was down, but I know that it was definitely an officer driving."

"And the sedan?" Suhren asked, realizing that the crime committed appeared to have been more orchestrated than a common murder.

"People from Berlin, I imagined," the soldier answered, shrugging.

The commandant was ready to dismiss the young guard, though he had already dismissed his promise to grant the lad a promotion. It was not a priority for the angry commander.

"Now think hard. That is all you can remember. There is nothing else. Any strange behavior—involving overseers, outsiders, strangers, Captain Wurtzmuller, himself? Think!"

"Well sir. Something odd happened a few weeks ago, but Sgt. Eigerhahm handled it. We were at the gate together.

"I do not want to get any more people involved with this investigation," Suhren sighed. "Can you relate the story to me with accuracy?"

"I can, sir."

The guard felt relieved that his personal account had ended. He began as a secondary source to what he remembered on a Wednesday, a few weeks ago, when Sgt. Eigerhahm called Captain Wurtzmuller.

"Sir, this never happened before. A woman, about twenty or twenty-two, arrived at the front gate in a taxi cab from Furstenberg—quite distraught—in fact hysterical. She wanted to speak with Captain Wurtzmuller. She would not leave or take "No" for an answer. She was completely irrational. The cab left. We did not know what to do. We managed to locate the captain."

"Did he accommodate her?"

"Yes sir. He came almost immediately. It appeared that she was an acquaintance from The Lorelei Rooming House in Furstenberg. We think the captain may have been sweet on her. It may have been a lovers' quarrel, or something. It was pretty funny to see an officer with girlfriend problems."

"What did he do with her?" Suhren asked, rather amused by the scene he now had whirling in his imagination. "Did he leave with the woman?"

"Yes sir," the guard continued. "He drove her back to town. That is the whole story."

"And you probably do not remember the woman's name now, soldier, do you?"

"Yes sir."

The dutiful sentry pulled a piece of paper from his jacket and presented his superior with it. The officer studied the scrap.

"Very good, son. I will probably want to speak with," he said, bringing the note closer, "with this Greta Junkwalter at The Lorelei. This is most helpful. You are dismissed. Wait out here, and Lt. Volsgaard will bring you back to your post."

CHAPTER 28

Passing through two nighttime roadblocks was almost uneventful for the newly freed trio. A captain was not going to be delayed and certainly not questioned. Gates raised and respectful German salutes followed as Isaac, Flora and Risa bolted through the checkpoints. Even Rolf Lizst, (aka Wilhelm Goerthe), who held the driver's stolen identification paper booklet out the window, was waved on without being stopped. He trailed the escapees, sometimes closely and sometimes far behind, turning off his headlights in order to conceal his pursuit.

They passed through Neustralitz at three o'clock in the morning. Isaac stopped every ten kilometers to check that their direction favored a northwest vector, heading toward the Jutland peninsula. Risa kept her foot on the wrapped body of their prisoner, overseer Dorothy Boerner. Both she and Flora had covered themselves with the remaining blankets. The night weather in the northern German country had turned chilly.

"I can feel her getting stronger under my foot. I think she may need another shot of "dope" to slow her down again. She is also starting to grunt. I would love for her to realize that it is me who has a foot on her head, that bitch. I am also starving. Can we stop and get some food?"

"We will keep going for another two hours," Isaac answered, looking back. "These roads are slow. I will stop somewhere around Waren. That seems to be about half way from Ravensbruck to the Denmark border."

"Why do we have to go to Denmark? Don't the Nazis occupy Denmark also? How will that solve our problems?" Risa asked. "Would it not have been better to flee to Switzerland?"

"I feel better traveling 100 kilometers as opposed to nearly 250," Isaac reasoned. "Plus, it is only a matter of hours before Wurtzmuller's body is found and our charade may be jeopardized. My plan is to head for the quickest border, other than Poland."

"I still cannot believe that this has happened," Flora added with the exuberance of a child. "Only eight hours ago, we were in our bunks, bedding down for the work week!"

"This hasn't happened yet, Flora. Please understand that we are always moments away from being in grave danger. One screw up, or one observant soldier—and we could be found out. I will not rest until we are in a safe foreign country. I am already worrying about crossing the border."

"Well, if I were to die right now, I would be okay with that, because we are together. I did not want to live when the other women told me that you had been killed. Now that we are both alive and together, I feel we have already escaped, and won."

"Speak for yourself, Flora. I cannot wait to get out of this shithole country," Risa Resto interjected, "but not before I take care of this bitch!"

The Romani woman dug her boot into the blanket covering Dorothy Boerner, not knowing what part of her body suffered the injury. As the jeep approached a sign, indicating that they had reached the town of Waren and its large body of water, Lake Muritz, Isaac noticed a wooden placard, announcing the local autumnfest carnival and fair that happened to have begun its one week festivities one day earlier, on September 26th, and was continuing until Saturday, October 2nd. The sign read that it was one-half kilometer ahead, in the Saggerhauft fields.

"Here is where we will stop and get lost in the crowd," Isaac announced to the women. "Flora—you and I will get something to eat and drink. Risa—you will have to stay with the overseer. You can then have some time alone when we return. We have to think of getting rid of her. We are far enough away from the camp. I will inject her one more time to slow down her responses—in case someone tries to assist her."

Risa said nothing as they entered a large field of harvested corn. The area was being used as a parking lot for all the visitors at the autumn festival.

"I cannot believe how crowded it is for a Monday morning," Flora pointed out. "Look at all the precious children with their parents, Risa." The field had numerous vehicles, parked in a line, a few hundred meters from the attractions. The group sighted a carousel, a Ferris wheel, horse rides, numerous games of chance booths and a copious variety of food and drink stands. The wealth of treats, Isaac thought, certainly supported the fact that it indeed was a seasonal celebration of the bounties that the harvest bestowed to the residents of Waren.

"Get me pastries and some beer," Risa asked as Isaac and Flora exited the jeep. "I have not had a pastry in three years. Get me as many as you can carry. I can feel our friend on the floor starting to kick a bit. She knows that we have stopped."

The attractions and crowds had distracted the three. They felt normal again to be mingling with society. None of them noticed the inconspicuous presence of Goerthe, nearly twenty cars away stationed in the second row of parked vehicles, that spread over the dormant cornfield.

"Whatever you do, Risa, do not leave the jeep and the canvas bags unattended," Isaac warned. "They are our only aids for surviving."

He prepared another syringe of morphine, and pushing aside the army blanket covering the still delirious overseer, located her arm and injected a second dose of the painkiller.

The young couple, infused with a lust for living, behaved like two starry-eyed lovers as they left the jeep, hand in hand. Isaac found a booth offering beer and Bavarian pretzels. Sharing the salty treat with his wife, he focused on a bakery kiosk that offered local strudel and crusty pastries.

"Do you think Risa would approve?" he asked his wife, whose fatigue had been eclipsed by a delirious state of joy.

"Let us sit a bit. I have something for you," he suggested to his young wife, motioning to an empty picnic table. "Taste my beer—it is refreshing."

Clad in military uniform, he then displayed character that would not have been demonstrated by a Nazi captain. Families with tykes in strollers, teenagers home from school, as well as adults, oblivious to the fact that their country was at war, stared at the loving couple on the bench. He removed one of the black boots he had been wearing during their escape, peeled off his sock and tried concealing the removal of white medical tape from his toe.

His toe had been harboring Flora's wedding ring that Isaac had found the very first week of their imprisonment. Cleaning the excess glue, he presented the band, as if proposing, once again. Flora was speechless, astonished.

"Isaac, how did you get this, my wedding band?"

She wept as she slipped it over her finger. Passersby looked with melancholic approval of what seemed to be two innocent locals in love, as Isaac quickly got back into his sock and army boot.

"I will tell you, later. We better get back to the jeep and relieve your friend."

"Let's get some food for the ride. I need some fresh fruit in my body, an apple or something. It has been three months since I have had any."

* * * * *

Within fifteen minutes of Isaac and Flora's visit to the fair, Risa Resto began to fidget and observe the pastoral surroundings. She felt exposed in an SS uniform and paranoid, as if she was being watched. Dorothy Boerner was starting to mumble louder and flail her arms with more conviction. The Romani woman could not resist. She unwrapped the top portion of the captive's blanket and grabbed her cheeks, forcing the overseer to face her abductor.

"Look at me, you piece of shit. Look who has the upper hand now. How do you feel to be treated like an animal? Ha!"

The gypsy threw the blanket back over the guard's body. She studied the grounds, noticing all the tents that had been erected by the various vendors and concessions. Risa assessed that her view was of the backside of all the booths. She could make out the commoners, working behind the scenes. Trucks of farm goods, baking trays, even a sausage smoking hut had been erected to produce items foreign to most of the fairgoers. Some grown men, in their butcher whites, were passing the time playing soccer by the temporary smokehouse.

Large-wheeled bins, randomly dotting the parking lot, sat waiting to be used by festival shoppers. A boy was lining them into a more assembled row. They reminded the gypsy of baby carriages, making her remember her mother, years ago in Bucharest, wheeling her sister while she held onto the handle. She wondered if the two were still alive. It had been nearly twelve years since she had last seen either of them. The Romani cleared her head, returning to the present. She had a plan.

The gypsy, in the uniform of an SS policeman, stood in the back of the open-aired army jeep. The crowds had dissipated. She exited the vehicle and brought the closest bin to the point between her and the car parked to the right. She took an invigorating breath, gathering a blast of oxygen for energy, and began moving Dorothy Boerner from the backseat floor. She held the overseer's dead weight by lifting at her armpits, using the raised panel for supper, and dumped the blanketed body into the bin she located near the jeep. Dorothy Boerner lied in a dazed state at the bottom of the wheeled cart.

"Let's go for a little ride, aufseherin. I will apologize early for the bumps."

The field was quite uneven since its recent harvest. Boerner was now shouting every time her head hit the metal side of the bin as they crossed the plowed stretch of land.

"Aaaw, are you uncomfortable, Overseer Boerner? Well, we will be at our destination soon. Just think of the all the pain you have brought on the women prisoners over the years. What is a little bump on the head?"

Risa Resto made it past the men playing soccer in their white butcher attire and stopped at the rear of the smokehouse and sausage tent. There were about a dozen employees—some working, some sitting and arguing and three at a table, drinking hard liquor as well as tankards of beer.

"Who is the boss, here?" Risa shouted with Gestapo authority.

"Since when are women allowed in the SS?" the grey-bearded elder shouted. "You are a woman, yes? You are Gestapo as well? How can that be?"

He threw back his head as he downed a shot of some hard brown alcohol.

"I am Borchweiss, the chief of this crew. We make the finest smoked meats north of Berlin. Why did you bring a harvest bin over here? I hope you are not looking for free goods. I cannot afford to give anything away. You are a Gestapo?"

"You do not even wait for an answer, Herr Borchweiss, before you ask your next question," Risa followed. "I am a prison guard and yes, there are women in a select group of Gestapo, solely involved in the hunting down and capturing women prisoners who escape from their facilities."

She sounded convincing as she fabricated the total lie.

"Well, okay, I uh, was unaware of that. What can I do for you, Frau Gestapo?" the swarthy butcher said before taking another swig from a stein.

"Come here. I want you to see something."

The Romani beckoned him to look into her harvest bin that had still been covered with one of the army blankets they had taken from Wurtzmuller's chalet.

The chief butcher rose from his bench and walked to Risa with somewhat of an arthritic gait. She threw back the woolen cover, where Dorothy Boerner sighed an unhealthy groan, mostly due to the annoying sunlight that radiated into the pail's interior.

"Hmm, pretty! Who is she? Why do you wish for me to see her?" Borchweiss asked. "Is that a prison uniform?"

"She escaped from a nearby facility," the gypsy answered. "We apprehended her about four kilometers from here in the woods. My superior notified the camp and we were issued orders to kill her rather than bring her back. I am a bit short on cash, Herr Borchweiss. She is yours, if you want her."

The old butcher looked at Risa with a suspecting grin.

"You want me to employ her?" he laughed.

"No I want you to pay me two hundred Reichsmarks to fuck her. Collect as much as you can from your men and treat them to a free fling with an honest to goodness prisoner who would have been killed—only for a poor SS woman who wants to make a few dollars."

"I am not a killer, Gestapo. I do not want to kill her even if she is a prisoner." He looked back into the metal abyss. "Anyway two hundred Reichsmarks is too much money—even if she is a pretty young thing. Is she injured or even conscious?"

"I never said you had to kill her," Risa answered, noting that he seemed interested. "Collect the money from your men. Let them have their way with her. Then, just put her back in the pail, or better, find a truck and dump her far away. She is drugged right now. She has no idea where she is. Two hundred Reichsmarks— what do you say, Borchweiss? She is an enemy of Germany. Here is your chance to do something patriotic."

The seasoned merchant presented a pensive glance into space then turned and walked back to his crew of younger and more agile workers. Risa studied the quorum assessing the business deal. Most of the workers were laughing and appeared to be eager for an agreement. No one, however, was visibly presenting money to their boss. Borchweiss finished and returned to Risa.

"I cannot get them to agree on your price. How about we settle for half your offer? It is I who must dispose of the woman. That is part of the deal I find somewhat unacceptable."

"I tell you what, Herr Borchweiss," Risa bargained. "Half it is, and you throw in that attractive hunting knife resting on the table—the one with the bone handle." She nodded in the direction of the weapon. "Being a butcher, you must have many knives you can part with?"

The elder man called one of his laborers to fetch the blade. The novice retrieved it and passed the impressive weapon to his boss. The butcher held it up to her face, displaying its craftsmanship and sporting look.

"You have good taste, Gestapo woman."

He flipped the knife, which tumbled three revolutions in the space, between the two. Borchweiss caught it by the flat of the blade, presenting the handle to the Romani. He then reached into his apron pocket and doled out several Reichsmarks.

"Count it. That should be one hundred."

The merchant quickly grabbed the bin handle, turned it toward a tent and ordered two workers to conceal the receptacle. They wheeled the pail, along with the dazed body of Dorothy Boerner, into the temporary linen shelter.

Risa bade "Good Day" and headed back over the barren field to their escape vehicle. A flash of fear ran through her body as the gypsy realized she forgot about the covered duffle bags buried behind the back seat. A quick relief consumed her body when she felt the storage area and saw the bags still safely in place.

A farsighted Goerthe still waited for an opportune time to attack what he thought to be Dorothy Boerner as Isaac and Flora returned to the jeep, minutes after Risa Resto's return.

"We bought you some pastries, Risa," Flora called as the couple jumped into the vehicle. "Look Risa— Isaac found my wedding band when he was working in the captain's house."

"Where is the overseer?" Isaac interrupted. "She is gone? What did you do to her?" he shouted at the gypsy woman. "You should have told us if you had a plan!"

Irate, he started the vehicle and pulled out to depart in haste.

"You said I was in charge of her. I got rid of her. You are angry? You did not want to kill her. So, I did not kill her. We now do not have her burden upon us, and she was not killed. That is good, yes?" Risa answered, using simple logic. "I sold her for one hundred Reichsmarks to a group of men to do to her as they wish. They think she is an escapee and an enemy to Germany. Hopefully, they do to her what she has done to everyone else for the past five years."

The Romani began laughing, causing Isaac and Flora to smile, caught up in contagious laughter until the gravity of the moment filled Isaac's mind. It was imperative to leave the area at once. He removed the folded pages from his pocket, pages that came from the atlas he had torn them from Wurtzmuller's study, and he focused on their current location.

"There is an autobahn about two kilometers north of here. We will get on it and head west."

The thorough man ran his finger left on the page to the most highlighted city, Lubeck, which appeared to be about fifteen kilometers northeast of Hamburg.

"After Lubeck, we will turn north on the local roads of the Jutland, past Kiel, to Flensburg and the border."

While he stared into Flora's eyes for approval, she returned a sober look, fully aware that the border would be a challenge and might require a plan that neither had yet to design. He backed the jeep onto the field and moved out. Goerthe followed, leaving a safe distance between vehicles. The large spare tire "W" made his pursuit a bit less difficult, as he tailed the trio.

A kilometer from the fairgrounds, Isaac could see the approaching sign for the autobahn. He advised Flora that they would be using the highway road, and he turned to relay the same to Risa, only to find the gypsy woman licking her fingers and humming at the enjoyment of the first sweet pastry she had eaten in over three years.

CHAPTER 29

With arms folded and a stern expression, Major Fritz Suhren looked down at Greta Junkwalter with disdain, considering she may have had some association in the death of Captain Heinrich Wurtzmuller.

"Why did you show up at the prison camp a few weeks ago, demanding to speak with my second-in-command"? I must have the truth to everything I ask of you, young lady. If I do not, I will have you thrown into my facility immediately. Do you understand, Miss Junkwalter?"

Still exhausted from her weekend appointments, Greta sat on the side of the bed in room 206 at The Lorelei, wiping back tears, promising to cooperate fully. The young prostitute poured some scotch into a filthy glass, resting on the drawer next to the bed. Gulping, panting, crying, she began.

"The two women guards burst into my room a few weeks ago..."

"While Captain Wurtzmuller was in here with you?" Suhren interrupted.

"No, no he had already left. The captain never asked for sex. I want you to know he was always a gentleman."

"I am glad to hear that," Suhren nodded, his sarcasm evident. "Then why was he here?"

"Is the captain in trouble, because... he was always respectful to me, sir."

"The captain is not in trouble. And as long as you provide the truth, the troublemakers will be the only ones that will be held accountable. Continue."

"The two women guards were very forceful in questioning the captain's business in this room. The one guard beat me, while her boss just let her do it. They were quite ruthless—unlike any of the men that would visit me for my services."

Suhren knew at once that the overseers Greta had identified were Deitzl and Boerner.

"Okay, Miss Junkwalter, you must tell me everything. Why was the captain visiting you? And please understand. I do not give black eyes. I imprison or execute. If you want to live, tell me the truth."

"The captain visited me every Saturday night….er, until this recent incident. He then employed a Gestapo courier to do the business in place of him. But that has only been for a few weeks."

"What business? Quick, Miss Junkwalter! What business?" Suhren asked, aware that speeding up an interrogation usually guaranteed factual enhancement and truthful responses.

Greta rose from the bedside, approached the toilet door, and opening it, she walked inside and unlocked the door to room 207 as Suhren watched, somewhat puzzled.

"See—the two rooms have a common toilet.

"This is where Pierre stayed on the weekend, waiting for the captain. They held their meeting in my room. When they were finished, Pierre would come back to 207 and I would return to 206. Everyone thought the captain was seeing me for sex, but he did not want anyone to know of their business venture involving funds for the Alsatian underground fighters."

"Wait a minute!" Suhren said, stunned by the flood of information that Greta had shared. "I need to hear this again, and please include all of the things you may have left out."

Greta then began to document her role in the transaction and her observations;, always reminding the major of her innocence, in case anything had been illegal.

"He would bring me food for my family. I would have to leave, so he and Pierre Bergeron could conduct business. They exchanged bags. The captain would bring a large duffle bag filled with food for me, and a smaller one. I do not know what was in that one. Pierre would give Heinrich a briefcase, and in return, he took the duffle bag back to 207. When their meeting was done, sometimes the captain would tip me or give me some relaxants from your camp."

Greta nodded toward the disposable syringes on her bureau—which included those she had recently pumped into her body. That is all I know, major. You must believe me."

"You reported that after the overseers paid you their visit, a courier began conducting this meeting with Herr Bergeron?"

"Yes, a Gestapo policeman. But he did not act like one. He was kind of shy, cute, but not very military-looking. Kind of… I don't know—un-Nazi-ish?"

Suhren immediately recalled the guard's story earlier, involving an SS policeman releasing the two prisoners for questioning at Wurtzmuller's chalet. It had been fifteen hours. What was going on?

His officer and a prominent overseer were dead, Oberaufseherin Boerner was missing, and two female prisoners had escaped—obviously with the assistance of some SS charlatan.

"Am I in any trouble?" Greta asked. "Do you believe me? Will I still get food or money from the captain? Is he okay? Please, Major, I was told that I was being a good German patriot for helping them conduct their meetings. I have told this to no one but you, sir."

She began to hyperventilate, realizing that her gratuities for the Saturday night meetings might have just come to an end.

"Speak of our session to no one. Do not leave the area. Conduct your business as usual. If you disobey any of my wishes, I will have to have you killed. I can do that, and I will do that if I have to."

As Suhren was leaving the sobbing prostitute, who feared for her future, her addiction could not be quieted.

"Major? Can someone still supply me with the needles, if the captain will not be around?"

"No, we cannot. Is not your profession enough of a disgrace? You have to be an alcoholic and drug addict besides? I am advising the manager to contact me should you decide to leave the area. If you do, I will find out where your family lives, and I will have them executed for accepting military supplies. Do you understand?"

His threat carried the severity to frighten Greta to sobbing again uncontrollably. The commandant left room 206 and descended to the front desk of The Lorelei. Herman Wohl stood at attention once the major stopped. He recognized the importance of Suhren's rank and became nervous at his presence.

"Yes, Major?" the clerk said in a pleasant tone. "I trust the woman you had requested to speak with was in her room. She usually stays here until late Monday."

Suhren did not answer.

"The salesman who visits room 207 on the weekend—do you know how I may be able to contact him?"

The obedient desk man turned to the mail and key cubicles for the corresponding rooms and pulled a business card from the wooden square, marked "207".

"Here you are, sir—Herr Bergeron's card."

Wohl handed it to the officer, who studied the company name and address.

"Could I use your phone, Herr Wohl?" Suhren asked in a more polite tone.

"Why yes, sir, by all means. There is one on the first table in the dining area. The room is now idle. You will have more privacy there."

Suhren tipped the business card to his cap, smiled at the clerk and entered the vacant hall. He dialed and waited for the phone to connect on the receiving end.

"Hello Lt. Volsgaard?—it's Major Suhren. Write this down: *Frankfurt Leather Works, Pierre Bergeron, 266 Wasserstrabe, Frankfurt.* I want you to leave for Frankfort immediately. Drive through the night. Find this location. You are to surprise this man.

"Arrest him. Bring him to the camp for questioning. Take two sentries with you. If he is not there, you wait for him. Arrest anyone who may try to warn him as well. It is imperative that he does not know he is being apprehended. Do you understand? He may have ties to Captain Wurtzmuller's death. This order must be followed at once. Has anyone heard from Oberaufseherin Boerner? Okay then, I will be back in the office shortly. I want you gone by my return."

Suhren hung up the phone, sat in a relaxed posture then reached once again for the black, metal receiver. He dialed the military operator for the northern German Jutland region.

"Commander Heinz Huberer, Mecklenburg-Schleswig, Regional Infantry Patrol." Suhren removed his officer's cap, threw it on the pre-set table top, sat back and awaited the long response that he knew all too well as customary delay for military communication.

After several personnel clearances and identification codes, the major of the Ravensbuck Camp was finally connected to his cohort from early military life.

"Heinz, my old friend, how are you? How have you survived the Hamburg attacks?" Suhren asked, speaking like the two were still junior officers of the Wermacht.

"I must ask a favor, and please keep it between us, Heinz."

Huberer seemed glad to connect with his past military chum and assured him that his request would be held in the strictest of confidence.

"I may have had a breach of security, Heinz. I had two or three women escape from my facility, with the aid of a male town worker. I believe they may have stolen high profile uniforms to create a diversion. Why pass yourself off as a soldier, when you can impersonate a high ranking officer, right?"

The officers laughed, though there was an underlying seriousness that both understood.

"How many Shutzstaffel captains are there in Germany right now—travelling the countryside with an SS officer and an overseer? Anyway, that is what I am pursuing. I have reason to believe that they may be in your territory, heading for the Denmark border, and they maybe driving one of our jeeps that has a large whitewashed "W" on the spare tire. Could you create an immediate alert for such a group? I would be greatly appreciative. If you come up with something, please contact me personally. One, I would like to punish them myself, and two, I would rather not have the CCI notified… for obvious reasons. Best if this matter is kept between just us.

"So how is Marta? Give her my love. When this shit war is over, we must do a vacation together—just the four of us. Okay? You can reach my office directly. Have the military operator identify your name. I will advise them to pass you to me personally. Heinz, I hope you can come up with something. And please, this is in confidence."

Huberer took all the information and promised to feed it to every checkpoint and platoon leader within his region. He assured his friend that precise information would be made known to the entire northern military presence under his command within the next twelve hours.

Suhren assured his gratefulness, hung up the phone and returned to the lobby.

"Good day, Herr Wohl."

"Good day, sir. Were you able to reach Frankfurt?" the clerk shouted out as the Major barreled with a frustrated posture through The Lorelei portal.

Suhren heard Herman Wohl, but he did not respond. He just wanted to leave the stench of sex, scotch and stale beer that had invaded his olfactory nerves ever since he had entered the seedy lobby and rooms of The Lorelei. He welcomed the fresh air of the Havelstrabe—the fresh air of autumn. He reached his jeep and climbed into the driver's seat. Still in a quandary, the commander wondered how long he could keep Wurtzmuller's death quiet. Perhaps he would have some answers by the morning.

CHAPTER 30

Hilda Luftheiser, secretary at the Frankfurt Leather Works, answered the office phone. It had not been a busy day, and that was good, because most of the workers were making sales calls or engaged in meetings. She was left alone to manage most of the company tasks.

The clamor of the ring was annoying. When she worked alone, it always seemed that the bell resonated to an ungodly level.

"Hello, Frankfurt Leather Works. May I help you?"

At first there was a greeting of silence, followed by a breathy and suspicious hesitation from the caller.

"Hello, please advise Pierre Bergeron that the commandant of the labor camp in Furstenberg was inquiring about his meetings with Heinrich Wurtzmuller. I think he may be in trouble."

An abrupt click followed, along with the shrill of permanent disconnection. Hilda jotted down the exact wording, as she had been trained to do, took the piece of paper, and walked it down the hall to Pierre Bergeron's main floor office. Typically, the veteran would not show up to the company headquarters until Tuesday mornings.

The dutiful secretary placed the note on his desk and she supplemented it with her own: "Pierre, this message was received at 3:15 p.m. on Monday. Very strange. I thought you should see it at once."

The phone at her front desk rang again. Hilda Luftheiser ran to answer it, as one of her unwritten jobs was to retrieve all calls before the third ring.

"Hello, Frankfurt Leather Works… Oh, hi Stefania… Yes, I want to go… I do not know what to wear… Who else is going?"

The suspicious call that the worker had just handled was history, lying on a pile of mail, memos, and invoices—forgotten until it would be read by Pierre Bergeron.

* * * * *

Goerthe felt helpless, trapped in the slower, right-car lane on the stretch of the autobahn between Waren and Keil. Crawling along, still in pursuit of Dorothy Boerner, or at least her persona, the criminal kept track of the "W" jeep, four car lengths ahead and in the fast lane. Traffic had come to a halt, as both vehicles were now within ten kilometers of the Hamburg city limit.

Stray bombings, from the July allied invasion of the northern metropolis had destroyed many roads and bridges in nearby hamlets. Two kilometers of highway were dotted with hundreds of crevices, each fifty meters, in diameter. Traffic was being diverted to neighboring and smaller, regional roads.

At 100-meter intervals along the autobahn, the infantry had stationed troops acting as traffic guards, monitoring motorist tempers due to the extensive delays.

"Soldier!" Isaac shouted to an available military guard, standing by the center grass section of the highway. "Can you help us? We need to be in Kiel by sundown? At this rate, we will not make it, and it appears we are heading into a storm. We have no canvas roof, as you can see. I would like not to get caught in the rain without a top."

The private approached the trio, all too eager to assist a captain of the Shutzstaffel. He saluted vigorously with the outstretched Nazi arm.

"Sir, all traffic is being diverted at Shoenburg, onto local roads. There is much destruction to the autobahn. What I can advise you, is to turn here, southwest, to the first exit. Head north, and take any farm road that runs parallel to the autobahn. The roads are only dirt, but you will get to Kiel at a rate much faster than here. The storm is coming off the Baltic. They are usually treacherous and last for days. You do not want to be in a car with no top. I can assist your turn if you like."

Isaac looked at Flora who just shrugged, before Risa's chimed in.

"I have to shit, and I would rather not do it in the rain."

The captain-in disguise nodded to the private, and the young soldier held up his hand to the car behind Isaac. "Back up, allow this vehicle to cross the divide."

Goerthe could see the unannounced maneuver, but was unable to react. The old villain began beating the steering wheel of the stolen BMW, screaming to surrounding cars, ordering them to let him follow. No one accommodated his foul and selfish requests, leaving the pursuer trapped and foiled in his completion of Wurtzmuller's contract. He watched helplessly as the whitewashed "W" vehicle sped away, heading south, beyond his sight—after he had tailed them successfully for nearly 100 kilometers. The frustrated murderer damned the British and Americans for causing their escape. Still pounding the wheel, Goerthe wondered if he would ever see the second part of his payday.

The autobahn lanes heading in the opposite direction were unobstructed. The trio arrived to the exit ramp in less than two minutes. Isaac motored east and into the docile milk farm country of the Schleswig-Holstein Region. At the second intersection, he headed left and northwest.

The soldier was accurate describing the driving conditions. They were moving, but at an extremely slow speed. The bumpy, tree-lined dirt road was pastorally magnificent. Rock walls, livestock fences, silos, barns, animals and farmhouses stretched to either side of the lane, painting a primitive folk genre.

"Post card Germany—what the rest of the world thinks it is… Bullshit!"

Risa's sarcasm made the couple laugh, though all three admired the scenery, and felt how the storybook landscape calmed the nerves and created a much-needed sense of whimsy.

"We have been on this road for nearly six kilometers," Isaac observed. "Where are the people? The fields, the animals, the homes—everything is unattended. There are no people."

"Yes, I was just thinking that, too," Flora agreed. "It is beautiful but, at the same time, eerie."

One half hour, (and five kilometers) later, the disguised group finally engaged a boy who was walking his bicycle along the path. It had been too rough of a surface to pedal the delicate two-wheeler.

"Hello, son, how are you today? It appears we are heading into a storm, yes?"

Isaac could see a defeated, cowering demeanor in the pre-teenager.

"Would there be any place to get shelter, around here, boy?"

"I suppose if you are military, you can stay anywhere. No one is around. The army forced all the residents out of the area due to the Hamburg raids. They were told to listen to the radio for the lifting of the evacuation."

"Why are you still here?" the skeptical Romani woman spoke up from her back seat.

The boy looked to the ground showing only the top of his cap to the group.

"My mother and father went to Hamburg two months ago for their anniversary dinner... They have not returned."

Isaac stretched the moment of silence.

"I hope they are only wounded, I lost both my parents on the same day—similar circumstances—many years ago. It will get better, trust me."

"We can stay in any house, as if it were ours?" Risa asked. "Isaac, I need a toilet immediately. I just felt some rain drops. Please pick one. We need shelter, and we must also keep the jeep dry."

The group bid farewell to the forlorn youth. He continued his journey on the path, unable to pedal over the rocky lane. The three escapees decided to pull into the graveled path of the farmhouse where they had just conversed with the boy.

"I wish we could have taken him with us. You know his parents are obviously dead," Flora sighed.

"Hopefully, someone who is as kind as Commodore Ahrens was to me will enter his life and treat him as family, Flora. We cannot change our plans. We need to be strong and act covertly."

The residence was plain, made with wooden beams and mortar. The outside showed it had been a working farm, possibly a dairy. The windows were clean, and the front door ajar. Whoever lived there took pride in its upkeep, but they were obviously forced to exit its comfort in a matter of minutes.

The women exited the vehicle, took the canvass bags that had been concealed in the space behind the back seat, and ran for the comfortable interior of the farmhouse. Isaac heard Risa scream, "Indoor plumbing!" as he found a large rubber tarp in the adjacent barn. He hurled the cover over the jeep, protecting the interior seats and flooring as best he could.

The droplets had progressed to a steady shower. The weather was becoming more treacherous as they faced an uncertain delay. He ran inside to the women. As proof that the residence was abandoned rather quickly, rotten fruit lay in a bowl on the kitchen table. The ice, fueling the perishable food box, had melted, and a foul odor was emanating from the porcelain appliance.

There was, however, an ample supply of canned foods, root vegetables, apples and fresh cider to nourish the three.

"I would like to take a bath and spend at least two private hours in the toilet," Risa announced to Isaac and Flora. "You two can have some time alone, if you know what I mean. I would like a long period of privacy, thank you," she said, winking at the couple.

Flora and Isaac climbed the creaking stairway to the second level. Finding a bedroom with a large double bed and mattress, Flora flopped atop the soft cushions and stretched her arms, as if floating on a celestial cloud. She kicked the overseer boots off from her aching feet, removed Dorothy Boerner's uniform and stretched, bellowing a sigh of emotional release.

Isaac studied his wife's movements. He had not seen her so relaxed, so beautiful and so inviting since the day of their Gestapo prison notice three months ago in Bremerhaven.

He tore off Wurtzmuller's uniform and threw the cap across the room, watching as it landed on the bureau. He whispered to Flora.

"Stay just as you are," he locked his eyes on hers and the two, no longer able to contain the irrepressible, pent-up passion, took Risa Resto's "winking advice."

* * * * *

Driving all night from Ravensbruck to Frankfurt, Lt. Volsgaard and the two soldiers were determined that their mission would be successful. The military abduction team sent to bring Pierre Bergeron back to Major Suhren for questioning wanted to complete the mission, get back on the road and be in the commandant's presence by sundown.

Upon locating the Wasserstrabe business address at 9:20 in the morning, the three men entered the Leather company office, surprising Hilda Luftheiser.

Exercising his best SS intimidation, the novice lieutenant was severe

"Pierre Bergeron, where is his office?"

At the same moment, he drew an automatic handgun from its holster. The young secretary wheeled her chair away from the desk and raised her hands high into the air.

"What is wrong? Why do you need Herr Bergeron? Please! We are just a business."

After Volsgaard pointed his German luger more directly at the worker, she nodded down the hall.

"Second door to the right! Please! What is happening?"

Her question went unanswered.

The two soldiers preceded the officer to the door. After Volsgaard nodded, one kicked the wooden portal by the lock and knob. It swung open with force, recoiling on its hinges. The Nazi group was greeted by an empty room. The desk was a disheveled mess and the phone was pulled from the wall and thrown to the floor, lying in front of an open safe. Exccept for some papers and receipts, the vault displayed a velvet abyss of darkness. To the rear of the street-level room, the window with torn lace curtains confessed that someone had recently used it for escape.

Volsgaard looked out to the ally. There was no sign of anyone. In anger, he spun, pushing a soldier to the side. He stormed back to a shaking Hilda Luftheiser.

"Bergeron's address—I want it now. If you contact him in any way, you will be considered an accessory to whatever crimes he may have committed. Do you understand, young lady?"

The hysterical office worker shook her head, agreeing, and taking a deep breath, she scribbled Pierre Bergeron's home address on a piece of paper and handed it over to Volsgaard.

At the same moment, in Frankfurt's national bus terminal, a portly, aging, Bergeron had just handed the driver his ticket to Munich. He lifted the two large, bulging leather briefcases—the best that his company manufactured, and hobbled down the aisle to an empty seat.

His plan was to lay low in the Bavarian city, find an underground means of fleeing Germany, and maybe go to Austria—maybe Switzerland, maybe even the Balkans—and live off his small retirement fortune.

However, the sweet period was finally over. He wondered what would happen to Wurtzmuller as a result of the investigation. They had agreed: in the end, it would be every man for himself. The gentle vibration of the bus motor calmed the old salesman he removed his fedora and placed it on the seat. He sighed, watching traffic pass in the opposite direction. He had escaped.

Hilda Luftheiser went back to the ransacked office after the unannounced visit. She was afraid to enter, but she did. Amidst all the force and bravado of the soldiers, they had been too focused on Bergeron and did not consider any clues that may have helped.

The young woman picked up the note she had written from the anonymous caller one day earlier. It was still on the salesman's desk. Volsgaard had failed to see it or read it. The secretary located

Bergeron's abandoned cigarette lighter. She walked to the window, lit the evidence and dropped its ashes into the debris below.

The receptionist at the Frankfurt Leather Works was unaware that she just saved the lives of two strangers, Herman Wohl and Greta Junkwalter, 100 kilometers away in Furstenberg.

CHAPTER 31

The rusted and run-down dented bus from the metropolitan transportation system had been retired from hauling crowds through Berlin two years earlier. One week ago, however, it had been resurrected, inspected and cited to transport fourth-year medical students from the Charite University of Medicine to the five field hospitals that had been temporarily erected in order to handle the casualties from the Hamburg attacks.

The massive medical tent facilities were located in Noderstedt, Rahlstedt, Harburg, Bergedorf and Lubeck—five cities adjacent to the destroyed metropolis.

The Lubeck field hospital, the destination for this group, was erected on the grounds of an old convent, St. Gertrude's, about twelve kilometers northeast of the Elbe River and the bombed city. The students, all too eager to leave the classroom and practice actual medicine, were ordered there by a direct mandate from Hitler himself—a sign that a tired Germany seemed desperate and was handling important, domestic matters, using unqualified personnel. Dr. Joseph Lowderstern, teacher and supervisor for the group of medical plebes, directed the driver to stop in Schwerrin, before the last segment of the journey to Lubeck.

Running through the pouring rain that began during the previous night, the students made their way to a general store and bakery. Some relieved themselves in the municipal building toilets across from the city square. The driver threatened to leave anyone behind who was not back on the bus in thirty minutes.

"Excuse me, sir, one of the young men said that this was a busload of physicians, is that true?" a woman asked as she held an umbrella close to her head, trying to keep it from inverting its protective arch. "Well yes, you could say that," the teacher answered, thinking the woman was going to request some advice pertaining to a personal illness.

He remained inside the bus, protected from the hard drive of the Baltic storm.

"I do not like to be unchristian, but there is an extremely indigent-looking woman, lying under a tree in the park. I told her to move, but she advised me that she had been drugged and raped at least eight times yesterday by a group from a harvest festival. She says that she is a director of women guards at a facility in Furstenberg, near Schwedt.

"She said some escapees sold her to a group of transient workers and they raped her over and over. I think—no matter what happened, she needs medical attention. Perhaps you can offer some assistance and have her relocated to a hospital? It really does not look good for our town to have such characters occupying the public grounds."

"Do not dare leave without me, driver," the senior physician advised the impatient and grumpy chauffeur. "I am checking this out. If this is true, and the woman is a member of the military; we will bring her to the field hospital."

Dr. Lowderstern shared the woman's umbrella. They walked quickly to the area where Dorothy Boerner had been left in the pouring rain by a truck driver paid by the butcher, Borchweiss, to dump her somewhere.

"There she is, under a woolen army blanket. It is soaked. She needs medical attention," the woman advised, seeming more interested in the dispensing of the human eyesore than actually aiding or comfort.

"Who are you? Why are you here? Do you have any identification?" Lowderstern asked.

The Oberaufseherin retold her circumstance, omitting her own act of murder and slanting the abduction as one of victimization.

"Please, contact Ravensbruck Labor Camp in Furstenberg. Ask to speak with Major Fritz Suhren or Captain Bitten—they will vouch for me. I was kidnapped by several escapees. They sold me to rapists, who left me to die. Please help me. I will give you a military phone number to contact!"

The physician took a pad from his coat pocket and jotted the number Boerner recited. The woman told the doctor to enter the municipal building and inform her friend, Elsa Ruisch in room 101, that she advised him to use the phone for an emergency.

The older medic moved easier in the rain unprotected by her umbrella. He darted up the building stairs, found the inside room and requested cooperation so that he could make the call. Dictating the number to Elsa Ruisch and advising her that the emergency involved a female officer of the camp in case anyone asked, he managed to reach administration offices within ten minutes.

"Yes, I am a physician from Berlin. I am bringing a group of doctors to the field hospital in Lubeck. Would you want me to transport this woman to that location? She can travel with us. I will see that she is given immediate medical attention… Yes, she appears to be in shock. No, I cannot get her to this phone. She is outside in the pouring rain. She is quite weak. Okay, very good, we will probably arrive by noon."

Captain Horst Bitten, who took the call from his civilian secretary, immediately contacted Fritz Suhren and apprised him of the recent break in events.

"I am not contacting the CCI until we gain more information. It has only been twenty-four hours since we discovered Heinrich's body. I will wait until we get some answers. Hopefully, Dorothy Boerner can supply them."

Major Suhren was also informed by his young lieutenant that they had missed capturing Pierre Bergeron. The frustrated commandant ordered the officer and his two soldiers to return to Ravensbruck immediately. The twelve-hour journey suggested their arrival would be sometime late Tuesday evening.

"When Volsgaard returns, I am afraid he will now have to visit Dorothy Boerner in Lubeck. Hopefully, she will not escape before he gets there," he quipped to Captain Horst Bitten, who had been idly flipping the pages of a magazine that had just reviewed the best accordions available in the musical trade.

"We have to keep Heinrich's murder under our hat a few more days, Horst… For God's sake, put that damned book down! Act more like a Nazi officer than a musician for once in your life!"

Bitten threw the journal on a pile of papers, but once his commanding officer left for the room, he picked it up and studied the new line of Hohner's.

* * * * *

Flora stared at the six or seven cows that sought cover under a large grove of trees in the far section of land where they spent the evening. The rain continued all night and into the morning. The stationary bovine group seemed annoyed at the weather conditions as well. A bale of hay left mid-field was drenched and untouched by the animals. The storm, compliments of the Baltic Sea weather pattern, extended into Tuesday, detaining Isaac, Flora and Risa. They remained in the vacant farmhouse, hoping for a break in the weather.

Flora sided up to her husband with a coy grin of embarrassment, the afterglow resulting from their first night of lovemaking in three months.

"How much longer do you think we will have to stay in hiding?" she asked.

"The boy had said these storms could last for days. We just cannot travel in a jeep without a cover. But if it continues through tomorrow, I do not want to stay here. We will have to move on—take our chances with the car flooding. It is not good for us to be on 'the run' and not running. For now, the weather has us trapped, but we would look equally suspicious in soaked uniforms, travelling through a downpour with no shed. I will give it one more day."

Risa had found a Belgian whetstone in one of the kitchen drawers. She took the rectangular knife sharpener into her room behind the kitchen. There, on the bed, the Romani began to hone the new blade that she bartered for from the festival merchant a day earlier. Patiently, meticulously, the gypsy glided the knife across the hard surface, occasionally thumbing the results. Smiling as she checked both edges of the steel shaft, Risa Resto displayed as much affection for her weapon as Flora did for Isaac.

Nighttime fell on the abandoned farm. Once again, Isaac lit candles, keeping the flames from windows, to stay hidden from stray visitors. The three laid out their uniforms and bedded down, hoping for an early and dry evacuation in the morning.

* * * * *

At four-thirty a.m. Wednesday, the rains ceased. The cool air, still thick and humid feel, formed a dense fog, covering the farm. The couple, as well as Risa, had not awakened. However, two German soldiers, patrolling the area, were closing in on the farm. The men emerged from the shelter of a tractor garage, one kilometer up the road.

"Let us see if the boy was telling the truth, Roonskamf," the taller of the two began.

"If it has a jeep with a marking on its spare tire, then it definitely has to be the group Huberer's directive warned about."

The infantrymen, Roonskamf and Buchwald, headed down the treed lane on foot, their BMW Wermacht bike still parked safely within the farm tractor shed.

They came to the third piece of property—the farm cited by the boy, as the one the trio had taken for shelter during the Baltic rains. Buchwald, the leader, held his finger to his lips. From that moment on, they would only communicate using silent gestures.

The duo slopped through the muddy tire track approach to the farm house, raising rifles and tiptoeing as they neared the home. Roonskamf threw the tarp off the rear of the covered jeep, raising his eyebrows to his counterpart upon discovering the tire marking. Quietly, they climbed the three exterior wooden steps to the farm house door, hoping to avoid any creeks that would ruin their element of surprise.

Buchwald motioned, indicating that he would search the second floor. Roonskamf was to do the same on the first level. Turning the knob on the old door, they entered. The moon, which was erased from the sky for the past few evenings, at last provided partial light, enabling the two soldiers to see their way through the shaded and darkened rooms.

Buchwald, with rifle extended, slowly ascended the rustic stairway and climbed to the upper level, where Isaac and Flora remained asleep in the main bedroom. Roonskamf peered into the living room and dining area. Assessing that it was empty, the soldier walked around to the bedroom behind the kitchen and discovered Risa under a blanket, sleeping on her back. He then noticed the Gestapo uniform draped over a chair, displaying the familiar red, black and white, swastika emblem. With rifle now at strike position, Roonskamf moved closer.

Buchwald stood in full view of Isaac and Flora as they slept in a loving embrace—they welcomed the much-needed sleep after the past few hectic days. Buchwald took note to the officer's uniform that hung on the closet door, but he failed to clear a table; knocking over its contents to the floor. The sudden noise startled Isaac. The couple awoke to an immediate awareness of their grave situation.

"Roonskamf, I have found the imposters! Up here, he has a captain's uniform. Roonskamf!"

The muffled answer from the lower level assured Buchwald that his partner was equally occupied.

"You are both under arrest, and I have been given orders to kill if given reason. State your names."

Isaac complied, identifying both he and Flora to the excited soldier. Flora recoiled, naked, into her husband's arms. Losing her breath, panting hysterically.

"Stop it, lady, or I will shoot! Roonskamf, can you get up here? I swear! I was given no reason to keep you alive!"

The distracted soldier moved back and forth, trying to communicate with his partner while holding the bedded couple in a captured position.

"Roonskamf!"

Nervous about his cohort' silence, Buchwald aimed his rifle and prepared to squeeze the trigger.

"I do not care if you people stay alive. Who wants to die first? I am a gentleman, so, you—lady—do you want to go first? Ahh, Roonskamf! You are here—just in time to see the completion of our mission."

The harried Private Buchwald, never losing sight of his victims, pulled the trigger and a shot rang throughout the farmhouse, echoing out to the green pastures, stirring the livestock, which had risen and had begun to move about in shower-free daylight.

CHAPTER 32

Private Sigmund Roonskamf had proceeded through the downstairs bedroom with caution. The body asleep in the bed appeared to be slight, perhaps a woman. He approached the blanketed victim and listened as the gentle rhythm of breathing suggested a state of sleep.

Risa Resto had actually awakened on hearing the soldiers' footsteps in the kitchen. Knowing that a startled offensive act on her part might lead to an impromptu gunshot, she played possum instead as the soldier approached. It was still dark. The Romani woman squinted, keenly seeing every move that Roonskamf made.

She noted when the trooper moved his rifle to one hand, holding the forestock with his left, the barrel facing the ceiling. His right hand was clearly off the trigger and reaching to pull the covers away from her. It seemed too easy for the street-smart gypsy from Bucharest. A thought raced through her mind, *This man is a professional? Never take your finger off the trigger!*

As the infantryman came within arm's distance, Risa pulled the soldier's neck toward her. This aided in the raising of her upper torso. The ten-centimeter, newly sharpened blade of her hunting knife penetrated her own blanket; as well as Roonskamf's uniform, chest, heart, lung, stopping only when it rested on the anterior portion of his vertebrae. He died in an instant, falling without a sound, atop of her thin body.

When Risa heard the soldier in Isaac and Flora's room, shouting his partner's name, she pushed the dead Roonskamf off her bed and on to the floor. The vigilant Romani, hunting knife in hand and arm dripping with blood, quietly climbed the farmhouse stairway. The blood-stained blade faced out and downward as it extended from Risa's palm, with her thumb securely positioned on the bottom of its bone handle.

As the already engaged infantryman, Buchwald welcomed what he thought was Roonskamf to view Flora's execution, Risa had instead plunged the knife from behind—Roman centurion style—through the clavicle opening between his neck and shoulder. The downward motion severed the soldier's aorta. The gun rang out, and the serviceman's bullet lodged into the bedroom ceiling. Flora shuddered into her husband's arms as they watched Risa Resto appear behind the fallen German.

"You were expecting Roonskamf?" the gypsy quipped in a morbid, matter-of-fact tone.

Isaac shot out of bed and hurried to the fallen infantryman.

"Help me remove his uniform. They are on to our charade. He knew that I was wearing the disguise of a captain. I must now be a common private. Quick, Flora—get his boots off. I want the uniform before it is soaked in blood. Risa—get back into your Gestapo outfit. Flora—you find a dress from the farm closet. We cannot stay in our former uniforms. Risa—it may be good if we parted. I will give you money. Perhaps we can meet together at a later date."

"No, no Isaac—she must remain with us. She just saved our lives. We will need her. I told you that she would be an asset to our escape," she begged as she removed the dead soldier's second boot.

"No Flora, Isaac is right," Risa conceded. "We are even. You saved my life back at Ravensbruck, and just now, I saved yours. I have paid my debt. It is time I leave. Besides, I would rather die in Romania than live free in the Baltic. I mean, that is where you are headed, right?" she shrugged. "Let us just get out of here fast. We can discuss our fate in the jeep."

The three assembled at Wurtzmuller's vehicle within a few minutes. Isaac threw the two duffle bags in to the back storage area. They took their seats—now as a soldier, an SS policeman and a female civilian.

The tarp had protected the motor as well as the interior cushioning and dashboard panel. They drove up the muddy path and headed north, once again, 38 kilometers from the Denmark border. Isaac had only driven a few hundred meters when they passed the open tractor shed, where the two servicemen ditched their BMW sidecar motorbike.

"Stop, Stop!" Risa yelled.

"That must have been there transportation!" Isaac surmised.

"Not anymore," she laughed as she leapt from the back seat. "Eureka! The key is still in the ignition. They must have helped themselves to the farmer's gasoline as well. The tank is full."

"You can drive such a machine?" Flora asked the woman who had just saved her life.

"Are you kidding? We used to steal these bikes from the Nazis when they began occupying Bucharest. When no one was around, at two o'clock in the morning, we would park them in front of the Gestapo barracks and set them up into flames—but not until we filled the sidecar with dog shit!"

Bowing his head, Isaac smiled, while Flora wiped tears and laughed at the remark.

"I guess this is where we say 'goodbye', Risa sighed, tilting her head toward her bunkmate, smiling. It was a melancholic moment, ending in a tearful hug. They had crammed thirty years of sisterly affection into ten short weeks of hell. Their meeting was the only good that had come from the situation. Yet they knew that having gained one another's acquaintance was not worth a single day of life at Ravensbruck.

Isaac retrieved the canvas duffle bag where he had stowed bands of Swiss francs and German Reichsmarks. Grateful to Risa for saving their lives, he handed her a healthy sum of both currencies.

"We are forever grateful to you for your bravery just now. I understand your desire to go back home. Unfortunately, Flora and I have been forced to leave ours."

Risa accepted the small fortune, throwing the stacks of paper money into the sidecar.

"I wonder how much will be left after I am forced to bribe all the bastards I will meet on my way to Bucharest?"

She hugged Isaac and then took Flora's hands, looking into her eyes.

"You have helped me discover inner pride and dignity—something I never thought I had. I will never forget you, Flora, for as long as I live. Good luck with your escape."

As a tear rolling down Flora's cheek was evidence of her inward response, though she tried to be stoic, she had tender words for her Romani friend.

"And I thank you, for giving me the strength to deal with all the negativity and personal defeat that the camp threw in our faces—especially when told about Isaac's murder. If not for you, I would have died of a broken heart."

The gypsy straddled the motorbike, turned the key, kick-started the BMW vehicle and guided the machine from the shed on to the road. Turning in the opposite direction of where they had been heading, Risa Resto kissed her palm, rubbed it on Flora's cheek and began a journey that she hoped would lead to her destination, Romania.

Looking on, Isaac put his arm around Flora and squeezed his wife's shoulder. Flora gazed back at him and smiled.

"There she goes—just another Gestapo courier… in search of freedom."

CHAPTER 33

Goerthe had spent the two stormy days depressed and angry after losing the trail of Heinrich Wurtzmuller's jeep. After going through a large sum of his money in the bars of Kiel, the criminal combed the streets of the port city in search of the monogrammed spare tire.

Unsuccessful, the hired killer decided to head back to Furstenberg, optimistic that Dorothy Boerner would have to return soon. He located the stolen BMW that he parked in the alley two days earlier and began his journey south.

St. Gertrude's Benedictine convent in Lubeck had sat idle for the last eight years. The monastic order had been making a local soft cheese to support its existence since the 1800s. Situated in dairy country, the nuns' business had been a natural means for taking in a modest income that helped the religious community survive. Their cheese was good, so the entire Baltic community accepted the product as a valid and necessary commodity to the Lubeck economy.

In 1935, however, the Nazi government took control of the convent and its two hundred-acre farm, forcing the twenty-six women to seek other venues to follow their beliefs and spreading the religious message of the thirteenth-century Gertrude of Helfta.

Three months earlier, the convent's brick building and adjacent land were selected as one of the field hospital sites that the Reich would temporarily erect to treat victims of the Hamburg bombings. They constructed sixteen circus-type tents in the nearby city of Lubeck, for temporary medical purposes. Within forty-eight hours of the first allied mission over the industrial metropolis, it seemed the field had sprouted giant mushrooms—a large, billowing pole-and-canvas hospital was treating nearly five hundred wounded a day.

En route to Furstenberg on late Wednesday morning, Goerthe passed the surreal medical facility, the brick convent being dwarfed by the temporary white city that blossomed from the side of the nunnery. When the dejected villain came to the fork in the road, he chose the route "Berlin, and all points south." He could not believe the size of the effort, the activity and the number of motor vehicles parked on the grass lot in front of the first row of tents. The visitors had even defined the patient demographic: one side of the grass was for civilian autos; while the other side was for military jeeps and troop transports. The scene was impressive and unfortunate at the same time.

Goerthe slowed to let an ambulance pull into the gravel driveway. Bored from the delay, the vagrant gazed toward the military section of the hospital parking field.

"Oh my God!" he shouted from within his own vehicle. Parked on the front row of army jeeps—he could not believe his eyes, was the monogrammed "W" of Captain Wurtzmuller's vehicle. He had been unsure if the woman in the aufseherin uniform was Dorothy Boerner, but as he pulled into the area behind the second ambulance, he knew he was about to find out.

The villain guided the stolen BMW into an empty slot, hopped out and ran over to the captain's jeep. He had not been as close since the night in the cornfield, when Wurtzmuller explained the assassination plans for Olga Deitzl and Dorothy Boerner. It was indeed the officer's vehicle—the same jeep he had followed for a hundred kilometers earlier in the week. A surge of adrenalin rifled through the old man's body, as he was began to feel better about completing the second part of his contract.

Revitalized, the criminal headed toward the main tent opening. Passing an outdoor group of injured civilians and army veterans, Goerthe bounced along, initiating a conversation with the line of wheelchair victims.

"Good day, gentlemen. Can I ask if anyone saw who might have come out of that particular army jeep, earlier—the one that has the large 'W' symbol written across the spare tire?"

An elderly dual amputee, wearing a veteran's army cap, volunteered an answer.

"Yes sir—a soldier and a young woman—a pretty little thing. I remember because of her dark, dark, hair and bright blue eyes. Pretty, she was."

"Was the man an officer?" Goerthe asked.

"No, no—just an infantryman. They took their belongings and ran inside rather quickly," the old man answered while boosting his torso higher in the chair. "They did not speak to us, but I did not see them leave."

"And we see everything!" another added, as the row of seven veterans all broke into laughter.

Goerthe nodded before entering a maze of canvassed bedlam and chaotic frenzy.

The floor within the tent was laid planks of oak, creating a roadway of level surfaces, allowing easy passage for wheeled gurneys and chairs. Actual working areas were still atop pastures of green grass. The wooden flooring made the search easy for Goerthe, who followed the timbered path to the next medical tent.

* * * * *

Isaac and Flora settled in the area that had been designated as the cafeteria and supply depot of the St. Gertrude Field Hospital. They thought the confusion of the harried emergency facility would offer anonymity before their journey, north.

"We can blend in to the faceless chaos this place offers," Isaac pointed out. "So far, the only danger we faced was seeking full concealment in the farm house. Public arenas seem to be more protective. I will get you some coffee from the counter, and then we can figure out our next move. You sit on the floor. Do not leave the sacks unattended, whatever you do. I will be right over there," he said, nodding toward the table with cakes and three large urns of beverages.

Flora tried not to stare as several blood-ridden gurneys passed through the supply tent atop the highway of oak planking in front of her. Moans and the flailing arms assured her that the victims were in a far worse place than she and Isaac were. Yet these people were injured by the enemy, but she and Isaac were running from their own country and government. It seemed the Nazis sought no defined enemy. Everyone was their foe. Nevertherless, she knew it would not be long before she and Isaac would be in a life-threatening confrontation. Isaac returned with her coffee.

"Flora, I noticed there is an area behind those linen screens where the hospital staff is entering and changing into new uniforms. See—those nurses who just emerged from the area—their white clothes were stained with blood, but now they are exiting all fresh and clean."

Flora noticed portable shower pipes, exposed above the dressing area—an option for staff members to regain composure and a chance to sanitize before their next shift.

"I think our disguise should take a new look," Isaac suggested. "When the area is empty, you rush in and find a nurse uniform. Discard the clothes you are wearing. I will stay with our bags. When you are in the new disguise and return, I will then do the same."

It took several minutes to complete their identity transformation. Isaac, dressed as an ambulance driver, approved of his wife's metamorphosis from farm girl to krankenschwester.

"We will walk out of here, find an idle ambulance on the grass lot where we entered earlier—one with a key in the ignition, and leave freely amidst the upheaval and confusion of this place."

They assembled their two sacks of valuables and supplies, with Isaac carrying the heavier. As they passed through the supply tent to the adjoining surgical station, two women, both on stretchers, who seemed to have been forgotten, cried to Flora for help to ease their pain. Guilty though focused, Flora ignored the pleas and hurried toward the first canvas medical unit, which had been the official entrance to the Lubeck field hospital.

As the couple reached the midpoint of the second "circus-like edifice," they cowered as a howl bellowed over the din. The shrill came from the far side of the tent, but had all heads turned in the couple's direction. It happened again, and this time Isaac heard a more audible message.

"Stop them! Someone stop them. They are kidnappers! They sold me to rapists! They killed a Schutzstaffel captain! Do not let them get away—they are killers."

Dorothy Boerner, the hysterical aufseherin, had been admitted one day earlier, compliments of Dr. Louderstern and the medical student group from Berlin. She screamed, hoping that someone would find credence to her frantic request.

"You! You—calm this patient! She is having a delusional seizure!" an administrating nurse called to an army medic. "Restrain her. Tie her hands to her chair." She filled a syringe with an unknown agent and threw it to the medic. "You inject her. I am too busy here."

The elderly man, wearing a white full-length lab coat of a field hospital medic, caught the open-needle syringe in a clean terrycloth towel. Smiling back at the busy administrator, the charlatan practitioner, Willhelm Goerthe responded.

"It will be my pleasure."

CHAPTER 34

Whatever sedative that the portly krankenschwester boss flipped to Goerthe was discarded into a nearby waste basket by the excited criminal. Finally, he had caught up with his mark—the second part of his payday. But first, *what do you mean those people killed a Shutzstaffel captain?* That remark caught his interest. *Who are they, anyway?*

"I had visited Captain Wurtzmuller to discuss business," her lie began. "They are escapees who burst into his house on Sunday, shot the captain, kidnapped me and sold me to rapists. They stole much money and valuables from his chalet. They drugged me, but I heard everything. They are trying to get to Scandinavia."

"You said they stole money from the officer… and killed him?"

"Yes! Yes, you fool—get them before they escape!" the wild Boerner shreiked at her nemesis.

Goerthe pulled out his third packet, housing a disposable phenyl syringe. He ripped the acetate bag with his teeth, bit off the protective plastic needle cover, adjusted the presently less attractive chief overseer's body so she faced the wall, and in a cold blooded manner, he injected the chief aufeherin in her jugular.

Instantaneously, the overseer's body slumped in her wheelchair, lifeless. Her heart had stopped before the empty syringe landed in the waste pail. The seasoned killer then directed his effort to finding the couple before they escaped with the money and valuables Dorothy Boerner claimed they had stolen.

* * * * *

The right side of the graveled driveway was reserved for the angled parking of military ambulances. Most vehicles arrived with wounded or with rerouted burn victims from the other area field hospitals. Some of the medical transports were serviced by the motor pool, fueled and were sitting idle, available for the eight-kilometer journey back to Hamburg.

Inconspicuous, Isaac tried to check the cab dashboards for keys that may have been left in the ignition. He was checking the sixth one when he met with success. The window was down, so he grabbed the chain that was dangling from the ignition slot. After securing their new mode of transportation, he circled back to the dual panel doors that opened vertically. Pulling the handle down, he swung the door on its hinges, sticking his head inside.

The ambulance had been a common, Phenomen Granite—equipped to transport four patients. The stretchers were attached to the side walls. The center portion presented a space for the attendant or krankenschwester to tend to any one patient, or all at the same time.

Isaac helped Flora up and into the back of the medical vehicle and then threw the two canvas sacks that had survived their escape atop one of the stretchers.

"You stay safely back here. We will drive on the main road, going north. We are now about twenty-two kilometers from the border. I will lie to any guard who stops us, and say we are being relocated to Denmark. My only fear is that they will report this ambulance missing and notify the nearby checkpoints. But if security is anything like this field hospital, we should be okay for the next few hours."

Flora positioned herself on the lower stretcher that was suspended from the right inner wall. She could see the back of her husband's head as Isaac took control of the wheel. A chain link pattern of metal separated the driving cab from the patient area, so they would be able to converse freely.

As Isaac put the Phenomen Granite in reverse, he observed a blast of light enter the otherwise dark interior of the rear section of the ambulance. Flora screamed as the back door slammed closed and a voice intruded.

"Get out of here fast. Do as I say or I kill the girl!"

Goerthe forced himself into the vehicle, clenching one arm around Flora's delicate neck as he held something to it.

"I just killed the overseer with this poison needle. Your nurse gets it as well if you try anything funny," he warned Isaac while lifting his arm and elbow to reveal the syringe.

"I am warning you—this kills in an instant," he said, reinforcing the threat.

"Take it easy, please," Isaac pleaded. "I know what you have in your hand. I will give you my full cooperation. Please do not injure the girl. What do you want from us? Who are you?"

Isaac had never met the vagrant and had no knowledge of his association with Wurtzmuller. The nervous old man pressed the needle so close to Flora's skin that she yelped as its point broke the skin of her slender neck. *So close was lethal poison to entering her body!*

"Get out of here, turn south then stop at the first chance you get."

Isaac stopped at the end of the driveway, facing the direction he was ordered; afraid that a sudden road bump would be fatal to his wife.

"I am stopped, please—not so close with the needle point. Why are you doing this?"

From the windowless back portion of the Phenomen, Isaac could make out shadows as he looked over his shoulder through the iron lattice partition.

"Who are you and what do you want?" he asked.

"The overseer said that you took money and valuables from Wurtzmuller's house after you killed him. Show me what is in the bags," he demanded, kicking one closer to Flora, keeping a hold on the woman's neck. "Open it! Let me see its contents."

"We did not kill anyone. She is the one who did the killing. She shot the captain in the head. I lived with him as his helper. I went into the prison, under a disguise, rescued my wife and we are trying to escape to the north. That is the truth."

"Hey Mister, I do not care who you are or what you did," Goerthe sneered in that moment Flora showed him several bundles of the money. "Okay, which way are we facing?" the he asked, assuring Isaac that he had no sense of direction—especially in the rear of a windowless van.

"We are facing north, right now," Isaac said, lying.

"I thought I said to head south!" Goerthe shouted.

"I don't know. There is a sign in front of me that says, 'Kiel–six kilometers,' Isaac answered, confusing the old man.

"Then turn here—head south, back to Furstenberg," he ordered.

"Sure, just be careful with that needle. I was in charge of ordering them for Wurtzmuller. They are quite lethal. I am no threat with an iron bar between us."

Isaac turned north and the direction they had been following all along.

"We may come to a checkpoint. I want to make sure you know how you will handle that moment," he continued, trying to distract Goerthe's attemtion from his wife.

"I will worry about that if it should happen," Goerthe snapped back. "How much money is in the sacks?"

"We do not know. After the overseer shot the officer, I saw an opportunity to escape and I acted on it. We did not kill Wurtzmuller. You have to believe that."

"Hey, I do not *care* who killed that bastard, but it seems you just made me a lot more money than he offered me. And now I can still live in Furstenberg and not be on the run."

Isaac knew Goerthe was an unscrupulous man. In fact it was proven every moment the husband looked at his wife in a neck hold fearing that she was only centimeters from death.

In a windowless compartment, Goerthe pondered a strategy heading south as the vehicle drove north.

* * * * *

"What do you mean she is dead?" Volsgaard scolded the head nurse who had presented him with Dorothy Boerner's death certificate. "She supposedly endured multiple rapes and was left to die. She is brought here to receive attention, and she dies under your care? This is negligence and incompetence! I want to know what happened!" he barked in his best impersonation of Major Suhren—after his unsuccessful visit to Pierre Bergeron's office.

"The report indicates 'cardiac arrest,'" the heavy krankenschwester answered, reading from the form. "I do remember telling a medic to give her a sedative. She was hysterical. She was accusing a driver and nurse for killing someone and selling her to be raped. Soon after the medic sedated her, an aid reported her death. It was only about a half hour later. Do you want the death certificate?"

"Yes, where is the medic who gave her the sedative?" he asked.

"You think I even remember what he looked like? Hmm… he was old—I know that."

"And the ambulance driver and nurse that she accused of those actions?"

"I don't know, Lieutenant. Look at this place. I cannot even get a bite to eat while I am here. The couple she was yelling at appeared to be leaving. Maybe someone saw where they were going?"

Desperate, Volsgaard ran through the tent and out to the chaotic front lawn of St Gertrude's. He saw no white-coated driver with a nurse amidst the confusion. He approached the seven older gentlemen. It was the same group that had greeted Goerthe and had observed Isaac and Flora earlier.

"Hello gentlemen, I hope you are feeling well this afternoon," the Lieutenant began. "I was wondering if you may have seen a medic or ambulance driver leave with a nurse some time ago."

"Only about twenty-five times a day," the amputee, who seemed to be the spokesperson of the group followed in a wise tone. "This is a hospital. What do you think?" he added, obviously unimpressed with the young officer." We see lots of men in white uniforms and nurses walking together." The other six patients laughed at his brash response.

"Sorry sir. Are you a veteran?" Volsgaard asked, a bit more respectfully.

"Verdun, First World War," he responded with pride. "Now you may want to ask if we saw anything strange, involving a nurse, a driver or a medic?"

"Okay, yes. If you did, it would be helping my search greatly… one military man to another."

"See that jeep over there?" the keen old observer began. Volsgaard's jaw dropped after he turned to see where the man was pointing. Wurtzmuller's monogrammed jeep was plainly in sight! How could he have missed it?

"Yes sir, I see it now."

"A soldier and a woman came in that jeep a few hours ago, they went inside but surfaced later, dressed as you inquired—he as an ambulance driver and she as a nurse. They studied several parked medical transports and finally selected a Phenomen Granite, and as they were leaving, another man in a lab coat hopped into the patient section, along with the nurse."

"You are sure that it was the group who came in that jeep; the one with the "W"? Volsgaard insisted, pushed his limit with the veteran.

"I did not say that. I said the couple came in the jeep. She was quite pretty, you know. I am old, but I can still recognize a pretty woman." His friends chuckled at his anecdotes. "The other fellow—the one in the lab coat, seemed to force himself into the ambulance. And not for the reasons someone takes a pretty girl into the back of an ambulance. I do not think he was a friend of theirs."

"What do you mean? For what reasons?" Volsgaard asked, perplexed.

"Come on, Lieutenant—the times haven't changed that much, have they? Everyone knows a military ambulance is a mobile brothel, when not in use," the elder answered, causing his friends to snicker.

"Which way did they go?" Volsgaard asked, ignoring the racy commentary.

"North—probably to the border," the old man volunteered with conviction.

"How do you know that?"

"Because when the driver helped the nurse into the patient section, I heard him say to her, 'it is about twenty-two kilometers to the border.' I may be old, Lieutenant, but I still have my hearing."

"Yes sir. Yes, you do. I wish we had men like you serving the Reich during this war effort. That is for sure."

After Volsgaard stepped back and saluted the elder with a "Sieg Heil!" the legless informant sat tall in his wheeled chair and responded with a salute.

CHAPTER 35

The border checkpoint vehicle line on the main highway outside of Flensburg had grown to nearly one kilometer long—twice the length of the pedestrian cues. The guards turned most of vehicles away, despite angry drivers and cars, popping with all their earthly belongings. Fearing more northern raids from allied forces, some nationals thought it would be acceptable to relocate in the German occupied state of Denmark. Recent lines of desperate civilians were growing. For every group, or vehicle that was allowed to cross the Jutland border, twenty-five were turned back.

Isaac sat in the crawling motor cue, barely moving forward. He did not want to jump his place, for fear it would bring attention to an inspection of the back compartment of their ambulance. He could see Goerthe in the rear view mirror, still grasping Flora around the neck with his left arm as the right held the chemical weapon to her neck.

"Where are we now?" the old villain shouted up to the disguised ambulance driver. "We have been traveling for about two hours."

"We are just coming into the city of Mecklenburg," Isaac lied.

"Mecklenburg, I saw that town on the way coming up here. That is about one seventy-five kilometers still to Furstenberg. Why the big delay?"

"We are facing the heaviest security area that I have witnessed since our journey began," Isaac answered. "Perhaps we can request emergency military courtesy to speed things up."

"Do not raise their suspicions—if you care about your wife's safety, that is," Goerthe warned.

Isaac did not want the killer to discover that they were actually traveling north, near the Danish/German border, just outside of Flensburg. If the killer discovered the betrayal, he would surly execute Flora.

"If I see a guard along the road, I will I will ask for preferred status and request to be rushed through. Are you in agreement?"

"Just as long as they do not come back here... If they do, you will be widowed!"

"Listen," Isaac reasoned, "if they decide to inspect the patient area, you should lie on a stretcher, under a cover, and at least look ill.

They won't want to get close to anyone sick or injured. You can still hold my wife's hand under the sheet, if that is so important to you. And should we get in trouble, you do as well. So why are you so worried about killing my wife? If guards realize something is wrong, we are all going to get killed for impersonating medics, whether you inject her or not."

"Just keep driving. Try to get through this shit quickly, okay? And do not preach to me about who will die and who will not. After we get through this checkpoint, I may release you. If you are lucky, I may even spare your wife, but I am not going to free you together. It will be up to you to find her," Goerthe laughed. "I can drive this truck also. In the meantime, no funny stuff, or I will inject this poison right into her neck, okay?"

The unmoving traffic added to the tension in the ambulance. Isaac could see the familiar sight of checkpoint guards in the distance, pre-inspecting the vehicles, ordering immediate turnarounds and answering the questions of impatient drivers. He grabbed a clip board from the front seat, turned a 'patient inquiry' form over to its blank side, and began writing a note.

"There are guards walking through the lines," he apprised Goerthe. "They are ordering drivers out of their cars, and looking for stowaways or something. I am going to have to get out of the vehicle," he whispered back. "Now would be the time to get on a stretcher under a blanket and look ill."

"You *know* what will happen if you try anything stupid!" the old criminal, warned, grabbing Flora's wrist while holding the loaded syringe to her arm. "Convince this guy not to snoop any more than he has to." That's your job!" he called as he settled down onto the lower left stretcher.

Isaac met the rifle-toting, guard at the front hood of the Phenomen Granite. Before he could say anything the soldier pulled him to the side of the road, and spoke in a low steady tone so none of the civilian drivers could hear him and take advantage of his directions.

"We are sending all military vehicles to the checkpoint situated on the Baltic Shore Road. It is about three kilometers east of here. No civilians even know that it exists. You will have no wait. Pass into Denmark. Drive for ten kilometers, turn left and you can continue on a major highway. Take the road just behind you, here. "You do not want to stay in this line, believe me. Take my advice and you will cross the border in seconds. The booths there are empty all of the time."

Isaac decided not to present his clipboard note to the guard. He would take his chances at the less-frequented border passage. The uneventful return to the ambulance would also win the trust he sought from Goerthe.

"The checkpoint soldier is letting us pass onto a military line with no traffic. He said that with any luck, we would be in the Furstenberg area by noon tomorrow," he continued in the lie.

The lateral direction change took only a minute. As Isaac drove the ambulance through the changing seaside terrain, he felt the looming severity of the upcoming border inspection. Where the road pavement ceased, sandy soil, as well as large, three-meter reeds, created a mazelike path down to the banks of the Baltic Sea. It almost felt surreal.

As the Phenomen Granite came to a clearing, they came to the perpendicular Shore Road cradling the Baltic's edge. The giant saltwater vegetation stalks created a canyon-like gauntlet as the dwarfed ambulance slowed up to the isolated checkpoint.

The soldier on the highway was correct. The less-frequented booth was manned by two German soldiers. Both appeared annoyed that a military vehicle arrived, to which they had to respond. Isaac whispered back to Flora and Goerthe.

"Stay still. They may want to search the back compartment. You keep covered. I will get us through the gate. Whatever you do, sir, remain calm."

He left the driver's seat and summoned the two guards to return to the booth area. Holding his index finger to his lips, Isaac handed the clipboard to the closest guard. The note on it read:

> "I am from St Gertrude Field Hospital. My nurse is being held hostage by a madman mental patient. He is holding a syringe of deadly serum under the covers in the back of the ambulance. He will kill her if you or I disrupt his escape. Please do not startle him. She is my girlfriend. I do not know what to do. We were on our way to transport a patient from Denmark back to Lubeck. Please do something, but you must protect my nurse. He is crazy!"

Once again, Isaac put his finger to his lips and continued to speak, as a distraction.

"How many kilometers to the next big city"?

"Only about twenty-two," the leader of the two responded in a loud voice. "Are you transporting any patients today?

"Can we take a look?" the other followed.

"Just an injured man. My nurse is back there with him," Isaac answered, hoping that Goethe internalized his remarks as a benign clue to prepare for an inspection.

"Very well. Let me see, driver—please open the doors."

Isaac was impressed at the theatrical prowess of the guards. He unlatched the vertical hatch and swung the doors open. The soldier with rifle in hand, barely outranking the other, stood on the back step of the Phenomen Granite.

"Nurse, please exit. I need to ask if you have any aspirin. We have run out, and I have been experiencing some major headaches."

Flora looked with fear in her eyes. She tried to comply and leave Goerthe's grasp, but he would not let go.

"Nurse, you can return to your patient momentarily. You must have medicine, at least aspirin, somewhere in this vehicle, no?"

He could see the concealed arm of Flora and her non-responsive behavior, verifying that the man was holding her beneath the cover. The guard tugged at her other elbow.

"Come on, now. I am not going to hurt you."

Flora felt the point of the syringe enter her forearm. She closed her eyes and swallowed. The only thing separating her from life and death was an accidental quiver in Goerthe's thumb.

"Now, now what is wrong? All I want is two aspirin. If you…"

Goerthe sprung from his supine position and jammed the entire dose of fluid from the deadly syringe into the chest of the young guard. At the same moment, the soldier' partner, waiting at the side of the ambulance, presented his rifle and fired into Wilhelm Goerthe's face.

The madman fell from his perched position on the stretcher and rolled onto Flora. The second guard rushed to the aid of his fallen cohort, but to no avail. His death was chemically induced, almost immediately.

"Help me get him to the ground," the frazzled guard begged Isaac as he bent over his buddy, attempting to locate a vital response.

Isaac looked at Flora for forgiveness of what was about to happen. She returned it with an understanding that she would. They both knew what had to be done.

"I am calling the command center to get someone over here" the guard said. "Both of you stay put."

"Wait!" Isaac shouted, "I am sure I just saw him move."

He seemed to be trying to revive the still body of the dead soldier.

"What? Are you sure?"

The guard responded by kneeling again over his friend's body and slapping his face, as he had seen done in the movies. Picking up the unattended firearm by its barrel, Isaac swung in a chopping motion, attempting to knock the soldier unconscious. The soldier moved slightly forward at the last instance so that the butt of the rifle crushed the guard's first three cervical vertebrae. After the young private collapsed onto the body of his partner, Isaac recognized the cold, glossy, blank stare of death in his eyes. He had just killed a man.

"Oh my God, Isaac! Is he dead?" Flora screamed. "What are we going to do?"

"We are going to cross the border and get out of here. That is what we are going to do. Take the stretchers off their racks. Help me!" Isaac ordered, trying to remain calm. "We will move the bodies over the road and dump them into the reeds along the water edge."

They removed the cot-like framed beds from the rear compartment—first moving Goerthe's body and then those of the checkpoint soldiers.

"We may have only seconds. Hurry!"

Flora strained to help carry the cots as best she could. Walking deep into the wall of grassy stalks, they dropped the bodies, stretchers and all, amidst the marsh-like forest of vegetation.

"Lift up the reeds. Try to hide the bodies from the road," Isaac ordered.

When they finished hiding the bodies, Isaac told Flora to raise the border gate, which she did, putting all her force on the counterweight portion of the bar. As the pole lifted to the sky, Isaac started the Phenomen Granite engine and moved their escape vehicle officially into Denmark. With Flora safely inside, they continued on the Shore Road, heading for the fishing town of Sonderborg.

CHAPTER 36

Ditmar Klitzenhaus, commander of the Feldgendarmerie police unit of Flensburg, was making his final daily routine check of the outer regions. Occasionally he would find a vehicle in distress or an unruly drunken fisherman, taking advantage of the freedom offered by the Shore Road's desolated environment. That day was quite different.

Klitzenhaus, an officer with the Wermacht's only approved civilian police force within the Reich, had just driven from the hamlet of Norstadt to the remote Shore Road and Danish border. As the constable drove to within five hundred meters of the isolated checkpoint, the very spot that Isaac and flora had passed through a half hour earlier, his eye caught three schoolboys, darting into the waterline vegetation that separated the road and sea.

The police lieutenant, annoyed that his tour was nearly over, floored the accelerator to his Benz jeep and skidded to a roaring stop by the boys.

"You three, halt where you are—now! What in God's name are you doing?"

The trio, about nine years of age, obeyed the intimidating officer. They stopped in their tracks—one boy wearing a German soldier helmet, and the two others toting regulation army rifles.

The ones holding weapons dropped them instantly, while the other seemed reluctant to remove his helmet.

"Sir, we did not steal these—we found them. Really," the leader of the group volunteered. "We found them by the bodies, lying in the sea grass. Really!"

"What did you say? Show me!" Klitzenhaus ordered, knowing his day would now extend well into the evening. The lawman picked up the army rifles that the boys dropped, as all three climbed into the jeep. The policeman glided his car into the area of question, until one called out.

"Stop! There!"

"You three, stay in my car. If you run, I will find you, arrest you and put you into my jail. We won't call your parents. That is unless. We just send you to prison first."

One of the boys began to cry and only stopped when Klitzenhaus told him he would also send him to prison if he didn't stop crying.

"When did you find these bodies?" the lieutenant asked as he got out of the jeep and rolled his cuffs, midway to the knees.

"We were catching frogs in the marsh and spotted the bodies and cots in a pile. We just took the guns to play war. We did not hurt them, I swear."

Klitzenhaus waded with boots on, past the road and into the watery buffer of vegetation. Flies that had survived the early fall frost were displaying an attraction to the decomposing flesh, partially submerged at the base of the saltwater reeds. The policeman recognized the two dead guards. He had waved to them nearly every day on his rounds.

Who was the third older man in a lab coat? He sought identification from Goerthe's pocket, but there was nothing. And then there were stretchers. He deducted the three victims were killed and carried to the weeds. As Klitzenhaus removed his police cap and scratched his head, he heard an approaching noise and commanded the boys to stay put. A car motor was getting louder and coming from the same sandy road that Isaac had taken from the highway.

Appearing on the road from between the wall of three-meter sea stalks, Lt. Joseph Volsgaard's jeep was closing in on Isaac and Flora's trail. The junior Ravensbruck officer-turned-sleuth spotted the three remorseful lads and the Feldgendarmerie policeman.

Noticing an un-manned, border checkpoint crossing, the Nazi officer yelled to the law official.

"What do we have here? Where are the guards? Is all okay?" he asked, though he sensed all was not well.

"Hello sir, I'm Officer Ditmar Klitzenhaus of the Flensburg Feldgendarmerie. The boys have discovered three dead bodies, two of which, I am sorry to report, are the Wermacht soldiers that were manning the border point. There is a third medical man."

"Medical man, did you say?" Volsgaard asked, remembering the lead given him by the St. Gertrude amputee.

"Yes sir, you are the first to come by the crime scene. The boys discovered the bodies and several stretchers, lying in the marshes here. The medic seems to have been shot at point blank range and one soldier has a broken neck, I believe. There is no sign of injury, however to the other guard. I do not know how he died. This is quite terrible. I have always criticized the military for having this border point in such an isolated area. I have always expected something like this to happen, out here. Unfortunately, now it has."

The officer called to the boys.

"You three, go home. If you ever play with dead soldier's belongings again, I will have the three of you hanged by the necks."

The urchins departed, yelping screams of relief, disappearing into the maze of Glyceria sea stalks, all happy that their parents would not know of the incident.

Volsgaard approached to the place where the bodies lay, wading toward the murky grave site.

"We had an incident in Lubeck. Prison escapees killed a woman overseer and hijacked an ambulance. I have been following them for several hundred kilometers. Those stretchers tell me they were involved here. I will have to now extend my search into Denmark, but I must first document these murders to my superior. Tell me, do you have full communication resources up here? I need to contact Furstenberg in the Schwedt District."

Klitzenhaus was still looking for any other clues that might be useful.

"I will have to get a crew up here at once, before sunset. My office is only five minutes down the road. We have full military phone access. You can reach your supervisor from there quickly. I can promise you that."

"What is on the Danish side, sir, if he wants me to extend my pursuit into Denmark?" Volsguaard asked, seeming reluctant to travel into a whole new country.

"Flat, boring, scenic farmland and seashore," Klitzenhaus laughed, "filled with nice people who are scared shitless of Germans!"

CHAPTER 37

Flora was entranced with the late afternoon sun's reflection bouncing off the crests of the rough Baltic Sea swells. Glancing over, she could tell that her husband was struggling with the thought that he had killed a man. It showed in his watery eyes.

"Isaac, you did the right thing. They would have uncovered our charade in minutes. We would probably both be dead by now. If I told you how many people died daily in the camp at their hands—how many people were executed for no reason by them—I know it would not change your feelings right now, but you have to know you did the right thing."

There was no response from Isaac, who clenched the Phenomen Granite steering wheel, as the stress of the last two days began to erode his confidence. The fatigue was becoming overwhelming.

"What if we drive up to a road block that has been warned of our actions? We may be in the same situation as we were in the farm house."

Flora rubbed his shoulder, hoping to keep the discussion positive, nurturing.

"It is fifteen kilometers to the next major town. We will get close and abandon the ambulance. We'll walk there on foot, okay?"

She had no sooner made the suggestion that they rounded the jutting shoreline to encounter an isolated booth and a Nazi checkpoint guard, in the virtual center of *no man's land.*

* * * * *

"Boerner died of cardiac arrest? I find that hard to believe. But I cannot belabor this. I want the whole issue to go away. You do not know who this dead medic was?" Major Suhren asked Volsgaard.

"No sir," he answered on Kiltzenhaus' office telephone. "They cannot be too far into Denmark. If they are using the road that I think they may be, it is a very slow, sandy, shore road. The Danes refer to it as the Fjordvejen. My guess is that they are using it to stay hidden from the populated area."

"Just follow that road to the first town. If you are correct and find them—kill them. If you cannot, then turn back. Say nothing to anyone about them escaping Ravensbruck. I do not want the

Concentration Camp Inspectorate on my ass about that. I am going to release a statement to them that Wurtzmuller committed suicide. We will cremate his body today. They will not even know about Boerner. In any case, you are back here by Friday. This issue will be over. Do you understand?"

"Yes sir, Friday."

Volsgaard did not share a similar desire to pursue the matter any further. However, he followed that one last order and summoned Klitzenhaus, who was typing his report in the next room. He wanted to return to the murder scene.

The criminal unit of the Norstadt Felgendarmerie had picked up the three bodies by the time Volsgaard and Klitzenhaus reached the unmanned border booth. As they were lifting Wilhelm Gorthe's lifeless corpse into the rear panel of a common troop transport, Klitzenhaus called to his men.

"One of you—stay here until the main road division sends soldiers back to this booth. Lieutenant Volsgaard, you have about one more hour of sunlight, if you are on this road after night fall, be careful, because it can be tricky. One wrong turn or overreaction and you could be stuck in sand, immobilized. The next checkpoint booth is about seven kilometers away—halfway from here to the fishing town of Sonderborg. I hope you find your people. As for us—the border is where our lives end."

Klitzenhaus shook the Nazi's hand and lifted the checkpoint beam's counterweight. Volsgaard accelerated the army jeep, driving into Denmark.

* * * * *

The helmeted though unarmed guard peeked out of the remote booth and raised his hand, pointing to the "Achtung" warning, ordering the green vehicle with 'red cross' markings to stop. He walked slowly up to Isaac and Flora, sitting in the front cab, still clad in medical garb.

"You know there is a better road about three kilometers west of this one? Where are you headed, Sonderborg?" assisting Isaac with the lie.

"Yes, we are. My nurse and I have to deliver some medicine to an army clinic up there. It's about ten kilometers up the road, right?"

Isaac asked, his smoothness at lying, impressing Flora. "We had decided to take the pleasant route, since it was not an emergency."

"Not an emergency? That is good. You know, you are the third vehicle to come by my booth today. Ten hours, and you're the third!" he removed his helmet and scratched his blond hair. "Can I look in the back?"

"Of course," Isaac slid from the driver's seat, walked around to the back panel and opened the vertical doors."

He noticed some of Goerthe's blood had splattered on to the interior wall of the ambulance, though he said nothing.

"Is that blood?" the soldier asked.

"Blood in an ambulance; go figure." Isaac interjected with benign sarcasm.

"Those sacks—that's the medicine? Show me."

Isaac could feel his body react to the invasive inquiry. He gulped as he opened one of the canvas bags. Flora was in fear she spied on Isaac through the linked partition within the vehicle, as he buried his hand in the wads of currency and boxes of valuables that he had taken from Wurtzmuller's house.

"Here, see?"

Isaac's blind search found what he had hoped would be an acceptable for a response. He presented the guard with a fistful of prepackaged syringes that they had also removed from the captain's living room stockpile of vendor samples.

"This is a new invention. The medicine is already in the needle. Within a few months, the whole army will be using this form of injection."

The satisfied soldier allowed Isaac to return the packets to the satchel and tie it closed.

"Listen, I have to borrow your ambulance."

The abrupt request caught Isaac by surprise.

"What? What? Uh, no! I could not do that. We are under orders to make this delivery. Aren't you bound by your command to stay on this post at all times? If you leave and your commanding officer discovers you missing—is that not grounds for treason?"

"Look," the annoyed guard began. "I have been here for a week without a leave. An average of two vehicles pass through here each day. I haven't seen my girl in eight *full* days! I cannot take it. No one gives a shit about this checkpoint because it is useless, okay? And I will not leave it unmanned, because you will man it for me. All I want is two hours. She is a waitress—up that road," he explained pointing to the sandy lane that was perpendicular to the checkpoint station. She works at the 'Sun and Sail' bar in Broager. It is a village, three kilometers inland from here."

He pulled Isaac aside in order to keep his next remark inaudible to the nurse, still in the ambulance.

"If I do not get laid in the next forty-eight hours, I may have to kill someone at this booth, just to get an officer out here to be relieved from this post."

Isaac could see the carnal desperation in the boy's eyes.

"What about my nurse?"

"She can stay with you. I have a uniform, hanging on the inside hook. Put it on if someone comes. She can hide under my cot in the booth. There are rations on the shelf and there is a latrine out back. No one will come by, I promise you. Two hours—and I will bring you back food and beer. My girlfriend can get it for free. Oh, and I may use your ambulance… you know?" the soldier asked, making a universal hand gesture that suggested a sexual encounter would occur.

"What if I still say no?" Isaac asked, all but ready to concede the argument.

"Then I blow two of your tires out with my rifle, and neither of us gets laid," the guard smiled with a mischievous sneer.

"I need to hold on to the sacks of medicine. If they get lost, I will be killed for insubordination," Isaac countered, bargaining with the lad.

"By all means," the soldier nodded as he removed one bag and helped Isaac carry it to the booth.

"What is happening, Driver," Flora called to Isaac as the men entered the wooden hut.

"The guard has to go on a brief mission. He will return in two hours. We are going to stay in the booth for him, until he returns with our vehicle. Please join me inside, Nurse—just for two hours."

"What, are you crazy? I have to be in town by nightfall!"

Flora was acting, but she was truly frustrated by the sudden change of plans. How could her husband relinquish their escape vehicle? She slammed the ambulance door, realizing they were stranded with no transportation.

The soldier hopped in to the driver's seat and felt the play of the ambulance clutch.

"Oh, one more thing, if you really are in a jam: see that house right there, sitting alone on the rocky section of the sheep pasture?"

Isaac could make out the roofline of a quaint farm structure at the end of a winding sand driveway.

"That is the home of Herr Lydaaker. He is a retired merchant from Sonderborg. He commutes there every day. He is home now. If you need anything, he will help you. Sometimes, his wife brings me stew. You probably will not need him, as I will return in two hours, and I mean that. But if you do require his services, just remember he *has* to say 'yes'.

"Why does he have to say 'yes'?" Isaac shouted as the vehicle pulled away.

"Because right now, we own Denmark, and if he says 'no', we can kill him."

The sex-starved private kicked up a pile of wet sand on to Isaac's foot as he sped off, howling.

* * * * *

The sun was setting on the low grassy terrain of southern Denmark. It had been nearly forty minutes since the hormone-motivated guard convinced Isaac to be part of his recreational joust. Flora rested on the soldier's iron-framed military cot, knowing that she had to be alert for any emergency. She tried to nap, but was unable. Isaac folded his arms and set his sights down the road to Broager, hoping for the ambulance to appear through the forest of saltwater reeds. Even he knew that two hours would probably mean four or five at best.

"What are we to do when we get to Sonderborg, Isaac?" his wife asked, staring up at the pine ceiling of the booth. "It appears that Denmark is as much of a Nazi occupied state as Poland or Czechoslovakia. Does it not?"

"I cannot tell. Before we were imprisoned, someone in Bremerhaven suggested that the people here seem to go about their business in a normal fashion. The Germans only need this place for its geographical position—a strategic area in case of allied attacks. We should see more tomorrow. I know one thing—the rest of the country will not be as remote as this road."

No sooner had Isaac commented on the quiet of the shoreline, when his eye caught a glimmer of light in the distance, along the

Danish Fjordvejen. It flickered between the marshy groves of vegetation bordering the water edge. Isaac knew what it was. About a kilometer away, he made out the headlights of a vehicle approaching the checkpoint booth—the fourth car of the day.

"Flora, Flora, quick—under the cot. Someone is approaching. I can see the headlights about a kilometer down the shoreline."

Flora rolled her slender body between the iron springs and the wood flooring. Isaac threw a green military blanket over the thin mattress, its edges falling to the sandy bottom of the check point booth.

"Keep still until I complete business with the oncoming car."

He removed the uniform top and field pants from the hook next to the cot, quickly putting them on, covering his white ambulance attire. Nearly ready to greet the vehicle, he grabbed the rifle, leaning against the inner framed doorway, and threw on a soft cap—as the soldier had taken his helmet to Broager. Thus the transformed private of the Wermacht strode to the middle of the road to meet the oncoming vehicle, hoping to keep business far away from Flora's concealment.

The jeep rounded the point and rambled to halt a few minutes later. Finally—on the third day of his escape from Ravensbruck, Isaac Bloom, the fugitive, was presently face-to-face with Lt. Joseph Volsgaard, his pursuer.

After the men formalized their greeting with Nazi salutes, Volsgaard, pressed for time, began.

"At ease, Private."

He exited the car and walked about the clearing, looking into the booth and then back at Isaac.

"Did you witness a military ambulance passing this point within the last hour or so? We are trying to locate the vehicle. There was an incident at the border, and it is a matter of national security that we find this ambulance. The occupants could have turned back to the main road, but my guess is that they continued on the Fjordvejen."

Isaac pondered the question, biting his lip because he realized his initial hesitation exceeded a response time that was reasonable to the impatient officer.

Volsgaard interrupted before he could answer.

"I know this may seem to be a tough question, private, considering the amount of traffic that appears to come by here daily. Must I repeat myself?"

"No, sir…" Isaac stammered, trying to salvage credibility. "There *was* an ambulance that came to the booth about an hour ago, but it did not pass."

Isaac had been stunned by the sudden inquiry, realizing that the military was in active pursuit of him and Flora. They were now cornered, along that stretch of sandy isolation.

"Well if you encountered an ambulance," Volsgaard continued, "and it did not pass your security point, then where did it go?" His voice was sarcastic, as an officer speaks down to the common enlisted man. "Who was in the vehicle? Can you at least remember that, private?"

"Uh… yes, sir," Isaac responded. "There was a driver and a nurse. They asked if there was a town nearby where they could get something to eat and whoop it up a bit. I directed them up that pass, to Broager—a town that is about three kilometers inland."

Volsgaard turned, studying the direction in which Isaac pointed.

"I do not see any road, soldier."

The reeds on the left side of the lane had blended into those on the right side, creating an illusion. The stalks painted a forest of growth, hiding the path that so delicately cut between them.

"It is there, sir," Isaac insisted, sounding like a native. "The path becomes more of a road once you clear the shoreline grasses. It opens up, and the road takes you into Broager. I sent them to the "Sun and Sail" Bar. They are probably eating and drinking there right now."

He kept an eye toward the overgrown clearing, praying the ambulance was not on its return as he spoke.

"Very well, soldier… but I have to say this—as an officer of the Shutzstaffel…"

Isaac squirmed as the junior lieutenant hesitated, and spoke.

"I noticed your bed. It looked like a pig had slept in it—a cover just lying on top, draping the floor? And you obviously just threw your uniform on over your pajamas," Volsgaard continued, pointing to the white cuffs of the ambulance driver uniform that peeked out from under the army greens. "I know you probably think this not important, but you represent the Wermacht. You are responsible to uphold an image, even if you guard virtually nothing in the middle of nowhere, and even if that be in another country, like Denmark. Now spruce up! Three kilometers you say?"

"Yes sir!"

Isaac was happy for the officer's departure as he watched Volsgaard round his vehicle, start the engine, and aim for the concealed road of sand that led to the town of Broager and the "Sun and Sail" tavern. He watched as Volsgaard left the Baltic Fjordvejen and disappeared between the green columns of vegetation.

"Flora, Flora, we have to get out of here. Quick! Get up. This Nazi officer will return soon. We have no means of transportation."

Isaac then realized the Nazi pursuit was not only a reality, but it was far closer to him than he had ever imagined.

The couple ran across the road and to the driveway that the soldier pointed out, who would certainly return to aid in their capture after Volsgaard confronted him. They hurried up the gentle incline of the path that led to the only residence within sight.

"Herr Lydaaker, Herr Lydaaker!" Isaac screamed as he approached the small cabin. Smoke billowed from the cobblestone fireplace of the log framed dwelling as he pounded on the door again, hoping for a response.

I am in charge… I am in charge," the humble fugitive kept assuring himself, motivated by an apparent date with death. The door opened, and a bald, elderly, fair skinned Danish man greeted him.

"Why the pounding? Who are you?" Tag Lydaaker asked, seeming annoyed as he looked at Isaac and Flora, reading the fear that radiated from their faces. "Where is the booth guard? What do you want?"

"Herr Lydaaker, you must take me and my nurse to Sonderborg right away."

"There is no chance of that happening. My wife and I are just sitting for dinner. Where did you come from? And where is Victor, the booth guard? Speak to him about your situation."

"That is why we are here. Victor needed our vehicle to go to Broager. We have important serum for the military clinic in Sonderborg. It must get there immediately. Victor will not be back in time."

The old man thought a second and felt the pressure of Isaac's remark.

"I tell you what—I will drive you after I finish my dinner. You will be in Sonderborg by eight o'clock. Yes?"

Invading his space, Isaac closed to within ten centimeters to Tag Lydaaker's nose.

"Sir, the life and death of a Nazi Major, Commander of the Danish Occupational Forces, depends on the quickness of getting this medicine. My nurse was given full responsibility to get it there on time and administer the dosage. If you and you alone want to delay his chance of survival and he should die, I would not want to be in your shoes when you answer to the authorities."

Tag Lydakkar gulped, taken by Isaac's performance, and he then ordered his wife to eat dinner without him.

"I will return in one hour. Keep my meal warm. Do you hear me?"

*****

The remote town of Broager was typically structured in the serene pastoral fashion of all seaside villages in Denmark. Its main edifice was a dual spire folk church on one side of the sandy soil road. Broager's business district sat on the other side of the lane. Five shops represented its entire economy: a bakery; a tailor shop; an animal feed depot; and general store were all closed at the end of the day. At six p.m., they did not contribute to the town's traffic. Only the Sun and Sail Tavern displayed signs of life—mostly locals, who were celebrating the end of the workday. The real laborers of the area, the farmers and fishermen, reveled in the three-hour drinking celebration before returning home to retire for their next four a.m. workday.

The brick and mortar tavern bustled with a crowd of regulars. The open front door helped amplify groups of hearty voices, singing local Danish sea tunes and regional favorites. In front, the carved wooden sign of a schooner passing through the golden globe of a setting sun, was emblematic of the tavern's name.

Lt. Joseph Volsgaard slowed his jeep as he drove past the twenty or so vehicles parked randomly on the front lawn of the active tavern. It did not take long to realize there was no sign of a military ambulance. Could the stammering guard at the checkpoint have been wrong? Had the couple not liked the location and gone elsewhere? Should he go inside the tavern to inquire? His reception would certainly not be appreciated by a group of rowdy drunks, and Danish ones at that.

He walked to the edge of the property line, thinking of his next move. While thinking, he directed his gaze upward, admiring the magnificent wooden religious structure on the opposite side of the lane. *How regal a building,* he thought, *and practically in the middle of nowhere. These people are committed. It's a good thing they are peaceful pushovers.*

His mental compliment abruptly halted when the astute Nazi observed the rectangular rear compartment of a Phenomen Granite nestled between two chestnut trees in the rear parking area of the folk church. He had located the escape vehicle! The murderers of Wurtzmuller and the border guards, just ten kilometers south, had parked in secrecy from the active bar. He felt his pursuit coming to finalization as he removed his automatic Luger from its black polished holster.

Volsgaard crossed the lonely street, as he was the only living soul around. The party-like noise blasting out the front door of the Sun and Sail tavern juxtaposed a surreal tone to the moment. Before he decided to enter the tavern to arrest the couple, the officer had a hunch they might still be inside the dark green medical van with a red cross that sat in the remote church lot.

After the officer arrived at the quiet ambulance a moment later, he placed his hand on the metal fender by the back compartment, feeling a gentle, pulsating squeak from the car's shock absorbers. He placed his ear on to the metal side panel. He could hear the guttural pants of sex, groaning from within.

The Nazi smiled, remembering the remark of the World War I veteran at St. Gertrude's Field Hospital earlier in the day—how the military ambulance was always viewed as a mobile brothel whenever the opportunity arose.

He was sure that his victims were vulnerable and would certainly be in an uncompromising position if he surprised them. So in one quick motion, the lieutenant twisted the two handles on the back doors of the Phenomen Granite wagon, releasing the latch posts. He swung the vertical panels open and straightened his arm, aiming the luger automatic pistol at the surprised couple inside. The amply-bosomed, bare-chested twenty-something woman, wearing nothing but a German soldier helmet, screamed in fright as she dismounted, unlocking from her partner's sexual union.

Volsgaard planted two slugs of lead into her torso even before she had gotten fully off her partner. He had mistaken the barmaid as one of the escapees and watched her collapse onto the cold metal ambulance floor. The innocent checkpoint guard grabbed on the linked partition of the cab section and seemed to crawl up the far end of the compartment. Cowering, he said nothing to Volsgaard, who spoke out.

"This is for Captain Wurtzmuller and whoever else you may have killed in your escape!"

The only thing standing at attention was evidenced in the inappropriate penile salute. The sentry, who had never even heard Captain Wurtzmuller's name, never got to respond. Volsgaard pumped two more bullets into the chest of the still-erect checkpoint guard, who dropped over the body of his girlfriend—Romeo and Juliet, Nazi style.

Volsgaard closed the back panels and walked around to the front of the church to the sounds of laughter and music. No one heard or saw the incident.

The proud, young officer, convinced that he had solved the murder and executed the culprits, returned to his jeep and headed for the faster traveled road back to the German border and eventually Ravensbruck.

* * * * *

"It is eight o'clock. Do you want me to cross the King Christian X Bridge on to the island, or do you want to walk from here?" Tag Lydaaker asked Isaac and Flora.

"Leave us here. We will walk to the clinic," Isaac advised the Danish driver. This is the isle of Als?" he asked, folding the atlas papers and putting them back into his pocket.

"Yes. Once you cross the bridge, you are on one of the many islands of Denmark. The city, which is right on the other side, is all of Sonderborg. Its main street is about a kilometer long. I hope you like fish?"

Laughing, Lydaaker stepped on his accelerator, pulling away from the couple, anxious to return to his dinner.

Isaac hoisted the large sack and threw it over his shoulder, handing Flora the smaller one. He acknowledged a "soldier to soldier' smile from the guard on the bridge, who was more interested in conversing with two Danish teenage girls. They would rather flirt with the occupant of their country than defy his presence.

Isaac and Flora sensed quite a relaxed demeanor from the people in the town. The German occupation was evident, but it was more informal than in actual Germany. Sonderborg was comfortable in size—not so big that it required a heavy presence of troops, and yet large enough for one to easily blend with the busy population.

The first city landmark to greet them was the spire of St. Mary's church, situated on the far side of the bridge. The rest of the village, dwarfed by comparison, extended down the Sonder Havnegade. To the left were stores, and behind them the residential neighborhoods. To the right were an equal amount of businesses, restaurants and taverns. All of these emporiums overlooked the extensive wharf and boat docks, which were so important to the fishing livelihood of the Danish village.

Isaac directed Flora's attention in the direction of St. Mary's.

"Let us spend the night in the church. Hopefully, it is open. If we are discovered, I am sure the religious community will understand our desperate choice. We will plan our next move in the morning."

Fatigued, as they had traveled seventy kilometers and witnessed five killings on Wednesday, the couple climbed the sandstone steps to the elevated building entrance.

The heavy oak doors with iron-ring handles were indeed open. The couple entered the rear foyer of the church and then into the main house of worship. A few large candles burned on the altar and along the walls, making Isaac wonder if its décor had not been changed since the Protestant Reformation of the seventeenth century.

He settled into a pew; the fifth from the last, while Flora plopped down into the one in front. She stretched out, using the prayer bench as her bed. He removed a can of beans that he had taken from Wurtzmuller's house three days earlier. Opening the lid with the opener, he helped himself to a large spoonful. He took another hefty scoop before leaning over the pew.

"Flora, have some. We will need energy. The morning will come early. We have no idea what tomorrow will bring."

He studied his wife's posture. Drawing back his arm, he downed a third spoonful of beans. Flora responded with a gentle snore.

CHAPTER 38

Reverend Kier Christiansen startled Isaac from his sleep. It was Thursday morning at 6 a.m. Isaac had been dreaming of his parents, something that was quite rare. In his reverie, they were alive and young. He was a small boy. Things appeared safe and happy. The family still lived in Gdansk, and it was springtime. His mother was beautiful, and his father played soccer with Isaac along the river bank lawn. The feeling of a secure and a healthy lifestyle had created warmth as he slept.

He was brought to his senses by a poking from the pastor of the church.

"Good morning, young man," the minister began in a definite and somewhat annoyed tone, speaking German. "I trust that your sleep was comfortable?"

"Good morning, sir," Isaac answered, somewhat embarrassed.

"Reverend," the man of the cloth corrected Isaac.

"I… I mean, Reverend," Isaac replied.

"You know there are military accommodations for German soldiers, like yourself, in Sonderborg, and I am sure they are a lot more comfortable than the hard oak wood of a church pew."

Isaac stood up, and in a hurry to leave, he nudged Flora.

"Uhh, yes sir… I mean, Reverend. I was unaware…"

"Please young man—Sit. Sit—the Lord never turns away anyone who seeks refuge within the walls of a church."

Flora awoke from her sleep and sat dazed as she glanced toward the morning light that began to filter in from the east. It cast a spectrum of colors filtered through the stained glass windows on the western wall of the room. The Reverend Christiansen sat in the pew directly in front of Flora, slinging his arm over the backrest.

"Now, what brings you to St. Mary's of Sonderborg, my children? Are you passing through, or are you to be stationed here?"

Before Isaac could answer, the door from the church lobby opened, startling the couple.

"Ah Kurig, come in, come in! Please get our guests some coffee and porridge from the kitchen. They look like they need some nourishment, yes?"

The pastor called the orders to his assistant, who nodded and hurried back out of the church proper. The minister felt safer about the presence of a German soldier and nurse spending the night in his church. He sensed hesitation and innocence in the couple. They did not seem to exemplify the typical arrogant and assertive traits that he had observed in other Nazi personnel.

"We will leave immediately after finishing our coffee, Reverend," Isaac assured him.

"Not to worry, but we are having a service here at nine a.m. You are both welcome to stay. It is a one-hour prayer for European peace."

"Thank you, all the same, but we will leave at once—after the coffee."

"So why are you in Sonderborg? It is not often one sees a soldier and nurse traveling as companions."

The pastor seemed genuinely interested in their plight. Isaac looked at Flora then back to the minister.

"Well, you are a man of religion and a seeker of peace, yes?"

"Obviously, my son, by mere neutrality, as well as profession, I seek an end to this horror."

"I can speak in confidence?" Isaac asked, seeking moral support, from the first person he believed he could confide in since leaving his surrogate father, Adolf Ahrens, in Bremerhaven.

"Of course," the religious head of St. Mary's assured him, realizing Isaac had something he needed to share.

"Reverend, we are husband and wife. We were part of a Nazi "round-up" in Bremerhaven, Germany. We were sent to a Nazi labor camp. We managed to escape and we are trying to get to a neutral country. Can you help?"

Christiansen responded in silence. He had never expected a summation so profound in such few sentences. He took a deep breath, glancing toward the gothic-arched ceiling of the church.

"Are you Jews?"

"Yes, by birth. But we were both orphaned by adolescence and do not practice Judaism."

Isaac was amazed how this always seemed to be the first apparent conclusion by anyone who sought the reason for his imprisonment.

Kurig returned with two mugs of coffee and matching porcelain bowls of porridge for Isaac and Flora, placing the tray on Isaac's pew and retreating to the lobby of the church.

Isaac sipped the coffee, while Flora scooped the pasty cereal into her ready mouth.

"You know, my boy, as it turns out—this is a very bad moment for those of Jewish heritage to be in Denmark. A few weeks ago, right after the holiday, *Rosh Hashanah*, the Germans began an effort to exile all Jews from Denmark. There are ferries and hired steamers leaving Copenhagen daily, for Kiel and Gdansk— all with Jews on board. Where they are taking them, no one knows.

"People fear they are treating the Danish population of Jewish residents similar to those in Germany. Our King had an agreement with the Reich, protecting all Danish citizens from such acts of violence, but recently, Germany seemed to have broken this pact. Your timing is quite poor. There are guards at every train terminal, ferry, road block and street corner. They are checking Danish identification papers. I suggest you maintain your disguises if you even want a chance to succeed at escaping. You do not want to be a Jew in Denmark anymore."

"I have money, Reverend. Would you know where I may be able to purchase papers from some underground service?" Isaac asked.

"You mean counterfeit identification… No I will not be a party to such a fraudulent practice, my boy. I do not want the Nazis after me as well. They are not softhearted on religious people either. If they found out that I have spoken with you and did not report it, they would immediately accuse me for assisting in your escape. So it would be best that you eat up and be on your way."

Christiansen stood and walked back to the lobby where he had his small office to the side, next to a toilet and clothes closet. Isaac could not figure the minister's mood. He was warm, and yet indifferent, hospitable, while sterile at the same time. Flora finished the entire bowl of maple-laced porridge and sat, cradling the coffee cup.

"Wait here," Isaac told his wife "Do not make any noise."

The husband scooted from the church pew and tip-toed back to the swinging wood door that separated the church proper from the lobby and Christiansen's office. Getting a glance at the side of the reverend's head, Isaac put his ear to the opening between the swinging doors.

"Now, I do not want any problems, Sergeant. Just come by, remove them from my church and do as you wish with them. I cannot be accused of harboring fugitives of the Nazis. We both know that if I did not report this to you, and they were caught, I could very well be facing a firing squad in two months. I cannot afford to be accused as an accomplice to any crime of your state. I will detain them as long as I…"

That was as far as Isaac listened. He hastened back to Flora's pew.

"Quick! No questions. Pick up the bag."

Isaac retrieved the large canvas sack, his eyes spotting a side exit from the church that appeared to lead out to a garden and lawn facing local homes. They fled through that exit, rushing into the modest neighborhood, where their disguises of soldier and nurse might betray them.

"What happened?" Flora asked as they made it to the second street of private cottages in Sonderborg, behind the spires of St. Mary's.

Isaac held her arm, hoping to accelerate her motion.

"Never again, Flora. Never again, will I be so stupid as to tell our story to a person. Denmark appears just as bad as Germany. You cannot trust anyone you may be speaking to. I thought a 'religious' leader would be a sure confidant. Never again will I speak of our escape."

"What do you mean?" she asked.

"Man of the cloth? Right! Do you know what he was doing? He was selling us out to the Nazis!"

Flora had never seen Isaac so irate—even with all that had happened over the last few days.

"A patrol was on its way to capture us and bring us back, fearing he would get into trouble if he associated himself with our predicament. Look at me, Flora—look at me!"

He stared directly into his wife's eyes.

"Never again will I confide our true identity to anyone. You do not know who you are dealing with. A minister would assist a Nazi before he would help a persecuted Jew? And what is worse, neither of us have ever been inside a temple! We are guilty! For what?"

Isaac looked down one of the streets, where he could see a troop transport of soldier's making their way to the entrance of St. Mary's church. The couple hiked up the next cross block, Amkilgade, penetrating deeper into the maze of Danish cottages and lawns. At last Isaac spotted what he needed—a clothesline, offering new freshly-laundered clothing and an opportunity to transform their disguise.

The white cord extended from the home's back porch and completed its suspension to a dilapidated shed at the far end of the property. Isaac saw a generous selection of both men and women clothes hanging from the rope. The couple pushed through the privet hedge border and hid inside the open hovel, trying to distinguish any human movement inside the main house.

They waited thirty minutes. The home seemed vacant for that period of time, so. Isaac shuttled out to the line and grabbed a pair of men's overalls and a sweater. He ran back to the shed, changed into the clothes then ran back for a sweater and skirt for Flora. The couple then continued their trek through the neighborhood, dressed as locals.

At the end of the neighborhood on Sankt Jergens Gade, there sat a park and playground for children. The couple ran through the grounds and into the adjacent woods bordering the playground. They traveled deep into the thickets and trees, away from any sign of human life.

"We will stay put until the search by any Nazi patrol squad ceases," Isaac advised. "Our canvas bags may still give away our identity. Sometime this afternoon, we will make our way down to the Sonde Havnegade, and seek refuge in a store or tavern. There, we can feel out the locals and perhaps acquire information concerning water transport to Sweden."

Isaac took heed to the warnings of Christiansen related to the Nazi occupation of Denmark and its treatment of Jews. However, there was an innocence and stability to Sonderborg. Perhaps the strong arm of Germany was more present in the larger towns, *but not there*, he thought.

CHAPTER 39

People scurried across the Sonde Havnegade. Sonderborg was an "early" city. Its day began with the fishing boats leaving the docks at four a.m., with some returning by mid-afternoon and others on longer ventures out into the Baltic for days, some for weeks.

Just before nightfall, activity winded down. Workers hurried, completing their daily chores, preparing for the next four o'clock day to begin. Isaac noticed a platoon of German soldiers at the next corner of the main thoroughfare, engaged in what appeared to be jovial banter.

Rather than pass them, he pushed Flora into the open door of a fishing supply company. As he nudged her into the shop, he took notation of the large spools of fishing lines, netting and hardware, certifying the main trade in Sonderborg. Inside, Flora was startled by a mannequin who sported an entire outfit, similar to the one's being worn by most men on the Sonde Havnegade. Its permanent stillness cast an eerie museum-like spirit inside the shop's walls. Neither had ever seen the fishing attire as was now presented in the small Danish town. Their beloved Bremerhaven boasted a vibrant shipping community, but it was hardly a port that possessed any fishing trade.

"Goddag," the proprietor greeted them. He was an elderly merchant with a head full of unkempt white hair. His red and ruddy complexion admitted years and years of salt and solar damage. The arched scar on his left cheek blended into the wrinkles of his aging face. A brown-bowled mahogany pipe, emitting a ghostly swirl of aromatic smoke, rounded out the nautical character of an old mariner, obviously turned land merchant.

Isaac answered through the haze of burned tobacco, using his best Danish-German vocabulary. The region was still near the border. Many words were close in speech, so they were able to communicate.

"We would like to purchase fisherman gear: boots, slicker, jacket—whatever is needed," Isaac told to the shopkeeper, who blew a billow of smoke to the ceiling as he tilted his head back.

"Are you intending to join a crew, young man?" the elder followed.

"Well, we hope to, yes. Is that possible?"

Isaac sensed there would be ensuing questions.

"If by 'we', you mean the woman also? Fishing captains do not take women on as crew—even for kitchen chores, young man. Around these parts, it is strictly a man's job. Before you invest in an outfit for the woman, I must tell you that."

He seemed stern but respectful of their patronage, and of Isaac's ignorance about the profession's protocol.

"Uh, thank you. Can I speak with you aside, sir? Do you have a moment?" Isaac asked, beginning the lie. "You see, we are to be married. We are eloping. We need to leave Denmark to go to Sweden. Her parents cannot know. If her father discovers this, he will destroy our wishes and our lives. I cannot let that happen."

Isaac hoped that a romantic plea may find some tender quarter in the "old salt's" heart.

"I see," the old businessman said, raising and lowering his bushy white eyebrows. "Then, did you know there are ferries out of Odense, Copenhagen and Nyborg that go directly to Malmo. You need not get dressed up as fishermen if you just want to go to Sweden."

"Sir, I must tell you," Isaac continued, "her father is very influential. He foiled our departure once before. We cannot take chances. I am from Germany, and I do not want any legal battles. I would rather do this as inconspicuously as possible."

He actually felt proud of his explanation. It seemed valid to his own way of thinking.

"See sir, I work in a military motor pool in Haderslev."

"Ahh, Haderslev! My wife was from there," the merchant volunteered.

Little did he know that Isaac had memorized the Danish town name that very afternoon while studying the Atlas.

"I was employed by the civilian mechanics division," Isaac continued. "The army assigned me there in '41. That is where I met her. We have been dating since. Her father does not want her marrying a German. We are in love and will leave the country to wed if we have to." You see now, sir?"

"Yes. Yes, I see what you are saying. Tell me—is Gundersen's Bakery still operating in town?"

Always expecting a trap, Isaac answered carefully.

"I did not get out much, sir. Was that on the corner in the main part of town?

"No, it was on Sokol Gade," he replied.

"Yes, if it is the one I am thinking. It is still there," Isaac said, muddying the trail of accuracy, if indeed the old man was attempting to catch him in a lie.

"Well, let me ask you, this: you and your girlfriend are not Jews, are you?"

It was the supreme question, and Isaac was actually expecting to hear it from the old man.

"Because if you are, I cannot help you. Last year—no problem. Today, I could get killed for helping Jews escape to Sweden."

"Look at me, sir." Isaac said, stressing his plea. "We are not Jews. We are lovers. All I want to do is buy clothes from you and discreetly take my girl to a new land so we can live happily ever after."

"What size shoes, sir?"

He fed the merchant with as much information as he could. One hour later, the couple faced the store mirror, clad in proper Baltic Sea fishing attire. Isaac giggled, looking at Flora. Her sizes were so large that the overall bib covered half of her face.

"Thank you, sir. You have been most helpful."

"Olaf Arnstaadt," the elderly seaman blurted out to the couple in a surprising *non sequitur.*

"Excuse me?" Isaac asked, bewildered.

"Olaf Arnstaadt," he repeated. "Go next door—to the "Northern Lights" Tavern. Ask for Olaf Arnstaadt. He should be getting there by six p.m. He is leaving at three a.m. tomorrow. He has a seven-day run up the coast to Stockholm—drops off his catch there and returns seven days later to Sonderborg. He was in here earlier, picking up supplies. Tell him Sven Ingman told you to speak to him. Do you have money?"

"Uh, yes sir. We can pay you in Reichsmarks. That is what they pay me at the motor pool."

"No, no—I mean do you have *lots* of money? If you need to go as fishermen, perhaps he will help you. But it will cost you lots of money. Not every captain would take a chance, but Olaf might."

Isaac kept repeating the name, "Olaf Arnstaadt," in his head. Somehow he knew, he would never forget it.

"I can pay you in Reichsmarks, sir? Isaac repeated.

"Yes, yes, of course. Let me figure out what you need to pay me."

Sven grabbed a pad from the counter and began converting the cost of the purchase. He was amazed when Isaac drew a thick bundle of paper bills from the large duffle bag and waited for his tally.

"You have been most helpful, Sven," Isaac said, shaking the old leathery hand of the merchant while providing the appropriate amount from his wad of bills. He called to Flora, who was resting in a chair, due to the excess weight of the fishing clothes on her slight body. They assembled their bags and headed out the door to the Sonde Havnegade, dressed as official Sonderborg natives.

"Wait!" Sven Ingman shouted before they reached the street.

Then the veteran seaman and shop owner reached into a large glass bowl on his counter that contained woolen stocking caps.

"My wedding gift to you. Thank you for the sale and have a good life."

He puffed his pipe, creating a cloudy swirl of fumes that circled his ruddy face.

Isaac grabbed the gifts in mid air and shoved them into his sack, tipping his head at the smoke-engulfed figure who seemed to resemble an ethereal apparition that had come to their rescue.

As the couple made their way onto the Sonde Havnegade, two German soldiers stopped in their tracks, yet only for the reason to let them pass first. Looking at one another in awe of the polite gesture, they remained silent. Isaac nudged Flora, pointing to the street sign, "Northern Lights Tavern," next door.

*****

The dimly lit pine-walled bar reeked of rancid sea odors and a mixture of beer, which had soaked into tables and floor planks. Occasionally, a waft of fried food infused a positive smell to the room that presently hosted twenty fishermen—some celebrating the end to their days and others getting ready to embark on a "longer run."

Isaac and Flora settled into one of the many vacant booths, noting that the regular clientele seemed to stand near the active bar, enjoying the professional interaction.

"Two pilsners please, and could you also point out which gentleman is Olaf Arnstaadt. We would like to speak with him if that is possible," Isaac asked of the waitresses, who began to laugh at his request.

"Did I say something wrong?" he inquired, feeling a sense of paranoia.

"No, no— it is just that I never heard of *anyone* from that crew being referred to as 'gentlemen'!"

Though the couple was comfortable with her explanation, Isaac wondered when he would cease feeling threatened by people's remarks and some hidden meaning in them.

"We would also like a plate of fried cod."

"Good, ours is the best—especially with salt and vinegar," the Danish girl added. "I will tell Olaf that you want to speak with him. He is the big guy with the red beard—the loud one."

She spoke candidly about the boisterous hulk of a man who dominated conversation at the bar, but she also seemed to admire him.

Flora watched the waitress whisper into Olaf's ear and watched him look back toward Isaac and her while he continued conversing with his fellow fishermen. At the first lull in their conversation, the burly man, clad in booted overalls and slicker walked over to their booth.

"You have reason to speak with me?" he asked, sneering down on the two. Flora still had a tag on her sweater.

"Yes, Mr. Arnstaadt. Please, can we have a moment?" Isaac asked in a respectful tone.

Olaf scooted in to the cubicle, next to Flora.

"How do you know who I am?"

"Mr. Arnstaadt," Isaac began, "we acquired your name from Sven Ingman next door. We are eloping to Sweden. We need transportation, and were hoping that we could pay you to deliver us to Stockholm. We have saved money for this opportunity, and we are willing to pay well for your services."

Olaf withdrew an ivory-bowled meerschaum pipe from his shirt pocket and placed it in his mouth. The tobacco-stained facial carving on the reservoir completed the man's nautical persona. He possessed the whittled face of a Turkish sultan.

"You know, I generally do not get involved with women. You are both engaged to wed?"

"Uh well—yes sir, her father does not approve of the marriage, so we are eloping. It's problematic because I am German and she is Danish, but we can pay you."

"Yes, you already said that. You are not in any serious trouble. The police or Nazis are not after you?"

Isaac waited, but Olaf never asked the usual question—if they were Jews. It was refreshing.

"And, you do not have identification papers?"

Isaac told Olaf that they fled her father in a hurry and had no way of proving who they were.

"That is why we cannot use public means to travel to Stockholm, sir."

"You are aware that if I get caught sneaking you out of Denmark, I could get killed. Jewish residents are using fishing vessels, and fishermen are getting killed along with them, just because of helping."

"We are aware of that, sir. Name your fee. I think we can meet it."

"Oh you can?" Arnstaadt laughed. "Well, then it just went up. Now listen. You come aboard my ship—you work. Do you understand?

"Yes, yes," Isaac answered, feeling reassured.

"You will need fake papers. The key is to not let the Nazi marine guards look at them too closely."

"Nazi marine guards?" Isaac gulped, realizing there remained risks ahead. He was expecting to blend in with crew and face no more scrutiny. "What do you mean?"

"Although Sweden is neutral to any war activity, they will advise the Germans of any fraudulent activity that may happen concerning stowaways—just to keep the peace. Not to worry—it is very informal, and I can handle the Swedes. The problem is getting out of our own marina right behind us," Olaf commented, pointing with his pipe toward the back of the bar. "They know that there are to be no women. If I leave with four fishermen, I had better arrive in Stockholm with the exact number that I left with from Sonderborg."

"You said that you needed *identification* papers"? Isaac asked, worried.

"They do not check them in Sweden—they only make sure the man count is correct. They will check papers right outside, however. You leave the Nazi marine police to me. Most times, they do not scrutinize the photos. My fee is five hundred Koners per person, up front, and another five hundred upon arrival."

"Will you accept Reichsmarks? That is the currency I was paid when I worked at a German military motor pool in Haderslev."

"Yah, I will. I have a bank account in Stockholm. They accept Reichsmarks. You prepare the fee."

Isaac knelt, going through his satchel.

"No, no—not now!" Olaf shouted. "I will leave in about an hour with my men to finalize our purchases of some last-minute supplies. We will meet at the bottom of the tavern's dock at two a.m. sharp. That is important—not sooner, not later. I have a crew of two. They work like dogs. You will work as well. I have a second business on board."

Isaac and Flora seemed puzzled.

"I have my own pickled herring business. That is what both of you will work at while we are at sea—filleting and pickling. It is easy: Gunnar, Leif and I will fish. You will help with the barreling of some extra herring. Believe me, I produce the best pickled herring in Denmark. When we get to the Stockholm port, I can make an extra 200 kronas just from my pickled herring. Restaurant merchants will be down on the docks, fighting for it. On one run, we completed thirty small wood kegs and caught five ton overall, on the round trip. That was my most lucrative journey in twenty-two years."

Olaf seemed stern but understanding in allowing Isaac and Flora onboard his vessel, notwithstanding the two thousand Reichsmarks he would make on the job. He nursed his meerschaum embers back to a healthy glow, tobacco burning within the bust of the nicotine-stained sultan's face. The smoke generated was not as defined as that of Sven Ingman's, but the sculpted novelty of his pipe certainly elevated Arnstaadt to a unique level of nautical mysticism.

"How will you explain my wife's presence to the authorities?" Isaac asked.

"Your wife? I thought she was your girlfriend?" Olaf countered, noting the contradiction.

"I am sorry. I meant 'soon-to-be' wife!" Isaac blurted.

Glancing down, he was too embarrassed to make eye contact after such a careless mistake, yet he was thankful that his error landed on the ears of an ally and confidant rather than a Nazi sympathizer.

The fisherman stood, calling out the names of his crewmen.

"Leif! Gunnar! Come here."

Two young Danes broke from a group conversation and walked to the booth just as the waitress brought the couple their order of fried fish.

"This is... I am sorry—your names?" Arnstaadt asked, addressing the couple.

"Heinrich and Dorothy," Isaac said without hesitation, inserting a dash of irony in his response by choosing the dead Captain Wurtzmuller's and Chief Overseer Boerner's first names.

"They will be accompanying us to Stockholm. They are eloping. I will have them work the fillet table as we fish. Okay?"

Taking off their blue stocking caps, the men bowed to the couple without speaking. They seemed to be subservient and loyal to Olaf Arnstaadt.

"You two stay here. Get some rest after you eat. We must pick up spices and fill our fresh water tank. He turned to the taller of his crewmen. "You had the food delivered?"

"Yes, and the ice blocks were placed in the hold about eight p.m. I ordered twelve hundred kilograms."

"That will be enough until our drop-off in Visby," Olaf nodded. "I am going back to Landhauers—hopefully they now have white vinegar..." he sighed, looking down at the couple, "one of the necessary ingredients for the pickling."

Isaac offered the men some fish, but they refused.

"Enjoy it," Gunnar advised. "This time next week, you will not want to see another fish for two years!"

After a laugh, Olaf Arnstaadt slapped his worker's back.

"Let's go do what is necessary. And if it was not for the fish, you would be poor, no? So do not complain."

Isaac turned to Flora, smiling as she had devoured the third bite of fried cod.

"This is good," he said and kissed her forehead.

CHAPTER 40

The two young entrepreneurs tried calming the dozen people who pushed and shoved one another, desperately trying to put the money into the hand of the shorter male. One man fell into the sandy soil amidst the flailing reeds along the banks of the Baltic Sea. Two others just kicked him out of their path. All had convened in an attempt to make the twelve-kilometer excursion from a point just south of Dragor, Denmark, to an undisclosed dock, near the city of Limhamn, Sweden.

The men had purchased a mail-order out-board motor from the Elto Company, which was originally-founded in America by Norwegian, Ole Evinrude. They pooled remaining resources and secured a five-meter rowboat as well. Attaching the eight horsepower motor to the vessel would enable them to reach the south shore of Sweden in two short hours.

For the last several weeks, the men set up near local synagogues in Amagervest, Dragor and Kastrup, offering safe delivery to Sweden for the local Jewish population. Their fee: fifty kroner per person. The venture was conceived as a result of recent martial law policies inflicted by the Nazi occupation, a reality all too well exemplified to Isaac and Flora by the minister of St. Mary's and Sven Ingman.

The young Danish partners tried to keep their advertising clandestine, which remained possible for only the first three weeks. Over time, however, the level of hysteria rose to such epidemic proportions that the casual booking system was overwhelmed. Just that night, the young businessmen had to turn four people away.

"First, keep your voices down. If you create a scene, we will not accept you—tonight or any other night. I am letting the mother and her baby on board, no matter. The remaining ten will draw straws for the six spots. If you are one, pay my partner and get on board."

He then tore ten stalks from the shore's tall grass, creating six-centimeter segments. Putting the grass lots behind his back, the seaman snapped four to shorter lengths, which would be the losers. By the third draw, an elderly man realized he had drawn a short straw. He was desperate.

"If you do not take me tonight, I will report your business to our local Nazi police unit. You will be shut down and murdered!"

"You fool, listen to what you say!" the other loser answered. "After you report him, they will kill you for attempting to flee as well. I would kill you myself, if you were to do such a thing!"

"I tell you, what, old man—keep your straw. Come back Saturday night, and I will let you on the boat first—like I did for the mother and child. Okay? And if you attempt to report me, I will somehow find you and kill you myself. Now, is that a deal?"

The elder, irate and defeated, stormed through the maze of sea grass and flattened rock paths, back to the town of Dragor. As he reached the sea road, he made peace with his anger, placing the short straw into his overcoat in the hope that he would be a free man by Saturday.

With the eight passengers sitting still in the tiny craft, the land partner in the smuggling escape business launched the two-man boat, as it was advertised, into the first few meters of the turbulent Baltic Sea. It rocked violently until the helmsman pulled the cord on the new Elto engine. The eight-horsepower motor responded as a noisy blast erupted from its casing. The novice seaman switched from neutral into motion gear, and the overweight, unqualified craft began its twelve-kilometer journey.

His partner retreated to their apartment, counting the 400 kroners. Reaching the room they had been living in for the past month, he combined the small fortune with money in a shoe box that held profits from eight previous ventures. He would wait there for his friend's return in the morning, while in the meantime contemplating how they could keep their business a secret from the Nazi rule.

* * * * *

Hans Vitmaar kept the tiny craft pointing toward a northeasterly direction. His nautical aid was a mere pocket compass that he recently acquired at a hunting shop in Copenhagen. He selected the path for reasons based on time and distance at sea. Neither man took the turbulent movements of tides that menaced the Oresund Pass into any consideration. The six meter converted rowboat chugged along, its hull rim only centimeters from the waterline. Nonetheless, Hans and his partner had managed the feat eight times before, so he felt confident that the passengers would reach Sweden's shore by midnight.

The protecting land mass of Saltholm Island, about one kilometer north of the boat, eventually ceased at keeping the waves to a modest roll. Hans knew that the last five kilometers of the journey, in open waters, was the most dangerous portion of the trip. The self-deemed boatman took a deep breath and held steady. The lights of Malmo, Sweden, the sister city to the Copenhagen ferry, were the only friendly sight on the horizon.

Frightened by the shaky voyage, the mother held her weeping son to her breast and rocked him.

"How much longer? Are you sure this boat can make it?" one of the men shouted.

"Shh!" Hans ordered as he adjusted the engine to neutral. "I think I hear a noise, another motor. Be quiet everyone."

Then he killed the engine entirely, so that the small vessel bobbed at the mercy of the aggressive Baltic swells. The drone of the oncoming vessel indicated that it was larger than the refugee scow. It also seemed faster. The pounding of waves onto its hull echoed intermittent slapping.

Hans sensed that it was coming in from the north, probably recently launched from Copenhagen. He sat still, reconfirming his order of silence. The oncoming thrust grew stronger, but its source could not be located in the black of night. The amateur seaman wondered why the noise seemed true to their location—it had not passed them. Instead, it became louder—as if it knew of their exact coordinates.

Hans waited several more seconds until the oncoming motor was too deafening for anyone to think. Then, suddenly realizing what was happening, he stood, shouting.

"Shit! Radar!"

He grabbed the cushion that had been protecting his bottom and dove into the cold unrelenting waves of the Oresund Sound, abandoning his new boat, motor and eight innocent lives. Frantic, he propelled his body, holding the cushion and kicking his feet, setting his sights for Saltholm Island, which seemed to be just under a kilometer away. A few lights and shoreline fires steadied his focus as he kicked, now two hundred meters from the chorus of screams that helped to pinpoint the craft's location. Although it would later haunt him, the coward saved his own life for freedom rather than risking it for profit.

* * * * *

Speeding at 35 knots, the Nazi Kriegsmarine Schnellboot switched its floodlight on when it came to within fifty meters of the defenseless vessel. Commandeered by the notorious Captain Klaus Rassmussen— known in the area as The Baltic Blitz—the ship's radar had picked up the tiny boat on its screen long before Hans even heard the hum of its huge engines.

Rassmussen laughed with the sadistic snicker of evil so common to those Nazis who enjoyed inflicting pain on their victims. With the "death raft" in his sight, he shouted down to the pilot who still had the boat located on the radar screen.

"Ram them! No one leaves Denmark like this—for good reasons. They are escapees. Kill them all!"

The pilot aimed the wooden-hulled patrol boat at the easy target. It crashed into the small craft, sending severed timbers of the converted fishing vessel high into the windy night, instantly killing the mother and child, as well as two of the other passengers.

The remaining four, in one last effort to evade the impact, dove into the violent sea. Hoping they had escaped the murderous act of the schnellboot crew, the drowning quartet swam to the nearest flotsam as pieces of wood showered into the turbulent wake of the ramming patrol boat.

Rassmussen, noticing some passengers had bailed before impact, ordered his pilot to circle the wreckage. He personally climbed up to the kollote steel bridge over the steering cabin and manned the loaded and mounted machine gun.

"Keep on spinning, Rolf," he called to his second-in-command. "We will show these Jews that no one insults the Fuhrer and leaves the party early!"

He laughed, in an irrational, criminal tone, and began firing into the churning wake of circular foam. He killed all four, but it only took two complete revolutions and over three hundred rounds of automatic fire. The captain seemed to salivate at executing people who had done nothing to warrant their deaths. He descended to the pilot's booth.

"Schmutzi, all this killing has brought on a hunger. Open some wine and fix us all knockwurst and potato. When we get out of this sound, we will enjoy a late meal and celebrate our small victory, yah?"

Schnellboot-51 patrolled the Baltic Sea primarily to defend German interests from the Russian fleet out of St. Petersburg. Rassmussen and his crew were in the middle of a three-month tour, purposed to accomplish anything required to assure German defenses, especially within one hundred kilometers of their shoreline. Compact, yet comfortable, the Schnellboot boasted a kitchen, radio room, radar station, five bunk areas and a captain's quarters.

Its weapon arsenal was equipped with four torpedoes, six depth charges and two S-38 machine gun stations. The 2500-liter gas tanks allowed the crew to patrol uninterrupted for a 700 kilometer range, which was about a week. If needed, they could refuel at sea from one of the dozen petrol scows situated off the German/Danish shores of the Baltic.

Rassmussen had just exercised his right as skipper of the patrol boat and would have received accolades from his upper command with regard to his aggressive action in this small incident. Instead, he chose not to radio into Nyborg to report what had just happened. Rather, he considered it just a drill.

Two hours later and a kilometer from the drifting debris and floating bodies, Hans Vitmaar crawled onto the cold, rocky shore of Saltholm island. Panting for dry air, vomiting salt water and guilt-ridden because of his cowardly actions, the money-hungry hustler feared only how he would explain the losses of their new motor and boat to his partner, once he made his way back to the mainland.

CHAPTER 41

Isaac and Flora stood on the back deck of the Northern Lights tavern. The wooden structure presented a vista of Sonderborg's fishing docks and nautical pilings that created a lattice work of pathways from all the business rear doors down to the water's edge.

It was cold. It always seemed colder around the sea. The hour of 2:00 a.m. offered little mercy to the couple, who would withstand harsher conditions, if necessary, to cross the Baltic for a chance to regain their freedom. Flora removed the military blanket from her bag, wrapping her petite body to retain as much heat as possible under the protection of the green wool.

The back door to the tavern opened at 2:05. Olaf Arnstaadt and his worker, Gunnar, soon appeared. The crewman was carrying several sacks on his shoulder.

"Put the spices on the stern side, where it will not get wet," Olaf ordered, holding a folder of papers in one hand and a case of bottled beer in the other.

"Okay."

The captain peered down the dock, observing four vessels. Each seemed to be waiting for their crews, as well.

"Good. No one is here yet. Heinrich, you will get on the ship. Try to look busy, but keep your head down. Look tired and bored, but mainly—just keep busy. Dorothy, I am going to stow you into a secret compartment in a panel behind the pilot wheel. Stay in there until we leave the harbor, and then go back to sleep. I have a small mattress hidden in there. You can pay me half my fee once we are out of the bay.

With Gunnar already by Arnstaadt's boat, the couple saw that it was the third fishing vessel in line at the dock. Isaac read the name, painted in black, just under the bow: "The Nordic Princess."

"This will be your home for the next six days, no?" Olaf laughed.

The fishing boat emitted a strong sea odor, but it was nothing the couple could not handle. The vessel was fifty meters in length, with two wooden poles that maintained the trawling nets. A generous deck surface assured Isaac and Flora that Arnstaadt was right. They would have enough space to fillet the herring that would be used for pickling.

In the dead center of the boat, the pilot's shanty offered some modest indoor protection from the sea environment. It had a small kitchen, ice box, gas burners, toilet and four cots for the crew to rest on in between their shifts—all within an eight-meter by eight-meter space. The catch-hold sat behind the quarters, with a blue canvas tarp thrown over its ten-meter square perimeter and six-meter abyss.

Olaf pulled the cover to make sure the four large blocks of ice had been delivered for the coastal run.

"Leif, chip off some of the ice and put the blocks into a few of the fillet barrels. The couple will start their work by ten."

As he glanced at his watch, his eyes caught sight of a uniformed guard with a clipboard and papers, approaching on the dock from the direction of the ship's stern.

"Good morning, Captain. How many will be going out today? Do you have everyone's identification papers?" the tall Kriegsmarine policeman said as he filled in the form before the Nordic Princess embarkation.

He checked over the form that Olaf removed from a folder within his bib pocket. The astute Dane kept an eye on the far end of the boat, where Isaac was hunched over a fifty-meter coil of dock rope that hung over a deck cleat.

"There are you and three helpers, sir?" the Nazi sergeant asked as he wrote a large "4" in the middle of a form. "Let me see their faces?" he demanded, taking the sailor by surprise.

Arnstaadt hoped that he was not going to be as thorough, so breaking into a tirade in an effort to distract the soldier's questioning, he yelled.

"Gunnar Hoffneever, how many times have I told you—no beer on board while we are working!"

He walked over to the Kriegsmarine guard and Gunnar, who stood in front of the Nazi as he checked the crewman's photo. Lief was next, then Isaac.

"This beer is not leaving this port, Gunnar!" Olaf scolded, holding the case of Danish brew up to the sergeant on the wooden dock.

"Sergeant Knutzen, would you be so kind as to take this off my hands? Perhaps you and your men could put it to better use. If there are two things I do not need—it is a drunken fisherman or one with a hangover.

The interruption worked. Knutzen closed the folder, handed it back to Olaf, laughed at the captain's anger, and accepted the gift, unaware of the ruse. Arnstaadt shoved the folder, along with the strange photo of a fisherman who had not worked for two years, back into his pocket. The I.D. was the closest he had that may have passed for Isaac, but the beer diversion was a better option.

"And when I return, Sergeant, I will bring you a small barrel of my herring—the best in Denmark. It goes great with a pint of Carlsberg."

"Thank you, Captain. I look forward to that," said Knutsen as he went to the next boat, leaning over and looking into the pilot booth. "Ahh, this crew has not yet arrived."

"Gunnar, help the sergeant bring that case to the marine guard booth, now!" the cagey captain demanded, hoping to get the soldier on his way.

The crewman complied and returned after a few minutes he returned.

"Here, he forgot to give you the count docket, Olaf. It says a crew of four."

"Let us get out of here, in case he decides to return," the captain ordered. "Leif—untie us and we will be off."

Arnstaadt turned on the engines, which had never faulted him once in twenty-five years.

"Gunnar—sorry I picked on you. Good boy for going along with it!"

They laughed as Gunnar proceeded to store the dock ropes in a wooden chest that lie against the pilot shanty.

"Heinrich, you can let your lady friend know that we are on our way to Sweden, but not before we try to exhaust this big sea of all it's herring! Leif—show Henirich how to open the panel while I steer us into the sound."

Arnstaadt unmarried the fishing boat from its dock point, and they nosed into the Alsund Channel as he brought the speed of the churning motors up to five knots per hour.

Isaac removed the veneer wall behind the steering column within the pilot booth, calling into the dark space.

"Dorothy, Dorothy!"

There was no answer. He thought it best to let Flora sleep. In five hours, they would begin the work of a busy day at sea.

* * * * *

The novice fisherman could not refrain from vomiting remnants of the wretched fried cod fillets he enjoyed ten hours earlier. His head, bent over the stern of the Nordic Princess, entertained the three seasoned fishermen. They laughed at Isaac's weak stomach and stooping posture as he writhed in pain from the greasy bile that interacted with the rolling waves.

"Get it all out of you!" Olaf Arnstaadt called as he began setting up the fillet pickling table toward the stern of the fifty-kilometer vessel. "I need you to be free from that sour stomach and cleaned up before you get to work. You can tell Dorothy to rise for the fillet station as well."

The last thing Isaac needed was to smell more fish, and raw fish at that. He took a mouthful of ice from the pickling barrel and breathed the friendlier salt air on the boat's starboard side, hoping the sickness had left his stomach.

The Nordic Princess rounded the Isle of Als land mass, making the slow journey from Sonderborg Bay into the greater Baltic Sea. By nine in the morning, the crew had journeyed thirty nautical kilometers and reached the open waters toward the southern shore of Sweden—an area usually known for great runs of herring. Leif and Gunnar manned the trawling nets, lowering them from the two great poles that stretched diagonally over the sides of the fishing vessel. Leif worked the winch, releasing the thirty-meter scoops into a dragging position behind the Nordic Princess, while Gunnar kept the lines free from tangling. Olaf piloted the rig, maintaining a speed optimum for collecting the great wealth of Baltic herring, a known delicacy to anyone living in the Scandinavian region.

By noon, the couple had been given a quick course on "How to Fillet Herring" by Olaf, so that by the second dozen fish, they had mastered the process.

"The main trick, Dorothy, is not to puncture the herring's innards—or all its guts and blood will invade the fillet…"

The sight of the blood and the odor from the fish innards caused Isaac to return to his stooping posture over the starboard side of the vessel.

"Clean up before you come back to the table!" the captain ordered.

By the end of day, the fillet duo finished three small wooden kegs of herring.

"Rinse them with fresh, hose water. I will add all pickling ingredients and seal the top lid. Three barrels—not bad for a start! Let us see if you can complete seven tomorrow, okay? Now go wash up."

Leif cooked a dinner of beans, knockwurst and sauerkraut. Flora ate more than either crewman, but Isaac refused food and rather welcomed the early evening breezes, which he inhaled standing at the ship's bow.

Saturday brought an identical schedule for the crew of the Nordic Princess, a day in which Isaac and Flora found no attraction to the life of a fisherman.

"Tomorrow we will complete the first part of our run and drop off our current catch in Gotland, on Monday We will refuel, get more ice, take a shower, enjoy a good meal and be back on the water by 4:00 a.m. Tuesday, yes?"

"Isn't Gotland Island a part of Sweden?" Isaac asked, remembering that detail from the torn pages of the atlas.

"Yah, but it is desolate. The only city is Visby, about half the size of Sonderborg, and nothing else. Believe me—you do not want to spend the rest of your life in Gotland."

As the captain rolled his eyes, the couple nodded. After all, they had waited this long. A few more days to reach Stockholm would be fine.

* * * * *

Friday was to be the last full day at sea. At 2:00 p.m. on Saturday they were scheduled to reach the Swedish capitol's port. Isaac realized the method to Olaf's fishing business—work no more than three days at sea and then relinquish your catch for money. This created four small fishing jaunts: Sonderborg to Gotland, Gotland to Stockholm, and then the trip in reverse. The two-day rest in Stockholm was a welcome holiday. Isaac wondered, in light of the German occupation of Denmark, *why didn't the fishermen flee there and make Sweden their permanent home?* as he and Flora were attempting to do, but he never asked.

"This time tomorrow, Flora, we will be Swedes—living in Stockholm."

Isaac filleted a Baltic herring without even looking at it.

"I think I will buy us the best beef dinner and champagne I can find. Celebrate our freedom! Do you realize what we have done? We have beaten the bully. So many odds were against us. We should still be prisoners… perhaps even dead."

"Captain, we have visitors! Starboard, five o'clock," Gunnar yelled as he pulled one of the netting lines, straightening its lie under the boat's salty wake.

"Crap! What are they doing this far north?" Arnstaadt responded, with definite concern in his voice. "Everyone keep to your stations. I will do the talking. Heinrich—you hide Dorothy where she has been sleeping, behind the pilot wheel panel."

The German patrol vessel was approaching at a tremendous speed. Nervous, Isaac had difficulty getting the thin mahogany board back into its metal track, so he was forced to rest the slab of polished wood against the compartment before running out to the stern to continue his tasks at the fillet table.

The schnellboot cut through the Baltic waves as if it was gliding through a serene glacial lake. Captain Klaus Rassmussen's patrol boat, reaching a speed of 50 knots an hour, ventured into waters that were usually dismissed by Kriegsmarine interests. Its 2500 liter tanks, recently replenished with fuel nearly one hundred kilometers away from this area, assured the skipper that the "Baltic Blitz" could harass any vessel in any part of the vast Scandinavian sea.

The Schnellboot S-51 slowed to a modest speed, overtaking the archaic pace of Olaf Arnstaadt's trawler. The wooden-hulled destroyer circled the Nordic Princess and slowed as the Nazi officer called across the water, using a megaphone, ordering the fishing captain to cut all engines.

The nautical attacker was twice as long as Arnstaadt's ship. Its hull, strategically constructed to avoid the Russian magnetic mines that laced the eastern Baltic, sat much higher in the water than its defenseless prey. The crew stood armed at various points of the deck. Only the pilot remained hidden within the metal-reinforced steering cabin.

Isaac's heart sank. What was the purpose of the invasion? He cursed himself for not deciding to leave the Nordic Princess in

Gotland and taking a smaller ferry to the Swedish mainland. He kept his head facing the table and filleted the herring at a rapid pace.

Gunnar and Leif stood on either side of Arnstaadt, who broke the silence as one of the Kriegsmarine sailors through lines to the fishermen. Each crewman connected the rope to cleats at the bow and stern of their vessel. As the braided connections were pulled taught, both ships locked as one, only protected by their dock bumpers.

"Ahh, captain, you are quite far from home, yah? I fish these waters every week. We have not seen the Kriegsmarine in these parts, ever. I have been doing this for over twenty years. To what do we owe this pleasure?" the gregarious fisherman began.

"Hello captain," Rassmussen bellowed from midship. "I noticed your Danish flag, flying proudly. And being stationed in Copenhagen myself, I thought maybe you were a Russian decoy. You are quite far from Denmark as well. Surely there are enough fish in Danish waters?"

"I have been following this run for quite some time—the best herring are in these waters. We trawl up the Swedish coast, release our catch, and then we complete the same route in reverse."

"Would you mind if I come on board, Captain?"

Rassmussen seemed amiable—not in character of the ruthless Nazi who rammed a rowboat several days earlier, killing eight Danes attempting to regain their freedom.

Olaf gulped. He was hoping that the obvious sight of poor fishermen would be of no interest to the schnellboot officer. It was not the case. He looked back at Isaac, working his station in a frantic motion.

"Of course, Captain. Denmark has always welcomed our German neighbor into its Scandinavian fold. My ship is no different."

Rassmussen motioned to one of the crewmen, and the obedient sailor lowered a metal plank that bridged the decks of the two vessels, creating an easy midair path for the seaman.

The komandant of the Schnellboot S-51 crossed the levered bridge, his wireless officer's cap clung to his head, unaffected by the gusts of sea wind blowing between the hulls. Two armed crewmen followed the smooth-talking Nazi officer as he reached the deck of the Nordic Princess. Once on board, the crewmen flanked their commander, affirming his dominant presence on the fishing vessel.

Rassmussen saluted Olaf Arnstaadt and followed with a handshake.

"How has your success rate been on this trip, Captain?" the tactful officer questioned, glancing around the deck surface. "I see you have another business besides fishing."

"Yes, yes I do Captain, I produce the finest pickled herring in all of Denmark. As long as we are on the waters, why not? Its freshness and spices make it perhaps the best in all of Scandinavia as well."

He called to his crewman

"Gunnar—bring the Captain a filled barrel that we produced on Saturday."

He turned to the officer.

"The seasoning process has begun by now. My gift to you, captain, for you and your men this evening. It goes excellently with a cold Carlsberg.'

"Thank you, Captain," Rassmussen nodded, directing one of his men to accept the offering.

Gunnar placed the small keg at the sailor's feet.

"So this is a routine fishing voyage, Captain?" Rassmussen asked as he began scrutinizing the deck more closely. He walked over to Isaac's table, turning sharply away in disgust at the bloody fish and the smell.

"Do you have the Kriegsmarine police marina form, sir?"

He moved into what appeared to be a skeptical mode—all too common in the demeanor of any Nazi officer. Arnstaadt's bribe of herring, although accepted, did not curtail the inquiry.

"Certainly, sir," the fisherman said as he went into the pilot shanty and returned with the docket that displayed a large number "four"—indicating the total number on the boat. He prayed no more paperwork would be required to satisfy the Nazi's questioning.

As Rassmussen followed Olaf back into the pilot quarters, the burly seaman bit down on the stem of his pipe, annoyed that the komandant's behavior was blossoming into an act of provocation.

"What is under here, Captain? Ahh your sleeping quarters, kitchen and stove. Very tight conditions for you and your crew, yes?"

Rassmussen picked up Olaf Arnstaadt's tobacco pouch, untethered its leather straps and sniffed the aromatic blend. He picked up some cans of food, studied the labels then placed them back into the box.

As astute as the officer appeared, he never caught the unsecured panel resting on the front cabin wall, behind the steering post.

"Hmm, a Wermacht issued duffle bag?" Rassmussen said aloud, examining Isaac's canvas satchel, thrown on the bunk where he had been sleeping. "Were you in the German army, Captain?"

In this question, Rassmussen had finally found a flaw in his so far benign and boring inquiry.

"No sir. That is not mine. It belongs to one of my men," Olaf responded in a matter-of-fact tone.

"Which one?" the officer asked picked it up and bringing it out to the open deck.

"Heinrich, the man filleting the delicious herring you will be enjoying, this evening."

Olaf knew his answer sounded patronizing, but he was getting annoyed at the intimidating delay and total imposition on his schedule.

"You, Heinrich, come closer. Please," Rassmussen beckoned Isaac to meet him, calling him to the center deck. "Why do you have a Wermacht army duffle bag? You are a fisherman—not a soldier," his voice echoing from the amplification caused by the wall of the schnellboot.

Isaac followed with his seasoned explanation, which he had used on Sven Ingman and Arnstaadt.

"I worked in a motor pool operation in Haderslev for two years, sir. Although a civilian, I received many military privileges, such as food, tools, supplies and such."

Rassmussen looked out to the vast ocean, breathed deeply and responded.

"Very well, young man."

He picked up the bag, and just as Arnstaadt put his hand out to take the sack from the Nazi, the captain threw it back on to the deck surface.

"Then you would not mind if I reviewed its contents, would you, young man?"

Isaac felt the glow of the mid-morning sun blind his vision as well his thought process. It had finally happened—so close to his and Flora's success. They had overcome so many difficult situations that week, and over the last three months—only to fail thirty-five kilometers from the shores of Sweden. He quivered as a tear rolled down his boney cheek, watching the Kriegsmarine officer loosen the ropes of the duffle bag collar.

Rassmussen knelt after widening the canvas straps, reached in he began to uncover Isaac Bloom's many survival items, accumulated from his imprisonment at Wurtzmuller's.

"Well, well, well, what do we have here?"

The Nazi revealed one of the gold candelabra sticks from the top of the bag. He held it up for his crew to see. They all laughed simultaneously—at such a ridiculous item to be drawn from the sack.

"Neitzheimer, can you read the wording at the base of the candlestick?"

Rassmussen was setting up for a more theatrical demonstration. His crewman looked at the decorative lettering toward the base of the golden candelabra.

"No sir," the sailor responded, playing along.

"Do you know why you cannot read it, Sergeant?"

"Why, Captain?" the cooperative crewman answered, as if some vaudeville straight man.

"Because the decorative writing is written in 'Jew.' That is why sergeant?"

Rassmussen laughed with a sinister cackle, enjoying the discovery of the questionable item just drawn from the bag. He held up the gold sticks, presenting his find to the other crewmen, who were leering down from the higher deck of the Schnellboot S-51.

"Hmm, Sergeant, it appears that there are several more. And what do we have here?" the Nazi officer called out, revealing three banded groups of paper money. "There appears to be a treasure of Reichsmarks, and Swiss francs. Tell me young man—why no kroners? In my next life, I think I would like to return as a lowly fisherman. Certainly, I am doing something wrong with this life. Your wealth intrigues me."

As Rassmussen was having a lark at being nasty, Olaf Arnstaadt stood frozen, unable to muster an explanation. He knew this was an event for higher authority and he was responsible for the character of his crew. He knew he was in serious trouble.

"Captain, would you be able to offer an explanation?"

The Schnellboot captain reached in and removed a box from the canvas sack. Opening the cardboard top, he discovered a generous pile of watches, gold jewelry and baubles, which greeted his inquisitive eyes. "Okay, I have seen enough. Schmutzi!" he called to his cook. "Bring this sack down to my quarters. I will study the rest of its contents this evening, over a cold pilsner and the best herring in all of Scandinavia," he smiled, dripping the sarcasm into Arnstaadt's face.

"Wait, I can explain!" Isaac interrupted. "Please! There were some neighbors in Haderslav. They asked me if I could take a package to their relatives in Stockholm. I did not even know what it was."

"So you handed them your empty bag. They filled it with all these valuables, and handed it back to you. And you never once looked inside?" Rassmussen queried, not believing the explanation.

"Well, I did, but it was not my business," Isaac said, thinking the excuse made sense.

"Are you aware that the Reich controls Denmark, young man? Everything within the country is owned by the Fuhrer, Adolf Hitler. If you try to remove it, you are stealing from Germany—a crime subject to death."

"Captain—please take the bag! My apologies for my fisherman in making a poor decision," Olaf pleaded. "I will punish him for creating such an inconvenience. Just please let us complete our run. I promise you, I will see that he never works these waters, again."

"I would love to take the money and run, Captain," Rasmussen said, "but what example would I be setting for my men? I am afraid that I will have to bring your ship back to Copenhagen to let a higher authority review my findings and let them decide."

Flora heard all. She wanted to run to the side of her husband, but she thought better. She had to stay concealed in the dark hold, behind the pilot wheel. She knew her discovery would only magnify the severity of the situation.

"How fast can your scow go, Captain?" the officer asked Arnstaadt.

"Six, maybe seven knots, top speed. This will take more time than it is worth for you," the fisherman responded, annoyed.

"Please—let me be the judge of that, sir," the Nazi commander replied with as much arrogance.

He shouted over the bridge, which still connected the two vessels.

"We will tow them to increase their speed. You men—connect the line from our stern to their bow!"

He motioned for the two armed sailors with him on the deck of the Nordic Princess to secure the towing line on to the fishing boat's bow.

"Give them two hundred meters of line. It will take us three days at this speed. When will we get in range of any German radio contact?" he asked the communications sailor.

"Sir, we will not be in any range until tomorrow afternoon. No one will know we are bringing them in until then."

Isaac caught Olaf Arnstaadt glaring at him in hate and disgust. The fisherman felt betrayed because Isaac had lied to him. Isaac looked to the deck. What would happen when Flora was discovered?

He spoke out to the Kriegsmarine captain.

"Sir, before you take my duffle bag, can I get something from it?"

"What? What do you want? Are you intending to beat me over the head with one of your candlesticks? Or perhaps you need a few thousand Swiss Francs?"

"No sir," Isaac answered, unsure of what he was even asking. "I just need to get something."

"Very well."

The officer motioned to his sergeant to drop the duffle bag as Isaac bent down, putting his hand deep into the oversized canvas, reaching around its base.

"Sergeant, hold your rifle steady. If he should try something funny, shoot him in the head.

Flora listened to the dialogue and began to cry into her overall bib, though she maintained silence.

"You better make it quick, boy. Sergeant, if he surfaces with a weapon, kill him instantly."

The entire crew, as well as Olaf, Gunnar and Leif, watched.

Isaac felt his way around the bottom of the huge canvas bag, in the area Rassmussen had not touched. Pushing aside the canisters of hand grenade explosives, flairs and food, he felt what he had hoped would be their salvation.

The smooth metal control panel—the one he had received from the salesman who startled him in Wurtzmuller's chalet, sat at the bottom of the sack. He remembered the day. He had signed for four units, but received a fifth transmitter and receiver, and he had secretly stored it in his survival bag.

His fingers danced across the control box, hoping to locate the toggle switch that turned on the unit. When he discovered its location, in the lower left corner, Isaac flipped it up. Miraculously, his hand felt the unit bear down, as electrical life jumped into the battery-powered receiver.

Without showing any emotion, he rejoiced at the subtle indication of its potential, pleased that he had decided to move its transmitter to Flora's bag. He understood all along that if they were to be effective, they had to be separated from one another and not locked into the same location. His arm scurried around, feeling through the rest of the contents.

"I will tell you what, Sergeant—if his hand surfaces empty, kill him anyway for wasting our time," the impatient officer ordered in jest.

Slowly, Isaac's arm slid from the bag, making its way to the cinched opening. Clearing it, he stood, presenting a stocking cap. He stretched the woolen hat over his cranium.

"I needed my cap, it gets cold at night."

He pulled down hard on the wedding gift given to him by fishing supply proprietor Sven Ingman. Handing the bag back to the sergeant, Isaac followed with a more self-assured response to his enemy.

"Now, I am ready."

CHAPTER 42

Kriegsmarine Captain Klaus Rassmussen ordered one of the armed sailors who had accompanied him aboard the Nordic Princess to remain on the fishing vessel to guard the four fishermen while their boat was towed back to Copenhagen. He promised the helmeted and battle-ready crewman that he would be relieved by one of his six comrades at eight p.m. The orders were to let them trawl if they could while being towed to allow the fillet station to remain productive, to let the fishermen continue their routine activities—and shoot to kill "if any of them tried something stupid."

The stoic and annoyed sailor, upset at the boring orders, stood with his rifle slung over his shoulder. He was certain that a group of ordinary fishermen would not attempt anything offensive—especially while being towed two hundred meters behind the floating fortress of a schnellboot. If necessary, both 37 milimeter cannons, situated on the deck of the German destroyer, could sink the defenseless trawler within seconds.

All the while, Flora Bloom kept in hiding behind the unsecured mahogany panel of the fishing vessel's pilot house. Every so often, she would peek through the crack of the wall to see all those on board, including the sole Nazi guard left behind. Helpless, she remained isolated and unnoticed.

After twenty minutes of silence, Olaf Arnstaadt finished helping Gunnar and Leif drop one trawling net into the sea. He surmised that the speed the vessel was moving, faster speed of ten knots, was too fast to catch any herring, but he refused to remain unproductive.

Upon completing that task, the captain of the Nordic Princess approached Isaac at the filleting table.

"Well, my friend, first let me thank you for ruining my run, maybe my profession, and perhaps even my life. What do you have to say for yourself?"

"I am sorry, sir. We should have left your boat in Gotland," Isaac sighed.

"Do you forget? According to the papers, I had to arrive with four fishermen to the Stockholm fishing docks. However, it makes no difference now. So tell me some truth here—are you and your girlfriend Jews? Are you criminals? Were those things stolen? Why did you lie to me?"

The sounds of the sea, along with the monstrous shnellboot engines and the more docile fishing motor, created a cushion of privacy as their conversation remained inaudible to the armed sailor.

"My name is Isaac Bloom. The woman is my wife, Flora. We were prisoners in a Nazi labor camp. We managed to escape. It was our goal to start a new life in Sweden. There were many obstacles. We almost made it. I am sorry that we caused this problem for you."

"And all that gold, jewelry and money?" Olaf asked.

"I managed to steal it back from the Nazis to use it for bribery and bargaining opportunities. It was also to be used for your fee. By the way, I still have more," Isaac said, wondering if Olaf had any last-minute ideas.

"You have more?" Olaf asked, puzzled.

"Yes, in my wife's sack."

"Ahh yes, your wife—stowed away in the hull—the wife who will be the reason we are all arrested and killed when we get to Copenhagen. I almost forgot about her seculusion."

Olaf stared out to the vast sea as he reminded himself of the grave situation.

"For a second, I thought maybe we would be released, once at dock. The Nazis will scour this boat. She will be found. We, my friend, are all doomed."

Chomping on his pipe, Olaf turned to rejoin his crew.

"Wait, sir—I have an idea!"

Isaac glanced aside, making sure he was not speaking too loud.

Olaf took Isaac by the nape of his neck and directed his skull to Schnellboot S-51.

"Whatever your idea is, will it be capable to deal with that six-man armada? I think you better account for that before you try anything that might make that ship's captain any more angry with us than he already is!"

"Please distract the guard. I must get to my wife. She has something in her satchel that might help us," Isaac begged the defeated skipper.

"After all this—now you are giving me orders?" Olaf responded with legitimate annoyance, hesitant to act. "Fine, do what you have to do inside, but I want you back on the table in five minutes. We are still a working vessel. You have to produce, even if we are returning home."

The captain turned to the armed sailor, shaking his head.

"After the war, do not ever get involved with the likes of fishermen. It is tough finding good help these days."

The German stood unresponsive, holding onto a boat cleat that doubled as a handle.

Once in the pilot booth, Isaac bent over the wheel, pretending to search for something. He knelt, picking up papers, rags, rope and rearraging their place within the shanty. As he came close to the open panel he whispered.

"Flora, can you here me?"

Two piecing blue eyes peered out from the crack in the wall.

He turned to note that Olaf was blocking the direction of the armed sailor and whispered to his wife.

"In your canvas bag, there is a metal panel with switches, lights and dials. Can you locate it?"

Seconds later, she held up an item s he squinted through the opening.

"Is this it?" she asked, pressing against the veneer mahogany wall.

"Yes!" he responded. "Just move it through the crack quickly. Press the opening so it passes through, and then conceal yourself."

"Hey, you get back here! I want everyone visible!" the guard yelled toward the pilot house, ignoring Olaf. "If you cannot find what you are looking for, forget it. I want you outside, right now!"

"Very well. I found what I was looking for…"

Isaac reappeared on the open deck, holding a strange contraption in his hand.

"What the hell is that? Give it to me! What are you doing? Get back to fisherman work."

The guard approached Isaac and went to grab the transmitter, but Isaac pulled it away.

"Hey, I will show it to you, but it is very fragile. I spent a lot of money on this in the nautical supply shop in Sonderborg."

"It will not hurt you, Sergeant," Olaf said, playing along. "Heinrich—tell the sailor what it is?"

The captain had hoped his weak endorsement of the square device would put the guard at ease.

"It is an electronic locating device," Isaac explained. "It works like sonar. It tells us if schools of fish are swimming near our boat and if we should put out out trawling nets or not. It is basically the same as used by the military—only it locates modest differences in water density, not submarines. It is a new invention for fishermen."

Isaac had read in a magazine that people were working on such devices, but he fabricated a total lie.

Olaf grinned, but the sailor was not amused.

"It sounds too futuristic, put it away. You are not fishing now, anyway."

"Your captain is letting us trawl," Arnstaadt reminded.

"Can we just see if there are any schools down there?" Isaac asked. "Then I will put it away."

The guard motioned with the barrel of his rifle.

"If this conflicts with the radio waves of our ship, I will personally throw it into the sea."

"It does not," Isaac assured him. "It runs on much lower frequencies. That was my first question to the man who sold it to me. We have radios on board as well."

"Ten minutes only, and then put it away," the guard sneered. "You are in enough trouble, fellow, believe me. You do not want any more."

Isaac stood on the port side, facing away from the Schnellboot. He flipped the transmitter to the "on" position. A red light immediately glowed atop the panel. Like its complimentary receiving unit, Isaac felt a flow of energy from its battery as it overtook the hunk of metal. A charged, vibrating current brought the green box to life.

"Hey, fisherman!—over here where I can see you! Conduct your search on starboard side."

Isaac complied, hoping the sailor would give him more time. He pointed the transmiter and its aerial toward the sea, as well as at the Schnellboot-51. Standing in plain sight, Isaac began his slow mock search, turning the dial of the frequency indicator. There were twelve settings, but unfortunately, he had no idea which number had been set on the receiver. He rotated the dial to the twelve different frequencies, but all for naught. The red light remained red at every integer.

Dejected, Isaac tried to remember what salesman Rutger von Blacom had instructed several weeks earlier. He had informed

Wurtzmuller through Isaac to be concerned first with safety—not to hit the toggle switch if both the transmitter light and receiver light turned green.

Determined, Isaac decided to give the indicator one more revolution.

"You have five more minutes to search for fish. Then that contraption goes back to your shanty," the impatient guard shouted.

As Isaac twisted the dial a second time, at number "five," the green light appeared, but then, just as quickly, the red bulb indicator glowed in place of the green one. Nonetheless, something had happened. His body bristled with hope. "Five" was the lucky number. But why wasn't it retaining its frequency connection?

He kept the dial on the fifth selection. Once again it flickered green and immediately returned to its red crystallized state. What was going on? Again, he tried to remember the Siemens salesman's brief explanation of the device.

"Okay, let's go! Enough play time. Put your toy fish-finder away," the armed sailor shouted, as he was not going to extend his experiment time period.

Then Isaac remembered: von Blarcom said that if the controller was out of range, the frequency might not reach the unit to adequately perform. Isaac looked at the tow line. When it was taught, they were at a distance of 200 plus meters, and then he understood.

Look toward the Schnellboot-51, there was a pattern: when the Nordic Princess rushed down a swell in the water, the rope created a reverse arch, bringing the vessels much closer. Isaac deduced that the change in the position between swells must have created the flicker!

"Okay, sir. I think I found a school! A few more seconds please. This is amazing. What a leap for the fishing industry!"

Isaac did not even realize what he was saying. When the eager young man studied the rise and fall of the tow line—sure enough, the light was crimson in color when the line was extended to its full length. But when there was a slack in the hemp, the green light briefly appeared.

He keenly observed a defined wave approaching. The huge swell would create a tightening of the line, but immediately afterwards, the response of a rush toward the German craft would be equally accentuated. He felt the adrenelin rush through his veins as he tried to time his attempt perfectly.

"Let's go, fisherman! Put that away. You have been wasting time."

As the sailor approached, Isaac felt the wave's zenith prepare the boat's velocity for its decent on down to its trough.

The soldier lost his step, not paying attention to the Baltic's agitation. He rocked back, reganing his balance. As he resumed toward Isaac, the proximity to the schnellboot lit the green indicator for a full five seconds.

It took Isaac Bloom only two of those five. He bridged the frequency radio waves, and the transmitter detonated its packed charge of modest explosives built into the receiving unit. What made the magnification of the response more significant was the numerous hand grenade canisters also at the bottom of the canvas sack. The delayed reaction created an explosion so forceful that it blew the armored pilot house shell off the German vessel thirty meters into the air.

Fires erupted. The crew of six ran for hoses, buckets and extinguishers. The blaze grew almost immediately, quickly becoming out of control. Isaac saw no sign of the captain who had apparently been down below where the sack had been placed.

"Shit! Shit! What did you do?" the guard yelled raising his rifle to Isaac's chest.

"I… I did nothing. Nothing!" Isaac claimed in innocence. "I just looked for fish. This is a simple machine—it is not anything dangerous. I did nothing! There must have been an accident on your boat. Maybe it overheated from dragging us and the motors exploded! I do not know. Please, I did not do anything!"

The schnellboot alarm signaled. It signaled across the waters, but no one could hear it, except those on the Nordic Princess. Olaf, Gunner and Leif were stunned. The guard grabbed the transmitter and hurled it into the Baltic waters. They could see the men onboard the Nazi destroyer, frantically working on the section leading to the crew quarters, the area of explosion. Isaac knew—it was exactly the area where Rassmussen had stowed his bag.

"We have to save them!" the guard called to Olaf, who had run into his control room and placed his vessel into neutral to keep a distance.

"The fires are spreading, I am afraid…" Arnstaadt never finished the sentence. The fire reached Schnellboot-51's huge gas tanks. There was a second explosion, which was exponential to the first. The fuel created a blast, splitting the hull of the sleak Nazi boat, hurling its oak slated sides into the salt air like matchsticks. Wood fires rained down on the water, some hitting Arnstaadt's fishing boat. Gunnar and Lief, responding, picked up two pieces of the ship's debris and heaved them over the side.

"Gunnar, untie our towline. If her stern sinks, we get dragged down as well. Hurry! Untie us!"

The crewmen responded to Arnstaadt's order, desperately trying to free the bow cleat from the sinking German attacker. No sooner had Gunnar untethered the line when the four-centimeter braided hemp whipped out of his grasp and trailed the back portion of Rassmussen's vessel as it sunk to the floor of the sea—a second later, and the Princess would have been dragged down along with the stern of the schnellboot.

The only things visibly afloat were individual fires of random debris, fueled by the oil and gas soaked devestation—that used to be the "scurge" of the Baltic.

"Circle around, quickly! Circle around the wreckage. I want to see if there are any survivors!"

The armed sailor was in shock, but he kept his gun on the crew of the Nordic Princess, hoping he might discover the live body of one of his fellow mates.

Olaf obeyed the sailor, but he conveyed the danger of getting too close to the still-fueled islands of flaming debris that scattered the widening circumference of the explosion. He snaked the Nordic Princess through smoke and fire, bumping into pieces of hull and other boyant wreckage.

"I cannot locate any survivors. I think we should leave this area. You can never be sure if something else may ignite, even under water.

At that moment, a subaquatic explosion erupted from the turbulent swells, rocking the fishing boat. The spurt of salt water, created by two errant depth charges, shot fifty meters into the air, from its port side. The deluge showered on the Princess. Gunnar slid across the deck, striking his head on the pilot booth. Leif and Olaf managed to stabilize while holding on to the starboard railing.

Isaac toppled onto the armed guard, who prompltly threw him off his fallen body.

"Get off me, you fool! Stand against the side of the hull rail, all of you!"

"I am getting us away from this sight before we are all killed!" Arnstaadt advised rather than asking permission. He received no resistance from the sailor.

"Captain, I want all of you to line up in front of me once you clear danger. Do you hear me?" the guard said, trying to maintain a tone of authority.

The explosions had briefly generated a convenient brotherhood of survival, but he wanted the crew to remember that they were still his prisoners.

"Set your course south, Captain. Then all of you, in front of me."

Arnstaadt locked into course direction, while the drenched Gunnar, Leif and Isaac lined up in front of the lone Nazi.

"You to the side," the befuddled gunman directed, pointing to Isaac with the barrel of his rifle. "You are somehow different. You do not seem to be of fisherman stock. Somehow your behavior has caused all this. Captain, is this man a valid crewman or a Danish escapee? I will not bring you harm. Just tell me the truth. I would sooner kill him and have only three men to guard on our return trip."

"I am an escapee from Ravensbruck, a German concentration camp, just north of Berlin," Isaac blurted in answer, surprising Arnstaadt and his men. "I lied to the Captain. He thought I was leaving Denmark to meet up with a girl. Neither he nor his men had any knowledge of my past."

The sailor was caught up in Isaac's candid voluntary explanation.

"I take full responsibility for my own actions, and for orchestrating the explosion and sinking of your ship. I detonated a device that I smuggled out of an arms warehouse. So, it is I that you want—not these honest fishermen. Please spare them any punishment that you have planned."

"The three of you—step aside from this individual."

The guard raised his gun to Isaac's head, aiming one meter away from his left temple.

"I will let you apologize to your fellow crewmen before I pull the trigger. You are a Jew, yes?"

Isaac took a deep breath. Before he spoke, the crash of an empty pickled herring barrel came down on the Nazi's neck and shoulder, compliments of one, Flora Bloom—who had discreetly exited her hiding place and whose intentions were not betrayed by the four captives, staring at her actions behind the guard's back.

The rifle scampered across the deck as the wounded sailor fell to his knees. Leif ran to claim the loose weapon while Gunnar picked up the stunned Nazi and brought the guard to his feet. Olaf faced him.

"Now who are you going to kill? Whose life are you going to ruin? Haven't you and your people inflicted enough misery on the world?"

"Whether we dock in Denmark, Germany or Sweden, who do you think the authorities will believe? You or me?" the arrogant sailor sneered at his captor.

Olaf Arnstaadt turned to walk away from the bewildered guard, and then, like a man possessed, he spun his huge frame around and picked the Nazi up by the scruff of his neck and the seat of his pants.

"What makes you think that you are returning to a dock?

As the fisherman hurled the German soldier over the side of the fishing vessel, he shouted.

"You really thought the authorities would have to choose? Now, how do you feel, Nazi? There are no choices. Say hello to your friends."

Arnstaadt jumped on to the edge of the deck rail and held tightly to the wooden trawling pole, standing fifteen meters above the helmeted sailor, who could barely stay afloat. The guard treaded Baltic waters that seemed to beckon his weighty uniform and sogged boots.

"Look at me! Look at me, you arrogant German piece of shit!" Olaf jeered.

Gunnar snuck a laughing smile to his buddy. They had not seen the Captain so wild since the previous May, when he became so drunk in the Northern Lights tavern that they missed their fishing run.

"Look at me, sailor! Thank you for taking our Danish freedom from us. Let this be the last thing you see before you die!"

Olaf spun while still holding onto the trawling pole, dropped his overalls, unbuttoned the trap door of his "long John" underwear and slapped his buttocks with his huge fisherman's hand. Looking at the drowning Nazi, the animated captain shouted.

"Kiss my royal Danish ass!"

Flora buried her head into Isaac's chest, still in shock over the morning's events. Leif and Gunnar were convulsive. The sailor's head bobbed for one more gasp of air, as truly, the last thing he would see on this earth was indeed Olaf Arnstaadt's behind. Isaac held Flora, kissing her scalp, whispering.

"It is over."

"Leif, what is the time?" Olaf asked, regaining his composure as he jumped back on to the deck.

"Eleven-forty," the fisherman answered. "What course, Captain?"

"After this, even I do not want to work. We are about 30 kilometers to Nynashaumn. Take me to Orlo's. We will drop our guests off there and continue to Stockholm tomorrow."

He looked at the embaced couple and smiled.

"The outcome was good… but I still want you off my ship as soon as possible."

Everone laughed—even Flora.

CHAPTER 43

The Nynashaumn cove narrowed to a docile passage as the Nordic Princess transitioned from the wild waves of the Baltic. The inlet had a smooth, glasslike sheen to its waters, the reflection of the fishing boat an inverted mirror image as the Princess glided through the sheltered fjord.

The welcoming arms of fifty-meter conifers on either shore seemed to embrace the tiny vessel as it edged deeper into the Nordic cove. Rock formations sculpted in the last ice age stretched from the green banks like the slender fingers of a hand, beckoning the craft to become a part of the nautical serenity.

As the sun set in the western sky, the corresponding tranquil mood created was a reward to the day's frenzied happenings. Over time, the distance from shore to shore narrowed to one hundred meters. Blue water, green vegetation and amber rocks set the scene for the occasional hut residences of local Swedish fishermen, living on the banks. Small homes, lacquered in brilliant colors of azure blue, loganberry red, lemon yellow and forest green dotted the treed shoreline. Other buildings had been constructed on oak pilings, extending human life out and over the waterway, allowing the inhabitants to be one with the harbor.

Wooden cabins in joyful hues married the natural beauty of the shoreline to the calmness of the sea. The structures brought life and happiness to what already seemed to be the perfection of nature.

"My friend, Orlo, is just around this bend. His house is red," Olaf explained, anxious to see his old fishing crewman. "I have not seen him or his wife for at least a year. He will help us. We are now some thirty-five kilometers due south of Stockholm. This is where I will leave you. He can assist for the rest of the way, no?"

Perhaps it was the therapeutic powers of the fjord, but Arnstaadt seemed to have totally forgotten the earlier day's events. He appeared calm and rejuvenated—as if some higher spirit was guiding his boat into the ethereal cove.

Isaac and Flora felt the spirit as well. A sense of release, calm and love warmed their cold, broken hearts, a good sign. The scenery was simple and pure, but it made them forget the hell that had once consumed them.

A young boy of about twelve years, watering flowers on the cabin widow sill, dropped his bucket and began running down the long wooden dock. The end of the structure blossomed into a platform of X-shaped racks.

"Those are for Orlo's cod drying business," Arnstaadt told Isaac and Flora, who stared at the geometric oddity.

Lief threw the docking rope to the youngster, who began to wrap it around the metal cleat on the last piling.

"Ahh, Riga—you must have grown a half of a meter since I last saw you!" Olaf called, jumping off the Princess.

He hugged the lad and looked up to discover two adults now running along the rickety pier to greet him.

"Orlo, Liv! How are you?" the captain shouted, climbing the dock stairway.

An older gentleman who could have passed for any Germanic or Scandinavian interpretation of St. Nicholas waddled to the dock edge, followed by an aging Swedish woman, her blond hair in a bun and alabaster skin still displaying pure Nordic beauty. The white-bearded Swede called to his unexpected guest.

"Olaf, my friend—it has been too long."

The two nautical figures embraced for several seconds, displaying a genuine comradery that had been the result of years at sea together.

"I have brought guests that I would like you to help get to Stockholm in the morning, yes?" Olaf said, pointing to Isaac and Flora, who were climbing over the edge of the hull.

"It would be my pleasure, Olaf. Your friends are immediately my guests."

Orlo went to the couple and hugged them as well. In that moment, Isaac felt they had finally succeded in reaching their goal of freedom, Orlo's embrace a symbol of success.

"Welcome to my house, welcome to Sweden, welcome to the rest of your life!"

Flora felt in the girth of Orlo's grasp. It had been years since any man besides Isaac had embraced her frail body so intensely.

"This couple has escaped the wrath of Nazi imprisonment. Show them what it is like to be a Swede!" Olaf urged, smiling, knowing he needed to say nothing else to his old friends.

"Come with me, young woman!" Liv said, grabbing Flora. "We will clean you up—you can take a sauna in our new cabin—and I will get you some fresh clothes. Then we will celebrate your arrival to our beautiful country."

They headed back to the red shore building, like they had been longtime friends, as Orlo continued his conversation with the men.

"You will join us as well, no? We were just getting ready to eat supper."

He removed a corn cob pipe from his lips as he offered the invitation to the three fishermen, who were securing the boat to the water's edge dock.

"Orlo, I need a favor," Olaf whispered. "I must arrive with four men in Stokholm harbor. Can I borrow Riga—just to confirm the head count? I will make sure he does not dance with the ladies on Saturday night."

The men laughed as the young boy tugged at his father's trousers, begging to go.

"Can I, father? I will behave. I promise. I have done all my schoolwork for Monday," he asked, clasping his hands in a praying motion.

"We must fish all day tomorrow and arrive in port by four o'clock p.m. I guarantee he will be tired, Orlo. I will put him on the bus to Havershamn myself by Sunday noon.

Orlo just looked at the boy.

"Go pack. Tell your mother what is happening."

The lad jumped with glee and ran back to the cabin.

"Will you eat with us?" Orlo asked.

"Orlo, I will. I must have Lief and Gunnar prepare for the morning. I will bring Liv's meals to them. But we—even Riga—must sleep on the boat. We will shove off at three a.m. You can assist the couple as you see fit."

He nodded toward Isaac, who smiled.

"Sir, we have some business to finish," Isaac reminded Olaf.

Orlo motioned that he was returning to the cabin. He could see his wife assisting Flora, washing the young woman's short locks under the exterior shower.

"Wait until you try the sauna. We just erected it. It is so rejuvenating! I will check on the stew," he shouted to her as he entered the scarlet cabin.

Liv wrapped her guest in several towels and directed her into the wood-hewn sauna booth.

Isaac needed some private time with Olaf.

"Sir, again I am sorry for the lie I told you to get on board your ship. There are no more lies."

Olaf put his claw of a hand around the back of Isaac's neck.

"In the end, all was okay. We will never speak of this again. We never encountered Nazi's on the water!" he said, letting out a big laugh.

Isaac opened the smaller bag that Flora had carried for most of the adventure. Reaching in, he removed stacks of Reichsmarks and handed them to the captain.

"This should be more than enough—probably more than we agreed."

He grabbed two additional bundles, yelling to Lief and Gunnar.

"Catch!"

They grabbed the wads of paper money, smiling and bowing to him.

"Do not treat them so good or they will not want to fish anymore!" Olaf bellowed, thanking Isaac for the generosity toward his men.

"If you are living in Stockholm, come by the docks. We may be in port and we can go for a beer," Gunnar yelled.

"Let us eat," Olaf said, putting an arm over Isaac's shoulder, and they walked the length of Orlo's dock to his crimson residence. By that time, Flora exited the sauna, dressed in Liv's clothes. They entered the tiny house together.

The small home consisted of three rooms. The living quarters had three chairs, stools, a wood stove and an area rug over its pine-planked floors. Behind Orlo's chair was a galley kitchen, which was part of the living area. The Swedish couple's bedroom was at the rear, and Riga's bedroom was a closet with a mattress on its floor.

"It is small, but nature is our main living quarters," Orlo explained, holding his arm up toward the window that overlooked the cove.

"It is beautiful," Flora exclaimed. "You and Liv are lucky to reside in such picturesque setting. You both are very happy. I can tell."

"I will take our plates down to the boat, Liv," Olaf said. "I will eat with my men. Has Riga had his dinner?"

"Yes, he ate earlier," Liv nodded.

"Well, I will leave you. Everyone must be tired. It was a full day… to say the least."

Olaf winked at the couple, as no one had mentioned the incident at sea to Orlo and his wife.

"I will leave the plates on the dock," Olaf explained.

He kissed Liv, hugged and rocked Orlo, who stayed in his friend's arms for a few extra seconds. The fisherman gave Flora a paternal kiss on her forehead.

"Stay as brave as you are pretty, young lady."

He faced Isaac and embraced his friend of just a few short days.

"Somehow, I feel we were meant to know one another, my friend. Like Orlo, I think we will be friends for life. My man, Gunnar, was right—scour the docks every once and a while if you remain in Stockholm. Look for the Nordic Princess. The three of us can stay in your home when we finish a run if you are lucky."

The group laughed at Olaf's self-invitation. He had picked up the plate when the rumbling noise of men running down Orlo's dock caused everything in the tiny cottage to vibrate. It sounded like a stampede of wayward livestock. Looking out the window, Isaac saw men holding rifles.

"Oh no!" he called, grabbing Flora, as they ducked within the standing group.

Orlo picked up a piece of firewood, holding it up over his head to defend himself. However, when the door opened, Orlo shouted.

"Lars Jacobsen—what is going on? Why are you on my dock, with rifles?"

"Sorry Orlo, but there has been another hijacking of an iron ore barge on the sea. We observed the vessel at your dock, and the shore vigilante thought that it may have had something to do with the theft."

"No, these are my friends, my visitors. Please remove your firearms. I get very nervous around guns."

He turned toward Isaac and Flora.

"Sweden is rich with iron ore mineral. Pirates steal barges filled with the rock and sell the ore to the Germans for the manufacture of weapons and ammunition."

He turned back to his neighbor.

"You will not find any iron here, Lars, so have a good evening."

"Sorry Orlo. We will be on our way. Good evening."

The jittery watchman motioned to his three cohorts, and they left the now dark premises.

Olaf, once again, kissed Liv and took the plates down to the Nordic Princess.

"I promise not to be a stranger, Orlo. I will return to your cove before Christmas. Perhaps we can have some part of the holiday together, no?"

"That sounds wonderful. And remember, Riga is to have no booze and no ladies!" he laughed as Liv slapped him with her towel for his fresh remark.

After Olaf left, Orlo locked the door as Liv took blankets and pillows from Riga's closet.

"You will have to sleep on the floor. Is that all right?"

"If I told you that I slept on a floor in a closet for the last three months, would you believe me?" Isaac asked.

"If you were a Nazi prisoner, we would believe anything!" Orlo responded. "What is important is that you are free, alive and our guests. Now get some rest. Tomorrow, I will take you into our town. There is a bus that leaves from the library stop, to Stockholm, at eleven o'clock. You will be at Town Center by four-ten. Liv has a cousin, Haggar Weymeyer, who works for the Swedish Red Cross. I will have a note for him to set you up with an immigrant sponser until you get on your feet. He owes me many favors."

"But do not tell *him* that!" Liv scolded as Isaac and Flora chuckled.

Dinner took all of fifteen minutes. Orlo pushed back from the modest table, rubbed his stomach and made an announcement to his guests.

"Well, I am expecting a delivery of cod early tomorrow. I must be at the dock by seven a.m., so I am retiring." Yawning, Orlo went into his small bedroom, with Liv following him.

Isaac and Flora arranged the pillows and bedded down for the night. They crept under the floral down blanket that Liv provided. The crackling stove radiated heat, and the holiday aroma of burning pine logs reminded the couple of childhood in a benign Germany.

As they embraced, Isaac wanted to make love to his estranged wife of three months, but he realized it was not the moment for romantic expression. They hugged, kissed, cried, laughed and in full exhaustion, held each other as they fell asleep.

EPILOGUE

June 26, 1963

President John F. Kennedy's hair blew in the summer Berlin breezes, but it always seemed to return to its rigid state of perfection. In his pure, British-influenced, Boston accent, the young leader of the Free World challenged the communist nations to quit all propaganda rhetoric and, like him, to come to Berlin.

He was loud at times, as he insulted the Russian regime of bullies, who needed to create the divisive schism of the Germanys as well as the capitol. His message was clear. He praised the strength of all who lived in the divided city and demanded freedom for all nations.

Thousands who were gathered in the public square of the Rathus Shoneberg responded with deafening cheers for Kennedy every time he completed a thought, using the tag line, *Ich Bin Ein Berliner!*

* * * * *

The poorly transmitted sound and the snowy reception on the small portable television set, sporting one broken rabbit-ear antenna was still able to convey the message of hope and the invincible quest to achieve peace and freedom. The battered television seemed to be a symbolic vehicle, proving that no matter how poor its transmission was, the message could not be stopped. Freedom would eventually win.

Summer solstice had just passed. The Scandinavian day still stretched to twenty-one hours of brightness and excitement on the 26th of June. The haberdashery shop, nestled off the lobby of the Grand Hotel, situated on the main Stromgaten in downtown Stockholm, had just presented the famous John F. Kennedy Berlin speech to an audience of one—namely the proprietor, Isaac Bloom.

The hotel shop had two entrances—one off the sunny waterway street in the heart of Stockholm, and the other from the elegant hotel lobby. The store, open to the public, sold fine men's and women's clothing and accessories, but its main value stemed from the continuous flow of business, generated by the six hundred guests who visited the majestic residence, while in Sweden.

Isaac and Flora Bloom had run the emporium for the hotel management for the last seventeen years. The two provided tailoring, dry cleaning and garment mending for the high-class residents who frequented the up-scale establishment. Living in a back room, equipped with a stove and refrigerator, the couple was able to work late hours, assuring guests that they would receive the ultimate quality and service expected of such an establishment.

Isaac worked at hemming a pants cuff while he watched the cheering Berlin crowds rally to the American president's words that "they must wave a fist of defiance into the face of communism." Fifty-year-old Isaac was so engrossed with the speech that he did not notice the street door to his shop open. An elderly, well-dressed, professional man entered, stepping down to the warm tartan plaid rug that stretched across the tailor's floor.

"Ahh! JFK in Berlin—how did he do?"

Isaac was startled at the definite German accent mouthed by the well-dressed and distinguished businessman. His wavy white hair resonant voice caused Isaac to take a long and pensive examination look at the customer.

"He did good," Isaac answered. "The people of Berlin seemed to strongly connect with him."

"Times have certainly changed. Have they not, my friend?" the older gentleman volunteered, recognizing a similar German flair to Isaac's tongue.

"How do you mean, sir?" the shop keeper questioned.

"Twenty years ago, Adolf Hitler stood at that very same spot, demanding the annihilation of Great Britain and America, as he spoke to a deafening crowd of screaming Germans. And here we are, twenty years later. The people are even more supportive of the political representative who used to be the enemy!"

The well-dressed businessman pulled back and took a long stare at Isaac's face.

"Do I know you, my friend? I have an excellent memory. I feel that we have met before."

"I do not think so, sir," Isaac answered as he studied the man's face in like manor.

"Were you in the war?" the senior volleyed. "I detect a northern German accent… Hamburg?"

"No, sir. I was born in Bremerhaven, but I moved to Sweden in 1935," he said, lying.

Then it hit him, like a bolt of lightening to his brain. The elder may have had an excellent memory, but Isaac placed their acquaintance first. It was none other than Rutger von Blarcom, the Siemens salesman who had startled the young Isaac Bloom when he was vacuuming the rug at Heinrich Wurtzmuller's chalet—the very same person who had given him the transmitter and detonating receiver that saved his life. Isaac said nothing to reveal the discovery.

"My wife and I have lived in Stockholm for over twenty-five years."

"Hmm, I see," the executive said, still trying to remember how he knew the tailor. "I am in town for a convention regarding a new industry—computers. My company, Siemens, is a manufacturer of electronic components. I was to give a lecture this evening when, lo and behold, I spilled some red wine on my suit jacket. Room 442?"

Isaac quickly responded to the information given to him by the salesman.

"Here it is; all clean. I trust you will find the stain completely eradicated, sir."

Isaac wanted to reveal their meeting. The older man seemed like a sincere person, even if he was friends with the man who held him captive outside the labor camp. He and Flora had vowed never to reveal their past… however, if indeed the opportunity had ever arisen…

Von Blarcom held the jacket up to the light. Pleased, he commended Isaac.

"Sir, you definitely know your craft. My compliments to you! I will now not look like the clumsy oaf I really am while giving my speech to the industry people. As the aging man began to exit through the other door that led to the hotel lobby, Isaac hurried to open it to let the customer walk through. The old man turned to Isaac Bloom and chortled.

"You have saved my life. Perhaps one day I can do the same for you."

The modest tailor smiled and quipped, "Well perhaps, sir, you already have."

Rutger von Blarcom took a long final study of Isaac's face.

"I do not know, but I feel somehow our lives have touched, if even for only a few seconds."

"Thank you, sir," Isaac responded as he closed the lobby door and drew the shade down its windowed section, flipping the "Out to Lunch" sign.

"Isaac, I will make us some soup and toast," Flora called from her workbench in the back room as she sat, mending a torn evening gown.

She was a woman of nearly fifty, her steel-gray hair twisted into a bun, which augmented the piecing blue eyes more than her younger, ebony color locks, if that was possible. She was still beautiful. Hotel guests occasionally mistook her for someone of more important stature as she passed through its lobby.

Flora dropped her project and began to prepare lunch in their one-room dwelling. Isaac, for his part, needed to be alone for a few minutes. The surprise of meeting von Blarcom's was benign, but he needed to do something—something he did only when a significant mood overtook the serious side of him.

"I will be there in a minute. I just need to do one thing more"

The seasoned Isaac Bloom hastened to his cluttered desk in the back room of the store, which doubled as their home.

Deep in thought, he reached down to the lowest of the three drawers. He opened the screeching panel that only responded to a shaking of the sides as it was drawn and looked into the messy abyss. There were a jar of buttons, a tin of pins and clasps, and the item he was seeking.

The emotional tailor removed a glass pickle jar of diamonds—the same diamonds he had taken from Wurtzmuller's desk nearly twenty years earlier. He vowed they would stay safely in his possession until the day he died—his personal and solemn oath to the women whose lives the precious gems represented.

He could not save the women, but the sparkling stones escaped with him and Flora. It had been his promise to the thousands of prisoners stripped of their possessions. Symbolically, the diamonds were the lives and souls of those imprisoned.

Under his guard, they would always remain free from Nazi rule and outside inerest groups. Isaac hugged the glass jar and buried his head between his extended arms. His own sacred rite, the older Isaac Bloom invoked a spirit, conveying a message, begging a manifestation to all the souls represented by the crystal contents: *They have not been forgotten! They are still being remembered.* They would always be a part of his and Flora's life. He would always take time to remember them and occasionally visit their souls that continue to live through the glittery anonymous treasure.

"Isaac! Lunch!" Flora called from their bedroom.

As he placed the jar back into the drawer, Isaac stood and heard a banging at the lobby door.

"Leave it, until we finish lunch," his wife called.

But she knew her husband. He would do no such thing. The tailor climbed the two steps of their sunken emporium and unbolted the shaded door, facing Rutger von Blarcom once again. The stately businessman stared at Isaac, tilted his head and smiled, raising his finger, pointing at him.

"Twenty years ago… house cleaner… Ravensbruck?"

"Sir?" Isaac reponded.

"Did you clean military homes during the war?" the keen salesman asked.

"No. No sir, I think you have mistaken me for someone else," Isaac answered, glancing down, hoping to avoid eye contact. "Twenty years ago, I was here in Sweden."

The older man did not believe the shy tailor, but all he wanted to do was to confirm his own memory.

"Well, okay then. I am sorry that I bothered you."

Von Blarcom turned, satisfied that his own recollection challenge had been solved.

Isaac returned to Flora, who had placed a bowl of soup and two pieces of toast on a plate atop their small dining table.

"Who was that, Isaac?" she asked.

"Just someone who thought he knew me," he explained.

"And did he?"

"No, he was mistaken."

"How did the American president do with his speech?" Flora asked, changing the topic.

"He did good, Flora, real good. I think he will bring many good things to this world. I hope he lives a long and wonderful life. Mmm-mmm, the soup is excellent. Is that chicken?"

ABOUT THE AUTHOR

Brian McManus was born and raised in the Bronx, New York. Graduated from St. Raymond Grammar School, Mount St. Michael High School.

Iona College (B.A.), Manhattan College (M.A.) and afterward for several years, attended Fordham University at Lincoln Center.

He lives in New Jersey with his wife Fran. They have two daughters.

In the 1990s Brian had been a "very occasional" paid freelance joke writer to Jay Leno and Big Dog Promotions. His regular profession for many years has involved sales.

This is his first novel.

www.ingramcontent.com/pod-product-compliance
Lightning Source LLC
Chambersburg PA
CBHW021034030726
47496CB00006B/1536
* 9 7 8 1 9 4 1 8 5 9 5 1 3 *